The Mountain

A Novel

By

RAYMOND J. STEINER

Other published books include:

The Vessel of Splendor: A Return to the One
The Girl Who Couldn't See
23 Woodstock Artists
Quarry Rubble (a book of poetry)
Heinrich J. Jarczyk: Toward a Vision of Wholeness
Heinrich J. Jarczyk: Etchings 1968-1998
The Art Students League of New York: A History,
Chen Chi Sketches and Drawings

RAYMOND J. STEINER is an art critic/reviewer for *ART TIMES*, a literary journal he helped found in 1984 and for which he serves as Editor. In addition to authoring hundreds of essays, reviews, critiques, and several books, he has lectured extensively on various topics. He is also an accomplished landscape painter and has exhibited his work in solo and group shows.

The Mountain

A Novel

By

RAYMOND J. STEINER

cSs

cSs **Publications, Inc.**

Saugerties, NY

Author's Note:

This is a work of fiction. Although some of the people, places, and events in this novel are historically authentic, liberties have been freely taken for the purposes of narration.

Published 2008 by CSS Publications, Inc. PO Box 730 Mt. Marion, NY 12456. Phone: (845) 246 –6944 email cs@arttimesjournal.com
www.raymondjsteiner.com
Book design by Cornelia Seckel

ISBN: 978-0-9675526-2-0

ACKNOWLEDGEMENTS

No book is ever written without the influence and help of others — this one perhaps more than most.

The Mountain was written over a period of ten years, but the inspiration and gathering of information had begun much earlier. Countless visits and conversations with artists — some now no longer with us — over the past thirty-odd years have formed the main substance of this book, helping me flesh out characters that, in the main, reflect bits and pieces of those that have shared with me their lives, their struggles, and their successes in the always-shifting world of art. Each will perhaps find that part of the book in which they so surely helped to guide my hand.

As for local history, lore, and trades, I've been gathering that kind of information at first-hand and through books since I moved to West Hurley, New York, from Brooklyn over sixty years ago, way back in the summer of 1945.

Many thanks are due those readers who added insights, offered suggestions, and corrected mistakes. In no special order, they were Elsie Seckel (proof-reader *par excellence*), Eva van Rijn, Susan Hope Fogel, Elaine Simoncini, Kate McGloughlin, Barbara Gill, Everett Raymond Kinstler, Jill Silber, Cheryl Post, Jörg Iwan, Linda Freaney, Ginger Lee Hendler, Linda Holmes Richichi, Eleanor Jacobs; Nick Peluso, Anthony Krauss, Ann-Marie (Annie) and Mark Hoffstatter, Robert Brink, Holly Post, Heidi Robertson, Alan McKnight, Jamie Barthel, Kathy Corpuel, and Kathleen Arffmann.

Finally, a very special thanks to Cornelia Seckel — my wife and partner — to whom this book has been dedicated. Without her encouragement and gentle guidance away from false starts and self-doubts, *The Mountain* might have languished on my desk as a perennial work-in-progress.

RAYMOND J. STEINER
High Woods, New York
April 2008

For Cornelia

BOOK ONE

1913

1

JAKE'S MIND WAS awhirl with images. He was confused, he was tired, and he was irritated.

He was disturbed because he was in the city, because he was being shoved by people waiting to board the ferry, and because he almost always found himself disconcerted when surrounded by too many people. His displeasure showed on his face, in his brusque movements, as he pulled away from the pressure of human contact. A solidly built man, he held his large shoulders stiffly, at times even placing his hands on his hips with his elbows akimbo to ensure the sanctity of his personal space. Perhaps most of all he was angry with himself for giving in to his anger. He usually had a better rein on his emotions — prided himself, in fact, for not allowing things to unsettle him.

He never liked crowds — as far as he was concerned five persons constituted a crowd — and this bunch was particularly discourteous, loud, and oppressive. On top of everything else, he was also dispirited because he felt he had wasted several days of his time and, further, that he had spent money he could not well afford to squander. Just a few days ago, he had looked forward to coming to the city because he felt it was important, indeed was convinced that he might come away with new knowledge, new information about art that he was not able to learn any other way. He could not afford the time or expense of art classes, so he figured the cost of the trip would be justified if he came back with some better understanding of what art was all about.

In no way, however, could he reconcile what he had seen over the past two days with what little he knew about art. Granted he was no expert — far from it, in fact. A handyman who had been messing around with a pencil since he was a boy, he was still a novice at wielding the brush, knew preciously little, in truth, about art in general. What he had seen yesterday and the day before, however, had flown directly into the face of everything he believed art ought to be — or at least what he wanted *his* art to be.

Worse, it made him feel stupid, the picture-perfect example of a hick from the country on his first trip to the big city. He had spent two long days at the International Exhibition of Modern Art, spending many hours touring, studying, and puzzling over the works distributed over some eighteen makeshift gallery spaces spread over the huge floor of the 69th Street Armory — and all he came away with was a confused jumble of images and emotions.

If that stuff was art — he thought — *then I'm as mad as a hatter.*

There were well over a thousand works in the exhibit — estimates ranged from about 1,050 to 1,300 separate pieces, depending upon whether you believed the organizers of the show or the printers of the catalogues. No agreement could be reached since many artists did enter paintings and sculptures after the catalogues were printed, and probably as many claimed that they were part of the show since, by all accounts, it was the show to be in. But however many there actually were, it seemed of little import to him since, as far as he could tell, the bulk of it was incomprehensible junk anyway.

Jake recalled snatches of some of the articles he had seen in the city newspapers the last two days. The *Times* felt that "no one within reach…can afford to miss it," while the *New York Sun* proclaimed that the organizers "wrought something very like a miracle." *The New York American* styled the exhibit a "bomb shell" and the *New York Evening Mail* declared that it "triumphed over all formal restrictions," claiming further "It was a privilege to get out of the artistic strait jacket."

A privilege?

Surely, the recollection of his visit to the Armory did not leave him feeling very privileged. And, it took the two full days he had given himself to see the show in its entirety.

To see it — perhaps. To absorb it, to comprehend what he had seen, to apply it to his own ideas about what an artist was or did, this was something still to be determined. And what did the *Evening Mail* mean by an "artistic straitjacket"? What was *that* supposed to mean?

He shook his head and pulled himself back to the present. The Weehawken ferry was already moored in its slip, steam from its stack blowing at right angles to her decks in the stiff breeze coming downriver. It stood waiting for its load of humanity and the subsequent fight with both the wind and the outgoing tide of the North River when it began to wend its way from the 42nd Street landing to the New Jersey shore across the way.

Jake filled his lungs with the cold air and turned to look north, automatically noting the heavy, gray clouds as they scudded across the horizon. The light seemed muted, as if filtered through cheese-cloth. He calculated that the ferry would have to head considerably far upstream in a wide arc if it intended to reach its berth, which was located almost directly across the river. Well, the few extra minutes that it might take would make no difference. He knew that it would arrive in time for him to make his connection with the upstate train — but now, every minute seemed to hang heavy on his mind and he was anxious to get back home. The gray light, the lowering clouds — and now a distinct dampness in the air — only made the seeming weight of time feel more real.

He took another deep breath, attempting to clear his head of unwanted thoughts, thoughts about the International Exhibit of Modern Art. He hunched deeper into his heavy coat, glad that he had not been fooled into wearing lighter clothing by the unusual warm spell that heralded the first few days of the month. Today, however, was a typical February day: cold, blustery, intermittent snowflakes whirling through the air, the wind cutting through clothes, reddening faces and ungloved hands.

Ships of all sizes and types, their sails full, precariously leaned over when caught in the crosswind as they plied their way up, down, and across the river. Jake noted dirty slabs of ice drifting on the river's surface, their unusual dark, bluish color making them almost invisible in the drably colored water.

So — he thought — *the ice must have already begun breaking apart upriver.*

Just one month ago, he remembered the river between Kingston and Rhinecliff being a solid sheet of ice, men walking across and working on it as if on a highway. The ice was still clean then — pristine and crisply light blue like the delicate cerulean of a summer sky. Not even the steady tramping of heavily booted men crossing its surface could besmirch the virgin expanse of frozen water. That unseasonable warm spell the first week of February, however, had begun the melting process, river traffic and ice-cutting hastening the progression of the break-up of ice before its slow journey downstate, the separated chunks picking up impurities and filth as they traveled south.

Today, though only a few weeks later, it felt as cold as ever, winter making its last attempts at hanging on. Still, the passing ice floes spelt winter's doom, and the river would soon be opening to traffic clear on up to Albany and Troy.

Turning away from the river, Jake let his eyes roam over the bustling hubbub that seemed to always characterize the New York City piers — day and night.

Did they ever sleep here?

Horses and carriages, automobiles, truckmen, porters, a constant carrying on and a carrying off of boxes and crates and sacks and barrels from the boats; men loading, shoving, unloading; raised voices, hand carts bumping into ankles, oaths directed at no one and everyone, rough workmen and genteel folks rubbing elbows, shoulders — and tempers — raw. From time to time, pocket watches would be consulted, accompanied by mutters and exclamations of "getting on with it." As impatient as he was to return home, Jake could not imagine his life being ruled by a timepiece. The shifting kaleidoscope of images and colors began to tense him up again and he longed for the peace and quiet of home.

Another deep breath; another slow release of air from his lungs.
How could they put up with this day after day, week after week?
The lowering sky and bursts of snow flurries seemed to further cramp the space, making Jake feel even more confined. Still, though he was uncomfortably hemmed in by shoving bodies, a part of him enjoyed watching the activity, especially the workmen as they went about their jobs, oblivious to the crowds getting in their way. He appreciated their economy of movement, their conservation of time and energy — a form of survival learned after long hours on the job — while getting on with their business of loading or unloading freight along the wharves.

He noted the shifting play of light across the water, marveled at how the intermittent shafts of sunlight that broke through the clouds picked out this or that object on the Jersey side of the river.

He tried to look at the scene as an artist might see it. Had he dared, he would have dug out his pad to make a few quick sketches — but he'd no intention of drawing attention to himself.

He also took in the sounds — so many and so varied a cacophony of noises that fell strangely on his ears. So different from the silence of the mountains. Grunts, oaths, thuds, scrapes. Voices raised in anger, in banter, in question. Hawsers, strained and released by shifting winds and tide, sang out from low to high pitch then reversed themselves, subtly modulating their mournful songs, reminding him of guitar strings being alternately loosened and tightened by turns of the key. Murmurs. Sighs. A harsh, hacking cough coming from someone nearby. Distant and indistinct sounds coming from shops and warehouses along the river, from vendors of ship's stores, from chandlers, restaurants, and bars. He listened and looked for the sheer novelty of it, knowing that when he returned upstate all such sounds would soon fade from memory, impossible to reconstruct in his mind once he immersed himself again in his usual day-to-day life.

He glanced again up and down river, turning up the collar of his overcoat and yanking down his cap as the wind whipped along the shore. The sights would also fade. As engrossing as river life seemed to be, Jake knew he would never be a marine painter. He liked his woods, his fields — his mountain. There were too many man-made things on the river, too much bustle and movement. Too many people. He preferred to sketch directly from nature, trying to capture in line and shading both the intricacies and the awful immensity of it all — trying also, but never quite succeeding, in suggesting the slow and constant change of growth. Yes, he preferred to draw in quiet as well as in seclusion.

Cold air was coming down from the north in earnest now, buffeting the crowd around him, making people visibly shrink in size as they tried to hunker down deeper into their coats and mufflers.

Coming from home — he thought —*from down off the mountain.*

In spite of the intermittent flurries of snow that whirled in the air over the heads of the waiting throng, the day yet seemed to promise clearing. Out of his element here in the city, however, he couldn't read the signs, couldn't predict what the day would bring as far as the weather was concerned. He idly watched tenuous patches of shade and sunlight across the river, lightening or darkening the opposite shore, as the sun, still too low on the horizon to shine on the people huddled at the ferry slip, remained hidden behind the buildings lining the street. The long-cast shadows — barely glimpsed whenever the sun made its fleeting appearances — made the day seem colder than it was. His guess was that the wind would shift sometime mid-day, blow in from the west and bring better weather. Whatever it seemed to be trying to do now, he figured it would all blow out to sea before he got back home.

As he stolidly stood his ground in the swaying movement of the shoving crowd, his impatience to get back upstate grew. How long had they been waiting to board? A half-hour perhaps? Three-quarters of an hour? God! ... It seemed an eternity! He widened his stance for a firmer footing, expanding his already broad width, trying his best to hold his own in the crowd. The longer he stood amidst the jostling bodies, the more he craved the solitude he always found in the Catskills. He wanted to be back where he knew how to plan his day, could tell whether it would rain, snow, or bring fair weather; back to where nature confided in him and shared her secrets.

Well, shared them up to a point, anyway.

He still had not learned the trick of capturing with pencil and paper all of her infinitely varied effects, all of her moods, the solace of her quietude, the mad fury of her stormy days. Someday he would attempt oils — and maybe then he would be able to make the kind of art he dreamed of.

The bustling activity surrounding him, as interesting as it ought to be to the occasional visitor such as himself, couldn't hold his attention, couldn't erase the last two days from his memory. He again hunched his shoulders against the cold while his mind kept returning to the 69th Street Armory and the assault on his senses, which continued to plague him. The swirl of images seemed indelibly impressed on his mind, recurring again and again to tantalize and confuse him.

Not that any of it came back to him in any sensible pattern. No matter how many times his mind would replay the march of impressions that paraded before his inner eye, they came as disparate and incoherent sensations of color and form. He doubted that any of it would ever make any sense — at least to him.

An elbow jammed rudely into his side brought him instantly

16

back to the riverfront. He saw that the people were finally moving forward, beginning to board the ferry, their faces turned down-river as they tried in vain to avoid the biting wind. Flakes had now changed to icy pellets, the tiny missiles adding to everyone's discomfort. Ordinarily, cold did not bother Jake — he was used to working out of doors in all kinds of weather. But here, his body inactive, in the city, the cold seemed sharper, more penetrating.

Jake allowed people to shove in front of him. Why all the pushing? What was the hurry? There seemed to be enough room and even if you had to stand all the way, the trip across river was certainly not that long. As he moved forward with the mass of bodies inching its way to the dropped gangplank, his mind flitted back and forth between the Armory with its profusion of images to the shoving mass of humanity around him. Not much different, he thought. Confusion. Confusion seemed always to be part of being around people. So much disconcerting bustle and all of it seemingly self-inflicted.

What made them want to live like this? How could they absorb it all? How could the mind find rest, stand still long enough to digest and evaluate what it had to take in? How could anyone stay sane in such a state of constant turmoil?

Well, perhaps he'd sort some of it out on the trip back up to Kingston. If he were lucky, maybe he'd find a seat alone on the train, far from some overly talkative seatmate. Since it was not only mid-week but also early in the day, chances were good that he might just get his wish.

There was not much of a wait when they reached the New Jersey shore. He'd managed to get off the ferry fairly quickly, make his way over to the West Shore train station, and, since he'd already had his round-trip ticket, was able to board immediately and find a seat at the rear of a car. He chose a seat on the aisle in the hopes that it would dissuade anyone from squeezing past to sit next to him.

He also did not much care to have a window seat since the ride upstate offered little scenery to arouse his interest. Train travel generally didn't appeal to him. Granted it was convenient, saved time, but he preferred a slower pace, a human pace. The world flashed by too quickly while riding on a train to really take it in properly and, for the most part, what he saw was not often attractive, rails

17

from point to point most generally laid down in the less favored parts of the countryside. As the train passed through towns, slowing for safety — and making it possible to settle your eyes on something — it was always through the poorest sections, with shacks, scraggly-looking truck gardens, abandoned buildings, and rusting farm equipment making up the view for the most part.

Had it been summertime, Jake would have traveled back and forth to the city by Day Boat, the more leisurely trip by water an experience he dearly enjoyed. Ever since that June morning back in 1907, when his parents had put him and his brother Freddie under the care of friendly deckhands aboard the *Hendrik Hudson* for an upstate visit to Uncle Hans and Aunt Birgit, he had fallen under the river's spell. For Jake, the highlight of the trip upriver never ceased to be that first sighting of the Catskills as the boat swung left around the bend known as Crum Elbow, some eighty miles north of Manhattan and just above the Poughkeepsie landing. He could close his eyes now and visualize it as clearly as if he were actually reliving the experience.

As the train chuffed out of the Weehawken station, plunging almost immediately into the tunnel through the Bergen Hills of New Jersey, the sudden transition from light to darkness brought to Jake's mind another re-run of the images he had taken in at the Armory. The train ride upstate would only take a few hours; maybe enough time to review his impressions — but he doubted he'd ever sort it all out to his satisfaction. He removed his hat and coat and settled back in the hopes that he might relax.

Almost immediately, however, the thought that here it was halfway through Thursday and that he'd wasted so much time on coming to the city began to nag at his mind.

Well — he thought — *there'll be no sleeping on this trip.*

2

Jake had come to the city on the previous Friday evening, spending the weekend and the whole day of Monday with his parents in Brooklyn, and returning to Manhattan on Tuesday, February the 18th, to see the International Exhibition of Modern Art — what everyone was already calling the "Armory Show" since it was held at the 69th Infantry Regiment Armory on Lexington Avenue. He purposely avoided the formal, public opening on Monday night, unwilling to put up with the expected crush of people and the interminable round of speech making that was planned for the event. He came to see pictures, not listen to words.

Although Jake had spent his boyhood just across the East River in the brewery-rich German neighborhood known as the "Ridgewood Section" of Brooklyn, the island of Manhattan was not familiar territory to him. Occasionally, he would walk into the city across the Williamsburg Bridge with his mother when she went shopping on the Lower East Side, but most of those memories were already fading, lost in a childhood he had little desire to relive in his mind. When he was old enough to travel across the river on his own, the city itself was far too intimidating for casual exploration. He always felt safer — if not exactly comfortable — staying close to his familiar Brooklyn neighborhood.

Sometimes, during the summer, his parents would take him and his brother Freddie to the Aquarium down on the Battery. At other times they would simply stroll along the piers, sometimes staying on the East Side, along South Street and the smelly Fulton Fish Market, sometimes over to that part of the Hudson that the city dwellers called the "North River" where the bigger ships from around the world were berthed along its shore. If his father felt expansive, they might stop at one of the oyster barges moored along the street for a light "stand-up" lunch.

The best, to Jake, was walking along South Street, watching his father duck his head as they passed under bowsprits jutting and bobbing over the sidewalks. Once, while sidestepping a group of men lounging around a half-loaded cart, his father's derby had been knocked off by a low-hanging line causing Jake and Freddie to burst out laughing. They both knew the hazards of finding humor in any misfortune that occurred to their father — but it didn't stop them from keeping an eye out for a repeat performance each time they went.

Being surrounded by the exciting activity of river life was a fascinating experience for a young boy, and although neither he nor Freddie could tell a fishing smack from a barge — Jake doubted if his father could either, since questions from them never elicited much more than a non-committal grunt — Jake's young eyes drank in the impressions. The thick web of lines that crossed and re-crossed from spar to spar and from ship to ship appeared so dense that he wondered how the swooping gulls could pass through them unharmed. The idea of being a deckhand on one of those floating cities and having to learn what each rope did and what its name was and where its terminal attachments might be, would leave him dizzy with wonder.

Even the words heard along the river seemed to have a special life of their own. Every young man seemed to be named "Laddie," every older one, "Matey." Jib. Spar. Keel. Pike. Shouts of Avast! Aye! Ahoy! They sounded as foreign to him as did many of the languages these sea-faring men used, exotic tongues seemingly from every country in the world. What most of the wharf-side words meant, Jake would only learn in later years, years when he no longer frequented the east and west shorelines of the lower tip of Manhattan Island.

Whatever fascination the workings of the shoremen had, the sea would come to hold a dark side for Jake, a sinister side that would stay with him throughout his life. One gray morning, the overcast sky reflecting dully in the oily scum of the East River, he and his family had seen a young man, perhaps not much older than himself, fall from the tall mast of a berthed ship. A short, high cry brought their attention to the boy-man's body twisting and turning like a rag doll as it fell through and rebounded from intersecting ropes, plummeting downward to finally plunge into the river and disappear under its swelling surface. Not a mark registered on the water a moment after he fell in. It was as if the event had never happened.

Though the fall was noted by his shipmates scurrying about helplessly, the boy-man was not recovered, his body presumably already swept into the harbor by the swiftly moving outflowing tide. The silence and finality of it profoundly disturbed young Jake. If the water could swallow up a human so nonchalantly while still under the eyes of thousands of his fellowmen, how much easier it must be for it to claim its victims in the deep of night while far out at sea. Though he had no great relish for being buried in dirt, the prospect of being drowned in that great swirling mass terrified him. Could there be a God who so off-handedly allowed such things to occur?

In later years, the city's West Side and its "North River" would become a bit more familiar to Jake. Since he was a child he had traveled with his parents and brother to Pier 42 to board this same Weehawken ferry to catch the West Shore Railroads going upstate when the whole family went to visit Uncle Hans and Aunt Birgit "in the mountains" for a few days' vacation. Later, when he was a bit older, his father had begun sending him and Freddie upstate on the Day Line to live with his uncle and aunt during the summers. This was a much greater adventure than merely crossing the river, since traveling by Day Line meant they would be on the Hudson all the way up to Kingston.

But the southern tip of the island with its shoreline streets was pretty much the sum total of his knowledge of New York City, the inner and uptown streets as foreign to him as the boulevards of Paris. Even at the age of nineteen, "big city life" was still pretty much a closed book to Jake, and wending his way up Lexington Avenue to 25th Street was an uncommon experience for him. Whatever attachments he once had to the city from his Brooklyn days were mostly gone, his move to the little town of West Hurley a few miles west of Kingston to permanently live with his aunt and uncle over three years ago, already distancing him from both the life and the memories of city life.

Still, even had he not known exactly where the 69th Infantry

Regiment Armory was, it was easy to recognize its military aspect from blocks away. If he needed further assurance that he was at the right place, the many automobiles and carriages lining the streets in front and around the sides of the imposing building on that Tuesday morning indicated that some special occasion was taking place.

Though he had arrived at least a half-hour before the doors were scheduled to open at ten-o'clock, a large crowd waiting to get in was already gathered at the Lexington Street entrance. He had known the exhibit was going to be a "big deal" — it was all the buzz ever since the news reached Woodstock early last year — yet Jake had still not expected such a large crowd. From the snatches of conversation he overheard, he gathered that most of those milling around him were artists — many voicing the same curiosity he entertained in his own mind — what would they see? — though there seemed also to be many who were there just for the "fun" of it.

He had hardly joined the growing throng when a shout separated itself from the general chatter of the crowd, catching his attention.

"Jake! Jake Forscher!"

He scanned the crowd and saw a hand raised in the air.

"Hey! Over here!" he heard, and saw a face that was vaguely familiar.

It belonged to an artist with whom he had only a nodding acquaintance from the Rock City group up in Woodstock, a man about his own age but one who, unlike himself, had been busy at the art trade since he was a child. A city-dweller and summer visitor to the Woodstock Colony, he talked much and affected to know more — neither characteristic much to Jake's liking. Jake returned the wave, gave a hint of a smile, determined to avoid the fellow if he could. Judging from the size of the crowd, it did not seem likely that they would come across each other again inside the armory.

He knew that Sunday was set aside for the special press opening of the exhibit and, though he had not yet looked at any newspapers, assumed that many of the reporters must have already written about the event for yesterday's papers. He caught excited talk about a "bombshell," a "wing-dinger," a "spoof on art," and a "real shocker." The people around him were either quoting what they had read in the dailies, or repeating what they heard others say. He resolved to pick up some of the papers later and read them when he had a moment alone.

When he finally got to the front entrance, he saw a cloth banner stretched across its wide arch, gently flapping in the morning wind. Large letters across its span proclaiming "International Exhibition: Modern Art" promised a momentous occasion, and Jake found that he was growing excited at the prospect of taking part in such an event. He noted that at each end of the banner, a pine tree logo identified the sponsors of the show, the Association of American Painters and Sculptors. He had heard much about this group in the last several months, and looked forward to this exhibit they put together. Attached to tall lamps on either side of the doorway at the top of the steps leading into the armory were large posters listing some of the participating artists.

Though Jake recognized the names of such artists as Picasso and Matisse, most of those listed on the posters meant nothing to him. And, though he *recognized* the names of Matisse and Picasso, it was only through the conversation of others that he knew of them and he had no idea of what their art looked like.

The palpable excitement infusing the crowd began to affect him, and he found himself anxious to get through the doors, his curiosity whetted in anticipation of the "wing-dinger" he would soon be experiencing. To his annoyance, he saw that the artist who called out to him earlier was pushing his way to his side.

"Were you here last night?" he breathlessly asked Jake.

Jake could not recall his name. "No, this is my first time."

"Well, let me tell you, you are going to see *some* show. It's all the very latest from Europe, you know. Stuff that'll make your eyes pop."

"So, I've heard," Jake said.

"It'll be the end of the Academy, that's for sure! After this show, they'll have to close their doors. What student will want to study from casts and follow rules after seeing this?"

"Hmmm," Jake offered. What or where the "academy" was or what studying from "casts" meant was a mystery to him, but he had no intention of asking for an explanation.

"Too bad you missed last night. What a crowd! A brass band

23

blaring away and you still couldn't drown out the excitement. I'm telling you, you're in for a real treat!"

Sounded exactly why he had *not* wanted to go to the public opening the previous evening. He only said, "Well, I'm here to see for myself now," and was greatly relieved when the fellow pushed his way through to another artist he recognized.

"Hey," Jake heard him shout to the other as he moved away, "wait 'til you see the French painters..." his voice fading in the general hubbub as he moved away.

It was not only that Jake did not particularly care for the young man, but that he had no desire to listen to a running commentary as he viewed the work. He had chosen to make the trip alone because he preferred it that way; he had learned from experience that, for him, looking at art took considerable concentration and he needed his wits about him when he did so. He wanted to use his eyes and not his ears.

He'd been hearing nothing *but* talk about the Armory Show from the Rock City crowd back in Woodstock since early summer of 1912, almost a full year before its opening. Their constant chatter about the upcoming show finally persuaded him to make the trip to New York to see it, and he wanted to do just that — *see* the show. For him, looking at art was as attention absorbing as was making it, and he had no intention of wasting his time in conversation with some pretentious chatterbox.

When he got through the doors, he was surprised to see two living pine trees standing to the right and left of him. Apparently the Association that brought the show together took their trademark symbol seriously.

Immediately in front of him was a large space full of sculpture. Hanging from the ceiling were yellow streamers, forming an enormous "tent" over the entire armory. Behind the wall of this first "gallery" — which he soon discovered housed only American sculpture — was a series of octagonal "rooms" formed by burlap-covered partitions, some eighteen in all. At the extreme rear of the Armory, he found another large "gallery," which mirrored that found in the front — this one filled with European art. With each of the partitions festooned in greenery and bunting, the otherwise bleak setting of the building presented a festive air to all who entered the huge hall.

Although he could later vividly call to mind individual works, remember specific paintings or pieces of sculpture, at first glance the overall exhibit presented a blur of color and shape, a visual medley that refused to settle into any kind of harmony for him. Since drawing was the only medium with which he had any direct experience, he was naturally drawn to look closely at those included in the show. With the exception of a handful that had seemed little more than the random scribbles of children, Bellows' boxing scenes — although the subject held little interest for him — and Luks' studies of deer in the Bronx Zoo were much to his liking. The few others scattered throughout the show left him cold.

Since it was painting he most desired to learn about, he spent a good deal of time in studying those in the show but, much to his dismay, when he tried to recall them on his way back upstate he mostly re-experienced only discordant impressions. Uppermost in his mind was the unsettling thought that he was out of his depth, that whatever he had thought he knew about art was suddenly all swept away in a single moment. He saw his world turned topsy-turvy, and he was left feeling like a child confronted with a difficult lesson to grasp. Though he was comfortable with some of the paintings — the works of Goya, Delacroix or Ingres, for example — others such as those by Cézanne simply puzzled him. The cubist and fauvist "galleries" were especially disorienting, the fractured images and garish colors jangling his sensibilities and assaulting his senses in an unpleasant way.

He anticipated seeing new things — had expected to be surprised, even enlightened, ever since he had first learned about the exhibition one afternoon in late autumn. He'd overheard Putnam Brinley, one of the organizers of the exhibit, speak about it to one of the Art Student League instructors and his students in front of the League's summer studio on Woodstock's Tinker Street, and his curiosity had been piqued. Jake didn't know Brinley personally but couldn't help noticing his 7-foot tall frame haranguing the small knot of people grouped around him, and had hovered nearby to listen in.

Arms gesticulating and head bobbing, Brinley was attempting to get the League people interested in the upcoming exhibit. The Leaguers, however, mostly landscape artists, seemed uninterested and unimpressed with his exhortations. From time to time, the instructor, John Carlson, would nod and smile, but Jake could tell that Brinley wasn't making much of an impact on his audience.

Brinley's promise that the show would "open eyes" to what would fast become the "new wave" of painting, however, fell largely on deaf ears — though the promise did manage to stick in Jake's memory. Carlson, who had taken over the reins of the League since Birge Harrison's retirement two years ago in 1911 and who was well on his way to becoming a landscape painter of some repute himself, sauntered back into the studio after listening for awhile, his students hurriedly flocking after him like chicks following a hen. After all, they had come to Woodstock to study landscape painting, and Carlson was considered to be one of the best. If their instructor had shown no interest in "modern" stuff, well, then, neither would they.

If almost all the artists in town were eventually talking about it, it was the Rock City group who mostly drummed up the exhibit in Woodstock, several of them, in fact, expecting, like Brinley, to participate in the show. It was almost the only topic of discussion during mealtimes at Mrs. Magee's boarding house, and Jake would hear Brinley's pitch many times over during the months leading up to the show. And, though Jake remained non-committal, it was Brinley's animated discussions that slowly persuaded him to make the trip down to New York City if only to see for himself what all the fuss was about.

Though not associated with of any of the artist-groups in Woodstock, Jake, like many of the townspeople, was aware that the little colony mirrored the larger art world. New York City might have been the most important city for art in America, but the fact that most of the leading artists had a foot firmly planted in the colony made the little hamlet of Woodstock the second most important art center in the country. If this new exhibit was such a hot topic right here in Woodstock, then Jake would be foolish to dismiss its importance out of hand. Therefore, whenever the occasion would present itself, he did not hesitate to make it a point to ask questions. There was a lot he had to learn about this art business, and going to see what was consistently being touted as the "show of the century" was one way he could go about educating himself.

Jake, always a loner, had no commitment to any group. An outsider by nature as well as by preference, he would join in discussions — mostly by listening — whenever he had occasion to be around artists, but, as far as he was concerned, the making of art was pretty much a personal thing, and its progress not open to "schooling" or "proselytizing." How and why he drew pictures came from somewhere within himself and not something he felt easy talking about. So far, at any rate, he had no words to describe what he felt or thought about art.

He was a great listener, however, and as the talk in town about the upcoming exhibit steadily grew, he was determined to make the trip down to the city and get to see it. He felt pretty strongly that he knew "art" when he saw it but, as yet, couldn't reconcile or quite understand how artists could be divided into different camps. What did "modern" mean, anyway? Didn't each generation of artists merit the name "modern" by virtue of replacing the previous one? How could such a term have any special meaning? "Art," as far as Jake could tell, was identified by its honesty of intention, its conformity to the artist's impression, and, in the end, whether or not it "said" something to both the artist and the viewer. It could be "good" or it could be "bad." But "modern"? It just didn't figure — and he was hoping that the trip to Manhattan to see the Armory Show would help, as Brinley put it, to "open his eyes" and help him clear up the mystery.

3

Planning the trip to New York City had been no small thing. Aside from the cost, Jake had to arrange it so that it did not interfere with his job commitments. He had been hiring out as a day laborer ever since he had moved upstate, doing odd-jobs and handy-man work, his axe and his scythe always honed, always standing ready at the door to be put to work at a moment's notice.

He'd been living with his aunt and uncle, contributing towards expenses, the arrangement making things simpler for him until he could get along on his own. The fact that he liked both his Uncle Hans and his Aunt Birgit — his father's sister — and could get along with them much better than he did with his parents, only made things easier. Such basic needs as room and board thus taken care of, he needed only to make enough cash for his personal needs.

Hard-working people, Aunt Birgit and Uncle Hans lived simple lives. Hans Wolff, short and powerfully built, was a practical man, his needs and luxuries neither extended nor extravagant. A stone-worker in his younger days, he now drove a wagon that carried bluestone from local quarries to the Rondout Creek for final shipping down the Hudson River to New York City. Aunt Birgit, handsome and amiable, ruled her kitchen, her usual fare a hearty but plain menu. It was up to the men-folk to tend to outside chores and needs; it was her province — and pride — to keep her home spotlessly clean and her men content.

Hans and Birgit Wolff had built their home on a half-acre plot in the newly settled section of West Hurley, the little town moved from its former location further south in the Esopus Valley when it was necessary to make room for the construction of the huge Ashokan Reservoir. Situated just north of the easternmost extreme of the soon-to-be reservoir, the burgeoning town had an air of new-ness about it. Unlike its former higgledy-piggledy settlement along the winding course of the Esopus Creek, its streets were now neatly laid out in grids snugly located within the right-angle plot of land that lay north of the east-west stretch of the Plank Road and east of a well-packed dirt road that struck due north to the village of Woodstock. The two towns, only three miles apart, were quite different in character, West Hurley, a quiet residential village, Woodstock, once a picturesque village inhabited by farmers and tradesmen, fast becoming a tourist mecca and burgeoning art colony.

The Wolff's neat, white, clapboarded house stood back on a shaded and quiet lane of similarly built homes. A good-sized vegetable garden took up most of the "backyard," and several outbuildings, a fenced-in chicken coop, and a covered shed for the horses completed the ensemble. Twin flowerbeds flanked the path from the lane to the front door, the only portion outdoors other than the vegetable garden that fell under Aunt Birgit's jurisdiction. When not busy about the house, there was nothing she loved more than puttering about her flowerbeds, savagely attacking any intrepid weed that dared to show its head, nurturing and coaxing whatever latest bloom graced the walkway. Jake, long "at home" with both of them, had grown to love the place nearly as much as did his Aunt and Uncle.

From time to time, he'd add to their meals by doing some hunting in the colder months and occasional fishing during the warmer seasons — but much like his uncle, he was neither an avid hunter nor fisherman. He'd never heard his father speak about hunting or fishing, and assumed that he also was not much of a sportsman. Immigrants all and coming from peasant stock, chances were that there was never any such tradition passed down in either the Wolff or Forscher families, since hunting was pretty much of an aristocratic sport and privilege in the old country.

For Jake, it had little to do with the unpleasantness of killing. His father, after all, was a butcher, and Jake himself had no compunction about taking the head off a chicken with a hatchet when it was needed for the pot, or shooting a woodchuck or rabbit that was ravaging Aunt Birgit's gardens. He owned several guns — a handgun, a shotgun, and a deer-rifle — and even possessed fairly decent fishing gear. He was just not very good at hunting and had little patience to angle for fish. As far as thinking of it as a "sport," he had never understood the concept of taking a life simply for the "enjoyment" of it.

After moving in permanently with Uncle Hans and Aunt Birgit, he began clearing wood lots and mowing fields in and around the surrounding area, finding most of his work in the neighboring town of Woodstock, hiring out to both the locals as well as to the summer trade who came and stayed for the season. Some of the seasonal visitors were landowners who depended on him to oversee their property during the months they were gone — mending, painting, carpentering — others simply unwilling to take the time to do their own mowing, tending, or fixing while they summered in the town. With the hotels and boarding houses in Woodstock, summer work was always plentiful, his reputation for dependability and fairness well-known around town, word of mouth often bringing him more work than he could sometimes handle.

Winters, however, could be long and cold, and there would be times when Jake would find ready cash hard to come by. Since the Armory Show was to be held in February, it meant scrimping and saving up to make the trip. An obligatory visit with his parents — though almost always a troubling and painful experience — just made economic sense, so he decided to combine his trip to Manhattan with a 3-day weekend at their home in Brooklyn.

Fortunately, he had found work in December with one of the companies that provided New York City with their daily supply of ice, and he'd hired on for the season with an ice-cutting crew working on the Hudson. The steady work throughout a good part of winter made it possible to put away enough each week against his trip in February.

Used to laboring alone in the woods and fields, employment on the river was a new experience for Jake, and working as part of a team with a crew took some getting used to. Though he loved the river, the Hudson in winter showed a far different aspect than it did back on that balmy day in June when, as a boy of 14, he fell in love with it as he steamed up on the *Hendrik Hudson* from New York City. He couldn't help but notice the spectacular view of the Catskill Range from the middle of the river — clearly visible with the absence of foliage, it was starkly etched against the winter sky — but was soon so caught up with the work at hand that he found little time to enjoy the vista. Only at lunchtime could he take the time to study the outline of the mountains, note the play of light on their surfaces and try to commit his impressions to memory. All too soon, however, would come the shout from the foreman calling his men back to the task at hand and, as if a teacher swept her cloth across the slate, all images would soon be erased from sight.

Frozen over to a depth of nearly twenty inches — a "good crop" according to the seasoned ice-cutters on the job — the river's surface held about 200 men, each busy at his assigned task. The chosen floes were already marked out with hemlock boughs, and a crew of approximately twenty men walking in single file followed the boughs with their chisel-bars, making holes to allow water up and through the surface, thus coaxing each section to eventually separate from the larger mass. Other workers were distributed over the river-ice, marking, sawing, scraping, or hauling equipment. Although Jake had long been accustomed to using hand-tools as extensions of his arms, with the exception of the large saws they used to cut through the ice, several of the implements and most of the equipment used on the river were new to him.

He soon fell in easily with both the men and the work however, and already sweating though the temperature hovered around zero, was alternating between cutting ice or loading the elevators, the foreman moving him back and forth between tasks as needed. Used to cutting wood, he found handling the saws preferable to working at the elevators that conveyed blocks of ice from the river-surface to the shore. Noisy, ungainly affairs, the clanking and ever-turning apparatus of the elevators hoisted the ice chunks to the upper banks of the river where they then fell into "runs" attended by another crew that culled out the unsatisfactory blocks. The saleable pieces would then be routed up to the men who handled, hauled, and passed them on to still another crew of men who quickly stored them in warehouses until they could be loaded onto barges and shipped down to New York City.

Standing at the foot of the elevator, his feet feeling as if permanently affixed to the frozen river, Jake manhandled the blocks of ice onto the ever-moving, ever-hungry belt. Like many craftsmen, Jake was leery of the moving equipment, distrustful of any tool that did not fit his hand, always wary of being caught up in the gears and chains that kept the machine moving. Workmen ignored at their own peril the fact that machines did not distinguish between warm flesh and cold, hard blocks of ice. He was always relieved, then, when called back to man the saw, a tool which he could control and that did not have a mind of its own.

Jake worked through the month of December, laid off with most of the temporary workers in late-January when the sun began its work of "rotting" the ice. Not only would the rising temperatures begin the melting of the surface, but also shafts of sunlight would penetrate the ice, turning it finally into what the seasoned rivermen called "kindling wood." Once that process began, it was not long before the extras like Jake would be let go. Though he enjoyed the experience of learning about a new trade, he was glad to leave the river, happy not to be part of the year-round crew whose whole life was attuned to the relatively short period of ice harvesting, reserving the greater part of the year to the repair and maintenance of their tools, equipment and buildings.

For Jake, being locked into any one occupation would have been too limiting, too demanding of his time and freedom. He needed stretches of time to absorb, to think, to allow his experience of the world to sink in and take root. His was a solitary nature, and he doubted if he ever would fit into an occupation that meant working alongside others and always at the same place. Though he had no particular trouble getting on with others when necessary, he far preferred his own counsel and company.

He also needed time for his drawing — stretches of time that seemed to be growing as he increasingly tramped the woods to look for interesting flowers, plants, trees and rock formations that might help him hone his skill with the pencil. It was now habitual practice for him to slip a sketchbook in with his lunch pail, his flat carpenter pencil in service as much for his drawing as it was for his jobs of measuring and figuring. Hardly a lunchtime break would pass without a new sketch being made and added to the growing stack of them back in his room. The time spent on the river had been one of the longest periods of time he'd given over to one job, and though he was not anxious to repeat the experience, he was at least grateful that it had given him the extra income necessary for the trip.

Now, here he was on his way back home from his visit to the city, left to himself at the back of the railcar, left to ponder whether enduring the freezing wind sweeping down out of the Catskills across the Hudson throughout most of the winter and using the hard-earned money for such a trip had been worth it. Spending time with his parents was never easy — he and his father seemed always at odds — so that part of the trip was already entered in his mind into the debit side. Now, he had to decide whether the two days spent at the 69th Street Armory had also to be chalked up as a loss.

When the train pulled into Kingston's Union Station some three hours after he had boarded in Weehawken, Jake was no closer to a clear judgment of whether the trip was worth it or not. The Armory Show only deepened the mystery between what he thought art was and what others tried to make him believe it was.

He walked the few steps over to the U&D Rail station, bought a ticket to West Hurley, resignedly hoping that his uncertainty would resolve itself in the coming days and weeks ahead.

As he got off the train in West Hurley, he sniffed the air and looked toward the mountains. Already, he was feeling his muscles relax, his mind returning to its usual contemplative calm. Putting distance and time between himself and the last few days in the city might help him gain some perspective over the last several days. In any event, he felt more himself once he was back in familiar surroundings.

Jake shouldered his traveling bag and headed for home. After the long spell of sitting on the train, it felt good to be moving his larger muscles. The quiet of the small town of West Hurley closed in around him, giving him that sense of belonging he had so sorely missed the last few days.

It was only a short walk home from the train station, and the day had cleared as he had earlier that morning assumed it would, the late February sun managing to take some of the chill out of the air. Snow was still fairly deep alongside the roadways, but carriage and auto tracks had pretty much made short work of it on the road surfaces. It was still February after all, and one shouldn't put too much hope in these false, spring-like starts. Real spring would be some time in coming and it was still possible for a lot more snow to fall before winter would call it quits.

4

"So, Jacob, how was Mama and Papa — and young Friedrich?"

"Fine, Aunt Birgit. Mama sends her love."

"And your father? How was your time with him?"

Jake did not answer right away, busying himself with filling his plate with mashed potatoes.

"Fine," he said finally.

Uncle Hans snorted. "It is never 'fine' between you and your father."

Aunt Birgit tossed her husband a look as she passed the platter of meat to him. "It doesn't help when you add to it," she said.

"Ach, *Liebling,* who can get along with your brother? He still thinks he is in the old country, trying to run his house with an iron hand. This is America! Here we are free to do as we choose and Jacob is now a man. He can find his own way through life."

"Hans, Friedrich only wants what's best for his son. Is that so bad?"

Uncle Hans chuckled.

Jake refrained from contributing to what had become a familiar exchange between his aunt and uncle. He knew that, at bottom, Aunt Birgit agreed with her husband, but had to keep up appearances. Surely she loved her older brother and would defend him against any attackers. But just as surely, she was well aware of his domineering ways and knew, as did her nephew Jacob, that she was happy to live far from her brother's censuring eye. Both she and Uncle Hans were good-natured, open-hearted people, and, though they had no children of their own, seemed to understand Jake far better than did his own parents.

Turning to Jake, Aunt Birgit asked, "Did you speak to them about the exhibit you went down to the city to see?"

"Not a great deal," he answered lamely.

"Not at all, more likely," said his uncle.

"Oh, I am sure they would approve of your interest in art," said Aunt Birgit. "If they saw the beautiful drawings you make, how could they not like them?"

Jake was not so confident that this was true. His father, like his father before him, was a butcher. A stolid, pragmatic man when it came to his trade, he was convinced that Jake, like any man worth his salt, should learn a practical trade and stick to it. Is that not how he supported his wife and boys? What kind of an occupation is being a handyman?

Still, for all his father's insistence that he learn a trade as soon as possible so that he could become a "productive human being," Jake was not so sure that his father found any great satisfaction in being a butcher. For as long as he could remember, before his father would leave his store on Gates Avenue, he would briskly scrub his hands for a long time at the sink. After cleaning them with the large bar of Octagon soap he always kept nearby, he would carefully examine his fingernails to make sure that there were no visible signs of blood remaining. Then he would step into the tiny backroom and change into clean clothes; always a white shirt and tie, a neatly pressed dark suit, his shoes highly shined and either a straw hat in summer or a derby in winter set at a slightly rakish angle over his carefully combed hair. A last minute check to see if his carefully trimmed moustache needed any clipping, and then he would walk the few blocks home where, to most of the neighbors, he was privately referred to as "the Duke of Halsey Street."

On most days, he would make a short visit to the saloon he passed every day on his way home to have a "boilermaker" — a shot of whiskey, still in the glass, dropped into a tall glass of beer, the concoction tossed off in a single draft. The transformation from the red-faced tradesman with the bloody apron and hands to the foppish man who strutted down the street always mystified Jake. He often wondered why the freely given smile and tip of the hat to any passing woman was never in evidence in their home. Once the door closed to the outside world, the dandy would disappear into the closet with his hat and coat and out would come the dour man who only sought his beer, silence and, above all, obedience from his family.

Jake never knew his father's father, Jakob Forscher, the man after whom he was named. A butcher also — a *metzger* — in the tiny town of Polling in southern Germany, he had taken his oldest son, Heinrich, into the business when the boy turned 15. Since the town could not support more than two butchers, Friedrich, the second son, came to America after his marriage to Jake's mother to open his own shop and to find his own fortune. Each time Jake would ask his father about his grandfather, Friedrich Forscher would look into the distance and share the same two snippets of information with him: "He once broke a soup plate over my head for speaking at the supper table" and "He never held me." Jake knew even less about his grandmother. Whenever he asked his father about her, his only reply would be, "Ach! She died too young."

He knew more about his mother's parents. Her father, Gerhard Haas, was the head of a large family, and was, by her account, a kindly man who owned a small farm a short distance from Polling. When his youngest daughter Hannelore — Jake's mother — married and went off to America with Friedrich Forscher, it broke Gerhard's heart. The last of his brood, "Hanni" was his favorite, and, though she never failed to write him and Mama long letters about her new life, after she had moved to America they never saw each other again. Of her mother, Hedwig Cunnegunda — her father had always used both names when addressing her — she had fond memories of learning from her the two cardinal rules taught to all future *Hausfrauen* — the arts of cookery and that of pleasing one's husband.

Jake's brother Freddie, his father's first-born, was thus destined to stand by his father's side in the butcher shop on Brooklyn's Gates Avenue. The sign out front already read "Forscher & Son: Butchers" and, as far as he could tell, the arrangement suited his brother to a T. Freddie, in fact, was beginning not only to look but also to sound a lot like their father. Lately, he'd even begun adding his two cents to the lectures Jake would receive from his father whenever he returned home.

"When are you going to settle on a trade?" Freddie would echo their father. "By now you should have found something upstate. Aunt Birgit tells us that there are lots of opportunities up there.

She says a lot of men are finding work on that new reservoir they're building."

"You should have stayed with your Uncle Hans learning the bluestone trade," his father would say for at least the hundredth time. "When I sent you up there to stay permanently, I thought you would learn from him. If you had kept at it, by now you would have been a master stonecutter."

This was an old story to Jake. Almost every time he had walked to or from the butcher shop with him, his father would invariably stop along the way to point to the curbing and stamp his foot on the sidewalk.

"There!" he would say. "There is a solid future!" totally unaware of the unintended pun he was making. "Bluestone!" he would pronounce as if he had just made the discovery of the stone himself. "Bluestone from the quarries up in the Catskills. Now even the big shots in New York City are buying it for their front sidewalks and stoops. From Uncle Hans you could learn the trade and be set up for life."

As a matter of fact, Jake had already learned quite a bit about the bluestone trade, was already adept at laying up walls for foundations, cellar walls or property boundaries, but it was not an occupation that he chose to stay with — a decision his uncle understood and seconded. Ever since the discovery of cement, Uncle Hans knew that the bluestone business was doomed and had advised his nephew to seek something different for his future. However, Jake had learned over the years that arguing with his father or trying to explain himself was to no avail and as was his habit, chose not to answer either him or Freddie directly. Instead, he would turn to his mother and divert the conversation into other, safer topics.

Only once had he ever brought up his growing interest in painting.

Jake turned to his aunt. "Mama would like my drawings, Aunt Birgit," said Jake, "but it would be too hard to explain to Papa why I'm making them."

"All he knows is meat — and making eyes at pretty women," said Uncle Hans, his deep chuckle trailing off into a rasping cough.

"Hans!" said his aunt. "His boy is sitting right here!"

She rose from the table and began angrily clearing away the dishes.

"The 'boy' is a man, *Liebling*. He knows what I am talking about." His uncle gave a wink to Jake and, pushing his chair back from the table, began tamping tobacco into his pipe. "Your brother always had an eye for the girls."

"So, he is a friendly man, a business man. How could he keep his customers if he was not friendly to them?" She was furiously working the hand pump at the sink, filling the basin with water to wash the dishes. "I do not remember ever hearing Hanni complain about it," she added over her shoulder.

"Ach, Hannelore," snorted his uncle. "When did she ever criticize her Friedrich? In her eyes he could do no wrong."

"Hans, Hans! Their son sits right there in front of you!" She shook her head angrily, impatiently brushing back her hair with the back of her soapy hand. "And you should stop that smoking!" she added, as he alternately coughed and drew on his pipe. "It's no good for you!"

"And how does this change your brother?" he asked. "My not smoking will change his bull-headedness?"

Jake sipped his coffee, refraining from adding any comments. He listened to the sleet driving against the window behind him, February reasserting itself once again as a winter month. At least he did not have to slog through this weather as he walked from the train earlier that day. He was glad that it held before he reached home, thankful that the respite gave him the opportunity to replenish the wood boxes in both the kitchen and cellar. He knew his aunt's anger would blow over, confident that both she and his uncle were far too happy with each other to allow discord between them to linger.

So unlike the relationship between his parents — he thought.

Jake was used to his uncle poking fun at his brother-in-law — it was, in fact, one of the reasons that Freddie and he had liked it when their uncle used to visit them while they still lived in Brooklyn since he would say things that they could only think. Uncle Hans loved, as he put it, "getting Friedrich's goat," impervious to both Papa's glare and his extended bouts of condemning silence.

He also knew that, in truth, Aunt Birgit could not disagree with her husband's assessment of her brother. She had come to America to live with Friedrich and Hannelore when they had gotten settled, hoping, as did her brother that America might offer her more opportunities than the little village of Polling might afford. She earned her keep by helping Hanni with the housecleaning, by working the counter on busy days at the butcher shop, and by taking care of the boys when her sister-in-law was occupied at other things.

Ja, ja. She knew her brother and could not with honesty say her husband was wrong. She also knew her brother's opinion about art and artists since she, like him, could well remember their father's comments about those who came to the shop in Polling. *Luftmenschen,* her father called artists. Men who lived with their heads "in the air." And when would Friedrich ever contradict Papa?

When Hans came courting back in those early days in Brooklyn, Birgit lay awake at night wondering how long it would be before she could move out of her brother's home to begin setting up her own. She first met Hans at the butcher shop where he would come in, always with a smile, and always with some little joke. He would openly flirt with her, causing her cheeks to flame and her brother to grunt with disgust.

"Did you come to buy meat or make eyes at my sister?" Friedrich would grumble. Pushing Birgit aside with his shoulder, he would wipe his hands on his apron and stand with his hands on his hips. "What do you want today? This is not a beer hall where we have time to socialize! We are trying to make a living here."

Hans would merely laugh, brushing off her brother's bluntness as if of no account. Coming as he did from Munich, Hans Wolff had none of the small-town closeness about him, none of the suspicion of "outsiders" common to villagers such as Friedrich. A bluff and hearty man, Hans had worked in the Solnhofen quarries located north of his hometown of Munich, earning his living as a cutter of the *plattenkalk* the region was famous for. This rich deposit of limestone, laid down during the earth's Jurassic period, had long been famous for the fossils it contained. Known and visited by archaeologists from around the world, Solnhofen and its quarries had offered steady employment to local laborers for many, many years. Hans was, in fact, a third-generation quarrier, following in both his father and grandfather's footsteps.

In later years, the stone was also favored by the artists who had learned of the work of Alois Senefelder, the man who had invented lithography in 1798, his fame bringing even greater interest and more jobs to the Solnhofen quarries. Artists paid well for the finely grained stone that suited their printing purposes, and Hans, a skilled craftsman, had been most often given the task of cutting the thick blocks to their fussy specifications.

Though a stone-cutter by trade, Hans's innate curiosity prodded him to learn more about the *plattenkalk* he worked on and, when things were slow, he would spend a good deal of his time searching for the fossils which had originally made the place famous. He had managed to gather a small collection of his own and was always delighted to find a new specimen to add to the growing number of boxes in which he kept them. He even went out of his way to get his hands on a book or two and extended his knowledge about geology and paleontology through reading.

When he was put to work cutting and squaring off the stones for the lithographers, his curiosity turned to the study of this process as well. He had come to know some of the men who purchased the stones and, whenever possible, would sometimes go to the exhibitions they had in Munich. That such a simple thing as stone could be responsible for bringing such beauty into the world as both fossils and as art, was for Hans Wolff a thing to cause wonderment. He brought his openness to others and to learning with him to America, finding it always a sure way of meeting new people.

Birgit would steal glances at him as he good-naturedly bantered with her brother, smiling behind her hands as he purposely made Friedrich take out different pieces of meat, only to refuse them and ask for others. Her brother would angrily slap the chops or steaks onto the scale, scowl as Hans would pull a face and point to another piece, and mutter under his breath while the "big shot" stole more glances at his sister.

When Hans began coming to the house on Halsey Street to pay proper court, Friedrich would never give an inch, refusing to join in any idle conversation in the parlor, claiming his right as head of the house by dominating the conversation at meals. To Birgit he would only say, "You can do better," whenever she asked his opinion after Hans's visit would end. Hannelore, ever the good wife, not wishing to contradict her husband, would say nothing either way but was secretly charmed by the amiable Hans who never failed to bring her flowers when he came to share a meal at their table.

Hans Wolff lived only a short distance away in a little room he rented on Evergreen Street, almost exactly halfway between the butcher shop and the Forscher home on Halsey Street. Meetings between Hans and Birgit gradually increased, Hans sometimes taking Birgit to a picture show up on Broadway or accompanying her to a dance at one of the many beer halls in the neighborhood. Love quickly blossomed. Her brother Friedrich, however, remained non-committal, barely acknowledging Hans when they passed on the street, nodding his head curtly to his future brother-in-law, saving his smiles exclusively for the next female that came his way. When he learned that Hans intended to move upstate after they married, he felt neither joy nor loss.

So — Friedrich thought to himself — *I will wish them well when it happens and that will be that. After all, each man has to have his trade, has to make his own way in the world. America offered them that opportunity and it was a man's duty to take advantage of it.*

Why couldn't his son Jacob accept that fact? Why was he not like Friedrich Junior, eager to learn his trade, already shouldering much of the duties of the business, even anxious — Friedrich could tell — to run it by himself? He did not resent his eldest son's ambition, seeing it as an inevitable development, looking forward to retire one day and never again having to scrub blood from his hands. *Genau!* This was as it should be.

"Ach!" he would say to his wife in Jake's hearing. "Why must he be so obstinate? He will never be worth the salt in his soup if he continues with his foolishness!"

Jacob, the "obstinate" son, turned his attention back to the present, to the voice of his uncle.

"Your brother was always *dick*," Uncle Hans was saying to Aunt Birgit as he puffed on his pipe. "Always so bull-headed. Always he had to be right." Supper over, they had moved into the parlor, chairs evenly distributed around the fireplace, he and his uncle smoking, while his aunt busied herself at her knitting. His uncle nodded in his direction, adding, "You are not so different from him, you know. You can be as stubborn as he is."

Jake did not disagree. However, he preferred to think of himself as determined rather than *dick* — thick. He knew his own mind, was not easily swayed by others, steadfastly finishing whatever task was at hand. If this made him *dick*, then so be it. But, he was *nothing* like his father!

His aunt, anxious to turn the conversation away from her brother, asked, "Well, how was the *Ausstellung* — the exhibit? Tell us about it."

Jake leaned back and looked at the ceiling. "I'm not sure I can — at least not with a whole lot of sense."

"An exhibit is an exhibit," said his uncle with a shrug of his broad shoulders. "The work is either good or it is bad. You went to see pictures. What did you see?"

Jake furrowed his brow and, leaning forward, said, "That's just it, Uncle Hans. I'm not sure *what* I saw. There was good work, of course. But, you would not believe some of the stuff that they were showing. Crazy pictures of people with two eyes on one side of their heads, blobs of color that made no sense. As far as the sculptures went, I've seen better carving from the bluestone workers at the quarry."

"It was a waste of time?" said his aunt. "That's too bad." She shook her head. "You were so determined to see it and worked so hard to make the trip."

"I'm not so sure I wasted my time," Jake said. "I'm sure I learned something, Aunt Birgit — only I am not sure yet what it is. It is still all very confusing to me. The work of the Americans — though I certainly did not like much of it — was at least understandable. But the stuff from Europe...I just don't know what to think of it."

"Ach, Europe," said his uncle, sadly shaking his head. "The old country. They still think like they did in the Middle Ages." A hacking cough followed a few deep draws on his pipe and he put it aside.

"It is terrible what is going on all over Europe," said his aunt. "The politicians and journalists instigate so much hate, so much bickering."

"It will be war soon," said his uncle quietly. "And with all our new inventions, it will be worse than ever before."

The quiet seeped into the room, a log fell into the ashes, the wind and sleet buffeted the windowpanes. The clicking of his aunt's knitting needles sounded uncommonly loud in the lull that enveloped them. His uncle sucked noisily on his now unlit pipe.

"So many old hatreds," said Aunt Birgit after a long pause. "It's no wonder that the art they are making is confusing. How could it not be with the people in such turmoil?"

Jake, deep in his own thoughts, allowed his aunt's question to penetrate his consciousness. Was that what he was seeing at the Armory Show? An outpouring of anguish? Of hatred? Confusion? Surely there was nothing peaceful in the images that continued to haunt his mind. Fractured worlds, fractured people. Colors that swam indiscriminately before the eyes. Pieces of stone and marble carved into unrecognizable lumps of ugliness. What else could it mean if *not* anguish?

Still, what had art to do with the politics of governments? Why must the artist take on the job of the journalist and the politician? Did not art come from some inner self? Some higher source? Was it not meant to be balm to man? A beacon to better selves? Why must it be twisted to serve the ends of man's greed for wealth, for land, and for power? Why must the artist add to what everyone already knew, what anyone could read about in the papers? How could adding to the ugliness of life help to alleviate it? Jake couldn't answer any of these questions. He did not know how to begin — or even if he knew the *right* questions to ask.

Again, a familiar feeling of insecurity enveloped him. What did he know about art anyway?

Jake glanced over at his aunt, her hands still at work on her knitting. Uncle Hans had fallen asleep, his chin resting on his chest, his unlit pipe still held in his large hands.

"No, Aunt Birgit," he said softly, "I don't think I can tell my father about my wanting to draw." He rose and stretched and leaned over to kiss his aunt goodnight.

He looked out the window and saw that the wind had died down and that the slanting sleet had turned into a fall of large, slowly descending flakes.

He went to his uncle and laid his hand on his shoulder. "Good night, Uncle Hans. I'll bank the furnace for the night."

He stood for a moment, his hand on the knob of the cellar door and said over his shoulder, "Had Papa been with me at that exhibition in the city, he might even have been able to convince me that he was right. Maybe it *is* all nonsense."

5

Taken out of school by the time he was sixteen and sent up to his uncle's to "learn a trade and become a man," Jake knew nothing about the course of art through history. Even now he was only learning the rudiments of painting. What did he know about theory, about aesthetics, about the "purpose" of art? He was still trying to master drawing, still discovering the nature and use of his simple materials.

Not only was he unable to tell his father why he wanted to be an artist — he couldn't even explain it to himself.

For as long as he could remember, making pictures came as naturally to him as did breathing in and out. He had an innate talent for copying almost anything he saw, spending hours on the parlor floor in his Brooklyn home with pencil and paper drawing characters from the comic strips he found in the newspapers. At the Catholic school he attended on Bleecker Street, he called the wrath of nuns down upon his head by filling his notebooks — and often, the larger crime, the margins of his textbooks — with caricatures of them and of his fellow classmates. Art was simply not part of the school curriculum. Still, drawing was a compulsion he couldn't resist; not even when his father cuffed him as he doodled and drew on the brown rolls of butcher paper when he helped out in the shop. The magic of being able to suggest distance and shapes with only a pencil and a flat piece of paper mystified him.

Where had this ability to take a pencil and replicate people and things come from?

To his father it was nothing but foolishness. A trick one learned like pursing one's lips to whistle. So, you could whistle — but what could you do with it? Could you make a living at it? What kind of a man would spend his life whistling?

He would grab the paper from Jake's hands and crumble it into a wad. "Stop wasting paper!" he would yell. "If you must play with a pencil, better to spend your time learning your sums so that the customers will not cheat you!" This would inevitably be followed by his father's recitation of what he had learned about artists from *his* father. To Jake, it was a familiar refrain.

"Papa said they were bums!" his father would say as he busied himself at the butcher block. "And your grandfather knew what he was talking about, Jacob! Unable to hold decent jobs, they minced about town and pretended to be creative geniuses who needed to be supported by the sweat of others." Jake's father would then shake his head. "Ach," he would mutter, "How many times did he throw them out of the shop when they tried to pay him with pictures? *Donner Vetter!* What could Papa do with pictures! Pah!"

In later years Jake would learn that Polling, Germany, where his grandfather had his *Metzgerei,* was one of the forerunners of the art-colony concept that was beginning to take hold in America. Woodstock, New York, in fact, where he now spent a good part of his time, was one of its prime homegrown examples. Like Woodstock, settled on the Sawkill River with its Catskill Mountain backdrop, the Bavarian village of Polling was nestled at the foot of the Alps, its bucolic setting beneath the towering mountains serving as a lure for artists from nearby cities. They would come to Polling during the summers not only from the nearby Royal Academy of Munich, but from schools as far north as Düsseldorf as well, setting up their easels in the fields of farmers, their "taking over" the tiny town often bringing upon their heads the disdain and disapproval of the locals.

Jake would also learn that among the "bums" that earned the dismissive attitude of his grandfather were such American artists as Frank Duveneck and William Merritt Chase. Both of these men had studied at the Munich Academy and, along with their fellows, spent their summers in Polling. That both Duveneck and Chase would eventually return to America to make names for themselves in the annals of American art would not have impressed his father one iota. Though in all likelihood Jake's father never set eyes on a real artist himself, he had accepted as gospel the pronouncement of his father, the same man who had broken a plate over his head and who had never held him. How could one question such authority?

And how could Jake tell his father that, against all such admonitions, he still practiced his foolishness of making pictures?

It was not that he had purposely chosen to defy his father. Ironically, the early compulsion to draw was only enhanced by his father's decision to send him upstate. When he and Freddie traveled up the Hudson on the *Hendrik Hudson* back in June of 1907, it was the first time they had traveled up to Uncle Hans and Aunt Birgit alone. Freddie was 16, he 14. Though they had gone many times when they were younger with their parents to spend a few days up "in the country," they usually traveled by train to save time. Once there, under the watchful eyes of their parents, their time was mostly spent on their uncle's well-kept, half-acre plot. Mama and Papa went to visit, not to sight-see, trusting to the garden kept by Birgit, the pigs and chickens they raised for food and eggs, Uncle Hans's horses, and the nearby woodland to occupy their sons. Coming upstate without their parents opened to Jake a newfound freedom from restraint; furthermore, the trip by boat opened vistas of the countryside he never recalled seeing when they traveled by train.

Though Freddie was charged with serving as surrogate father while they were on their own, the experience of being afloat on the river proved too exciting for the two teenagers to remember all the commands and rules they were given. And although the deckhands and officers of the *Hendrik Hudson* tried to keep a watchful eye on all of the children aboard the day-liner, the boys found it too irresistible to keep from roaming the various decks, staring goggle-eyed at the huge steam-engine and its moving parts, asking as many questions as they could when they could find a deckhand that would pause long enough to answer them. Freddie became particularly absorbed in how the boat operated, curious to see the workings of the huge paddle wheel — its massive and moving bulk carefully shielded from the passengers for protection — and was soon taken in tow by one of the deckhands to be led below decks for a "cook's tour."

Less interested in the mechanics of steam propulsion and the operation of machinery, Jake spent most of his time on the top deck, moving back and forth across its planked decks to take in the constantly changing view of the countryside as the great ship plied its way up the Hudson. Though he found the taking on and unloading of passengers and freight along the various landings momentarily interesting to observe, he found himself impatient to be away from the towns and out on the river to once again be able to watch the hills, trees, and farms as they slowly slipped past the boat.

The shipping channel, as it sometimes approached the west shore, sometimes the east, offered the passengers a never-ending variety of close-ups and panoramas of the landscape on both sides of the Hudson. The forbidding Palisades, the hills and fields, the farms and mansions, the landings and warehouses, silently sliding past his line of vision in the constantly changing light, riveted Jake to the rails running around the observation deck. Long forgotten was the sandwich and cookies his mother pushed into his jacket pocket; equally oblivious was he to Freddie's periodic intrusions of "checking up on him" as Papa had instructed, his excited descriptions of what he had seen "down below" falling largely on deaf ears. Jake was too busy filling his eyes to spend time filling either his stomach or his ears.

As they pulled out of the Poughkeepsie landing, one of the deckhands keeping an eye on him told Jake that he ought to find a good place on the port side of the ship so that he could see "one of the most beautiful sights along the river."

"That's the left side," the deckhand added, but Jake had already learned from listening to the workmen that "port" meant "left" and had automatically begun heading towards that rail.

By now almost filled to overflowing with images, Jake could not imagine what could be more beautiful than what he had already seen. He looked eagerly up ahead, scanning the river over the bow of the ship, but could see only a row of low hills that seemed to signal an ending of the river.

"Coming soon," the deckhand called out to him.

Jake strained his eyes to see the "most beautiful" sight.

"We're coming to Crum Elbow," hollered the deckhand as he pointed ahead. "It looks like the river ends up yonder, but it takes a sharp turn to port. Once we get around that bend, son, you be sure to keep your eyes peeled!"

For the rest of his life, at will, and even in the dead of night, seated in his room some miles inland from the river and many miles distant from that bend in the river known as Crum's Elbow, Jake could still recreate that view in the shimmering June sunlight as it unfolded before his eyes when the *Hendrik Hudson* negotiated that curve.

Off on the horizon, some thirty miles distant, he saw the eastern peaks of the Catskill Mountains, their undulating mass appearing blue in aerial perspective. He held his breath, fearing that any sudden movement would make the vaporous image vanish from sight. Though he knew from earlier visits upstate that their massy bulk existed, from his view on the river and in this light they appeared dream-like, wispy, subject to instant dissipation if blasted by a strong wind. He was aware that somewhere at their base his uncle and aunt lived, and that he had often caught glimpses of the mountains when he rode with his uncle down to the several stone-finishing sites he worked at along the Rondout Creek. This was the first time, however, that he had seen the mountains *en masse*, the first time he had beheld them as a contiguous, unified whole. It was as if he had to step back in space to grasp their significance as an entity unto themselves.

The deckhand, now standing alongside him, said softly, "The Indians call it the 'Wall of Manitou' — 'God's Wall'."

Jake could not respond, and keeping his eyes on the mountains, merely nodded.

The deckhand silently moved off and, as time and distance slowly passed, Jake remained at the rail as if transfixed. He felt oddly gigantic, as if he had expanded beyond his skin, as if his body extended beyond the bounds of the boat, even beyond the banks of the river. For a moment he imagined himself hugely towering over the earth, and, almost at the same time, experienced a confined tightening across his chest and a swimming giddiness in his head. The idea that he might be suffering seasickness flashed through his mind. Abruptly, however, the unsteadiness left him and he found himself tightly gripping the handrail. And though he would not have been able to put it into such words back on that day on the Hudson River, his young mind somehow sensed that he had been experiencing a God's-eye view and that his first glimpse of the Catskill Mountains from the deck of the *Hendrik Hudson* had been some kind of revelation.

Jake had no frame of reference for the sensations that possessed both his mind and his body that day. Though he and Freddie went to Catholic school, the subject of religion was rarely broached in the Forscher home. His father, though born a Lutheran, was affiliated with no church. Jake and Freddie attended a parochial school only in deference to their mother's wishes and, though she was raised in a Catholic family, her ties with her religion were somewhat loosened by her marriage to Friedrich and by her move to America. Consequently, a sense of the Divine Power that the Dominican nuns tried daily to impress upon their charges found little purchase in Jake's young mind. Papa was all the god-figure he knew — or wanted to know. Whatever relationship he might have with some unseen, distant God was long ago superceded by the authority embodied in the physical presence of his father, the butcher Friedrich Forscher.

The power, then, of that distant airy vision of the Catskills to impact him so forcefully, to make his body tremble, stunned him. It was literally his first "religious" experience, an epiphany that spoke to him of a force outside of and greater than himself. Had the nun Sister Celine suddenly appeared at his side to say, "There, Jacob, *that* is what I mean," he still would not have fully understood the import of the experience. For the 14-year old Jake, he knew only that there, up in those ancient hills that to the world traveler hardly warranted the title of "mountains," was where he belonged.

Throughout the remainder of the trip upstate, in spite of the many new vistas spread before him, Jake's eyes never strayed far from the irregular silhouette on his left that moved in and out of sight as intervening hills came between that mesmerizing view and the boat. If anything, the attraction seemed to gain in strength as they loomed ever closer. At journey's end, as they finally neared the little town of Staatsburgh snuggled against the eastern bank of the Hudson just opposite Kingston, the Catskills dominated the western skyline. Jake could now see the whole eastern range from Overlook to the high ledges in the distance where he could just make out the Catskill Mountain House looking down on the river. Though details were still too far away to distinguish, Overlook's massive flanks held Jake's eyes in bondage, neither the ship's slowing and lumbering maneuvering into Kingston Landing nor the bustling activity on shore distracting him for an instant.

That summer was the first time that he and Freddie had stayed with their aunt and uncle for the whole season. For Jake, from the time Uncle Hans met them at the landing to take them home in the heavy-wheeled bluestone wagon until the time he took them back to meet the Day Boat going south to New York City the following September, the summer weeks and months flew by all too quickly. For him, each day was a time of learning more intense than any he had ever had at school.

That summer also witnessed his coming of age. It was as if a veil had been lifted from his eyes. Though most of his uncle's property was already familiar to him, each thing now presented itself to him in a new light. What had formerly simply been just "trees" now separated themselves into distinct varieties. He learned to tell oaks from butternuts, maples from chestnuts. He distinguished hemlocks from cedars, scrub oak from sumac. He studied the difference in the shapes of their leaves and how each of them reacted to wind or rain. He puzzled why some trees seemed to swallow the light hungrily while others threw it back into his eyes. He looked closely at the barks of trees and at the wood grain in the split logs in the woodshed. He found fossils embedded in shelf-rocks and noted the density of the grain of the bluestone that seemed to be everywhere he looked. Each new discovery was painstakingly drawn onto sheets and slips of paper that he kept in a box under his bed.

When he fed the animals, he noticed the difference in the way the feathers of his aunt's chickens rejected the rays of sunlight and the way the hairy skin of the hogs seemed to absorb them. Though these animals were not a natural part of their surroundings, he saw how they had adapted to their adopted homes in spite of their dependence on humans. At times, when he looked into the eyes of Uncle Hans's huge horses, he imagined that the animals knew him as another human would know him, that they could almost speak to him as they lowered their heads to nuzzle his chest. He knew that they had been brought there for their usefulness; knew that when they stopped laying eggs the chickens were destined for the pot, while the pigs — Uncle Hans always raised two each season — would be fattened until late autumn when they would be slaughtered for winter eating.

Wild animals — the squirrels, woodchucks, raccoons, deer, foxes, and birds of all varieties — all native to the Catskills, were self-reliant, fended for themselves throughout the seasons or took wing and left for warmer climates. All things animate and inanimate that he discovered that summer absorbed his time and interest.

As he learned to use his eyes and hands, he also began to sharpen his senses of hearing and smell. He heard and remembered the different bird songs, the snort of the startled deer, the sharp yapping of the fox, and the chhhkking sounds of chipmunk and squirrel. He distinguished between the smells of evergreens and hardwoods. Within the space of that summer, Jake had made the complete transition from city to country boy.

Throughout the remainder of the summer, whenever the image of the Catskills from the riverbend returned to his consciousness — though he could not have expressed it in words and had hardly thought it out in his own head — Jake felt that he had to make himself worthy of the gift he had received on that day. And, if he could not find words then he would use lines and shadows to record his feelings. As the summer progressed he somehow felt it necessary — felt it his *duty* — to connect that God-like view of the Catskills with its separate components. He came to believe that by making himself learn how to draw their individual parts that he might also comprehend their essence, their being, understand the overpowering hold the mountains had on him.

For reasons he could barely fathom, when he thought of that day on the Hudson he found himself thinking about what he felt when he looked at Joanna, a pretty girl he sat next to back in parochial school. He could never understand why her nearness stirred him inside and he would sneak looks at her in class as she made her letters in her composition book, imagining that by studying the way her nose turned up or how her curls swung forward over her face as she concentrated on forming her words, he might figure out how she could exert such power over him, how she could cause him to blush and stammer when she turned to speak to him. And, although he never really figured out the mystery of Joanna's attraction by attempting to take her in "a piece at a time," he still believed that if he knew how the things of the mountains worked, how they fitted together and operated in concert, maybe he could learn to know them — and discover how they had the power to influence him.

When he was informed during the winter of 1909 that his father meant for him to stay and live with his aunt and uncle when he turned sixteen so that he might apprentice as a stonecutter, he could hardly contain his joy. Though he did not know anything about the work of quarrying, he knew that living in the Catskills would make him more than happy. The summer he turned sixteen, he traveled on the Day Line alone, Freddie by then already a full-fledged partner permanently at Papa's side in the shop.

That summer left Jake with more time on his own, more time to dig deeper and to look closer. He learned to know the different sound of rain as it fell on the leaves of trees, onto the upturned earth in the garden, or as it spattered across the packed earth of the roadway. He felt and mentally recorded the slight give of pine needles as opposed to the crunching of dried leaves through the thin soles of his high-topped shoes. He ran his fingers over the barks of different trees, over the smooth hardness of stone, over the serrated edges of leaves, and over the backs of the few farm animals it was his daily chore to attend, trying as he lay in bed at night to recall the sensation that each imparted to his fingertips.

He discovered where and how different birds made their nests, where the deer lay down at night, how possum, skunks, foxes, rabbits, and raccoons favored the night hours to forage for food, while squirrels and birds preferred the light of day to look for theirs. He learned how to find wild columbine and to bite off their nectar-filled lobes for that small taste of pure sweetness, how to uncover from their blanket of dead leaves the rare trailing arbutus with its other-worldly perfume, where to find the cinnamon-scented wild azalea, and marveled at how mountain laurel preferred to root itself in rocky soil.

He also discovered that both Uncle Hans and Aunt Birgit were attentive listeners, eager to hear what he had learned each day. He was especially pleased to learn that his uncle knew much about the fossils he had brought to the house as he began to share with Jake his work in the Solnhofen quarries while he still lived in Germany. When Uncle Hans began telling him about the stones he shaped for the lithographers and about going to visit exhibitions in Munich, Jake was beside himself with joy, happy to find an ally in his burgeoning interest in art. When Uncle Hans and Aunt Birgit presented him with his first bound sketchbook later that summer, he could not keep the tears from springing to his eyes.

Most important of all, however, it was during that second summer that he had settled in his mind once and for all that it was Overlook Mountain that had claimed him. Of all the Catskill peaks, it would be Overlook that he would explore, Overlook that he would climb, Overlook that he would come to know, and Overlook that would reveal its secrets to him. He would explore her slopes, her ridges, her plateaus and, though he did not know it yet, would in time find himself attempting to uncover her mysteries through his own magic of capturing her on paper.

How could he tell his father such things? For Friedrich Forscher, reality consisted only of what could be hefted in the hand, of what could be measured and weighed according to well-established and authoritative rules.

As Uncle Hans put it, all Papa knew was meat.

6

Jake was not surprised to learn that, even three weeks after he had seen the Armory Show down in New York City, the exhibition was still the main topic of conversation among artists in Woodstock. Practically every artist in town — even John Carlson with several of his diehard landscape students — had gone to see the show and, whenever or wherever two or three gathered for any length of time, the topic of the exhibit would come up and each was sure to add his opinions and observations.

No one, as far as Jake could tell, appeared indifferent, each having strong feelings about the relative merits or worthlessness of the show. From time to time Jake would take part in these conversations — mostly listening in, however. Since it was known that he had gone to see it, he would sometimes be asked to offer a comment — but, for the most part, he had relatively little to add and, in spite of the often strongly stated feelings of others, was no further ahead in clearing his own mind about what he had seen.

The first week of March had been an exceptionally mild one, warm breezes wafting up from the south and streams swollen with rapidly melted snow giving proof that winter had lost its icy grip. Overlook Mountain was still capped in white, but Jake could tell that it would soon be time for him to be looking for outdoor work.

He had been in Woodstock for several days, building bookshelves for one of the "city folks" who had recently sought permanent residence in the village, an occurrence that was happening more frequently as the little town gained national — even international — prominence as an art "colony." Many of these newcomers had become enchanted with the quaint little village in its Catskill

Mountain setting after coming up for a summer of art instruction at either Byrdcliffe or the Art Students League, deciding after a season or two to either buy or build their own studio in or near the town.

Of the two main attractions that brought artists to the town, Byrdcliffe was the older, founded in 1902 and run by a man named Ralph Radcliffe Whitehead. Whitehead, an Englishman influenced by the aesthetic and socialist ideas of John Ruskin and William Morris, had envisioned founding his own colony of artists and artisans in America. Following the recommendations of two of his own followers, Hervey White and Bolton Brown who had scouted a good bit of the Catskills, he began building his community just outside the village of Woodstock on the southwestern flank of Guardian Mountain. White and Brown, armed with a general description of what, to John Ruskin, might be a perfect setting for such an art colony, had discovered a site that commanded a striking view of the Woodstock Valley. Whitehead, when he looked over the grounds, readily agreed on the suitability of the location and named his community "Byrdcliffe," a combination of parts of his and his wife's middle names.

Jake had often worked at Byrdcliffe, hiring out mainly as a day carpenter to Fordyce Herrick, Whitehead's chief carpenter on the premises, but at other times, happy to turn his hand as a laborer to the more menial chores that continually seemed to arise in the building of this little village. Whitehead, sporting a neatly trimmed mustache over his full lips, ran his colony in a somewhat lordly manner, his English tweeds, his accent, and gentlemanly mien greatly impressing Jake as the Englishman strolled around to oversee his workers. Though he at times appeared imperious with his guests and generally held himself aloof from the workmen, Jake found him to be a generous employer, always paying him a fair wage and always in a timely fashion. By 1913, most of the 30-odd buildings scattered over Whitehead's 1300-acre plot had already been erected, but Jake was kept busy either building interior walls and bookshelves or using his axe, scythe and brush-hook around the grounds to keep the many interlocking paths and roadways between buildings clear of shrubbery and unwanted saplings that seemed to spring up overnight.

As he had expected, the Armory Show did not play much of a

part in the general discussion among the Byrdcliffe residents. Neither the exhibit's much-touted anticipation nor one-month stay in New York City aroused much interest in Byrdcliffe since modern art in general and commercialism in particular was an anathema to the pure-minded Whitehead — an attitude to which most of his guests wholeheartedly ascribed. If Jake had heard mention of it at all at Byrdcliffe prior to his decision to go and see the exhibit, it was usually only in negative terms by the utopian colonists on Guardian Mountain.

Though Woodstock originally owed its genesis as an art colony to Ralph Radcliffe Whitehead and the founding of his Byrdcliffe settlement in 1902, it was the coming of the Art Students League of New York four years later to establish its summer sessions in the village that put the picturesque little hamlet on the artistic map of America. Already a force in the artworld, the League had enjoyed a solid reputation built upon its original founding in 1875 as a school established and administered by its own cadre of students. After some initial forays into Connecticut — mainly at Norwich and Lyme — the League had, under the urging of Birge Harrison, settled on Woodstock as the place to establish its permanent summer sessions. Harrison, a landscape painter and art instructor at Byrdcliffe, had left the employ of Whitehead to become the head of the League's new venture when, in 1906, it opened its first studio in what was once a blacksmith's shop in the center of the village.

By 1913, the year of the Armory Show, the League, already a powerful force in the colony, had moved out of its original home in the blacksmith's shop to put up its own building on Woodstock's main thoroughfare, and it was there that Jake would hear equal amounts of excited anticipation and dismissive derision in and around its studios on Tinker Street. Though most League students had come to Woodstock to study landscape painting — Harrison had, almost from its inception in 1906, been calling it the "best landscape school in the world" — they came from a wide variety of backgrounds, and many were open to anything they might learn about art.

As did many of the Leaguers, Jake had been gathering most of his information about the Armory Show from the artists over in Rock City. It was there in Bolton Brown's enclave that modern art reigned supreme and, among his entourage, the Armory Show a main topic of conversation. Brown, even before Harrison, had left as art instructor at Byrdcliffe but under more unpleasant circumstances. He and Whitehead sharply disagreed about his role at the colony and since their parting of the ways it seemed he had every intention to champion everything that Ralph Radcliffe Whitehead had held in contempt — especially any kind of art that could be called "modern."

Brown had chosen to build his own studio in what was commonly called "Rock City," situated down from Byrdcliffe at the crossroads of Glasco Turnpike and the Rock City Road and nearer to Woodstock's village center. Under Brown's guidance and prompting, his followers soon gained the reputation of "going their own way," finding fault not only with the "Byrdcliffers," but also with the more traditional landscape painters at the Art Students League as well. When Brown's group was joined by such like-minded artists as Andrew Dasburg and Konrad Cramer, the Woodstock art colony could boast a firmly entrenched "modernist" camp in its midst.

Dasburg, whose work already indicated a strong Cézanne influence, was also taken with the paintings of Matisse that he had seen at the Paris Exhibition of 1905, and had met both him and Picasso just two years earlier in 1911. Konrad Cramer, meanwhile, had just recently arrived after extensive contact with the *Blau Reiter* School in Germany. Both freely and eagerly shared their experiences about what was happening in Europe with anyone who listened.

It was from Dasburg that Jake began hearing about Henri Matisse and his *fauves* — the "wild beasts" — and though he had some vague idea of what these "wild beasts" were up to, he was certainly not prepared when he actually saw Matisse's work at the Armory Show. He found that artist's *Jeune Marin* and *La Femme bleu* particularly disturbing, the colors "all wrong" to his way of thinking.

It was the arguments of Brinley, however — his full name was Putnam Daniel Brinley, but everyone called him "Daniel" — the most vocal and most committed to the Armory Show of the group — that finally persuaded Jake to make the trip down to New York City.

Most often, the experiences and discussions of the Rock City group concerning modern art were shared at the communal dining table at Rosie Magee's, a boarding house just down the road from Brown's studio. Known as "Mother Magee" to many of the artists in town who found her table to be both bounteous and inexpensive, Magee, a local, presided over her guests, as would a mother hen over her chicks. Rosie's husband, Sanford, was a retired quarry teamster and a long-time friend of Jake's Uncle Hans and, it was through that friendship that Jake was able to make a special arrangement with the Magees, staying as a guest at a reduced rate when his work schedule made it necessary for him to be in town overnight. Also, while he was in town, Mrs. Magee always welcomed him as a non-paying guest at her noontime and evening meals. He would repay "Missus Magee" — Jake never referred to her as "Mother" or "Rosie" — for this extra kindness by doing odd jobs around the place, taking care of minor repairs that Sanford tended to let slide.

Jake would usually sit quietly over his plate, listening intently, trying to absorb what he could. Much of what was said at Mrs. Magee's table went far over his head, the discussions about art often intellectual and theoretical and centered on concepts and artists that he had little or no knowledge of. Having had no formal art training, the references to art history, to past masters, to trends and movements, appeared to have no direct relation to the actual act of painting and he had no frame of reference by which to understand or evaluate the discussions. At times, conversation would become heated, loud and querulous, unlike the quiet chats he would sometimes overhear up at Byrdcliffe from the small groups that walked by as he worked around the grounds. To Jake, it would often seem as if talking about art was as important to the Rock City group as *making* it.

Though he often felt at a disadvantage, Jake did not as yet fully appreciate the unique position in which he found himself. An outsider by nature, he was also one in fact by virtue of the unusual set of circumstances that had set him there, in that place, and at that time. Not being either formally or informally associated with *any* of the artistic coteries that were growing up around him in Woodstock, neither was he a "local," a born and bred Woodstocker who, by and large, kept themselves aloof from *any* of the art groups that seemed to be sprouting up in the once sleepy little hamlet like mushrooms after a rainstorm. Not only was Jake still regarded by the townsfolk as a "city boy," he also lived in West Hurley, some few miles distant from Woodstock. It did not matter that he had been working in and around the town, side-by-side with many of the local men since he was sixteen; the fact remained that he was born in Brooklyn — and Woodstockers, like many small-town inhabitants, counted as one of their own only those who could point back to parents, grandparents, and *great* grandparents who called the village "home."

Thus, though he might at times have felt as if he didn't "belong" — he didn't even "belong" in the home of his aunt and uncle, for that matter, in spite of the fact that he felt more at home there than in that of his parents — neither did he ever feel *obliged* to belong anywhere or to anyone. The only thing — if 'thing' it was — he felt bound to, was to understand what he had undergone when he was on the river and had seen the Catskills from Crum Elbow. Otherwise, he was in fact a free agent, able to pick up and go whenever and wherever he wished, at liberty to accept or refuse any job offered him, the only axe he had to grind the one he carried over his shoulder. And though he might nod respectfully to the local tradesman who railed against the artists who were "ruining the town" or sympathize with the artist who felt he had to pay too much to the farmer who rented his outbuilding to him, he could often see the up and down sides to both of their points of view.

Likewise, he would quietly hear out the opinions about art of Byrdcliffers, Leaguers and Rock City dwellers with equal attention and dispassion. In such haphazard fashion did his intellectual and art-knowledge grow. But he was quick and eager to learn, at liberty to pick and choose those ideas that most accorded with his natural bent, the almost slipshod "educational" process saving him from forming any hard and fast rules.

Although Jake could find things with which to agree or disagree from both the Byrdcliffe and Rock City groups, he found that he could learn most from the Leaguers who stood somewhat midway between the extremes of Whitehead's elitist and Brown's anything-goes approaches to art. He soon discovered that he had more to mull over when he took his noon-time meals over at Mrs. Cooper's whose establishment was just a few doors down from the League studios on Tinker Street and to where many of those students gathered to eat. So even though he had to pay full freight at Cooper's, he felt that the 25 cents he had to shell out for the food — which, in terms of portion and taste rivaled that found at the table of Missus Magee — was as good if not better a deal than paying to sit though an honest-to-goodness art course at the League.

He noted that both Leaguers and Rock City dwellers tended to look down on the Byrdcliffe residents — one Rock City wit referring to them as "fairies and old maids in burlap skirts." Despite their jibes, Jake found himself admiring the gentility of the guests who spent their summers over on Guardian Mountain. True, he found them a bit exotic, often decked out in what he considered outlandish costume for the rural setting they chose to live in; they nevertheless seemed to be a friendly and interesting group. Though as a paid laborer he "knew his place" — Whitehead was a firm believer in observing hierarchical distinctions — he often found the residents willing to engage him in casual conversation. Some might stop him in his scything to ask him the name of a wildflower or even join him for a minute or two as he settled under a tree somewhere on the grounds to eat his lunch.

If at first they startled him as they plumped down beside him wherever he was sitting, asking him questions about Woodstock or the Catskills or to simply pass the time of day, he soon looked forward to their impromptu visits. Many seemed eager to speak about their reason for being at Byrdcliffe, happy to talk about the craft they were either studying or teaching. They would tell him about looms and pottery wheels and furniture making — all of which he would listen to politely even though he had no real interest in these topics. Though he found any craft that necessitated the use of the human hand to be inherently interesting, he would wish that there were more painters around to speak to. Since Harrison and Brown had left Byrdcliffe, the little art instruction still being offered was largely taken care of by Carl Eric Lindin who handily managed the slowly dwindling population of artists coming to the colony. As far as Jake could make out, the colony seemed overly populated by too many weavers and potters and musicians and wood-turners to have much room left over for painters — and Jake wanted to hear about painting.

And not just theories — like he did at Mrs. Magee's. He wanted to hear about *how* and not *what* he ought to paint. He already knew what he wanted to paint. He was drawn more, therefore, to the conversations between the students of John Carlson that he listened in on at Mrs. Cooper's, for it was here that he could learn about landscape painting. Over a quick noontime meal, he might pick up such hints and pointers as to how that instructor primed his canvases, how he "broke" colors, and how he used blue in the shadows cast by trees rather than by using the deadening non-color of black. When, from time to time, Carlson would join his students over lunch, Jake would pay special attention, rolling over the teacher's words in his mind when he went back to swinging his axe or nailing shelves in place or while walking home from whatever job he had just completed. What little he had seen of Carlson's work greatly impressed Jake, and he tried to learn as much about the painter and his methods as he could.

* * *

All of what Jake learned during his handyman work in and around Woodstock, he would store carefully in his mind to mull over in the privacy of his own room. He dreamed one day to have his own studio where he could work out some of the ideas he was hearing from the artists and students he eavesdropped on. He had already imposed upon his uncle's generosity to allow him the use of one of the outbuildings on his property. Built as a chicken coop by the previous owners, the building was large and soundly constructed, with large windows ranged along the side opposite the nesting boxes. It had an old wood stove set up in one corner, which was used to heat the building in the winter. Since Aunt Birgit kept only about a dozen hens around the place, the building went largely unused and served merely to store some of his uncle's tools.

Uncle Hans readily agreed, and, whenever Jake could find the time and could afford the materials, he slowly began converting the coop into a "studio." He found the word a bit pretentious for someone who had yet to earn the title of "artist," but he soon had the place cleaned out, caulked and insulated for the winter months, new shelves replacing the nesting boxes which he'd removed and re-installed at one end of the woodshed for Aunt Birgit's small flock of laying hens. The old cast iron wood stove was cleaned up and old, rusted stovepipes removed and replaced. A coat of paint on the wooden siding of the building would serve as the finishing touch. Both Uncle Hans and Aunt Birgit agreed that the "gussying up" of the old chicken coop had greatly improved the looks of their property and heartily encouraged their nephew in his fixing up of the building.

Jake had noted many such buildings turned into studios by artists, several in fact, converted over the past few years by him, so the remodeling presented little difficulty. His frequent visits to artist's studios had given him a good sense of exactly how he wanted to set up his own, and among his many questions about painting would always be a question or two about space management and equipment placement. Although they all had their own individual sense of what a studio ought to contain or look like, all agreed that a primary consideration had to be light — which many insisted had to come from the north. Several even hired Jake to move existing windows from east, west, and south walls and rcplace them on walls facing north. Luckily, his chicken-coop windows already had a northwest orientation and, at least for the present, he saw no reason to change them.

If the outside looked presentable, Jake's "studio" still had a long way to go to resemble the studios he had remodeled or built for the "real" artists he worked for. For now, it was merely a large, empty space waiting to be made purposeful.

His easel — which still had to be built — already had in his mind's eye its designated space near the windows. He had all the plans for its making carefully stored in his room, its design based on one he admired in Birge Harrison's studio over on the upper end of Glasco Turnpike. Harrison had still been putting finishing touches on his new studio in the town of Shady since his retirement from the League two years before and had hired Jake to construct some built-in shelves. Jake had struck up an amicable relationship with Harrison, finding him straightforward and open to his many questions. Mr. Harrison had good-naturedly allowed Jake to take measurements of his easel and draw his plans during one of his free moments.

A large wooden palette hanging from a nail driven into an overhead ceiling beam of the nearly transformed chicken coop presaged the building's ultimate purpose. A wooden box unobtrusively stuck in a corner might have given a second clue, but from its nondescript appearance might have held anything. It was actually a traveling paint-box. The palette hanging overhead had been bought and paid for from his earnings and the paint-box one of his own constructs, built, like the easel would one day be, from drawings he had made himself. The box held no paints since he did not yet know enough about colors to know what to purchase. A glass jelly jar holding about a half-dozen used brushes — given him by Birge Harrison — stood on a windowsill. Palette, paint-box, and brushes comprised the full complement of his "studio" paraphernalia. Though it could hardly compare with the well-stocked, well-broken-in studios that he often found occasion to work in, it was his own place and he was inordinately proud of it. And, what he lacked in materials, he more than made up for with the steady amassing of knowledge that he was slowly gaining from day to day.

7

As spring turned to summer and the summer began hinting at autumn, Jake noted that talk about the Armory Show was beginning to fade, most of the artists with whom he came into contact concentrated once more on their own work. Whatever positions individual artists might have taken, either convinced or not of the show's importance, most objective observers had to admit that, in general, the work shown at the Armory did exert an impact — and it was mostly the moderns who dominated the lingering discussions and the significance of that impact. Especially over in Rock City, there was strong conviction that men like Cézanne, Picasso, Matisse — Post Impressionists of all stripes, in fact, had forever called traditional practices into question. These artists had made major breakthroughs — according to such men as Andrew Dasburg and Conrad Kramer — that would forever after alter the course of American art. Some even argued that the breakthrough began with the Impressionists themselves when they began breaking up brushstrokes; others that the trend started even earlier with such painters as Franz Hals, Velázquez, and their loosened brushstrokes. Whatever the truth of the matter — if one could speak of such a "truth" — few knew how defining a moment in the course of American art that the Armory Show would exert nor how far into the future it would linger in the minds of anyone connected to the world of art.

Whether or not these "breakthroughs" would permanently "close the Academy's doors," meanwhile, remained to be seen. Since his visit to the show Jake had learned more about the National Academy in New York City and its instructing practices, but as far as he could tell from his limited perspective, it was a long way from closing down. Students still flocked to its doors and artists still jealously aspired to the title of "National Academician." As far as he could determine, those who had gone to the Academy — or for that matter had any kind of formal training — seemed to continue to go their own way, unconvinced that the work they were doing was, as the Rock City crowd put it, "passé." Many, in fact, seemed more determined than ever to follow their own dictates, blithely ignoring those who were equally intent on forging new paths. In the end, it seemed to Jake that the Armory Show merely served to harden long-held opinions and prejudices.

Of more importance to Jake — at least for the present — was making sure that he could find enough work so that he had enough cash to tide him over the coming winter. Work at Byrdcliffe had been slowing down since Whitehead's main house, "White Pines," the theatre, and many of the major studio buildings had already been completed and in use.

Fortunately, Jake began getting new work from another defector from Byrdcliffe, Hervey White, who had purchased a farm on Woodstock's opposite borders, not far from Jake's home in West Hurley. White, chafing, as had Brown and Harrison, under Whitehead's regimen, had recently bolted from Byrdcliffe, determined to start his own colony on his new piece of land. The "Maverick," as it was soon to be dubbed, was not conceived on quite the grand scale as was Byrdcliffe, Hervey White being a completely different character from Whitehead, and his "utopian" plan reflecting that difference.

Somewhat of a Renaissance man, Hervey White was a poet, a musician and a novelist — but most of all he was a dreamer — what Jake's father and grandfather might call a *Luftmensch* of the first order. He envisioned his "Maverick" to be a place that would serve as home to a wide variety of folks, each free to pursue his or her own star, each free from any one overriding guiding principal. If less organized than Ralph Radcliffe Whitehead, White had the good sense to recognize that creative people — to be *genuinely* creative — needed to be free of constraint and regulations. In short, they needed a place to gather that had no "boss" who was intent on directing their course.

Jake's axe and scythe were put into service to help clear some of the wooded land on White's farm, and before the snow started flying, his carpenter's tools to help White put up cabins to house his guests. Unlike Whitehead's elaborately planned and sturdily-built structures over in Byrdcliffe, the Maverick's haphazardly situated and roughly-constructed buildings were extremely rustic, most having little more than a sleeping and working space to offer occupants. Running water was not available, so such luxuries as toilets or showers were non-existent, but this seemed not to bother Hervey White's rapidly expanding community. It was not long before artists, musicians, newsmen, anarchists, actors, social reformers, drifters, dancers, feminists, writers, and poets flocked to Woodstock's newest attraction, many coming from the bohemian crowd in New York's Greenwich Village, many already acquaintances of White's from before and during his days of tenure at Byrdcliffe.

Rough-and-tumble residents rubbed shoulders with young Manhattan socialites, all joyfully taking makeshift showers under watering cans attached to tree limbs when occasion and need demanded. White collected rent when he could and cheerfully waived it when he couldn't. No one complained about the lack of amenities; everyone thought it a lark to spend a summer season in the "wilds" of the Catskill Mountains. For many of the self-styled Bohemians, Hervey White loomed as some modern-day Bacchic/Dionysian figure that presided over and lent approval with a silent wink to their woodland romps. As word of mouth spread, the colony grew. The West Hurley woods rang out with impromptu song fests, discussions, declamatory voices raised during hastily written theatrical skits, joyous laughter and — for Jake — a ripe and ready new source of information about art as more and more artists were attracted to the free-wheeling style of Hervey White.

Unlike the more defined groups he was used to at Byrdcliffe, Rock City, and the League, Jake discovered that the people flocking to Hervey White's Maverick were a varied bunch indeed. Some, like the feminist Charlotte Perkins Gilman, and reformers like Clarence Darrow and Thorstein Veblen, had already garnered some notability and added their fame and yet another flavor to the ever-growing mix of burgeoning creative energy that added new luster to the Woodstock mythos.

Intermixing between the several coteries was inevitable in the relative confines of the small village of Woodstock, and as time passed it was soon difficult to separate them into their old, hard-

and-fast categories of "Byrdcliffers," Rock City Group "Modernists," or "Leaguers." White's unrelenting democracy simply became too irresistible, and it was not long before dividing lines of hard-held principles began breaking down. Byrdcliffers of the more daring sort were found romping in the West Hurley woods with artists and craftspeople from New York's Greenwich Village, Modernists were busily spreading their theories with whomever stood still long enough for a harangue, and the Leaguers were beginning to break loose from a strict regimen of landscape painting and happily partaking of whatever came their way. Artists rubbed elbows with anarchists, musicians with potters, actors with feminists, and all of them with the locals – who, like it or not, had to accept that their village's growing popularity with the "arty" set appeared irreversible. Whatever they might have privately felt about artists traipsing through their fields "in search of motifs," their Yankee good sense would simply not allow them to pass up the opportunity of lining their pockets with all that new-found revenue flowing like a golden river into their midst.

Such prosperity also affected Jake who, once worried how he would get through the winter months, found, along with his usual work for Mr. Whitehead and now, Hervey White, an almost steady employment in re-modeling farmer's outbuildings into artists' "studios." His handiwork as a skilled carpenter had become well-known through word-of-mouth and he was recognized as something of an expert when it came to building a studio — so much so, in fact, that he would often not only follow orders but could make valuable and welcome suggestions along the way. He got so busy that he found himself longing at times for the coming of winter with its relative inactivity that would allow him more time for his own work. In addition to his multiplying opportunities for making ready cash, Jake was also finding that the heady mix infusing the old hamlet and rapidly breaking down reserve between factions — including that of the locals — was beginning to work some of its magic on him. He began to feel less reserved in his interactions with artists, more willing to speak freely about his own interest in art, and more boldly putting forth his questions to those whose opinions he valued.

Meanwhile, Jake's attempts at what he silently called "capturing Overlook" steadily grew as he doggedly continued his progression of approaching it from part to whole. He had amassed a considerable collection of drawings, many of his sketches of the flora native to the Catskills pinned up in his bedroom and, lately, beginning to adorn the bare walls of his "studio." During those rare times that he had no obligations, he would take daylong hikes up into Overlook's upper reaches, armed with a light lunch and a sketchbook, faithfully and painstakingly recording his new discoveries as he explored the mountain's secrets. As much as possible, he stayed clear of the well-traveled road up to the Catskill Mountain House to avoid meeting up with summer boarders or other artists in search of subjects. Always, he preferred the out-of-the-way recesses, the less trodden ridges and hollows that were unknown to most of the outsiders.

With increasing frequency, the small-scale studies he had been making of individual plants, trees, rock formations, and the like, began to expand into wider compositions of tree-groupings, expanses of rock ledge and even modest vistas he could glimpse from vantage points on high. Though not very distant from the boarding house above, one of his favorite lookouts was from the top of the cliff that had stood as Overlook Mountain's major landmark ever since the landslide exposed it in the rockslide of 1831. From here, he had a magnificent view eastward that opened across the Hudson River and far away toward the Berkshire Mountains in the neighboring state of Connecticut.

When not up on Overlook, the slope upon which Ralph Radcliffe Whitehead had built his Byrdcliffe colony afforded a splendid prospect of the Woodstock Valley, and Jake would often use his noontime lunch breaks to try sketching the view from various locations on Guardian Mountain. He still had trouble replicating the effects of aerial perspective and found that his carpenter's pencil, though a serviceable enough tool for capturing the detail of a wildflower or rock ledge, did little justice to the effects of light and distance on valleys, buildings, trees, and watercourses.

His gaze would be turned away from the traces of human settlement, as he had no desire to draw buildings or the neatly patterned geometry of yards and plots and fields that man had imposed upon the landscape along the Sawkill Creek. Vistas from Overlook's crest, especially that facing the Hudson River, were a bit more interesting to him and he made several drawings of the view toward the East.

But it was always the mountains that held him. The image of the Catskills first seen from the *Hendrik Hudson* still haunted him, and it was their presence untouched by human influence that he meant to someday paint. For Jake, it was Overlook Mountain, aloof and separate not only from the human forays made upon its mighty bulk but also from its neighboring fellows, that attracted him. It stood there immovable, grandly disdaining both the spoiler and the lover.

One day toward the close of summer, he had been summoned to Byrdcliffe to clear a path to a spring that came bubbling forth from the upper slope of Guardian Mountain, a short distance from the pottery studios. He had spent the better part of the morning completing the job. Around noon, he settled down beside the spring, ready to take his lunch and decided to make a sketch or two of a small clump of trailing arbutus growing a few feet away. He'd sketched arbutus many times before, but the way the sun's rays cutting through the trees from almost directly overhead and glinting from the plant's glossy leaves as they lay flat upon the ground had caught his eye, and he was determined to make a record of it.

As he sat hunched over his sketchpad, he could smell the fullness of autumn on the air. Of all the seasons, he liked fall the best. Winter — though it afforded him more time to spend at drawing — and summer both seemed to dampen his creative urge, and spring with its profusion of growth and blossom, seemed impossible for any human to compete with. Autumn had its own colors of course, but the air always seemed crisper, clearer, more invigorating and conducive to stirring Jake's creative juices. Whether true or not, he always imagined he could see farther, discern detail better in late September and October. Autumn had its own smells and sounds as both nature and man began preparing for the coming winter. As the days cooled, the earth gave off different odors, the pungent smells of rotting vegetation augmented by man's fall ritual burning of leaves. The season even offered different sounds — wildlife actively scurrying through dry leaves in their preparation for the coming snows, their noises deadened at times by the saws and axes of men cutting and splitting firewood toward the coming cold of winter. For Jake, it was the season most rich in sights and sounds and smells, a time dear to every outdoorsman he knew.

He had just laid aside his sketchpad and had been bending over the spring, his hand cupped to catch a few mouthsful of water, when he was startled by a soft voice.

"Here ... oh! I'm sorry, I didn't mean to sneak up on you like that."

Jake looked up to see a young woman offering him a cup.

"For drinking," she said when he looked at the cup and then raised his eyes questioningly.

"Yes," he mumbled as he awkwardly took it from her hand; then, recovering somewhat, he said, "Thank you."

Jake recognized her as one of the regular guests at Byrdcliffe, first noticing her the previous year when he had been building shelves in the pottery shed, a small building which abutted the kilns. It was in the main studio that he had first seen her at work. Though afterwards she often nodded to him as she walked by with her friends while strolling through the grounds, this was the first time he had heard her voice, and he was suddenly and acutely aware that her presence, her voice, and her unexpected offering, thrilled him.

He knew that his face was coloring and, averting his face to hide his embarrassment, turned to the spring to fill the cup. He took several draughts and, feeling in control once more, turned to face her.

"Thank you," he said again, and raised the cup up to her.

"No," she said. "It's for you." She smiled. "To keep," she added.

Jake's face began to color again. He looked away from her eyes to the cup, staring intently at it as if he were studying it. It dawned on him that it was no ordinary cup, but a vessel that had been turned by hand at one of the potters' wheels down in the studio below them. He looked up at her again.

"Oh, no," he mumbled, "I couldn't," and tried again to hand it back to her.

"But I want you to have it," she said firmly.

Jake looked at it again. "It's beautiful."

That smile again.

"I don't — don't think I ought to," he protested. "It's so beautiful."

"Now it's my turn to thank you," she said.

He directed a quizzical look at her, and then pulled back his head as the significance of her remark penetrated his confusion.

"Yes," she said. "I made it."

Jake turned the cup in his hands and peered at it intently again. "You made this?"

"Yes," she said, then added, "… for you."

Now, a full-fledged flush reddened his face.

"I made it for you," she said a bit more forcefully. "I've watched you several times drinking from this spring, scooping up the water with your hands and I thought, well…"

Still crimson-faced, Jake began to handle the cup more gingerly, holding it as if it were one of Aunt Birgit's baby chicks. He couldn't look up at her. "I'm afraid I'd break it," he said. He held up one of his large hands. "My hands are so rough … and this is so beautiful."

She smiled again and Jake felt that thrill pass though his body once more.

What the heck is happening to me? — he thought.

Jake realized she was speaking, and turned to face her.

"Thank you again," she was saying with a throaty laugh. "You needn't handle it so delicately, you know. I believe it's pretty strong. Anyway, you'd be surprised how tough a clay cup can be."

His blushing once more under control, he looked at her questioningly. "Tough?"

"Oh, yes." Her face grew animated. "People dig them up all the time, and some of them are thousands of years old. Many are broken, of course, but it's amazing how many whole pots, vases, cups, and dishes are unearthed by archeologists."

Jake turned the cup around in his hands again, looking at it as if he had never seen a cup before.

"Made from the earth," she said, "Clay pottery has the resilience of the earth. Even early man knew how durable their vessels were. They not only used them for everyday use — like for drinking — but used them to store things in — even used them as burial urns. Oh, yes, even ancient peoples knew how strong they were."

"How do you know all this," Jake asked after considering her words. "Are you one of them — an arka – arky-ol-o-gist?"

"Well, no, not really," she said with a smile.

Jake seemed to suddenly take note of her age. "I guess you're too young to be a — a…"

That smile again. "Well, I'm not *that* young," she said with a laugh. "Both my parents are archaeologists, though, and I've been studying it at college."

He could think of nothing to say other than, "Oh."

"Yes," she continued. "I'm now a sophomore at N. Y. U."

"En why you?" Jake said.

"New York University," she said. "You know, in Manhattan?"

He did *not* know, but answered, "Oh, yes. And you are going to become an arch – a - archaeologist?"

"Well, I'm not positive. Not yet, anyway." She shrugged her shoulders, the movement sending another shiver through him. She inclined her head towards the cup in his hands and added, "I like *making* pots as much I do studying about them. This is also my second year at taking ceramics — that is, up here, I mean — taking pottery lessons. I don't make pottery at college."

"Yes," Jake said. "I remember you from last year. I saw you at the wheel once or twice."

"Uh, huh," she said. "And I remember seeing you, too." She held out her hand, "Hi! My name is Sarah. And now we have formally met."

Jake stood up and held out his free hand. "Jake," he said. "I'm Jake," feeling an almost electric excitement as he felt her firm grasp.

"We all know who *you* are," she laughed. "And your last name?"

"Forscher," he said. "Jake Forscher," then, tentatively, "… and yours?"

"Winters," she said and pointed at the cup. "My initials are etched into the bottom."

Jake turned the cup upside down and there, as she said, were the letters "SW" imprinted in the clay. When he turned to look back at her, he saw her already heading down the slope toward the studio.

"Bye," she called over her shoulder.

"Wait," he blurted even before he knew he was going to do so. "I've got something for you." He pulled the sheet he was working on from his sketchpad and held it out to her. "You know," he said shyly, "for the gift … the cup."

Sarah Winters stopped and turned back. She took the drawing from his hands, a quick intake of breath her first reaction. "Ohhh," she said after looking at it for a few moments. "This is really wonderful! It's *beautiful!*"

"So … I guess we're even then," said Jake.

"You know," she said, "I've often watched you take out your pad to draw but I never had the nerve to come over to ask you to let me see. I had no idea that you were an *artist* …" She left the "instead of a working man" unsaid.

"Well, I've got a long way to go to be an *artist*," he said.

"Well this says different," she said and held up the drawing. "Will you sign it for me … Jake Forscher?"

"*Sign* it?"

"Yes. I signed your cup, didn't I?" she said with a laugh. "All *artists* sign their works, you know," and she held the drawing out to him.

Jake blushed again. He had never signed or put his initials or any mark on his drawings to indicate that it was his work. Not even the few that Aunt Birgit asked for and hung on her living room wall after he had framed them for her. "Well, I guess … sure," he stammered and, taking out his flat carpenter's pencil from the pocket of his overalls, carefully made a "J" and an "F" at the bottom of the drawing. He looked at his initials and then looked up with an embarrassed glance. "Did I make them too big?" he asked. "They seem to take up a lot of space."

Sarah laughed again, sending the now familiar thrill through him once more.

"Not at all," she said. "They are very handsome indeed and do not in the least take away from your drawing."

Jake wasn't too sure about that and resolved in the future — if he were ever again to identify his work as his — to work his initials into the drawing to somehow make them less conspicuous. "Well, as long as you don't think they spoil the drawing …" and stopped abruptly, blushing profusely as he realized his comment placed too much emphasis on the quality of his sketch. "Not that it matters, I guess," he added haltingly.

"It matters to *me*, Jake Forscher. I love your drawing – initials and all – and I'll always cherish it. And, for your information, I think it a far better gift than the simple clay cup I gave you." She reached out to touch his arm, saying as she did so, "And I thank you very, very much"

Again, he felt that electric jolt, and before he could recover, she turned downslope again to return to the studio below. "Bye," she called out once again over her shoulder.

"Good bye," he said. Then added in a louder voice, "Thank you again for the cup. It's beautiful."

"You said that already," she called back and disappeared into the building.

BOOK TWO

1914 — 1917

8

IF THAT WINTER brought Jake no closer to a clearer understanding of what the Armory Show meant for him personally, it did allow him more time to spend on his own development. Neither mild nor severe, the winter of 1913-14 went about its business somewhat modestly, managing not to burden people with either exceptionally deep snows or gladdening their hearts by sending along occasional respites of warmth. Jake did his usual chores of taking care of the horses, the wood splitting and hauling of the chunks into Aunt Birgit's kitchen and cellar, finding that, as things went, he had few complaints about having to find his hands overly idle when it came to earning money. The previous season had been good to him, and his savings promised to comfortably hold him over until spring.

He was pleased that Birge Harrison had made good on a promise he made to Jake during the past summer, opening his studio to him during the cold months and spending some time in teaching him a few of the basics of oil painting. Harrison began by telling him about types of canvas, and the usual methods of priming and stretching them. Jake, always a quick study when it came to using his hands, picked up the lessons with little effort. More troublesome, however, was the mixing of pigments and their application to canvas. Wielding a brush proved to take a bit more dexterity than swinging a hammer, and dabbing at a piece of linen not quite the same as slathering paint over the side of a barn.

"Don't let it buffalo you," Harrison said peering at him over his wire-rimmed glasses. "Don't make it more difficult than it is. A fellow instructor at the League used to tell his students, 'If you stick your brush into the paint and then put it on the canvas and it sticks there, then, by gum, you're painting!' and, you know, he's pretty much right."

Harrison had placed a stretched and primed canvas on his easel and, with only the primary colors and a blob of black and white on his palette, began brushing in a scene of a tree-lined field with broad sweeping strokes. "Now, you see," he explained, "that I'm only using red, blue, and yellow here." He turned to Jake. "These are called the primary colors since between them, they contain all the colors we need. I want you to *see* that all you need are the primary colors" — he slowly and deliberately pointed with the handle of his brush at each of the separate colors — "and a little bit of white and black to darken and lighten when needed. You don't need to go out and buy all the colors. In fact, it's better if you don't at first, since by limiting your palette, you'll learn more about how color works."

"Don't you need to start with a sketch?" Jake asked.

"Depends," said Harrison as he stepped back to squint through his spectacles at his work. "I've painted enough landscapes in my time to be able to cobble something together here for the sake of illustration." He brought his brush to his palette and, dipping the tip into the clump of blue, dragged it over to the yellow, swirling his brush until he got the shade of green that he wanted. A touch of the mixture placed on the canvas seemed to displease him and he added a tiny bit of white to lighten the hue. "There, that's better," he said, then picked up his conversation. "It's all a matter of what you're comfortable with, Jake. If you feel you need a preliminary sketch, then you make one. Just remember, there are no hard and fast rules in this business." He paused. "I've always envied composers because they had the precision of mathematics to fall back on. And writers, well they had rules of grammar and the conventions of mechanics and usage to use as a guide." He looked at Jake. "Well, we don't have such niceties to fall back on. Oh, we've tried — the Renaissance painters worked real hard at it, but whatever 'rules' artists have come up with have been consistently bent or ignored by others." He squinted at his canvas. "And, when you come right down to it, it's probably a *good* thing — creativity — if it deserves the name — ought have no restrictions put on it. So, I guess I ought to stop envying musicians and writers and be happy I'm just a painter." He turned and pointed his brush at Jake. "So, whenever you get frustrated or angry with this business, remember to step back every so often and laugh at yourself— be happy that you have the freedom to march to your own drum."

"Got it," said Jake.

"Now, you'll find that a lot of people — and not all of them artists — will try to tell you that things *ought* to be this or *must* be that but they're talking through their hats. What you paint and how you paint it is your business — and no one can tell you different. What you do might not please others … and you might not be able to sell any of your stuff." He turned from the canvas and looked steadily at Jake. "It all depends on *why* you're painting in the first place."

Harrison paused to bring together some more yellow and blue and then touched the mixture to a tree beginning to take shape on the far side of the already brushed-in field. "You can always tell the amateur by the number of colors he thinks he needs on his palette. The famous Swedish painter Anders Zorn used only two colors in addition to black and white — vermilion and yellow ochre — and there are few who could outpaint him." He stepped back to review his work. "I also recommend a large tube of zinc-white — stay away from lead white for awhile — you'll learn more about that later — and a small tube of lamp black — the smaller size will remind you to take it easy with its use. These few colors and some pure linseed oil should do you for now. You'll need this for thinning out your oils and for mixing your pigments. Some prefer a mixture of turpentine and copal varnish, but I prefer the linseed oil. Remember — for now, keep it simple. You'll just have to find your own preferences as you go along, Jake. Whatever you do, I recommend you don't stint on purchasing the very best. You're enough of a craftsman to know the value of good tools and material, and you can afford to spend more if you know how to cut down on the extras."

"Uh, huh," Jake said as he watched Harrison's apparently random dabs and swipes slowly transform themselves into fields and trees.

"It's like I said," Harrison repeated. "It all depends on why you want to paint in the first place."

Jake nodded.

"And?" Harrison asked.

Jake pulled himself from his concentration on the canvas.

"And?" he echoed.

"Do you know why *you* want to paint?" Harrison prompted.

Jake visibly pulled into himself.

"It matters, you know," Harrison persisted. "It matters because what kind of a painter you become will depend on *why* you paint."

Jake remained silent.

Harrison returned to his dabbing, mixing and brushing, allowing the silence to settle over the room. Finally, he said, "Am I wasting my time here?"

"I – I hope not," Jake finally got out.

"Well, have you *thought* about it?" asked Harrison. "About why you want to learn how to paint?"

"Oh, yes sir!" said Jake. "I've thought about it since I was a kid."

Harrison turned his attention to Jake's eyes again. "Since you were a kid, huh?"

"Well, maybe not about painting," Jake said. "But I always made pictures — with a pencil, I mean. I still do. But I didn't know anything about painting back then. I never even *saw* a painting until I moved up here from Brooklyn."

"Do you have any of those drawings?" Harrison asked.

"Well, not any of the early ones. They were mostly cartoons and comic strip characters, anyway. Most of those were either ripped up by the nuns in my school or thrown away by my father." Jake smiled sheepishly. "If he caught me at it, I'd usually get a smack and told to get back to work." He shrugged. "They were just kid stuff anyway."

"Kid stuff," Harrison said with a chuckle. "Some might say that *all* art is 'kid stuff'. And as far as your father's disapproval, you might as well know right off that you weren't the first. Trying to put a stop to kids falling into the 'bad habit' of art is as old as the hills. Goes back a long way, Jake — did you know that Michelangelo's father *and* his uncle used to try to beat the notion of becoming a sculptor out of him? Seems to be a time-worn tradition in those families with the bad luck of discovering a budding artist suddenly cropping up in the family — maybe even God's way of preparing an artist for what he might expect out of life." Harrison chuckled, as if recalling some of his own confrontations with his parents. "But you have some drawings now?"

"Oh, yes. I've got a few from the last couple of years. I try to sketch every day — or at least whenever I get a chance."

Harrison turned back to his canvas. "How about bringing some around – say tomorrow? We can talk a little more about painting if you have the time." He stepped back to squint at his canvas once again. "I'd like to take a look at some of your drawings if you don't mind."

"I don't mind, Mr. Harrison," said Jake. "In fact, I'm honored that you want to see them."

"Well, let's not get too hasty here. Wait until I tell you what I think before you get *too* 'honored'. I might just tell you that we're *both* wasting our time." He grinned. "But I promise not to cuff you one if I don't like 'em."

Jake nodded and returned the grin.

"And do me a favor, will you?" Harrison added. "Spend some time thinking about the 'why', okay? We ought to explore that a bit before we go too far. I don't want to lead you in the wrong direction." His face turned serious. "Like I said, it really matters why, since the answer to that will indeed determine the kind of painter you will eventually become — and I don't intend to get in the way of that."

Jake gave considerable thought to Harrison's question through that evening, though he came to no clear answer. Not one he could give Harrison, anyway. Hadn't he been wrestling with that very question all these years? Though he knew that the urge to draw went back as far as he could remember, and that the idea of painting was somehow connected with his experience on the *Hendrik Hudson* when he rounded Crum Elbow, he could no more formulate the 'why' into any coherent explanation now than he could in the past. Still, he struggled with Harrison's insistence on some kind of an answer since he did not want to lose that man's friendship and guidance.

Nor was his struggling with the words to fit what he felt he must do made any easier by a new puzzle that had been nagging at him since the end of last summer. This was the perplexity he was faced with when he thought of Sarah Winters and his brief encounter with her over at Byrdcliffe. Sarah Winters. Even her name sent that shiver through him.

Ever since their exchange of gifts — how long could it have taken? A few minutes, at most? — Jake could not get her out of his mind. Of course, the cup, now sitting on the shelf next to his brushes in his studio, served as a constant reminder — but he well knew that he did not need the cup to recall her face, her words.

Her face? Her words? Nothing was really clearly remembered. His memory but poorly reconstructed their conversation; all he could recall were his own bumbling mutterings. What a fool he must have seemed! What a bumpkin! She was a college student – a sophomore! How she must have snickered when she told her city friends about the handyman who gave her a drawing.

She did, though, say that his drawing of the wild arbutus was 'beautiful' and that she would 'cherish' it. A very great part of him wanted to believe that.

And her face? It puzzled him that he could not remember it exactly. It was like trying to sketch from memory — like trying to recall how a vine climbed a tree, or a flower's petals unfurled, or a tree rooted itself amongst rocks. He'd think he had it in his mind, but if he didn't sketch it on the spot, when he returned to the studio he could not remember and had often found his pencil refusing to set down an image.

Her face? For the few minutes he was with her he had avoided looking at her directly, but his recollection — or was it his imagination? — was that she was extremely pretty. He thought that her hair was honey-colored — but could no longer say for sure. He had no idea what the color of her eyes was. None. He knew that he stood considerably taller than she and, from early memories of seeing her around the grounds, that she was slender, petite. And even though her precise image would flit tantalizingly out of his mind's reach, it did not stop him from believing her to be the most beautiful girl he had ever seen.

He knew that he dreamed about her — often — but upon waking only knew that it was Sarah Winters who visited his dreams without ever having left behind a definite image he could depend upon. And if the imprint of her image was not as clear as, say, his first image of the Catskill Mountains, Jake knew that its impact on him was as powerfully strong and that, in some way, the magic worked upon him by both was akin. Which was why, he figured, that now, at the very time he ought to be working out an answer for Birge Harrison, thoughts of Sarah Winters persisted in clouding his mind. Somehow, it was all connected.

9

When he arrived at Harrison's studio the following day, he nervously handed him two of his most recent sketchbooks. Other than his family — and the one drawing he had given to Sarah — he had not shown his drawings to anyone. That Birge Harrison was an artist, and an artist of some repute, made it even more difficult.

He walked over to the easel on which the painting that Harrison was working on the day before was still resting, trying to look unconcerned as Harrison leafed through his books. Harrison said nothing and, after flipping through them cursorily, began to slowly go through the two books page by page, sometimes holding up a drawing close to his eyes and at other times, holding the book away at arm's length, squinting his eyes as he did while he painted.

The silence seemed ominous to Jake and, as best he could, he concentrated on Harrison's painting. The landscape seemed to Jake to have "settled" down since he saw it the day before; perhaps he was just seeing it with different eyes. It did not seem as if the painter had done much — if anything — to the picture since Jake had last seen it. Though he knew little about painting, his feeling was that Harrison had somewhat of a light touch, his edges not sharply defined, colors merging into each other in a soft, cottony way. He wanted to see stronger outline, more dramatic contrast. Still, the greens seemed more defined, the shadows and lights more pronounced than he remembered.

He was amazed at how many kinds of green Harrison was able to produce from a palette that didn't have a speck of green upon it — at least not in the beginning. He remembered, however, how varying shades of green appeared the day before on the palette as Harrison worked his brush into the blobs of blue and yellow, adding at times minute specks of red, white or black. Knowing nothing of primary colors or of how pigments interacted and even less about color theory, the ability of Harrison to produce so many greens out of 'nothing' seemed almost magical. How long had it taken the artist to learn such sleight-of-hand, and how many years before he could make those colors appear as sun-lit fields, cloud-filled skies, and trees that threw back the effects of light and shadow to the viewer? Would *he* ever have that same skill to make paint do that?

"These are good," Harrison said, suddenly breaking the silence. "*Very* good."

Jake just nodded in acknowledgement of the compliment.

"And you say you mostly use a carpenter's pencil?"

"Well, I seem to always have one in my pocket or tool box. It's just handy, I guess." Then, not knowing whether Harrison's question was intended as a criticism, he added, "I suppose I ought to use proper tools, but I'm not really sure what kind of pencil to use."

Harrison tugged at his mustache. "And you've never attended an art class?"

Jake was beginning to feel increasingly uncomfortable under Harrison's penetrating look. That Harrison had brought up Jake's lack of schooling and the wrong tools were all he could think of.

"No," he said quietly. He wondered if the artist was going to squint his eyes at him as he did at his paintings and, simultaneously, he incongruously wondered what that squinting was all about.

"Hmmm," was all Harrison said as he laid the sketchbooks down.

Jake stood there and looked at him with apprehension.

"And the why?" said Harrison, looking at him intently over the top of his glasses. "Have you thought about that?"

Oddly, the question, which had been plaguing him since childhood, brought Jake great relief since it shifted attention away from his sketchbooks.

"Mr. Harrison," he began, feeling the tension in his body release, "I think about that almost all the time. I know why I draw pictures ..." His face colored when he realized he brought Harrison's attention back to his sketchbooks, then charged ahead, "Pictures of plants and trees and things like that, but I don't really know why I think I *have* to draw. It's kind of an urge I've had for as long as I can remember." He laughed. "I did it even though I knew I'd be punished and not even the nun's ruler or the back of my father's hand could make me stop. Even today, in the middle of clearing a field or cutting down a tree, if I see something that catches my eye, I'll stop to sketch it. But *why* I feel I have to do it, well, I just don't know."

Harrison was silent for what seemed like several minutes, and again Jake began to feel uncomfortable. Why did he have to come to him anyway? He was an important man and probably too busy to spend time with someone as ignorant as he was. He wished Harrison would give him back his sketchbooks and let him get on his way.

"First," Harrison's voice seemed to boom in the confined space of the studio and startled Jake from his thoughts. "First, you're not wasting my time — or yours. Like I just said, these drawings are good — *more* than good, they're first rate. I know few artists who have such a knack for draftsmanship as you seem to have." Harrison ran his hands through his receding hair. "And no schooling," he said, as if musing aloud. Then looking directly at Jake, "Probably best that you *didn't* go to art classes. Some nitwit who only knew how to *teach* art might have already talked you out of your natural talent. Not everybody is born with this gift, Jake, and some, even though they want to become artists — *do* become artists — never get the hang of it."

Jake's mind flashed to images from the Armory Show, but refrained from interrupting.

"So, again, first of all, we — *you* — are not wasting time — let's be clear about that. Judging from these sketches, you seem ripe for painting and I'm happy to teach you some of the basics." He squinted again. "But *only* the basics. I sure don't intend to be one of those nitwits I just told you about. There are a lot of middlin' artists out there who can't make a living off their art, so they end up teaching. A student has no sure way of knowing which instructor has it and which one doesn't. For most, it doesn't matter one way or the other. But for someone who comes to it naturally," he paused to point at Jake, "it could be disastrous. So ... all I'm going to do is show you some elementary stuff."

Jake opened his mouth to say 'thank you' when Harrison went on.

"Second – let me tell you that one of the finest draftsmen in

Germany, Adolph von Menzel, used a carpenter's pencil, and he is still hard to beat when it comes to getting down in line what your eyes tell you. He could get more effects with that unlikely tool than most can with a whole set of fancy pencils. So, again, second — don't load yourself down with a lot of expensive equipment. It won't help if you don't have it — and you," he pointed at Jake again, "*have* it. The best tools in the world don't make the craftsman — something you probably already know."

Jake nodded.

"So, again, just the basics — that's all I'm going to give you. Like yesterday, I showed you how to limit your palette to the primaries. Since painting landscape seems to be the way you're headed, you ought to find out how many greens you can make out of blue and yellow on your own before you go out and load up on all the greens those art suppliers can talk you into buying. From there, you'd do best to follow your own dictates." He handed Jake his sketchbooks. "Your instincts haven't let you down yet — and if you continue to listen to them, they never will."

Jake took his books back, still not sure if Harrison was finished speaking. He wasn't.

"And, third — finally — about the 'why'." Harrison rubbed his long chin with his paint-spattered fingers. "Why a feller paints," he said, "is probably the most important thing of all. And, let me assure you, Jake, that there are almost as many reasons why someone wants to be an artist as there are artists. I don't know how much stuff you've seen, but anyone can see that not everyone in the business of painting is on the same track."

Again the Armory Show flashed through Jake's head and he was tempted to bring it up, to ask Harrison if he had seen it and what he thought of it. He had no intention of interrupting him, however, and Harrison continued.

"Not only are there different subjects, but there are an infinite number of ways one can wield a paintbrush or knife — in short, there are *styles* of painting. Again, I don't know how much you've seen and I don't intend to rattle off a list, but there are a great many theories, and 'schools', and, lately, a whole lot of 'isms' cropping up."

Jake was unsure of what an 'izzum' was, but continued to keep his silence.

"Now a person might want to be an artist so that he can make pictures to sell. Now probably *most* want their pictures to sell, but that doesn't mean it ought to be the *reason* they paint because, if it is, then they are no longer artists, but simply people with a skill to make a product that they know how to market. They might be good at what they do — they might be *very* good — but *what* they make is not necessarily art." He paused. "Now, *there's* a subject that would take a lifetime to settle — what *art* is — or isn't. Generally speaking, history decides what's good or bad — what's art and what's not — but even history has proven wrong at times. People's ideas change, their tastes change. And I don't know much else that has changed as much as art has over the years — but then I don't know much about things *other* than art." He settled back in his chair. "Anyway, Jake, you'll learn all this sooner or later, but you ought to know this and that is that there is no *surer* reason for wanting to become an artist than, when you get right on down to it, you simply can't help yourself. You do it because you *have* to do it. You do it because, if you don't, you'll become sick over it. Mentally. Physically. You just can't ignore the impulse because it somehow comes from inside you, from your very nature. It's *who* you are. Now if you had rattled off some easy answer when I asked you 'why?' yesterday, then I might have suspected that you *were* wasting my time. But you didn't, Jake, and you have to know that that's important. I told you already that you have a gift — the talent to reproduce on paper what you can see. But the *real* gift — one that not many have — is this *need* to draw, to paint. Like I said, there are a lot of reasons people take up this business of making pictures, but the ones who do it because they have no choice are the *real* artists — and, you'll also find as you go along that they are a rare bunch indeed."

Harrison turned to set up a fresh canvas on his easel.

"Now let's talk a little bit about values. Did you ever notice the way I squint at my painting? Well, that's to better see the lights and darks in my composition. You'll learn to do the same thing when you're outside and trying to pick out a subject. Squinting simplifies things, weeds out the detail, shows you where your darkest and lightest areas are. Some of the old-timers use a Claude glass for the same purpose — but for now, Jake, you just try squinting the next time you're looking at a scene outdoors and you'll see what

I mean."

He squeezed out a dab of burnt umber and a sizeable blob of white.

"Now let me show you how to paint a picture with just one color — mixed with varying degrees of white. Get the hang of this and you'll know what I mean about values in no time at all." He smiled at Jake. "Other than reminding you again of which end of the brush to use, Jake, I doubt I'm going to be able to teach you much more."

10

During that summer and early fall, while Jake was making tentative forays into the mystery of pigments floating in oils, his uncle was also beginning a new if more sinister phase in his work. For perhaps the first time since he had moved upstate to turn his hand to working the bluestone quarries of Ulster County, it began to dawn on him that his German ancestry was something of an anomaly among American quarrymen. Though Uncle Hans had long believed himself to be an 'American', his fellow workers, predominately Irish, had been lately taking note of his accent, many going out of their way to mock him to his face.

At first he took it as the usual banter between workmen, the timeworn use of badinage and heavy-handed joshing just one of the ways men customarily relieved the tedium of hard work. He had found America to be no different in that respect from his days in working the quarries of Solnhofen. It was simply the way of men, as far as he knew, the world over. Undoubtedly, the workers who toiled on building the pyramids or building the Great Wall poked fun at each other in much the same manner. It brought laughter — at least to those who were not the butt of the jokes — and, at bottom, Uncle Hans thought it a healthy way to relieve the tension of labor that could often be hard and hazardous. He simply laughed it off, then, when he would be greeted with calls of, "Hey, velcome to der chob," when he showed up with his empty wagon in the mornings. Rather than rising to the bait, he would just clamp his teeth down on his pipe stem and offer a silent grin as greeting.

When they began adding 'Heinie' to the greeting, however, he began to sense a new edge to the humor and a direction in its intent that he began to dread.

"It's what's happening over there," his wife said as Hans told her about the new hostility he was experiencing on the job.

"*Ja*, of course," said Hans. " I know. But I have worked with these men for years now. They *know* me!"

"*Ja*, and how long has Germany known the Belgians? And the French?" Aunt Birgit referred to her native country as if she, too, considered herself no longer a part of it. Like her husband, she loved America for all it had given her, and would proudly say she was an 'American' if asked her nationality.

"But zhese Irishers," said Hans, his accent getting more pronounced as his anger increased, "zhey alzo come from across der oschean. Are zhey more 'American' zhan me?"

Jake, who had been quietly listening to the interchange between his aunt and uncle, broke in with, "Yes, but Ireland is not threatening anyone, Uncle Hans. And," noting his uncle's thickening accent, "they don't say 'chust vun more' when they order another beer at their shebeens."

"Ach!" said Hans and began another of his coughing fits. "I've had many a beer mit' zhem in zhere taverns! *Zhey* don't bedder schpeak American zhan me!" he sputtered between coughs and stalked out of the room.

Jake had never seen his uncle so disturbed, never remembered his usual calm manner so ruffled and his sounding so 'German'. He looked at his aunt. "Will he be all right, Aunt Birgit?"

"Ohh, let him settle down," she answered and began preparing supper. "Once he calms down and has his meal, he'll be fine." She shook her head. "Ach, this hatred. Now they have to bring it here to this wonderful country. It is a shame … a shame!"

Expressions of intolerance were certainly not new in the area. Jews had been feared and refused accommodations at local boarding houses in and around Woodstock for as long as Jake could remember. Even many locals, though they had little experience with them, would have nothing good to say about "Hebrews," often voicing fears of their "taking over." What exactly they might take over in the tiny hamlet, Jake could never quite determine. More surprising to him was to hear similar disparaging comments about Jews from the so-called 'cultured' people who had come to study at the League or to 'summer-over' up at Byrdcliffe — though he had never heard such comments at the Maverick, their members as free-spirited and open as ever.

However, like everyone else, Jake had been hearing about the looming war in Europe, had been hearing about Germany's alarming aggression, and with headlines growing increasingly more alarming, had been noting Europe's headlong plunge towards war increasingly more frequent on the lips of people. He had personally not experienced such open antagonism as had his uncle, and, by and large, felt the events in Europe held little meaning for him. His customary solitary nature made him avoid politics and he had little interest in the party or church affiliations of those he worked for or with.

He evaluated people by how they treated him and had no desire to know their beliefs. If he judged anyone at all, it was only by the quality of their work. He admired those who displayed good craftsmanship and disapproved of anyone performing or condoning shoddy work habits. In any event, both the slow fitting out of his studio and his — so far unsuccessful — attempts at making his daubs even faintly resemble what might be called a 'landscape', had occupied his attention to the exclusion of all else throughout most of the winter and early spring.

He attended to his chores at home, taking on outside jobs only when necessary to keep from jeopardizing further employment or when he needed the money to purchase something he wanted. Although still largely bare of furnishings, his studio began taking on a little more of the characteristics of what he started to think of as a "real" studio. A few more brushes — all newly baptized in oil pigments — graced his jelly jar and he now possessed a handful of tubed colors to work with. He had learned also that not all brushes were alike, and was able now to differentiate them as "flats," "brights" and "rounds" and, thanks to Harrison, began to see how each served a different purpose.

A fresh roll of canvas stood in a corner, several feet already cut off and stretched, all still virginally unblemished with the exception of the one set up on his easel. This one looked a little worse for wear with its indistinguishable smears and scrapes marring its surface. A painter would have seen at once that he was attempting a landscape; a layman might have seen only a confused jumbling of colors. Each time Jake stood back to assess his progress, he would shake his head and mutter, "Would've fit right in at the

Armory Show," and, cleaning his brushes, give up for the day.

His drawings now covered a good portion of his wall space, tacked up in no particular order. He had begun the practice of pinning them up when he came back from a sketching jaunt and, whatever their value as studies, they at any rate tended to hearten his flagging spirits when the handling of paints frustrated him.

On a pine shelf he had especially made to hold it, stood the cup that he had been given by Sarah Winters. The presence of that gift also heartened him, its solitary prominence in his studio proclaiming its importance to him. Would he see her again? By now their short encounter had attained mythic proportions in his mind, and he had fallen into the habit of reconstructing their conversation to include words, hints, gestures, and suggestions that, in his clearer moments, he knew never took place. He *wanted* those things to happen. He *wanted* to sound more confident, *wished* that he were more socially adept. But he knew that he had made a poor showing and fervently wished to see her again that he might make some effort at amending that first impression.

Meanwhile, the growing troubles in Europe hit a little closer to home one noontime in late spring as he took his lunch at Mrs. Magee's. He'd just finished a carpentry job over at Mr. Rose's general store — putting up a few shelves to replace those which were beginning to sag from over-stocking — and, not having brought any lunch, walked over to Rock City for his mid-day break.

He had hardly sat down to his plate when one of Brown's acolytes, a young man Jake had seen often during the past year, said loudly, "Well, what do *you* think about what's going on over there?"

Jake didn't realize at first that it was he who was being addressed. He looked across at the man sitting on the opposite side of the table and said nothing for a moment or two. The speaker was, like many of Brown's followers, a bit too forward, too full of himself and of his own opinions for Jake to ever take much notice of him.

"Are you speaking to me?" he finally asked after he noticed the silence that had settled around the table.

"Yep. What do *you* think's going on with Germany?"

Jake slowly and methodically filled his plate before answering. "Well, it's a bit hard to tell from here," he said evenly.

Sanford Magee, sitting next to Jake, gave a deep, snorting chuckle that seemed to annoy the questioner.

"Well, you're *German*, aren't you? 'Forscher' — that's a German name, ain't it?"

Jake looked into his questioner's eyes. "I was born here," he said quietly. "In Brooklyn. That makes me an *American* — not a German."

The table quieted down again.

"Where are *you* from?" Jake asked.

"I'm from New York City," the man answered. "And so were my parents."

"That make you more American than me?" Jake tossed back. "Seems to me the only *real* Americans here were already run off their land by the early settlers. You related to them? Maybe part Indian?"

"No, I'm not," the young man shot back. "My grandparents came from France — and what the Germans are doing in France is despicable!"

"No doubt about it," agreed Jake, "but what does that have to do with me? I'm just sitting here trying to eat my lunch. I've never even been to Germany — or France, for that matter."

Someone snickered and whatever tension seemed to be building, quickly dissipated as knives and forks went busily about their work. The topic was dropped and the usual chatter about art soon dominated the table.

Jake knew that he had been somewhat dismissive of the man's questions but, as he returned to work, the fact that he seemed to be summarily lumped into something called "Germans" or associated with a place called "Germany" troubled him. Assumptions about him seemed to be made based solely on the fact of his German descent. He wondered how it was for the Jew, so many years on the receiving end of the assumptions made about them by the townsfolk.

Still, he understood the razzing that Uncle Hans took from his fellow workers — after all, he *sounded* German. He didn't condone what the quarrymen were doing with his uncle, but he understood it. But *he* was not 'German' — no matter what his last name was.

On the other hand, he could also understand — and sympathize with — what bothered the man whose grandparents were

French. Whether or not they were still alive to see it happening, Germany had no right to invade their country. Or that of the Belgians, either. He also knew well that many of the Rock City group emulated the French — especially men like Cézanne and Matisse, the painters who were constantly talked about and championed by Andrew Dasburg. As far as the Rock City crowd was concerned, the French artists were the leaders in all matters of art — and Bolton's coterie, more or less to a man, justifiably resented Germany for what was taking place in that country.

More surprising to him was that he'd heard similar rumblings of anti-German sentiments from some of Hervey White's group as well. For all their flaunted, liberal bohemian way of life, some seemed as prejudiced as the most hidebound conservative local.

Truth be told, he himself could find no justification for Germany's aggression. But, again, what had that to do with him? In the first place, he knew almost nothing about Europe's history or how its nations had come to talks of war. Some of the arguments of the people he heard in and around Woodstock might have sounded reasonable, but neither his uncle and aunt — both of whom adopted this as their own country — nor he had any control over the actions of people that lived over three thousand miles away.

Not everyone, of course, confronted Jake on his 'German-ness'; most of the people he worked with or for probably didn't even *know* his last name was Forscher — a 'German' name. And, by and large, those who did know, never saw fit to mention it. Still, as events heated up in Europe, there was a growing unease across the land, and Woodstock, in its own small way, contributed its share to the unrest. While his Uncle Hans might have to suffer some harassment at the hands of his fellow workers for his obvious 'German-ness', Jake felt confident that by staying out of political discussions he could weather whatever storm might come his way.

Already a loner, Jake merely retreated further into himself whenever politics cropped up in the course of his dealings with others. And, though he might have felt some resentment at being considered suspect by some, he found that the occasional enforced isolation gave him more time to explore the vagaries of oil painting.

Confining himself to one canvas, he would, as Harrison, who knew Jake's modest means had suggested, merely scrape off the previous days' work and start anew. He, again as Harrison instructed, merely 'played' with the paint, exploring the way it mixed, how it behaved under different brush strokes and, from time to time, trying his hand at spreading the paint with the knife.

He had no specific 'picture' in mind, merely attempting to suggest a tree, a mountain, a field, by applying the colors at hand. He was still using the primaries, learning by practical application how they influenced each other, sometimes with subtle nuance while at others dramatically transforming them into what appeared to be entirely new colors. Recalling what he had heard from League students about Carlson's use of blue for his shadows, he tried to avoid the use of black in his mixtures though he felt freer with his use of white to lighten his hues.

When he found his attempts bringing him to frustration, Jake would put aside his brushes and take up his carpenter's pencil. Sketching, since it always came easy, offered him respite from the difficulty he was consistently experiencing in making oils do his bidding. He was often annoyed to find that the meticulous detail he might obtain through the use of the pencil stubbornly eluded him when he had a brush in his hand.

It puzzled him to discover that whenever he tried to embellish a tree with further touches of greens, what had originally began to *look* like a tree would quickly degenerate into an indistinguishable blob. The exasperation this caused would almost always drive him out of the studio — weather permitting — to seek solace in sketching — something that he knew he could almost always successfully accomplish.

Hunching over a sketchbook with a pencil in his hand might make him forget his frustrations with painting, however since his talks with Birge Harrison the simple act of drawing seemed no longer the automatic activity he had known since he was a boy lying on the parlor floor copying figures from the comic strips. A 'gift' Harrison had called it. Not the skill of being able to draw, but of being born with the impulse to do it in the first place. A gift? Jake wasn't so sure of that. How could something that seemed to drive him so relentlessly be called a 'gift'?

What was it that had happened to him when he was 14 and taking the boat upriver that day? How did his childish need to draw relate to that?

11

The summer of 1914 afforded Jake the most concentrated time with his art that he had yet enjoyed. He carefully regulated his work schedule to insure a steady trickle of income and the assurance of keeping alive his usual contacts with those who hired him from season to season. The more familiar he became with handling the brush and working with color, the better he could apply some of the ideas he had learned from Harrison, supplementing his few lessons with what he could pick up from others along the way. Now when he walked into his studio, it *felt* like a studio.

Uncle Hans, meanwhile, continued to bring home increasingly alarming tales of the abuse he was receiving at the hands of his fellow workers, and Jake, as much to avoid any hostility that might come his way in town as he might show his uncle support, spent more time at home to monitor things there. Not that they expected any overt display of vandalism. Nevertheless, they thought it prudent to keep a wary eye over their property as more and more incidents of anger began cropping up — so far only sporadically in the small towns of West Hurley and Woodstock, but happening in the nearby city of Kingston where people seemed inclined to let daily headlines inflame them. Those susceptible to rumor found their fears fed by occasional reports of bands of German sympathizers or support groups — "Bundes" — that were supposed to be settling in and around the area to carry out their nefarious plots to further the "German cause."

Although ferment about the war could be found in greater or lesser degrees amongst all of the Woodstock artists' groups, those up in the Byrdcliffe colony seemed most unyielding in their anti-German sentiments. Though he had no way of knowing the reason why — it might be that there just weren't any jobs — Jake had received not a single overture for work from that group throughout the season. He had, of course, hoped for employment with Mr. Whitehead since he was anxious to see Sarah Winters again. Her absence over the winter only made the memory of her loom larger in Jake's mind, and he found that rarely a day passed that he did not think of her.

He still had no clearly defined idea of what exactly their brief encounter signified for him. Other than his now vague memories of the girl who sat next to him in school, Jake had not as yet any experience in matters of the heart. He could not say that he *loved* Sarah Winters — he had no real knowledge of her aside from what he had learned in their brief conversation the day she gave him the cup. Although a simple design, the vessel seemed perfectly formed for its function — a fact that appealed to him every time he took it down from the shelf and turned it over in his hands. A skilled craftsman himself, he admired any handiwork that showed evidence of thought and care and this simple cup that came from her hands seemed to form a silent and mysterious bond between them.

The cup, he would sheepishly admit to himself when he saw it — which was every time he entered his studio — was beginning to take on the dimensions of some semi-sacred object that he was coming very close to revering. But what had that to do with what he felt for Sarah Winters? Like the day on the river at Crum Elbow, he had no frame of reference in which he might evaluate what he had experienced with her during the few moments they spoke together by the spring on Guardian Mountain. The mystery of Sarah Winter's hold over his thoughts was as deep as that imposed by his first view of the Catskill Mountains — and, rather than becoming more clear to him, had likewise deepened with the passage of time.

Late in July he had finally summoned enough courage to walk up to Byrdcliffe under the pretense of asking about work but in actuality, with the hope of spying Sarah around the grounds. When his search for her proved fruitless and he was told that he was not needed for any of the usual odd jobs, Jake surprised himself by boldly walking over to the ceramics studio to inquire about her whereabouts.

"Oh, she left a little early this year," he was told by one of the other residents. "I think she was taking a trip to Europe with her parents before she had to go back to school."

Jake was disappointed, but was considerably shaken when he realized how profoundly unhappy the news made him. Sickness was something he rarely experienced, and a dull ache in the pit of his stomach made him fear that he was going to be ill. The ache stayed with him as he made his way home, neither lessening nor increasing as he walked the several miles back to West Hurley. By the time he reached the house, the discomfort seemed to subside into a general sense of emptiness, a strange and indefinable feeling that he could not ever recall having.

When, over the next few days, Aunt Birgit began probing him with queries, he felt for the first time uneasy in the house he had called home since he was sixteen. When he overheard Aunt Birgit whispering to Uncle Hans words to the effect that "Jake seems maybe to have a girlfriend," he found looking either of them directly in the face almost impossible. After spending several full days in his studio, only coming into the house for meals or well after dark when he presumed they were in bed, Jake decided that a trip to see his parents might be a good idea. When he told his aunt and uncle of his intentions one morning, a knowing smile was surreptitiously exchanged between them as both Aunt Birgit and Uncle Hans heartily seconded his idea.

If anything, the weekend spent with his parents sent him into an even greater despondency. His mother, never very demonstrative in any event, greeted him as if he had just come home from a day away at work in his father's shop. He arrived at his old house on Halsey Street late Friday afternoon, the neighborhood appearing exactly as it had when he had left it. His mother had prepared his old room, pointing things out as if showing a visitor a room he had never seen before. He placed his bag on his old bed, a bit surprised that — as if he *were* some strange boarder — he felt no connection to it at all.

His conversation with his mother was strained, neither of them knowing much what to say to the other. She busied herself with preparing supper, constantly looking up at the clock in expectation of her husband and son's return from work. She had just said, "Papa and Freddie will be here soon," when the front door opened and in walked his father with Freddie a step behind.

Jake's first impression was that his brother had become a carbon copy of his father, both dressed almost exactly alike, his brother sporting an exact replica of their father's mustache on the upper lip of his equally ruddy face. A picture of both of them washing up at the sink in the back room, each vigorously attempting to make their bloodied hands white, flashed through his mind.

"Well, well," his father said brusquely. "Our star boarder has come for a visit." Standing foursquare before Jake, he presented his cheek for a kiss.

Jake allowed his lips to brush his father's face and quickly turned to his big brother. "Hello, *Herr* butcher," he said with a laugh, and both young men hugged each other. Jake detected the odor of liquor and beer on his brother's breath — so, now he also was stopping on the way home for a "boilermaker" with Papa.

"And you," said Freddie stepping back to look at Jake. "What do I call you? *Herr* handyman?"

As best as he could remember while puttering around in his studio the following Tuesday morning, the conversation never went much farther during his stay in Brooklyn. His mother hovered in the background, his father busied himself with reading the newspapers, and Freddie was spending most of his time with his fiancé. Jake briefly met her, Konstanze, a rather reserved young woman with plaited blonde hair. Other than spending Saturday evening with both of them to see a "moving picture" — all the latest rage, according to Freddie — about which he could not recollect a single scene, he did not really have a chance to know the young woman who would become his sister-in-law.

When he thought about it later, during the trip back upstate, he realized that, when it came down to it, he hardly knew his brother Freddie any better. As far as he could tell, Freddie seemed to be slowly transforming into his father, and the prospect of that coming to pass left him with little desire to reclaim whatever intimacy they might have once shared as boys.

The redeeming feature of the entire trip was the trip back upstate on the *Mary Powell.* Dubbed "The Queen of the Hudson" on her maiden voyage in 1861, the ship had been the pride of her owners for over 50 years. One of the fastest steamships in her prime — and one of the most handsomely appointed — Jake had been looking forward to sailing on her ever since he had heard rumors that the *Washington Irving*, put into service only the year before, would soon send her into retirement.

Scheduled to leave at 3:30pm on Monday afternoon, Jake arranged his day so that he had time to spend in Manhattan before heading back upstate. He had no specific plans, but welcomed any excuse to avoid having to go over to the butcher shop on Gates Avenue. Freddie had told him of some of the improvements made in the store, but the excitement with which he shared this news made no impression on Jake. He listened politely, pretended to be interested, but then told his brother that, though he would have liked to see what had been done, he was leaving early in the morning.

Jake spent the better part of an hour while in the city at the Metropolitan Museum of Art, taking advantage of the opportunity to seek out the work of some of the old masters whose names had come up in various conversations back in Woodstock. Ever so slowly he was learning how to adapt what he had heard to what his eyes were showing him on the canvas. Though he still found it almost incredible how some of these painters could do what they did, he could at least get some inkling as to how they accomplished their tricks with the brush. The Dutch and Flemish painters, however, continued to astound him with their uncanny ability to paint such tiny detail and with such amazing fidelity to nature. How they were able to paint the individual hairs on a dog's back while he still could not seem to capture an entire leafy branch made him grind his teeth in frustration.

Early afternoon found him down at the Mary Powell's berth on the 'North River'. He walked up and down along the wharf in an attempt to get different views of the steamboat, his developed sense of proportion and craftsmanship telling him that she did indeed deserve the appellation of "Queen." Built for the speed for which she had long been famous, the *Mary Powell* was lengthy and sleek, her body rakishly streamlined to reduce the resistance of water and air.

When he finally boarded her around 3pm, Jake, with his added years of maturity since his first steamship trip on the *Hendrik Hudson*, could now assess the thoughtful planning that went into the design of these Day Liners. Walking the decks of the *Mary Powell*, he noted the sturdiness of its construction and the elegance of its interiors. The main saloon was wainscoted in solid walnut, echoing the walnut furniture that was lavishly upholstered in blue velvet. Interspersed with the paintings — which, as far as Jake could tell, were first-rate originals — were large mirrors that gave the illusion of a much larger space.

He ran a practiced eye over the wainscoting in the saloon, noting the care with which the mitered joints were made in corners and angles of the room. It was the work of fine craftsmen and he wondered who the carpenters were who did the finishing handiwork. Despite her impending replacement, the *Mary Powell* appeared to be lovingly maintained, her spick and span appearance obviously meant to please the many well-dressed people who, like Jake, were sauntering along the decks, small groups and families staking out their territory along the rails for the journey up river.

Over the years, Jake had seen the final resting places of several of the old Day Liners, their rotting and rusting hulks testimony to the changing needs and tastes of man. As he stationed himself on the boat's left railing up near the bow in preparation for the rounding of Crum's Elbow, he was keenly aware that the old excitement was now tinged with a sense of sadness. Unlike his earlier trips, when it was the landscape which commanded his attention, Jake found himself paying more heed to the various landings on this trip — West Point, Cornwall, Newburgh, Poughkeepsie — knowing that, as the days of the Day Liners would pass, so also would these bustling little ports along the Hudson — and again, a whole way of life would pass into obscurity.

And this time, as the Catskills loomed in the late afternoon light, their eastern faces almost entirely in shadow, Jake, though as moved as he was when he first saw them at the age of 14, now registered a tinge of melancholy as the *Mary Powell* made that left-hand turn up the Hudson's channel.

How much must we lose in our determined press for progress?

Jake pushed away from the rail to find a seat inside.

12

Although autumn was upon them and Woodstock's summer residents beginning to leave, Jake still had enough to keep him busy. If there was no work for him up at Byrdcliffe, he found plenty of it with Hervey White who was not only continuing to put up his inexpensive cabins, but was now planning to build a concert hall.

As White's ideas expanded and the population of his Maverick grew, the need for a better water source began to make itself felt. Consequently, White contracted with a local drilling company to sink a well on his property that would properly supply the burgeoning little colony. This new project added to the already bustling activity around the Maverick, and White found enough odd jobs around the place to keep Jake busy through the whole of the fall season.

Unfortunately for White, the water table on the Maverick was exceptionally low and he would not learn until spring how deeply the drillers would have to go. What he knew for sure was that he had to come up with a plan not only to pay for his proposed concert hall but now also for the new well, and the idea of some kind of festival to help raise funds started to take shape in his mind.

Though anti-German sentiments would still be expressed from time to time, the overriding spirit of democracy that characterized Hervey White's Maverick made Jake feel a bit more welcome than he had at Byrdcliffe. He thus found himself becoming increasingly involved in the many projects that White dreamed up in an effort to raise funds for his colony.

The onset of winter slowed things down and, although it passed quickly, the cold days could not end fast enough for White. For Jake, however, having a few days off now and then meant having more time in his studio, more time to explore the mysteries of painting. But, like Hervey White, he also was anxious to get back to work, back to finishing up the many tasks still needing completion at the Maverick.

The final depth reached by the well-driller in his efforts to obtain adequate water pressure to supply the Maverick was five hundred and fifty feet — a record for the surrounding area — which considerably upped the ante for White, and this unexpected expense along with his other dreams pushed his already fertile imagination to lengths even he did not know he possessed. The nascent idea of a festival to help bring in money grew in proportion to both the size of the bills he incurred and to the interest his idea generated throughout the artistic community of Woodstock.

By the early spring of 1915, locals, who recognized the festival as another opportunity to make a few dollars, added to the schemes of White and his coterie of artists, musicians, actors, and craftspeople by planning to set up food and handiwork booths. A constant stream of workers was needed to help construct stands and clear undergrowth to make room for the ever-spreading festival to take place, and Jake found plenty to keep his hands and time occupied. An August opening date was planned, and excitement steadily mounted as the summer progressed. Woodstock was soon blooming with posters, banners, and an ever-growing crowd of boosters and promoters helping to spread the word abroad.

By the end of July, the Maverick colony, with its festooned booths and hastily put together "quarry theatre," began looking more and more like some medieval fairground, the string of electric lights strung around the theatre the only modern contrivance that spoiled the illusion. Plans for skits, pageants, dances, music performances, and costume making began proliferating as the festival fever spread. It was becoming increasingly obvious that the entire day would be taken up with activities, and everyone looked forward in anticipation to the day of the actual event.

Jake found his natural reserve relaxing somewhat as the day approached and, like most of the town, was caught up in the heady flow of excitement that coursed through the ordinarily quiet little hamlet. With all the notice Woodstock was getting during that summer of 1915, Jake felt sure that he would once again have occasion to see Sarah. Though he had avoided Byrdcliffe, he felt sure that with all of the increased activity he would come across her in town. Again, however, he was to be disappointed. He neither saw nor heard anything about Sarah Winters and, although now thoroughly unable to reconstruct her face in his mind's eye, he still felt the dull ache of her absence. As the day of the festival loomed closer, he began pinning his hope on seeing her at the Maverick — surely she would not miss such a momentous event.

On the morning of the Festival, Jake passed along his fifty-cent admission fee at the entrance, fully prepared to enjoy the day. Already, gamesters, jugglers, singers, dancers, actors, and merry-makers were roving the grounds, all hell-bent on entertaining the crowds who swarmed over Hervey White's colony. The Maverick was mobbed with costumed revelers but try as he might, Jake could catch no glimpse of Sarah. Though resolved to enjoy himself, he nevertheless could not quite get past his disappointment when, as the day wore on, he did not succeed in finding her among the throng.

In spite of his disillusionment, the day passed swiftly for the revelers and the coming of the evening's darkness did little to dampen the crowd's enthusiasm for having fun. If anything, the cover of night made some of the merrymakers more daring, and Jake noticed several couples disappearing into the surrounding gloom. As he moved about, he could hear muffled giggling coming from behind bushes and trees or from nearby cabins, but more often than not, he merely overheard the usual art-talk that was common whenever artists got together. Criticism and praise for the profusion of creative efforts that went into making the Festival flowed freely from the self styled experts. He still found it the best way for him to learn — that is, to eavesdrop on the conversation of others, listening in without adding his own comments or questions.

When the electric lights came on to signal the beginning of the dramatic productions, Jake, as was his usual habit, stood somewhat aloof, leaning against a tree a short distance away to better observe the activities of the crowd. He could see the actors perfectly well and could see no reason why he needed to be jammed into the front rows, only to have his movements restricted by the crush of those beside and behind him. Even if he did not catch every word, after awhile this was no problem. Not used to late hours, he was already beginning to fade and, at the moment he began thinking that it was time for him to start home, he felt the pressure of a warm body against his side. Though subtly insinuating, the suddenness of the unexpected contact nearly sent him tumbling over on his side.

His first reaction was one of anger, but when he turned to see who had taken such liberty he brought himself up short.

Standing there alongside him, her arms crossed across her chest, was a woman he had never seen before. She stood nearly as tall as he and, though he could not see her clearly in the reflected lights strung around the theatre, he could make out a mass of hair piled atop her head and a slightly mocking smile on her face. He could not at first tell whether she was handsome or not; her stance was self-assured, almost challenging.

He stepped away when he realized she was still pressing into his side.

"Pardon me," he said, not knowing what else to say and those, the only appropriate words he could think of.

"All right," she said. "You are pardoned."

Jake detected an accent, but his limited knowledge of languages gave him no hint of what it was.

"And now that you have been pardoned," she continued, "please be so kind as to follow me."

Completely perplexed by her behavior and at a total loss of coming up with any words of objection, Jake found himself dumbly following her through the woods. She led him away from the theatre and, after a few moments, into one of the many cabins spread throughout the Maverick.

Immediately upon entering, she pulled him down to a bed in the darkened room and said in that unidentifiable accent, "We will make love now."

Jake uttered not a word as she slipped her dress over her head and began undressing him, this latter task taking considerably longer since, in addition to his usual clothes he had on laced, high-topped boots while she, underneath her outer garment, was completely nude. When she was done removing his clothes, she fell back onto the bed and pulled Jake down on top of her.

Though he never found out her last name, Jake later learned that her name was Irina, that she was Russian, and that she was visiting the Maverick with a sister whom most thought was her twin.

No one was able to recall a surname, or even if they had heard one. At that, even the little Jake could learn about her left him with more knowledge of her person than he could understand about what had occurred between them.

Though he'd had some inkling of what was to transpire as she led him through the woods that night, at twenty-one Jake was still pretty much of a sexual innocent when they made love in the cabin. He was no longer one when he left her side at the first hints of dawn.

In the days following the Festival, Jake had ample opportunity to play back the events of the night in his mind. Irina was an able and enthusiastic teacher; he was — and still somewhat astonished when he thought about it — a pliable and willing student. The rudimentary understanding of what comprised the sexual coupling between a man and woman that he had picked up from the conversation of men had, within a single night, expanded a thousandfold. Had anyone ever tried to indoctrinate him in the mechanics of sexual intercourse, he would not have believed the variety of possibilities, the amazing flexibility, or the range of sensibilities that the human body was capable of experiencing. Weeks later, he could still find himself aroused by recalling the events of the evening and, though he could vividly re-play — even in slow motion — the things that Irina and he had done with and to each other, the entire night yet retained a dreamlike quality for him.

He could recall tracing her high cheekbones with his fingers, remembered the feel of her long, silky hair, which had come undone almost immediately after her head lay back on the pillow. Enough light penetrated the darkness of the cabin to allow him to see that her hair was blonde — almost white — and that her eyes, though he did not know their color, slanted exotically upward from her slightly pugged nose. He could still feel her legs wrapped around his waist, their velvety softness bringing him at times to frenzied bucking and twisting. He remembered her taste — the salty sweat of the back of her neck and at the hollow behind her knees, the sweetness of her lips and mouth, the musky pungency of her crotch. He imagined that he could recall the exact softness of her belly and buttocks. And he remembered that the odors wafting from the heat generated by the exertion of both their bodies intermingled not unpleasantly with the heady bouquet of oil paint and turpentine that lingered in the confined space.

Yet, itemizing these disparate elements, listing them one after the other as if he were writing out a list of materials he might need for a job, carefully considering the size, measurement, and exact quantity of each part that went into the whole, brought him no closer to comprehending what, in its totality, that night signified. Crystal clear in their hard-edged definition, the separate elements of making love with Irina refused to coalesce into a something he might hold up to his mind's eye to evaluate. All attempts to set it into a coherent, unified event merely caused each piece of the puzzle to swim in and out and through each other, all boundaries broken down, imitating, in a sense, what they had done to and with each other that night. He could not say it was a 'this' or a 'that'. To call it — baldly — "love-making" was, for Jake, completely inadequate — false even — for though he had reached full manhood, he was still not quite sure what "love" actually meant.

He was told that his parents "loved" him and that he ought to "love" them. The nuns never tired of reminding the students that God "loved" them — that His son, Jesus, even died on the cross for them because He "loved" them. He was pretty sure that what he felt for Aunt Birgit and Uncle Hans might well pass for "love," and was fairly convinced that what he felt — continued to feel — for Sarah Winters could also be called "love" — of some kind. Yet, in the end, he had no way of characterizing what had taken place on that Festival night at the Maverick.

To further complicate matters, as the night of the Festival receded into the past, all of what he had experienced with Irina seemed to merge with that surging swell of emotion he experienced when he had first glimpsed the Catskills from the river. Surely, such distinct events, people, and things were not interchangeably identical and such an indeterminate word as "love" could never be sufficiently clear in defining or clarifying them. Whatever might be the proper niche that his night with Irina might eventually assume in the context of his life, Jake knew that, at bottom, that night would forever remain an unrepeatable event — that though it profoundly affected him — as did the mountains — as did Sarah — it would, like Halley's Comet, exist as a once-in-a-lifetime experience.

13

1915 slipped into 1916 and gaining mastery over the craft of painting with oils was still proving to be largely beyond Jake's abilities.
For every canvas that resembled a landscape, there were a dozen
that looked like the slapdash daubings of an angry housepainter.
Somehow, the points and tips he managed to pick up in conversation with other artists or had learned directly from Birge Harrison
would not always translate into the movement of his brush over
the canvas.

One day, out of sheer desperation — and because he was weary
of cleaning his brushes after one more fruitless attempt — he tried
laying on the paint with the palette knife in thick slabs and slashes
throughout the entire canvas. He was astonished upon stepping
back to see that the effects of what he had done was not without
merit. It at any rate looked more like a landscape than many of his
previous attempts with the brush.

The knife gave him less control over the application of pigment,
and, in its almost haphazard clumpings, ridges, and mixtures, suggested, if not the definiteness of trees or fields, the *impressions* of
these things. Heartened by the unexpected results he had obtained
through the use of the knife, Jake began experimenting further
with its use. For the first time since he had begun using oils, he
experienced a genuine sense of play and, at times, instead of mixing the colors on his palette, tried applying globs of pure blue to
the canvas and then working dabs of yellow into it as he worked
the mixed pigments into the surface. The varying shades of green
that flowed from the tip of his knife melded into each other in indeterminate patterns, their ultimate arrangements seeming closer
to how nature appeared to the eye than did his previous attempts
at dabbing brushloads of color in a studied, predetermined man-

ner — attempts that consistently resulted in labored and over-fussy mélanges that looked, in the end, as if stuck on in patches across the surface of the canvas.

The edge of the knife blade also gave him the hard-edge definition that he admired in the work of Carlson — and missed in that of Harrison — the effect closer to how he himself saw a tree trunk, a creekside, or stone-edge in nature. In addition, the flat of the blade allowed him to apply the paint in thick slabs or thin layers, the variation in pressure giving an overall textured look to his painting. Where he might have once fussily dabbed with a brush to try to give a running stream of water highlights, the knife almost forced him to put on the paint in globs and smears — again, the effect of which was to give his paintings a realistic rendition of nature's often indiscriminate ebb and flow of color and form.

When he spoke about his use of the knife with Birge Harrison during a chance meeting at the village square, the painter merely said, "Whatever works for you, Jake. Whatever works. Just follow your own dictates and you'll rarely go wrong."

Heartened by Harrison's encouragement and with his confidence steadily growing, Jake was finding it easier to both frame his questions about art and to put those questions forth more boldly. He was learning an artist's vocabulary, and the more he learned about his tools and their application, the easier it was for him to put his questions clearly to others. He did not know how much — or even if — Birge Harrison had spoken to others of his faltering attempts, but it was not long before those who had only thought of him as a mildly interested bystander began to see that they had an up-and-coming artist in their midst. Though he still kept pretty much to himself and continued in his occupation of handyman, now when he stopped and asked questions he sensed a new kind of response from artists.

This was especially so at Mrs. Cooper's where many of the Leaguers still hung out, and where he was always sure to find a few hanging around during lunchtime. Several had taken a liking to Jake — and he to them — and they would always hail him whenever he entered the boardinghouse.

"Hey, Jake, come sit over here with us," said a young painter named Ted Deavers.

This was Deavers's second year at the League summer sessions, and during the course of the season he had found occasion once or twice to consult Jake about the best paths to take up to the crest of Overlook. They had first met near Overlook's summit late last August, Jake caught unawares as he was sketching a clump of mountain laurel against the sunlit face of a rock ledge. The brief encounter — and Ted's enthusiasm about the drawing Jake was making — opened the way to further interchanges between the two men whenever their paths crossed in town.

Jake gladly joined the small group of artists, and nodded silently as Ted introduced him around.

"Jake, this is Joe Bundy. He thinks he's going to take over Carlson's post any day now," said Ted as he gestured toward a freckle-faced, sandy headed young man who hardly seemed old enough to be out of grade school, let alone be taking art classes at the League.

"Well, watch out — I just might," laughed Bundy good-naturedly.

"And this," continued Ted as he indicated a tall, well set-up, handsome man, "is Ralph Smythe."

Jake nodded again.

"I think we've bumped into each other now and then — over on Rock City Road? — Anyway, glad to meet you."

"Same here," said Smythe. "Say, are you an artist? I thought you were a local."

Before Jake could answer, Ted broke in.

"An artist? With those hands? Why a brush would get lost in 'em!"

Jake flushed. He had almost risen from the table to stalk out of Mrs. Cooper's boarding house when he realized that he was being teased.

"Look at 'em!" Ted continued. "They're huge!" Then he made an exaggerated motion as if protecting himself. "God! I'd better watch out. He ever catches ahold of you with those mitts, you're done for!"

Jake blushed again, shyly attempting to hide his hands from view. He knew they were large — reddened and rawboned from working out-of-doors, the surfaces of his palms callused to a bone hardness from years of holding scythe snaths and axe helves. They were formidable and could indeed be used as weapons.

Ted, seeing Jake's embarrassment, broke in quickly.

110

"*I'll* say he's an artist! His drawings are top rate!"

Jake was beginning to think his face would never stop heating up. "Uh, thanks, Ted," was all he managed to get out.

"So," said Bundy, "who're you studying with?"

"No one," answered Jake, then added after a short pause, "But I did get a couple of tips from Birge Harrison."

"Oh," said Smythe. "Then you're already finished with art classes?"

"Well," Jake said. "I've never actually taken an art class. It just seems like I've always had a knack for drawing pictures."

"Wow!" said Ted, obviously taken aback by this admission. "I knew you weren't taking courses at the League — at least I've never seen you there — but I always figured, you know, the way you handle a pencil, that you've had some training — a *lot* of training!"

Turning to the others, he exclaimed, "He draws like a master!"

Jake shrugged his shoulders and shook his head 'no'.

"The drawing always just came," he said. "Now painting — that's a different story." He looked over at Smythe. "You get a look at my painting and you'll see that I *am* a local." He grinned and added, "A local yokel with big hands." He was surprised — pleasantly — that he could fall so easily into their banter.

"Well," said Smythe, "there *is* a difference between drawing and painting — that's for sure." He settled himself back in his seat. "One of my teachers made a great point to tell us that the lines you make in a drawing is the drawing, but the shading and cross-hatching that you add in, well, that's the *painting.*"

"Right," said Bundy, "Carlson pretty much says the same thing. Too much attention to line and your painting will end up looking like a colored picture — just a drawing that has color added to it."

A glimmer of understanding rose in Jake's mind.

"Yes – yes. I think I know what you mean. I've been drawing with a pencil for so long that I can't seem to get used to a brush."

"The trick is not to *forget* how to draw but how to avoid trying to do with a brush what you do with a pencil," said Ted. He looked at the others. "Did that make sense?" he asked with a frown.

"It does to me," Jake said. "I think that's exactly what I've been trying to do — *draw* a painting."

"You know," said Bundy. "Taking a painting class with Carlson wouldn't hurt. He really knows his stuff — and he's a good man.

We all think he's a regular guy."

Jake looked closely at the young man. He still looked to be only about 13 years old, but he reckoned him to be about 16. He certainly held his own amongst his older friends, and Jake admired him for that.

"Well, that's just not something I can afford to do," said Jake. "For now anyway, I'll just follow my own lead as Mister Harrison suggested."

"*He's* no slouch, that's for sure," said Bundy. "He was John Carlson's teacher, you know. I'd certainly take his advice."

"Besides," added Smythe, "there've been a great many masters who never went to school to learn how to paint. They were *natural* artists, *born* artists."

"Yeah, but most of us have to struggle along taking lessons," said Ted. "Who'd make it today in the art world without some teacher helping you along and introducing you to the old-timers?"

"True," said Smythe. "We are trying to find our way into what's becoming a pretty crowded club. I suppose there are a lot more artists around today than there were back in the days of old Rembrandt."

"But still," said Ted, "going to school doesn't automatically guarantee you anything. No school — no teacher — can make you an artist if you aren't up to snuff."

"Right," said Bundy slapping his hand on the table, "and that's why I like the League — and especially Mister Carlson. Here they don't hand out fancy certificates that say you are now a master artist after finishing a course. They don't ask for references or give entrance exams to see if you can draw from a cast. You want to be a painter, why then you just enroll in one of their classes. No one says you can't, or ought not, or even — when you're through — that you did right by *taking* the course. All Carlson does is show you what he knows and if you can become an artist from what he tells you, why then that's that. Becoming an artist is up to *you* — and *no* one but you can tell you any different."

"Here, here!" proclaimed Ted and Smythe simultaneously.

"You looking for a job with the registrar?" joshed Ted and, turning to Jake, added, "But he's right, you know. You either are or you aren't. Time, you know, sorts us all out. History alone makes the final judgment."

112

14

It would not be until some days later when he took his paint box and easel out of doors to paint on site that Smythe's words — "a drawing is not a painting" — would sink in for Jake. Although he constantly had his sketchbook with him, had sketched outdoors countless times over the years while sitting with his back up against a tree, he had not yet found the courage to *paint* outside the privacy of his studio. He still felt awkward with a brush in his hand, never confident enough to allow himself to be seen by others as he struggled to gain control of his materials. Although still a far cry from seeing himself as a 'real' painter, he felt that he'd progressed enough to at least give it a try. He knew enough places where the chances of his being stumbled upon were almost nil, so he packed up a few canvases and the rest of his gear one morning and headed out.

After setting up in a meadow high up on one of Overlook's flanks, he almost immediately felt a difference. Freer, more at ease, somehow. For the first time, he felt "in" the picture and not seeing it in his mind's eye as he did back in the studio. There it was right in front of him and all he had to do was copy it onto his canvas. Eager to begin, he quickly set about laying out his palette and was soon applying color to his canvas.

Hmm…just like lying on my belly and copying from the comics.

He was not painting for long before Smythe's words began to make sense. He gradually came to realize that one ought not attempt to "paint" a tree — as one might try to draw one with line — but rather to *suggest* a tree through the proper use of his pigments in indicating color and mass. Within an hour he completed a fairly presentable study, and quickly dug another canvas out of his bag.

Turning his easel ninety degrees presented a fresh vista and he immediately went to work. The sun was higher now and, for the first time, Harrison's 'squinting' lessons made complete sense. He noted how edges — the very details he sought to capture in his sketches — blurred when he peered through narrowed lids, and how areas of color, or patches of light and dark, lent an integrated and seamless structure to the landscape that lay stretched out before him.

He also saw how his use of the knife facilitated the rendition of mass rather than depending on the brushline to do it for him. Now, when he squinted to find the darkest areas of his motif, he easily slathered on swaths of the darkest greens he could mix, then with that as his starting point, would begin to add his surrounding colors with increasingly lighter tints. By stepping back from his canvas from time to time — as he remembered Harrison doing so in his studio — and comparing it with what he saw in front of him, he could better evaluate the success of its translation.

As he painted, snatches of other conversations amongst artists as they sat in Mrs. Magee's or Mrs. Cooper's came back to him. Now he knew what they meant by 'blocking' in a subject and waiting until you got back to the studio to add whatever touches or highlights that might be called for. By waiting, they had explained, it allowed for some gestation to occur and, more importantly, the practice precluded becoming either overly fussy with a brush or overly hasty in an effort to "beat the light" while still out in the field. All of this now made sense.

As his confidence grew over the next several weeks, he began doing less sketching and more painting on site, taking his canvases and paint box to the several locations where he had already found suitable subjects during his many explorations of the area. There were one or two that had long been his favorites, locations in and around the Woodstock area that offered advantageous views of Overlook.

One he found particularly to his liking was over in High Woods, a tiny settlement that had sprung up around the bluestone quarries in the nearby township of Saugerties. Only some five miles out of Woodstock, he located a field that offered a wide vista of Overlook's southeastern face, the outline similar — but much closer, of course — to that of the one he first witnessed as a boy from the observation deck of the *Hendrik Hudson*. The owner of the field, a local who raised chickens on his small farm, gave Jake permission to use his property in exchange for an occasional odd job around the place.

He discovered several new places where he could set up his easel in relative privacy — on the flats of Zena, on the outskirts of Saugerties, and from Glasco Turnpike over near Cockburne's Hill — each vantage point offering its own view of Overlook, each place's owner open to similar arrangements of barter. For Jake, having access to these sites in all seasons and at almost any time of day he wished, made his longtime goal of "capturing" Overlook seem increasingly to be within his grasp.

As he was slowly finding his way toward making paint do his bidding, a remark made by Ted Deavers as they were finishing up their lunch that day had taken root in the deeper recesses of Jake's mind.

"You either are, or you are not," Ted had said when they were discussing what made a person an 'artist'.

Harrison had implied something similar when he urged Jake to explore *why* he wanted to paint. He seemed to suggest that the urge to make art was not consciously chosen, but rather an inborn compulsion that, if not heeded could — how did Harrison put it? — cause one to be physically and mentally ill. If Harrison was correct, then the very fact that one's motive to create came *unbidden* would separate that person from the pretender — would mark that man or woman as a 'real' artist. How might one discern the difference?

Surely early prehistoric peoples — Sarah Winter's pot makers, for example — did not attend art instruction classes. Also unlikely was that stone-age creative urges gained recognition by contemporary critics or art historians. Did such a word as 'art' or 'artist' even exist back then? How were these early artists regarded by their tribe? Were they rewarded? Or shunned?

More to the point, what was *their* 'why'?

These questions teased at Jake's mind as he steadily progressed in his own work. Could they be answered? Surely someone had made inquiries into such things; he would simply have to expand his own line of questioning to include a much wider range than his interests had so far included. Perhaps, if he could arrive at some better grasp of these things, he might better understand himself — might even be better able to comprehend the still confusing experience of the Armory Show. Although it had been over two years since he had seen it, he had found little opportunity to discuss the exhibit in any depth with anyone and, even if he had, had still not an adequate vocabulary in which to frame his questions.

Still, if his familiarity with the artist's jargon needed further improvement, Jake was discovering that his visual vocabulary was growing from day to day. More and more he found that he did not have to get down every detail of a motif when he was out in the field, that he could readily draw from his memory when driven back to his studio by lack of light or bad weather. His years of sketching were now paying off since he could rely on the images he had recorded in the past to fill in when the present prevented ready access to a given subject. He had learned the lesson that, in the final painting, it need not be necessary for a one-to-one correspondence between art and reality — that it did not matter if *this* tree or *that* plant was, in fact, in that precise spot, but that they *could* have been because both were natural to such a surrounding.

Moreover, though he was beginning to discover how the visual image was taken in by the human eye, and how he might fabricate that impression on canvas, Jake was now faced with a problem that opened even greater obstacles to attaining his goal: nature, it was now becoming apparent, never showed the same face to its perceivers. How might he capture Overlook if that mountain continually altered her appearance? Overlook in summer was not the same Overlook that she was in winter. Nor was Overlook the same in morning light and in evening light — it was, in fact, never the same in *any* light, capriciously changing her visage from moment to moment, let alone from season to season and from year to year. Could one speak of 'an' Overlook at all?

He could still bring to mind the airiness of the Catskills in his initial sighting as he came up the Hudson in 1906. The impression he'd had was one of unreality; he had imagined back then that the slightest breath or blink of an eye might make it all vanish from sight. Now, here he was, after years of physical interaction, years of climbing her heights, touching her mantle, tasting her fruits — years of *feeling* her under his feet — still struggling with

Overlook's 'reality'. What the hell was going on?

As if this were not bad enough, Jake was still perplexed by the constant disparity between what he envisaged and what he managed to get down on canvas. In spite of his steady progress, he knew he still had a long way to go. He knew *exactly* how a shadow fell across a field — but still could never quite "get it right" on canvas. He knew his woods intimately — yet could not unfailingly approximate in paint what he *saw*.

Baffled by his inability to come up with clear-cut answers, Jake would turn his hands and mind to what he knew best — the commonplace practicality of physical labor. He knew how to cut and to measure and to dig and to hammer, applying all of these tasks to the building of Hervey White's concert hall as he joined other workmen to help in the fulfilling of White's dream during the spring and summer of 1916. The work sustained him throughout his mental perturbations, satisfied that at the end of a day's labor he could kick with the toe of his boot the solidity of a well-set pole or the permanence of two pieces of nailed wood.

This, at least, he knew was *real*.

15

The excitement heralding the second Maverick Festival, though he was once again involved in many of its preparations, had little effect on Jake this time around. He felt little desire to attend this second round of merry-making, his mind increasingly preoccupied with his painting and its attendant problems. He had enjoyed the festivities the previous year, but had little interest in a repeat performance. Fun for its own sake seemed somehow frivolous, the idea foreign to his usual self reserve.

And, as the much-touted plans for Hervey White's second and even more ambitious festival were being noised about town, so also did further rumblings and rumors of war come to the little art colony of Woodstock. Still a distant consideration to Jake, the political climate of Europe rarely entered his mind as he went from day to day, earning his living, struggling yet to uncover those deeper mysteries of the craft he was just barely getting to know.

The memory of his liaison with Irina had slowly receded from any semblance of reality, the night already relegated to some freakish aberration in his life, a once-in-a-lifetime happening that held no significant relevance for him or for his day-to-day existence. It took little effort for him to believe that the whole episode was a product of his imagination, a sort of fantastic wish fulfillment in lieu of his meeting up again with Sarah.

Though it was now thoroughly impossible for Jake to precisely reconstruct her features, the memory of Sarah had remained a constant fixture in his mind. Oddly, the very *lack* of physical contact with her — so unlike his encounter with Irina — made Sarah that much more "real" to him. Her cup, standing in full view each time he entered his studio, helped to keep the memory of their short meeting alive. If he could not remember her face, the recollection of her friendly gesture could not be erased from his consciousness — the cup constantly serving as tangible evidence of that brief encounter.

Still, Sarah was as remote from his everyday life as was Irina, and it was only their persistence in his memory that brought him to thoughts of other women. Aunt Birgit still teased him once in a while about his having a "lady friend," but other than his experiences with Sarah and Irina, he had little contact with women. He lived in a man's world, working alongside them or alone, spending most of his free time either in his studio or out of doors.

He was aware — in a general way — of women's interest in him. He could not fail to notice how some of them looked at him when he had worked around Byrdcliffe or now, in town or at the Maverick. Sarah herself said that she had "seen him around" and that they "all knew Jake." But women all seemed somehow beyond him — as if they had come from a different race. Other than his aunt and Mrs. Magee or Mrs. Cooper whom he somehow didn't 'see' as women, most of those he came in contact with were artists — city people. They were — to Jake — *aliens.* Thus the total surprise that day when Sarah approached him and offered him the cup.

Even the local girls intimidated him. His natural reticence became awkward shyness the few times he found himself in their presence. When the sisters or daughters of some of his fellow workers came to bring dinner pails to them on the job, he would note their sidelong glances at him, blush at their furtive smiles. In time, some even approached him to say "Hi" or to share a few words. Their tentative openness was different from the brashness of some of the women artists he had come across at Mrs. Magee's or Mrs. Cooper's, and it was only in gradual degrees that he eventually responded to their presence.

The men he worked with would sometimes rag him about a sister or daughter being "sweet on him," but Jake would just grin, blush, and shrug his shoulders, busying himself with whatever task was at hand. He never paid such banterings much mind, but lately there were times when old "Dutch" van Gaasbeeck's daughter would pop into his mind at the oddest moments.

Nicholas van Gaasbeeck — "Dutch" to almost everyone who knew him — was a master carpenter who had taught Jake much over the years. Their paths frequently crossed in and around Woodstock and they often found themselves working on the same jobs. His eldest daughter, Ruth, was a robust and buxom blonde who looked nothing like her gnarled and grizzled father. As time passed and Jake saw more of her, he could only assume that she must have favored her mother — though, since he had yet to meet Mrs. Van Gaasbeeck, he could make no such judgment.

Chance encounters with "Ruthie" on various jobs that Jake and her father had worked on steadily increased, and eventually "Dutch" invited him over to supper one night to their home over in Wittenberg where Jake had the opportunity to meet the whole family. Ruthie's younger siblings — two sisters and two brothers — all shared her red-cheeked freshness, while her mother — whom Ruthie *did* resemble in facial features and after whom she was named — was a rather somber and gaunt woman who, from her six-foot height, towered over both her husband and her children.

In their simple and straight-forward ways, "Dutch" and Mrs. van Gaasbeeck reminded Jake of Uncle Hans and Aunt Birgit and it was not long before he found himself comfortable enough to come back now and then to share supper at their table.

He enjoyed roughhousing with Ruthie's younger brothers, surprised that being with young children could be so pleasant. Having them around was a new experience for Jake and, sometimes to Ruthie's displeasure, they would occupy most of his time while he visited.

In time, however, Ruthie would induce him to take a walk with her down to the general store or over to Yankeetown Pond for an evening stroll along its shore. Ruthie would talk animatedly about almost everything and, generally, Jake was content to let her go on, rarely interrupting her in her conversation.

He might nod an assent or shake his head negatively from time to time in response to whatever she was speaking about, but found little to contribute in the way of words. Most of the time he would store up interesting images in his mind that he noted around the pond and, instead of thinking about Ruthie when he returned home, would go to his studio to reproduce them in his sketchbook from memory.

When she once persuaded him to accompany her to a barn dance, he reluctantly agreed, but the lively music and whirling dancers merely threw him into a mild panic. He spent the entire evening hulking in a corner, refusing to rise to her pulling hands when each new number began. When she tired of trying to get him out on the floor, she would dance with others, and he was happy to watch her kick up her heels — but even happier that while she was dancing it allowed him respite from her repeated urgings to "get up and stomp a little."

"Dutch" and Mrs. van Gaasbeeck made it plain that they were pleased that he was "seeing" Ruthie. Even though their "dates" were widely interspersed, Mrs. van Gaasbeeck would always offer him a somber nod of her head when they met in town, and "Dutch," whenever they worked on a job together, would go out of his way to give him a silent nudge with his elbow if they came into close contact.

As for Aunt Birgit, she made no secret of *her* delight in the whole business.

Jake, for his part, chose to keep an open mind.

16

The second Maverick Festival was as successful — some claimed that it was even better — than the first, its popularity firmly establishing Hervey White's enterprise as a permanent part of the Woodstock Colony. Jake, as he had resolved, had not gone to the festival, content in having experienced the first one, but seeing no reason or profit in repeating it.

The festival had served to cap another summer season and, as the dog days of August began to be freshened by the shifting air masses being pushed down from Canada, Woodstock settled once more into its other role as a rural village. Farmers took in crops and prepared their homes and animals for the oncoming winter while those artists who now made Woodstock their permanent home stocked up on supplies and envisioned grander schemes for the quieter months ahead.

From his long familiarity with artists, Jake knew that for all its vaunted zaniness, the Maverick Festival served a much deeper purpose than making money for Hervey White or giving the community an opportunity for "letting their hair down." Not only did it bring a closer spirit of — if not exactly camaraderie — then one of cooperation between townsman and artist, but it also served to satisfy an ancient need common to most creative souls. Though he still had much to learn about painting, he knew enough about artists — and himself, for that matter — to know that the path of creation was a lonely one, and that the journey to artistic self-expression was beset by a host of psychological problems that would daunt the bravest. In addition to the many and varied physical problems that can hinder the creative spirit — intractability of materials, illness, daily survival — the artist, whether he be painter, sculptor, composer, poet, writer, or actor, is constantly put on notice by society at large that what he does has no practical application in a world of cold fact. And, like Icarus, he knows the danger of attempting to fly too high — indeed, knows the danger of trying to fly at all.

Yet creative personalities, in the solitary isolation of their studies and studios, continue to face blank canvases, blocks of stone, sheets of paper, silent pianos, to once again bring something from within themselves that — in the end — no one has requested and that ultimately may yet prove stillborn. And, whether success or failure follows, each time the study or studio door is closed to the outside world for another descent into one's depths, the toll levied on the human psyche is immeasurable. Jake had seen more than a few empty whiskey bottles lying around studios as he put up shelves or moved windows — bottles that only the day before had been full. Many artists, their waxed wings melted by too close a brush with the sun, fall never to rise again. Others — the *real* artists — simply pick themselves up and try again because, as Birge Harrison had impressed upon him, *they had no choice.*

A much different business, this making of art than the making and producing of things that people required — like carriage parts, foodstuff, farm implements, or clothing. When Jake was hired to build a bookcase or mend a shelf, he already knew that the finished product — if made well and to the buyer's satisfaction — would be accepted and paid for — because it was *wanted.* Not so for the artist who created things out of some inner need and for no other reason than that he *has* to. Though Jake had made more shelves, cabinets, and bookcases than he could now count, he was well aware that not a single person had ever asked him to paint a landscape.

Those artists that survive the fray find, if not worldly success, then solace in such diversions as Hervey White's festivals. Swinging like reluctant pendulums between terrifying bouts of isolation and the comforting empathy of others, they seek haven in cliques and associations, in ever-shifting 'common' goals, in whatever social gathering might offer a respite from the constant gnawing of that self-expression that persistently and irresistibly craves to be released.

Some, desiring to find common ground with others, form clubs with formal rules and regulations that, as far as possible, sought a common cause and did not impinge on the sacrosanct areas of creativity peculiar to each of its members. Jake had heard of old, established New York City clubs that catered to artists with particular needs and goals. The Tile Club, for example, was established to arrange *plein air* group excursions for its members, the Salmagundi Club a place for painters to enjoy camaraderie and joint exhibitions, while the National Arts Club, a bit more on the 'posh' side, offered its sponsored members an elegant gathering place for socializing with artists of all disciplines. Then, there were the more specialized groups such as drawing, pastel, or watercolor societies, groups that called together artists who chose to work in only one medium.

Thus the banding together in such communities as that found in Woodstock's Byrdcliffe, Rock City, the Maverick — or in the towns and cities of France, Austria, Russia, Germany and in England — in short, wherever artists could meet and interact for the temporary illusion of not being alone. For some artists, the group became an extension of themselves, offering them an identity that, because of their calling, served in place of their own tenuous existence in a world that did not understand or accept them. Whatever religious affiliation these artists might have had — or still clung to — their true congregations would almost always be composed of the like-minded — and like-afflicted — comrades in their clubs, their associations, their federations, and their guilds. Sometimes, artists formed temporary 'movements' centered around a particular trend or idea— or, as Birge Harrison called them — 'isms'. Anything might serve, no matter how loose or short-lived, to not feel entirely cut off from a society in which they had to survive.

Even Jake, a natural isolatoe, recognized that though he may be reticent about his private life, he welcomed the quiet evenings at home with Uncle Hans and Aunt Birgit, their inbred European reserve exactly fitted to his own sense of proper boundaries between people. The openhearted acceptance of him by his aunt and the quiet talks he sometimes shared with his uncle were enough to last him through hours and days of working alone. Often, just knowing they were *there* was a comfort.

Still, his ingrained sense of independence made Jake wary of groups, and he was unwilling to attach himself to any club, party, or organization. Reliant on his own resources since early boyhood, he had little desire to submit to the dictates of others. Although he knew that there was strength in numbers, he was also acutely aware that being swallowed up into a group also meant giving up some portion of free will — and if anybody needed the freedom to go his own way, who else would it be but the artist? Of course, artists came in all stripes, as he was well aware. Harrison had alerted him from the outset that each artist had his own "why", and it wasn't very long before Jake saw himself as 'different' from a good many who claimed to be artists. He'd come across too many parroting their instructors or speaking in multiple voices — as did the Rock City crowd —and he couldn't take them seriously, couldn't really see them as "artists". Though it would be ridiculous to think that all artists had to travel up the Hudson to discover a "why", he was pretty sure that some kind of similar experience was necessary to set them on their way. Discounting those who only came to art as an occupation and were in it for the money, or fame, or whatever, Jake just couldn't see how the artist who felt himself compelled by forces larger than himself could find any real shelter or consolation in seeking acceptance into a group.

17

One afternoon in early September, when he had started to walk home after a day's work at Riseley's boarding house, Jake noticed his uncle's wagon, still loaded with bluestone, pulled over on the side of the road near Disch's mill. Pleased that he might get a ride home, he went to the wagon but saw no sign of his uncle. Puzzled, he stood wondering at this unusual state of affairs when he heard a rustling and muttering coming from the banks of the Sawkill beneath the bridge. To his amazement he saw Uncle Hans scrambling up the slippery bank, his face and head dripping with water that ran down his collar and shirtfront.

"Uncle Hans!" exclaimed Jake as he hurried down the creekbank to offer his help, his uncle wincing as Jake grabbed his hand. Jake then noticed the raw knuckles and bruises on his uncle's forehead and cheek. "What happened? Was there an accident at the quarry?"

"Ach! Today fisticuffs!" Uncle Hans panted as he gained the top of the slope.

Jake helped him up onto the wagon, turning his uncle's face this way and that in an attempt to assess the damage. "Shall I take you over to Doctor Downer's?"

"No, no," Uncle Hans waved his hand angrily, again wincing and reaching up with the other to massage his shoulder. "Dere is no damage — chust bruises."

Jake, noting the return of the heavy accent, could sense his uncle's agitation.

Uncle Hans wriggled his arm. "I think maybe only I hurt my arm a bit," adding with a deep chuckle, "from when I hit *him!*" His uncle's hearty laughter degenerated into a long, spasmodic fit of coughing.

"Well, you don't sound so good," said Jake. "And who's 'him'?"

"That wiseacre with the big mouth," said Uncle Hans when the coughing subsided.

Jake was relieved to hear that the accent was gone.

"The one who never stops with this 'Heinie' business."

"Ahh," said Jake, understanding what had transpired. Then, looking at his uncle's dampened clothes asked, "But how come you were down in the creek?" He glanced around to see if anyone else was nearby.

"I was cleaning myself up," said Uncle Hans. "I didn't want to go home looking like some brawling hoodlum and upset your aunt."

Jake surveyed his uncle. He took in the beginnings of what promised to be a fine shiner, the glowing red bruise on his cheek, and the scraped knuckles. Then, laughing out loud when he saw that his uncle was in no real danger, added, "Well, you did a fine job, Uncle Hans. Aunt Birgit will never notice a thing!"

"Don't *you* be a wiseacre, now," groused his uncle, relapsing once again into one of his prolonged coughing spasms.

Jake gently shouldered his uncle over and said, "Let me drive, Uncle Hans." Glancing sideways at his uncle's rapidly blooming eye, he added with a smile, "You probably can't see where you're going anyway."

Uncle Hans settled back in the seat and closed his good eye. "Schmart aleck," he said good-naturedly to his nephew, and remained silent with only an occasional coughing spell breaking their silence as they made their way home.

Neither given to idle chatter, both men retreated into their own thoughts.

The old stoneworker mulled over in his mind an idea that he had been speaking about with his wife for some time now. Birgit had been urging him to retire, pointing out to him in her practical way that, now that they owned their home free and clear of any commitments, they were 'well enough off' to take things a little easy. Hans, however, was not sure that he would like the idea of being idle. He thought of Sanford Magee, whiling away his hours on his front porch, doing nothing but getting in his wife's way. Even Jake had to attend to Sanford's chores under the pretense that he was 'paying' for the meals that he shared at the Magee table. He could not see himself turning into a 'lump'.

On the other hand, Birgit pointed out that with the free time he might find plenty to do. Wasn't he always going on about knowing more about those fossils that he always seemed to find? Now, alongside the small collection that he had so carefully carried with him from the Solnhofen quarries, he had added a considerable store of those he found here in America. Though they were different, of course, such remains of early life indicated that even here in the Catskill Mountains the whole region must have been under water at some time in the past. Yes, he would enjoy knowing more about this, and was sure that he might find books about such things in the Kingston library.

So, yes, it was true that he need not just sit around doing nothing. But, in his heart, he also knew that Birgit — his *Liebling* — wanted him to stop work because she was worried about his coughing. He silently shrugged his shoulders — noticing again that the movement caused him some pain — and resolved that, it was true, it was time.

I will quit working — and — I will quit smoking — he thought.

Almost immediately, however, his resolve was beset by questions of which he would miss more.

Jake, wrapped in his own thoughts, had also just arrived at the matter of his uncle's cough. Confident that his Uncle Hans had suffered no real damage in his altercation with whoever the 'him' was back on the job, he was not so sure that his persistent cough was not indicative of some deeper ailment. Both Jake and Aunt Birgit had been agreeing that the cough was becoming more alarming in its violence and increasing frequency. He really had to support his aunt in insisting that Uncle Hans make a visit to Doctor Downer. Perhaps a little medicine would alleviate those wracking coughs.

He'd given little thought to his uncle's interactions with his fellow workers. Name-calling, after all, was a way of life for workmen. Nicknames came fast and easy to men on the job as they picked up on each other's foibles, weaknesses, or physical characteristics. "Fatso" or "Squinty" might not have been particularly liked, but no one took them seriously or came to blows over them. "Shorty", "Lefty", "Red", and the like, were just easier than remembering a man's name that you might work with for only one day. Calling Uncle Hans "Heinie", however, went a bit deeper, given the way the wind was blowing these days. As for the politics that lay behind this latest dust-up between his uncle and his fellow worker, Jake still had no clear opinion one way or the other. He was disturbed of course that his uncle, ordinarily a peace-loving and cheerful man, should be beset by such trouble because of such a silly thing as a German accent. Weren't all Americans ultimately immigrants? Sure, Germany was causing distress with its belligerence in Europe, but what did that have to do with his poor Uncle Hans?

Two days later, all thoughts about his uncle or the politics of Europe were completely erased from Jake's mind.

The day dawned with the promise of being one of those exceptionally warm surprises one sometimes finds at the end of September. Though sultry, the air still had a tang of autumn crispness that gave it the illusion of all being well with the world. Jake gave himself a holiday, prepared to do nothing but hang around Woodstock, seeking out some of the old haunts to see if he might find an artist or two with whom he might exchange a pleasant hour or so, perhaps to discuss a little about painting.

After an uneventful morning and a light lunch at Mrs. Magee's where, as usual, the talk was too loud, too rambunctious, Jake decided to stroll on over to the League studio to see if he might come across any of the students there. Although he still did not feel free to enter the studios — especially when classes were in session — he thought it possible that he might bump into someone coming or going to class.

He had just left Rock City Road and had taken only a few steps onto Tinker Street when there in front of the village green he saw Sarah Winters standing and speaking with a man.

Taken completely off guard, Jake stopped in his tracks. Sarah, speaking animatedly to her companion, had not seen him and, checking his first impulse to run up to her, Jake was undecided as to whether he should attempt to catch her attention or turn back up Rock City Road. Turning away seemed the best alternative, but before he could do so Sarah spotted him.

"Jake!" she called out. "Jake, Jake, it's *me*, Sarah!"

Jake turned to look at her and could not check the swell of emotion that seemed to fill his chest. He merely looked at her and could not speak for fear of blurting out something foolish.

"Jake! Don't you remember me?" She had come towards him,

leaving her companion to stand by himself.

"Of course," Jake managed to mumble. "Oh, yes – yes, I remember you. You – you just kind of took me by surprise."

"Just like the first time," laughed Sarah. Then, turning to the man still standing off by himself, she called out, "Cal, come here. I want you to meet Jake."

Ambling over in a loose-limbed kind of way, 'Cal' reached out to shake hands with Jake. "How do you do," he said.

Jake thought the greeting a bit formal and simply returned a "Hi." He noted that the hand held out to him was rather soft, the grip more tentative than genuinely intended.

"I met Jake up at Byrdcliffe last ..." Sarah turned to Jake, asking, "Was it last year?"

"The year before," answered Jake, not sure why it might matter to this stranger.

"Anyway, he's the artist I told you about, Cal ... you know, the one who gave me that exquisite drawing?"

'Cal' merely nodded.

"I've had it matted and framed, Jake. Some day I'll have to show it to you."

Jake smiled.

"How is your work going, Jake. Are you still making those lovely drawings?"

"Well ... yes ... but I've begun painting and that sort of has been taking up a good deal of my time."

"Oh, how wonderful! Cal's a painter also, Jake. He's been studying over in France for the past several years, but that frightful war has interrupted his instruction." She looked up at 'Cal' and, facing Jake, continued. "He's studying at the League now — in New York City." She turned back to 'Cal', then, once again, to Jake. "This is his first trip to Woodstock and I was showing him around."

"Are you studying here at the League, uh, Jake?" asked 'Cal'.

"No, I'm not," said Jake. "I live here ... actually the next town over ... West Hurley."

"Must be interesting," 'Cal' said tonelessly, "living here way out in the sticks year 'round Jake – uh – Jake ... What is your last name anyway?"

"Oh, what has happened to my manners," Sarah broke in. "I ought to have done this properly at the beginning ... I was just so

130

pleased to see you. Anyway, Jake, this is my fiancé Calvin Steele. Cal, this is Jake Forscher."

Further stunned by this unexpected announcement, Jake hardly heard what followed.

When he left them standing at the Green, he could recall little else of their conversation — could not even remember how he had taken leave of them. To see her after so long! To feel that same thrill, that same constriction in the chest — that same inability to open his mouth and speak confidently.

Some kind of pleasantries must have passed between them, but as Jake moved off to continue on his way, a single query from Calvin Steele came back to play itself over and over in his mind —

"Forscher ... that's a German name, isn't it?"

Jake could not remember his response.

18

The winter of 1916 was especially cold, especially forbidding — or so, at any rate, it seemed to Jake. He rarely went off by himself that fall and early winter to seek those lonely spots where he might find a new motif, experiencing no joy as the bare trees of winter offered new vantage points from which he could discover different views of Overlook.

The mountain, he had learned over the years, revealed new secrets to him from her varied aspects, at one time appearing as young and brash with new things to tell him, while on other days seeming as if tired and old and weary of its earthly role of standing sentinel for its fellow mountains. For the first time, Jake could not be lured to its flanks and summit, paintbox slung over his shoulder, eyes eagerly searching for a new subject.

He told himself that it was too cold, that the snow was probably too deep, that the winds would make it impossible to draw or paint — though none of these things had ever deterred him before. Many a day he had slogged through fields of knee-deep snow, settling himself against the trunk of a tree and working on his sketches until his limbs lost all feeling, and his fingers could no longer grip his carpenter's pencil. His long years of working out of doors had inured him to either falling or soaring temperatures, and he blithely accepted visitations of rain or fog or snow as merely new veils through which he might study his mountain.

Though his disinclination to brave the winter gave him more time to spend in his studio or at home, he found the same disinterest in doing those things that had for so long been a vital part of his life. He went about his chores sullenly, avoiding extended conversations with Aunt Birgit and Uncle Hans. Hour after hour might be passed by splitting wood, a chore that he dearly loved, its rhythmic ritual lulling his mind to empty calm. When the woodboxes were filled, the animals taken care of and any other jobs Aunt Birgit had asked him to do were finished, he whiled away time by seeing to his tools, honing his axe and scythe, meticulously arranging his tool box. When he could find nothing to occupy his hands, he would spend most of his time in his room, lying idly on his bed, either dozing or daydreaming about nothing in particular.

When he stirred himself to go into his studio, he listlessly stood around or aimlessly rearranged his easel, straightened a drawing hanging on the wall, or checked his brushes for the hundredth time to see if they were clean. How could they be otherwise since he had not painted a single canvas in many weeks? He would sit in the straight-back chair that comprised the only piece of non-essential furniture that he had allowed to clutter his studio, tilting it against the wall and staring out of the window — but seeing nothing.

If, by chance, his eyes strayed to the little shelf that held the cup that Sarah had given him, Jake would immediately snap out of his reverie, slam all four legs of the chair back onto the floor and stalk out of the studio. Waves of anger, of humiliation, of consternation, of helpless despair would take away his usual calm, driving him either back into the house to put up with Uncle Hans's increasing complaints about his fellow workers or Aunt Birgit's persistent attempts at "cheering" him up.

Sometimes, he would walk into Woodstock to lose himself in idle chatter with whomever he might find around town. He even teased himself with thoughts of perhaps seeing "her" one more time, but knew that the chances were slim of coming across any of the summer visitors, least of all of Sarah Winters and her fiancé, Calvin Steele.

And, if he did, what might he say? Would seeing her again with 'Cal' alleviate this unfamiliar feeling of malaise that robbed him of his usual self?

Running into Sarah that day in late fall had done more than just upset him. His seeing her again brought back all the emotional turmoil that he thought had long been buried. That she had so calmly introduced him to her "fiancé" left him desolate.

Worse, that brief encounter on Woodstock's village green had put the final touch to his budding relationship with Ruthie van Gaasbeeck. Not that it had been going all that smoothly.

Although he enjoyed spending time with "Dutch" and his family, he was simply not all that much of a "lady's man." Ruthie loved square dancing, but when she finally persuaded him to accompany her on the dance floor, he was all left feet. As much as he tried, he was just too stiff, too self-conscious to let himself go and respond to the lively music.

It never got much better on their walks together. His long silences and inability to carry on a normal "boy-girl" conversation had increasingly annoyed her, his non-committal grunts often sending her marching to her front door in a huff. Her petulant outbursts and pouting lips only served to send him deeper into himself. Running into Sarah, had merely closed a book on a story that never really had a chance to begin.

* * *

Winter eventually gave way to spring, the annual rebirth of nature affecting Jake whether he wished it or not. He could not resist seeking out the first blooms of arbutus, tramping to those deep recesses in abandoned quarries where one could still find snow in spite of the arrival of warmer temperatures, checking to see if the trees were budding on schedule.

Though he still had little desire to draw or paint, he found renewed energy to divert into his "paying" jobs. The coming of warmer weather meant there would soon be plenty of shelves to put up in the studios of others, still a thousand and one repair jobs for the hotels and boarding houses in town.

Fitting in a new bookcase or a set of shelves into a confined area was a pleasing challenge to him, the careful measuring and cutting requiring his close attention and skills. Whatever such concentration might do for the job at hand, it had the added benefit of keeping his mind off other things. Once completed, Jake would step back — even find himself squinting — surveying the artistry of his work.

Good — he would say to himself — *Joints are well-mitered, rough corners sanded off, and the finishing touch of paint makes the new addition seem as if part of the original whole.*

Proud of his work, Jake never failed to experience a sense of accomplishment when he built something from raw materials, cut a clean swath of hay with his scythe, or took a tree down with a minimum number of strokes.

He prided himself on knowing his tools and only wished that he had equal control over his brushes — but time and practice — at least Birge Harrison led him to believe — would finally tell. He felt the desire to paint returning once again; now all he needed was the know-how. He knew he was improving, but if he could paint a picture with the same ease that he might split a pile of stove-wood, he would feel a whole lot better. The smooth flowing motion of axe, arm, and shoulder was eminently satisfying.

Had he known of it, he would have readily agreed with Henry David Thoreau's observation that learning how to split and stack wood was a far surer way for a man to be educated than by sending him to school. Once one learned the inner structure of wood — the individual grain of oak or maple or butternut — one merely had to allow the axe to fall where it must; common sense and gravity did all the 'work'. Like all labor involving wood, it was clean work and Jake could spend hour after hour splitting logs, going through cord after cord, feeling at the end of a day's toil only a slight weariness in his shoulders. His mind, however, always felt clearer, the rhythmic swing of the axe a meditative balm that cleansed his thoughts of whatever troubled him. If only he could feel the same while he painted!

The spring of 1917 also brought Uncle Hans to the final decision of leaving his job.

On April 6th, America declared war on Germany and he could only envision more hostility from fellow workers coming his way. Aunt Birgit was delighted with his decision, already planning out the many leisurely projects for her husband that she felt he so deserved after a lifetime of hard work. Now he was free from the harassment of his fellow workers, free from a job that kept him away from home for long hours every day, free from worrying what might happen when the already dwindling bluestone trade finally ceased altogether. Now her Hans could take the time to read about his fossils — or do whatever else took his fancy.

Jake, too, was pleased with his uncle's decision — and even more so when Uncle Hans turned over the use and care of his wagon to him. Not only would it give Jake a permanent mode of transportation, but now he could add hauling to the list of services he could offer his employers.

Since he was a boy, he had been taking care of his uncle's horses, feeding and brushing them down after a day's work and keeping their stable clean. Now, he would be doing these chores for himself. If he could not yet see himself as an artist, now at twenty-three, he at least saw himself as a moderately prosperous businessman.

Fickle May inevitably transformed itself into a gently compromising June, bringing the sweet promise of summer to the Woodstock Valley. The definitive stand against Germany recently taken by President Wilson seemed to Jake to have narrowed things down to the point that everyone knew exactly where they stood. Still, the politics of Europe receded even farther from his thoughts. He already knew where *he* stood.

Once again, Jake picked up his brushes in earnest. The ache in his breast was gradually showing evidence of letting up, and he found joy in both his studio and his tramps up the mountain. Overlook firmly reestablished its claim on his attention and the world again seemed a good place to be.

Woodstock, as if in harmony with his inner mood and in spite of Europe's turmoil, continued to bring attention to itself as an up-and-coming art colony, growing ever more worthy of note as its fame reached even those in war-torn countries far across the sea.

Then, on June 5th, Jake was officially notified that he would be among those called upon for the first of the three draft registrations that would be sending American conscripts to Europe.

BOOK THREE

1920 — 1929

19

THE WAR HADN'T changed Jake as much as it had deepened him.

His mind already set before he was caught up in it, neither the war nor the politics in Europe which brought it about had any personal meaning for him, Jake refused to bring any of his experiences as soldier back home when he was released from active service. To his mind, he was now free of it and he had no obligation or desire to allow any if its boundless horror or arrant madness to become a permanent part of his life.

Though the official records indicated that he had served with the American Expeditionary Force as an infantryman in France, for Jake the war represented a meaningless nightmare from which, upon awakening, he could piece together no coherent story. He did not try to fit it into any reasonable pattern, nor had he any motivation to do so.

The obligation placed upon him by forces greater than himself to leave his familiar life and surroundings had served to bring him closer to his inner being, had intensified the path of his already reserved character into immovable and ironclad channels. Where he was once firm, he was now implacably resolute.

Like most of the conscripts who were already familiar with the use of firearms, Jake was given a perfunctory combat training course when he arrived in Europe and was almost immediately sent to the frontline trenches of France after he had completed the hasty preparation.

His training was brief and he remembered little of it. In later years all he could recall was a talk given by the chaplain on why it was all right to kill in the time of war. "Unlike murder," the chaplain had said, "which is a premeditated act, killing the enemy in times of war is a patriotic duty and condoned by God."

Jake had wondered how such training before battle could not be considered "premeditation."

He could not tell — nor had he cared to find out — where in France he was sent, which fields he had crossed or lain in, which rivers he had forded, or which towns he had passed through. If pressed — which he never allowed himself to be once he returned home — he might recall the name of a comrade or two, but could no longer remember in which shallow and muddy ditch, at what point in time, or even in what part of France, they had fallen.

In late autumn of 1918, *he* had fallen.

During the first few weeks of a lengthy convalescence in a field hospital, his sleep had been intermittently interrupted by a recurrent nightmare. In the dream, he foundered for days in the indifferent immensity of an ocean, utterly alone in a never-ending expanse of water where all boundaries of self merged into a limitless horizon. The dream would eventually recede into the deeper recesses of his psyche, and would return only sporadically at farther and farther intervals and ever-lessening intensity until finally it — along with his actual wartime experiences — had been put entirely out of mind.

At times, in the quiet of his studio or during a solitary tramp through his beloved woods, unwanted and un-summoned memories, disconnected details, would periodically visit him that, when called up in his mind, stood out in perfect clarity: the huge, looming troop ship standing in its berth in the New York harbor; the persistent and acrid odor of human excretions on the passage over the Atlantic; a raging thunder and lightning storm over the North Sea that had kept him glued to the rail throughout its duration; the initial feel of foreign soil under his feet; the sounds, sights, and smells of men killing and being killed; the overwhelming and chaotic sense of utter confusion.

Though these images would flit in and out of his consciousness to remind him of his time away from home, he would immediately shut them out. Since he was determined that the war would represent only an extended and general void, a period bereft of reason wrenched from his life, he never allowed himself to dwell on such images and thoughts, always turning his attention to the present when they came unbidden into his head. If in his studio, he would immediately attack a new canvas; if on a job, he would re-measure, cut, and build more deliberately; if in the woods, take out his sketchbook and draw. In time, even the few events that sporadically and stubbornly assailed his mind's eye in the years following the war would lose their sting and become dimmed in his memory.

He brought home a single, physical memento: a thin, white scar that began at the inside of his left knee and, traveling upward in a perfectly straight line, disappeared into his groin.

20

The Woodstock that Jake came back to was a far cry from the sleepy little village that he had first seen as a boy when he had driven in Uncle Hans's bluestone wagon through the town's two main thoroughfares on their way up to the California Quarry.

Woodstock, now firmly settled into its "art colony" reputation and preening itself on its newfound status, had taken on different airs, both long-time visitors and locals acting out the roles such a colony ought — or what they *believed* ought — to be exemplifying. Berets were now the favored headgear for artists and, judging merely from the varying degrees of outlandish get-ups, one could not always tell the difference between the bona fide artist, the affected tourist, or the enterprising townsman.

Many of the shrewder locals began looking for ways to ingratiate themselves with the increasing number of oglers coming to town by carriage, auto, train, and boat in search of local color. Even the most backwoods locals, however, knew the real article from the pretenders, and Jake had to smile when he saw someone strutting down Tinker Street trying with all seriousness to *look* like an artist. He, perhaps better than most, knew the deceptiveness of clothing, how what one wore could mask what one was. He had only to recall his father's transformation from butcher to dandy or his own from civilian to soldier in uniform to remind him that clothing, after all, was merely one more subtle form of disguise.

Some of the more serious artists began to avoid Woodstock on weekends, retreating to their studios hidden on the quiet lanes and roads that led from the town's center and away from sightseers. Though many of the landscape painters felt that the increasing number of onlookers and weekend tourists would soon spoil their rustic retreat, others argued that the traffic was not — in the end — a bad thing since it could only result in greater exposure of their work.

The Maverick was still a major draw, its laissez faire ambience and increasingly popular festivals — now established annual affairs — drawing visitors, tourists, bohemian types, and hangers-on from all corners of the globe. Hervey White's already densely populated little colony also drew in a heavy influx of theatre people in addition to the painters, sculptors, and musicians that had formerly dominated his ever-expanding complex of cabins and performance halls. As the summer seasons waxed and waned during the 20's, summer stock theatre rivaled the visual arts as Woodstock's prime claim to fame, and it was not unusual to find such upcoming film personalities as Helen Hayes or Edward G. Robinson sauntering down Woodstock's Tinker Street on a Saturday or Sunday afternoon.

For some of the old-timers — townsfolk, artists, and Jake especially — Woodstock also began to take on too much of a commercial aspect as the 20's progressed. To their eyes, the once quaint little village appeared to look more and more like an enterprising town *striving* to appear like an art colony.

The little village, once spread out rather thinly along the stem and arms of the "Y" of the two main roads which forked at the Village Green, began expanding into the surrounding countryside as ever more farms were given up to new businesses, homes, and studios. Main thoroughfares were widened and dirt roads began to be graded and packed to accommodate the growing numbers of tourists who flowed into the town. Bicycles — a new fad in Woodstock — became the favored transportation of artists as they traveled out of town for rustic "motifs," while automobiles — the newest rage of the more affluent tourists — were becoming more numerous on the roads.

Woodstock's former "commercial" enterprises, which consisted mainly of a general store, a couple of blacksmiths (which now had to re-tool their shops to accommodate the new gas-fed "contraptions"), and several boarding houses, were joined by a variety of "cafés" and new stores that catered to the summer trade. Shops featuring "genuine" Woodstock arts and crafts started popping up along Tinker Street, with items tagged in a wide range of prices to satisfy a wide range of pocketbooks. One might now visit Woodstock on a weekend and return home with an original "Woodstock" watercolor, ceramic pot, piece of woodcarving, or handcrafted jewelry.

Among the several artists' groups, the dialogue they shared about art, which had once been serious and passionate interchanges between professionals, started to take on an air of pretension; staged "discussions" were now bruited about town in cafés and bars by attention-seeking artists, their "art" openly and ostentatiously hawked on the streets as precious commodities. Weekends seemed especially noisome to Jake and, now even more of an isolatoe since his war experience, he began purposefully limiting his time in town to avoid the crush of people.

A major change in Woodstock was brought about by the discontinuance of the Art Students League's summer sessions in town. The slow drifting away from landscape painting by many of the younger artists — a move roundly applauded by the Rock City group who always advocated its irrelevance — made it difficult for the League to fill classes, rendering the upstate venture financially unfeasible. The pulling out of the League was not welcomed by everyone, however, and several of the older artists, still interested in exploiting the natural beauty of the area, began opening up their own studio "schools" to offer instruction to those who remained committed to landscape painting.

The League's closing, although viewed by many as an unfortunate turn of events, did not substantially affect the town's prosperity. The Maverick continued to boom, Byrdcliffe — though Whitehead was equally upset at the "new" Woodstock spirit of commercialism — still attracted summer residents, and the current popularity of theatre all added to the little colony's continuing path of success.

Woodstock's scramble to get on the economic bandwagon, of course, was merely a reflection of the general prosperity that was being experienced across the country. Change and excitement was in the air, and both nationally and globally, the world was transforming. Jake had been hearing some of the women artists speaking about suffrage, and though such notions were still foreign to most of the local women, the idea of a vote for women finally became a reality in 1920.

If such changes and economic prosperity brought about dreams of a positive direction for the country, the '20s also had their darker side. Old mores and morals were being pitched out in what appeared to many an alarming and reckless fashion. Efforts to curb the breakdown of morality were more often than not as pernicious as the "evil" they sought to prevent. Prohibition, for example, birthed its own woes, and clubs that featured illicit booze, jazz, and new dances were viewed by the old-timers as nothing more than updated dens of iniquity.

Woodstock, with its New York City connection already firmly established, mirrored the exuberance of a country coming out of a world war a bit more readily and a lot more openly than did its more rural neighbors. Eyebrows were raised when female ankles were flashed along Tinker Street, and, though others shrugged, Jake was still not accustomed to seeing a young woman artist light up a cigarette in front of her male colleagues. Woodstock was just being — well, *Woodstock*. Everyone expected artists to be a little strange. Still, it was a bit unsettling for some.

West Hurley, a mere handful of miles away, seemed like a different world, but Jake had discovered that things had also changed at home. While he was overseas, Uncle Hans had succumbed to what was known in the region as the "quarryman's scourge," silicosis. His uncle's years of working in and around the quarries of Germany and America had finally caught up with him, the slow build-up of inhaled stone-dust taking its final toll on his overworked lungs. Jake had not been home to witness his uncle's confinement and eventual death at the T.B Hospital in Kingston. That he could not be there to offer comfort to Aunt Birgit was just one more thing the war had taken from him.

"Always he was coughing, coughing," said Aunt Birgit, her eyes glistening with tears. "I thought it was his smoking that was making him ill."

"I'm sure it didn't help him," said Jake as he put his arm around his aunt's shoulders.

"It was his only enjoyment, that old pipe of his," she said sadly. "I shouldn't have tried to make him stop." Then the tears began to flow in earnest. "Finally he had the time to do his reading, and … and …" her sobbing choked off the words and she shrugged her shoulders helplessly.

Jake, already containing his own sorrow at his uncle's passing, could find no words to comfort his aunt. He merely held her tighter.

"Well," she said. "The work was good to him even if it did kill him. All those years it put a roof over our heads and food on the table."

Jake had learned that his parents had been up for the funeral and asked her more out of idle curiosity than real concern, "And Mama and Papa? They were all right when they came up?"

"*Ja, ja!* And Freddie and his little Konstanze also," said Aunt Birgit. "The whole family made a little holiday and stayed for a few days." She looked over at Jake. "I hope you don't mind, but I let your Mama take a look into your studio."

Jake smiled and shrugged his shoulders. He was long past caring what his family thought about his art. "That's fine, Aunt Birgit. After all, this is still your home."

"Well, your Mama was very pleased to see your studio." Then with a little shrug, "Your Papa peeked in and only grunted. Freddie and his wife also took a quick look."

Jake thought about his brother, now married and living in a rented flat on Evergreen Street just around the corner from the butcher shop on Gates Avenue. He'd made a brief visit to the homestead in Brooklyn after his release from the service, staying a weekend with his parents before leaving for upstate. Freddie was already looking like a successful 'burgher," his compliant little wife "yes dear-ing" him just like his mother did with his father.

Jake still found his time in his parent's house on Halsey Street wearying. He silently bided his time while Papa and Freddie went on about the "Future" — in Papa's use of the word, Jake always saw it with a capital "F" — and found himself absently and impatiently answering his mother's aimless questions until he felt free to leave catch his train.

Freddie — who had somehow avoided the conscription, Jake too unconcerned to inquire how — asked him little about his time overseas, which was fine with Jake who found himself unwilling to volunteer any information. Germany's aggression and eventual defeat were not topics dear to Papa's heart, so everyone studiously avoided discussions of the "Vaterland." When the subject of his time in the service was briefly touched upon — Mama had asked him if he had had enough to eat while he was in the army — father and sons avoided each other's eyes and, as quickly as possible, they would move on to other topics.

When he was alone with his parents, conversation was, as usual, sporadic and unsatisfying.

On Saturday morning he went off by himself to walk the old neighborhood. Having left his parents' home solely for a few minutes' respite to collect his thoughts, he had no particular destination in mind and aimlessly wandered the streets on which he once used to play. He barely took notice of people or buildings. From time to time, the clanging of trolley bells along Gates Avenue interrupted his thoughts, bringing back memories of placing cherry bombs and pennies on the tracks, he and Freddie squealing with delight as the fireworks exploded or the coins flattened into elongated lozenges when the trolley ran over them. He wondered at his own and at Freddie's daring when, as they got older, they would sometimes hitch rides by precariously clinging to the rear bumpers of the swaying trolleys. Mostly, however, he only felt even more of a stranger to the neighborhood as he let his feet take him where they would, sometimes heading for Broadway to walk under the el, at other times along the tree-shaded streets that paralleled or crossed Gates Avenue and Halsey Street.

Suddenly, a large shadow fell across his path, abruptly jolting him out of his reveries.

He looked up to find himself standing on the corner of Menahan and Bleecker Streets, directly in front of St. Barbara's Roman Catholic Church.

21

After its finishing touches were completed in 1910, St. Barbara's, an impressive example of Italian/Spanish Renaissance architecture, was the tallest structure in all of Brooklyn. In the warm, golden light of that Saturday morning, the church, with its dome and spires soaring up into space, looked particularly beautiful to Jake.

On impulse, he climbed the wide flight of stone steps that led up to the massive front doors remembering, as he slowly made his way up, how many times he had reluctantly gone to church in the past. As pupils of a parochial school, he and Freddie had to go regularly to Mass not only on Sundays, but were also required to attend services on every feast and holy day of the church calendar. Grouped into their separate classes, they would be marched from the school in single file, each class assigned to specific pews inside the church.

Jake pushed open the door, instinctively expecting at any moment to hear the chhkk-ing sound of the beetle-shaped, metal clickers the nuns held in their hands to alert their students when to stop, continue, turn, sit, stand, or be seated. As he strode through the outer entry, he noted the familiar tables set out with pamphlets and notices, and ignoring the holy water font, stepped through the central doors into the nave. He was relieved to find no one inside.

Deceptively compact from the outside, the empty church seemed huge, its interior gloomily cavernous since the only light that entered came filtered through stained windows set high above eye level. Like the inside of most large, stone buildings, it was cool, somewhat dampish, a bit off-putting.

Jake's steps resounded from the high walls as he walked down the center aisle of the marble floor toward the communion rail.

This place was designed to daunt, to awe — he thought.

He realized that places of Catholic worship were built more than human-size for a reason. They were designed to humble the human spirit. They were meant to impress — if not actually to press down upon — the visitor.

Well — he whispered — *It certainly worked on me.*

Jake halted his steps and stood in the center of the nave, letting the silence seep into his consciousness. While quietly standing there, he found it difficult to dissociate himself from the boy he once was. Back then, he never felt any of the warmth or safety that the nuns had assured him he would find in the house of God. He never felt any of the love that Jesus was supposed to have for him.

He closed his eyes and momentarily re-experienced that familiar sense of dread in the pit of his stomach.

With an abrupt shake of his head, Jake pulled himself back to the present.

Letting his eyes travel back and forth, up and down, he wondered at the impact such a structure — a place like Notre Dame, for instance, must have had on the visiting peasants from the outlying districts of Paris. Here was a single building that could contain not only the total population of their village, but also its entire physicality of homes, gardens, and livestock.

How insignificant they must have felt, how little in the eyes of God they must have imagined themselves to be.

He resumed his walk towards the altar. When he reached the communion rail, Jake turned to face the rear of the church. He let his eyes survey the rigidly aligned benches.

It's been a long time.

His eyes traveled up to the domed ceiling, to the stained glass windows on either side of the outer aisles, and lastly to an incredibly detailed carving that adorned the wooden pulpit.

He walked over to the raised platform, the wooden structure set in amongst the pews about a third of the way into the nave, purposely positioned to be amidst the people as the priest delivered his sermon.

Threats of darkness and fire descending onto the bowed heads of the rigidly seated parishioners, righteous punishment for misdeeds that separated them from God's love.

Taking a seat directly in front of the pulpit, Jake knelt on the bench and leaned forward to run his hands over its richly polished wood. Tracing with his fingertips the simulated trailing vine that seemed to grow up the side of the railed enclosure, he allowed his craftsman's eye to appreciatively take in the meticulous carving of leaf and tendril, of hidden bird, small animal, or blown flower.

Good work.

He glanced around the worn pews, at the pamphlets protruding from brackets attached to the backs of seats, at the padded kneeling benches, and the life-sized paintings and saw how judiciously — and fruitlessly, to his way of thinking — the space was made to make humans feel welcome in God's spacious house. He tried to people the space with imaginary parishioners in an effort to make the empty church seem less aloof — but he failed in the attempt.

With a touch of sadness, he could readily see why it was that he had never felt much welcome in a church as a child — even today, as a grown man, he could only muster a vague sense of emptiness as he quietly sat there.

He got up and began to walk around the perimeter of the nave, studying the figures portrayed in the stained glass windows, peering closely at the agonized and angry faces depicted in the carved reliefs of the Stations of the Cross. Finally, he returned once more to stand in the center of the church to take in a final sweep of the dome, the organ, the altar, and the pulpit.

Facing the rear, he noted the organ pipes soaring up towards the roof, the lofty ensemble punctuated by a circular, stained-glass window high up on the wall that allowed liquid color to stream down to the marble floor. Everything, he saw, tended to direct the attention upward, attempting by pointed arch, vertical organ pipe, center point of dome, to cause the eyes — the soul? — to rise toward the Supreme Creator.

Why had my soul always felt so leaden in such a place?

Though he was moved by its massive and stony influence, he knew he could now let go of the apprehension he once felt so strongly as a boy. He wondered at the change. It was, after all, not unlike the church he remembered as a boy.

Of course, as a child he had not appreciated the finer points of architectural beauty; never noted the sublime art in stained glass windows or statues or paintings. For all its beauty, however, the overwhelming sense of scale aggressively and unmistakably reigned supreme. His artistic sense told him that the intent to inspire a love of God was simply swallowed up in the overblown spatial composition.

In the end, human smallness set against the immensity and gravity of the apostolic church is the message it imparts.

As these impressions passed through his consciousness, images of the sea, of his first view of the Catskills, crept into his thoughts. How does one grasp such boundlessness? How can the limited embrace of human arms contain infinity?

He thought of the night he spent with Irina, and he thought of the war. How can one hope to understand such inexplicable mysteries? Unbidden, never fully understood, such things descend on one, flood one's mind and consciousness, obliterating all human standards of measurement to ultimately drown the self in a sea of unknowing.

Such things lay outside one's grasp.

At least, they lay beyond mine.

Since his return from the war, Jake no longer believed as he once did that one might comprehend the whole through coming to know the parts. Overlook Mountain, he now knew, could not be known by learning about her separate elements. Neither the horrors of war nor the transcendent ecstasy he had experienced that night at the Maverick would ever be comprehended by recalling in precise detail each and every action of each and every moment.

The answer was not found in the detail. It was not traceable to this plant, this exploding piece of shrapnel, this placement of hand on flesh, or this particular dramatization of "God." The answer lay somewhere above, beneath, within, beyond — outside of, apart from, the accidents of individual characteristics.

Comprehension did not come piecemeal nor did it come from outside oneself. It came unexpectedly, suddenly, entire, from somewhere deep inside.

One did not — could not — "embrace" the Catholic Church, or a war, or a mountain range, or even a woman during a sexual encounter. Such things perhaps embraced you, momentarily, their limitless boundaries intersecting with your finite human existence for a split second of time. They are random anomalies of the cre-

151

ation, gifts or burdens that, because of inherent flaws in the universe — through tiny cracks that God has somehow overlooked in the supposedly seamless flow of existence — are sometimes visited upon mankind.

Once experienced, inadvertently glimpsed in an unguarded moment, these intrusions into our beings — though never forgotten — are never retrievable to the human consciousness in their totalities. Just tiny bits of them float into a dream, appear before a daydreaming eye, flit into the mind abruptly and unexpectedly, tantalizingly keeping the memory of something "other" alive.

Turning, Jake once more faced the altar of St. Barbara's Roman Catholic Church. Shorn of flowers, stripped of its dyed and expensive coverings, the holy table where the priest re-enacted the transubstantiation of bread and wine seemed small, a cold, hard slab of marble dwarfed like everything else in the yawning space of the apse.

As he turned to leave, he could not help but feel its weight once again oppressively bearing down on him.

How am I to capture the looming enigma of Overlook Mountain on a blank, white canvas when a cunningly constructed pile of stones can so easily confound me?

22

The lump sum mustering-out stipend and small disability income that Jake had received upon his release from the army, allowed him to cut back on his day-laboring, enabling him to pick and choose only those jobs that he found most satisfying and least draining on his creative energies. He ran into "Dutch" van Gaasbeeck from time to time, their paths continuing to cross when they found themselves on the same job. Ruthie, "Dutch" told him, had gotten married while Jake was away, she and her husband now living out in Oregon.

His friendship with the van Gaasbeecks had largely been severed even before he had been conscripted into the Army and, though Jake missed the evenings and the meals he had shared with "Dutch" and his family, the loss did not overly trouble him. When in town, he continued to confine himself to spending as much time in discussion with artists as he could, his "social" calendar — especially in relation to women — almost non-existent. The few times he had been bold enough to ask one of the local girls to accompany him to the movie theatre in Kingston had been disastrous. In the first place, he found little pleasure in sitting idly watching images flickering across a screen for several hours and, secondly, since his injury from the war, he was even more awkward around women than before.

He was content in his own company, often taking his bedroll and a few provisions up on Overlook's flanks, bedding down for the night as he used to do when he was a boy, making camp near a convenient spring. The several fires and other troubles that the Catskill Mountain House had been experiencing for the past few years had made it a less desirable place for summer boarders to visit, and Jake had found the probability of running into anyone while up on Overlook occurring less and less — for his part, a happy circumstance.

Over the years, he'd found several camping sites that he was sure must have first been used by local Indians before the white man had driven them out. The proximity of a spring, flat rocks set up as "chairs," or the remains of old campfires within a circle of stone under overhanging ledges gave sure indication that some human had spent time in these places, and Jake delighted in finding discarded artifacts left over from their presence. Already, several arrowheads that he had discovered on his trips up Overlook had found room on the shelves of his studio.

Altitude seemed to induce clarity of his senses, as if distance from the busyness of men down on the farmed flatlands brought the ether closer to celestial powers, the air more conducive to spiritual thoughts. Jake could see how ancient belief always reserved the high spots of earth for the gods. Even today, such lofty sites were seldom visited by men, the effort it took to gain their inaccessible heights not worth their trouble. Climbing mountains seemed a waste of energy to the ordinary man, and only resulted in lost time better spent in making one's way in the world.

Though he could not endow his favorite haunts up on Overlook with any particular religious significance, Jake sought these elevated havens because they gave him space and time to think, to sort out those things that puzzled or troubled him "down there" during the day. The old-timers like Thomas Cole and Frederic Edwin Church who scoured the Catskills for motifs also knew these lonely spots with their magnificent vistas, had actively and strenuously sought them out, lugging their equipment up and down rugged hill and dale. Today, Jake found that so many of the younger landscape artists were content to remain in their studios, finding their inspiration in the work of these earlier artists rather than expending the effort to seek out their source and experience nature on her own terms.

But there were also those places that Jake had discovered in his explorations where he was sure that no human foot had ever trod. There he would hunker down and rest his back against a tree that he was confident had never felt the touch of man. These came to be his "special" spots, his "sacred" niches for conversation with whatever vestiges of Deity clung to them — or him. In his occasional stints as "guide" to those artists who prevailed on him to "show them the *real* Overlook Mountain," he would take pains to avoid these sites, unwilling to share them with anyone else. These were *his* places, consecrated by his conviction that only *he* was blessed with discovering their location. In any event, most of the artists he had led up Overlook Mountain never seemed inclined to stray very far from the well-beaten paths that others had made over the years.

Several of his favorite vantage points afforded him breathtaking views of the Esopus Valley and the now completed Ashokan Reservoir that shone like a dazzling jewel in sunlight — a view that the Hudson River Painters never saw. Some forty miles in circumference, the containment of the man-made lake that made up the reservoir, which now provided water to some three million people down in New York City, had been a major undertaking, dislocating countless families and introducing a host of new immigrants into the area. Whereas the bluestone quarries had brought in a large Irish population to the Catskills, the building of the Ashokan Reservoir had brought in a labor force made up almost entirely of Italians and Negroes. During its several-year construction, their little communities sprang up here and there throughout the mountains, adding yet another ethnic mix to that of the local populations.

Jake would often spend the whole weekend up on Overlook, sketching by day and at nights lying on his back to lose himself in the night sky. If the weather was right, he'd sometimes make a couple of oil studies that he could expand upon back in the studio. Some nights the vastness of space would bring to mind the immensity of the ocean, and he would feel fear in the core of his being.

What was his place in all of this?

Occasionally, during an overnight on Overlook, Jake would be surprised by a swiftly rising thunder storm and he would sit out the fury of a Catskill Mountain "thunder-boomer" under the protection of whatever ledge or shelter he could find. Ever since Washington Irving's story of Rip Van Winkle, the notoriety of the region's thunder and lightning storms had been known the world over. Such fierce storms as could be whipped up by winds racing through the mountainous undulations that surrounded him were probably long known by the Indians, and he could easily imagine that he was often sitting in the same sheltering place that many of them had also sought out for protection when the rains fell and the heavens thundered.

Ever since he was a boy, he enjoyed walking in a sudden summer rainfall and smelling the different odors that the earth seemed to give off in a downpour. He loved the feel of water running down his face, down his neck and over the flesh on his back. He'd come home soaked, shaking himself off at the front door as if he were a stray dog. Aunt Birgit would scold him as she took a towel to his head, "Look at you Jacob! *Du lieber Gott!* Even your underwear is soaked!"

The raging thunder and lightning storms, however, reminded him of the one he had witnessed at sea on his passage across the Atlantic with the troops on their way to Europe. As it had back then, the dramatic power and threat of such fury both frightened and thrilled him. He'd often seen lightning strike nearby — sometimes splitting trees from top to bottom — and had even felt an electric tingle pass through his body on more than one occasion as he sat on the damp earth.

He imagined the sensation of a fully charged bolt passing through his body, entering the top of his head as if the finger of God had specifically chosen him at that moment. If it felt no different from the tingly surges he experienced that had made the hair on his arms stand on end when it struck nearby, then he felt no particular fear of such an event happening. How much worse could it be from that sudden flash of light and instant shock that he had experienced when he was struck by shrapnel during the war? He felt no pain then — it was only later when he awoke in the hospital that he experienced discomfort. There would be no such awakening from the direct strike of a lightning bolt, however, but if the moment of annihilation was anything like being struck by flying metal, then dying would not be such an unpleasant thing.

Sometimes, during the height of a storm, he would step out from under the protection of his ledge and turn his face upward into the rain, the thunder, and the flashes of lightning.

This would be the way I should like to go — chosen by God and taken in an instant.

23

Although Birge Harrison had made it clear that he was not seeking students — insisting that he had already given Jake "all he could" — Jake would have liked to spend more time with that artist in his studio, but did not want to impose himself on the man. Harrison had, after all, retired from teaching at the League in order to devote himself to his own work. And though still very much a novice when it came to painting, Jake already knew the value of being alone with one's work. Even a little thing such as his aunt calling over to him to come and eat could stop whatever creative flow he was enjoying at the moment. The act of creation, he was discovering, was no easy undertaking, and one needed full attention to bring to bear on the task.

Once, during a conversation he sat in on at Mrs. Cooper's boarding house, one of the students said that he had asked Carlson during a critique if he thought that his work showed "talent." Carlson, he said, told him not to worry about "talent," but rather to ask himself if he could spend days on end by himself.

"The skill and expertise will come," Carlson went on to explain to the student, "if the dedication and the will to stand alone is there."

His listeners readily agreed. Granted one needed guidance from time to time, but there was simply no substitute for working out one's problems in isolation, no other means of becoming one's "own man."

Jake found that if he couldn't always talk to other artists, he was experiencing an increasing need to look at other paintings from time to time. By looking closely at how Carlson or Harrison — or any of the more accomplished artists — worked out their laying in of foregrounds and backgrounds, of positioning horizons for better effect, or bringing attention to this or that spot on the canvas, he could apply some of the same principles to his own work.

Unfortunately, since he did not feel at liberty to freely visit the private studios of artists, he did not always have this luxury. His opportunity to do so, however, was greatly facilitated when Woodstock's identity as an art colony was given a healthy boost by a group of artists who banded together to form an Association.

It was an idea whose time had surely come to the colony. Initial discussion made it almost immediately clear that, if such an association were to succeed, the organizers had to see themselves as artists first, and as proponents of a certain style or movement second. Once resolved to not allow differences of artistic opinion or style thwart their purpose of having a place of their own in which they might exhibit their work, the concept quickly took hold and the group's dream came true at the opening of their very own gallery. Built on the site of Rose's general store which had recently been destroyed by fire, the centrally located site was perfect for the new group. Originally calling themselves the Artists Realty Company, they soon changed their name to the Woodstock Artists Association and, in 1921, the "WAA" was officially launched at its first in-house exhibition.

The Association's goal of including all serious artists regardless of their individual style meant that exhibitions were mixed, and though Jake found much of what they hung not to his taste, he now had the opportunity to see more of the work of those artists he did admire. The presence of the Association and its gallery now made it possible for him to study John Carlson's snowscapes to his heart's content, carefully noting as he saw them hung alongside his students and colleagues how that teacher's influence was beginning to show up in the work of others. He also found new artists that he found interesting, such men as Frank Chase, Allen Cochran and Charles Rosen causing him to stop and reflect on their paintings whenever they were included in the Association's exhibitions.

So much to learn!

Jake also noted how some of these men were incorporating so-called "modern" tendencies in their work such as using an arbitrary use of color or fractured surfaces in their otherwise traditional landscapes. As he had when he first saw such techniques at the Armory Show, he still found the effects somewhat disturbing, preferring a more realistic rendition of the rich variety of landscape that his beloved Catskill Mountains offered.

One of John Carlson's maxims that Joe Bundy had told him about — one that he had taken to heart — was to "avoid the bizarre." Advising his students that they need not travel to Venice or Egypt to seek the exotic motif, Carlson taught them to see the miracles that lay at hand — "right outside your back door."

While he still taught at the League, Carlson had fought long and hard to make his students hew to the old line of traditionally representing nature. It was no surprise to many of the artists, therefore, when, disturbed by the extremes of the modernists, Carlson resigned from the WAA shortly after it had been formed to eventually open his own school of landscape painting in town.

When Mr. Ayres over at the Old Woodstock Inn on the village green started showing Birge Harrison's work in a special gallery he prepared for just that purpose, Jake was particularly pleased. Here, he could spend some time studying Harrison's work without having to bother the artist at his studio. Visiting Ayres's gallery was a particular pleasure for Jake since that gentleman championed traditional art, making it an ironclad policy never to show any modern art in his establishment.

As much as he'd learned from his talks with Harrison, Jake continued to find that painter's work a little too "soft" for his tastes. Harrison, of course, strove mightily for this "poetic" effect, having himself been influenced by the work of such artists as George Inness and James MacNeill Whistler, both of whom deliberately sought the ambiguity of obscure outline in their paintings. Harrison, therefore, who had also studied impressionism in Paris, tended to rely more and more on soft edges and lightly-hued "pastel" touches to achieve his end, preferring vaporous fields of color for the purposes of lending his paintings "atmosphere" — work that was far removed from the drama of contrast that appealed to Jake's sensibilities.

In his own experience, Jake found nature to be full of contrasts and conflict, their very tensions causing the trees, flowers, fields and watercourses to come alive. It was just this opposition of forces, this tension, to his way of thinking, that made Overlook Mountain possible as a visible phenomenon. Without contrast, without contention, without growth and decay, all of nature would become a flat, never-ending horizon of sameness, and Jake found such an idea repugnant to his sensibilities.

Though he had no way of proving it, without this undercurrent of tension between order and chaos lurking beneath the apparent stability of nature, Jake was doubtful if the making of art might ever have occurred to mankind in the first place.

24

Since his return from the war, Jake was spending more time in his studio, settling in more determinedly in his painting and approaching his work less feverishly, less haphazardly. Though he continued to lose his way, he periodically reassured himself that, as Harrison promised, it would only be a matter of learning his tools and materials. If he was still no closer to understanding the "why" of his painting, he *was* making some headway into the "how."

His studio now boasted a fuller complement of colors, a few more brushes and knives. He continued to like the feel of painting with the knife, discovering that the different shapes that the knives came in allowed for interesting variations in the laying down of paint on canvas.

In addition to the new art materials, Jake had built another shelf near the one that held Sarah Winter's cup, this one longer and wider to hold his uncle's fossil collection.

"He'd want you to have them," said Aunt Birgit to him one day, and he was happy to have this very personal side of his uncle as part of his studio.

He knew Uncle Hans's appreciation of their unique rarity and beauty, something he had long shared with his uncle as he himself began to discover nature's own creative side. He would often pick up an individual piece from Uncle Hans's collection, trying to feel through his fingertips the processes of time and nature that came together to produce such a marvel. Here, what was once animated life was now surrounded in inanimate matter — both object and context preserved as if a sign for all to see. Though he could not explain it even to himself, he knew that these mysterious workings of order and symmetry, of meaning embedded in apparent chaos, their contrivance hidden from human eyes, were in some way a key to man's understanding of his own attempts at making art.

Did man learn from nature? Or were both nature and man informed by some outside force that imposed such order?

If he could not impose a similar organization on his often-chaotic thoughts, Jake was nonetheless fussy about his studio — his work place — and, though it might not be apparent to a visitor, his tools and materials were laid out to his own sense of utility and satisfaction. Because he lived frugally, he kept his brushes scrupulously clean, reused canvases that represented failed attempts, and used his paints sparingly, squeezing out from the tubes just enough to meet his immediate needs. And, following Harrison's advice, he still kept his colors to a minimum.

Though he had never gotten into the habit of laying out his palette in any orderly fashion — Birge Harrison had warned him to avoid what he referred to as "formulas" — his few colors were nevertheless laid out on his shelves in an orderly manner. Tubes of white were kept at one end — near the yellows — and black at the other, after his reds and blues. Earth tones — ochers and umbers — were arranged from light to dark, all kept in a separate row.

Jake knew that many of the artists in Woodstock still ground their own pigments — several extolling the practice to him, claiming that it would make him more familiar with the properties of paint — but he had, after some thought, considered it an unnecessary step in his development. He wanted to *use* paint, not learn how to manufacture it and, again following Harrison's advice, had tried to avoid an over-attentiveness to method and materials, concentrating instead on the business of making pictures. At least for now, the tubed colors he could easily purchase in town served his purposes.

Still, he had to admire that some of the old die-hards continued the laborious task of purchasing dry pigment, grinding it on marble slabs set up in corners of their studios, and carefully mixing them with their chosen suspension mediums — each of course having his own recipes and measurements faithfully followed and stoutly defended. Such practices seemed to suit the studio-bound painter and indicated a commitment to their craft that Jake could only find admirable. Their arguments to him notwithstanding, Jake chose to ignore their urgings, having found that the ready-mixed and handily packaged tubes were simply more practical for on-site painting.

Familiarity with one's materials and tools might be necessary if he wanted to be called a painter, but Jake was becoming aware that it took more than skill with his hands to make a painting. He had seen what some of the artists who proclaimed the virtues of paint grinding had produced, and obviously there was more to being an artist than knowing the craft. As any tradesman knew, there were carpenters and there were carpenters — a bookcase built by one was not quite the same as one built by another. The same with painters. There were painters in Woodstock who made pictures, and then there were painters who made *art*. Still, he was enough of a craftsman to know how important it was to appreciate tools and means.

As impatient as he might be with discussions about materials, Jake strongly felt that the continuing arguments for and against what was still being called "modern" art could be even more fruitless. As far as he could tell, there were simply too many different styles and approaches made by individual artists to comfortably fit under any one label. Though the Armory Show had taken place almost a decade ago, the issues of "modern" versus "academic" could still draw a crowd, and still generate much heated debate — none of it, for Jake, coming near the heart of the matter.

Precisely what that "heart" was, however, persistently eluded Jake. Art — and its history — was still pretty much beyond his ken, and until he felt comfortable with his own painting, such matters would have to await his full attention. Meanwhile, he continued to ask an occasional question about technique, and kept his ear attuned to whatever relevant information might come his way.

For now, his traveling paint box was more fully equipped and, with a new collapsible easel as part of his gear, he spent more time than ever painting on the spot. His favorite part of the day was early morning, and he often spent an hour or so painting before setting out for a day of manual labor at some job he had been hired to do. He loved setting up his easel at some woodland spot before the dawn broke, ready to begin as soon as there was enough light to distinguish his colors. These early hours were precious to him, and he liked to think it was because they were not yet soiled by the busy industry of man. No human sound marred the stillness.

No hammer or saw broke the silence. No voice cried out to another. The very animals seemed to observe the moments of silence, even the birds halting their pre-dawn chattering as soon as the sun cleared the horizon.

He also began traveling further afield on days he was free from work — scouting out many of the sites favored by those earlier painters dubbed "The Hudson River School." He explored some of the other Catskill Mountain peaks, even taking the Otis Railway from Catskill up to the Mountain House to sketch or paint the Hudson River in the distance from the vantage point it offered. Once or twice, to get a different perspective of the Catskills, a view similar to one he had seen while working with the ice cutters in the winter of 1913, he paid fare on the "Skillypot", the little ferry that carried people from Kingston Landing across the Hudson to the town of Staatsburgh on the river's east bank.

However, he continued to find infinite variety in his old haunts, still discovering "new" Overlooks in different lights, in varying weather conditions, and in all seasons. As his work out of doors progressed, and as he repainted familiar scenes in the changing light of day, he was slowly beginning to realize that it was often his own moods that could conjure up "different" Overlooks.

There was certainly proving to be more to this business of painting than just making pretty pictures.

During those times he retraced the steps of such painters as Thomas Cole and Frederic Edwin Church, Jake found an increasing admiration for these artists with their fidelity to nature, and for their whole-hearted attempts at capturing the enduring beauty of the Catskill Region. And, although he found some of their paintings overly meticulous in detail, at times too fussily overworked to give an authentic impression of the Catskill wilds, he accepted these painters as honest craftsmen painting to the best of their ability in the only way they knew how.

That tradition of honest work common to the serious craftsman was still alive, in Jake's opinion, in present-day landscape painters such as Birge Harrison, John Carlson, Frank Chase, Allen Cochran, Charles Rosen, and Carl Lindin — all of them now beginning to be considered the "old masters" of Woodstock. Though none of them painted canvases as ambitious in size and design as those made by Cole or Church, they nevertheless attempted to remain true to their subjects, all of them depicting in realistic — though more modest — terms the landscape surrounding Woodstock. This was after all a new era, and despite the apparent prosperity that followed the war years, no one today purchased such huge canvases since few lived in mansions that might house them. That way of life — like so much else — was a thing of the past, and if an artist intended to make a living at his art then he must follow the current market trends.

To Jake's growing dismay, this consideration of "making a living" through art was increasingly cropping up in conversation around town, and he found it just one more troublesome aspect to contend with in his progress as a painter. Woodstock's "boom" during the 20's seemed to be making everyone more conscious of making money — and artists as well as businessmen seemed to be caught up in the frenzy of "getting their share."

Though he could understand it in the local merchants, the subject of "selling" seemed to creep into artist's conversations a bit too often, at times even dominating their discussions about art. Nowadays Jake was hearing as much about what was "saleable" as he was about what was "good" — as if the two concepts were interchangeable. This new idea of worth being measured in terms of dollars instead of in terms of quality nagged at Jake's mind and he did not know where to go with it.

It was at any rate of no immediate consequence to Jake since selling any of his work had as yet not been a matter of consideration. If he had a half-dozen canvases that he was willing to call "finished," it would have been a stretch — and, since they served him as indicators of his progress, he would not at any rate have dreamed of letting them leave his studio. Like trailmaster's blazons on trees, his paintings were signposts of where he'd been and where he was going — without them surrounding him, he still feared to lose his way.

He was still not signing his paintings, the "J F" he printed on Sarah Winters' drawing the only time he had ever identified any of his work with a personal mark. He was of course familiar with the addition of the craftsman's mark, his uncle's friends in the bluestone business doing it for as long as he could remember. In many cases the identifying mark used was simply a symbol — most often a crudely stylized emblem that the craftsman chose because it was easy to make with chisel or hammer — but whether it was symbol or initial, adding one's imprint to the product of one's hands had long been a common practice in the trades. In some cases, as with the lumberman who harvested the wilds of Maine, this mark identified one man's work from that of another as logs were sent *en masse* to downstream mills, ensuring that, when a season's work was done, each would be properly recompensed for his labor.

Still, signing one's name across the face of a painting — which seemed to be the accepted form for the artist — seemed to Jake to be not only pretentious, but as far as he could make out, a gratuitous intrusion that marred the integrity of the picture. This was particularly true with those artists who flamboyantly scrawled their name across the bottom of the painting. He was less repulsed by those who hid their names cleverly in foliage or in some inconspicuous place within the painting, but still felt that once the artist's "secret" was known, the practice was as obvious — and as objectionable — as if printed in block letters on the face of the painting.

Jake well knew the reasoning behind affixing one's mark to a piece of handiwork. Uncle Hans had early instilled in him the practice of pride in one's product, telling him on more than one occasion that he must strive to do work that he would not be ashamed to put his name to. According to his uncle, it was as much an indication of responsibility as it was of self-respect.

Still, he found a certain amount of ego in signing one's name on a painting in such a manner that it could be seen from across a room. This was as troubling to him as was this growing practice of turning art into a "business" venture and Jake, conceding only to place a date on the back of the few canvases he kept in an effort to track his own progress, continued to leave his work unsigned.

It was in any event a non-issue for him. Though he acknowledged the need of the master craftsman to identify his work with a sign or mark, Jake was still painfully aware that, as an artist, he was far from being a master painter. He had yet to find his "voice," his individual message or intent, feeling at times as if he were getting further from rather than nearer to getting a clear vision of his purpose.

If his paintings now clearly resembled landscapes, he was not at all sure they were communicating what he wanted to say about a particular motif. Indeed, he was still not sure what needed to be "said," nor what a painting must contain to convey what he felt a painting ought to "say." As a painter, he had to admit that he was no closer to depicting Overlook Mountain now than he was when it so forcibly entered his consciousness when he was a young boy.

25

In late autumn of 1922, Jake was offered the job of emptying out an attic of a pre-Revolutionary stone house in Old Hurley. One of the county's earliest settlements, this historic town once served as interim capital of New York State after the British had burned down Kingston, the state's original capital city. Headquarters had been temporarily moved to Old Hurley, outside of Kingston, before its final removal to a safer location upriver at Albany. Situated some distance southeast of his home in West Hurley, the trip to the little hamlet constituted a considerable distance for Jake to travel by horse and wagon. He gladly took the job, however, and looked forward to both the trip and the visit to this lovely old town with its numerous stone buildings and fine farmland nestled snugly alongside the Esopus Creek.

The day promised to be fair and, starting out early in the morning, Jake headed east on the Plank Road, intending to take it as far as the Hurley Mountain Road which cut back west and south along the Esopus Flats and to the town of Old Hurley. He planned to reach his destination in late morning with enough time to get the job done and still have enough daylight left to be able to head back home through the Dug Hill Road where he might unload whatever trash he was hired to remove at the town dump. If everything went smoothly, he figured he'd be home before dark.

It was one of those Indian Summer October days when the foliage was at its peak of color, the sky an unbroken sheet of cerulean blue, the air so pure and crisp that Jake felt as if he could take a bite out of it with his teeth. It was the kind of day that thrilled him, a day in which he felt he could see into infinity, a day that so made his creative juices flow that he found himself almost regretting that he accepted the job. Such days were rare indeed, days that seemed to bode nothing but good, days that, to Jake, seemed made for painting, days when mind, body, and soul were in perfect harmony with nature, all conjoining to make success at whatever one undertook inevitable.

He had committed to the date, however, and, giving the horses their lead, sat back and contentedly took in the day through his nostrils and his eyes. How the morning light raked the trees on either side of the road, leaving deep pockets of shadow at their bases! And how quickly did the sun move across the sky, just moments ago shining directly into his eyes and now, glancing off his left shoulder and the top of his head as the Plank Road veered southward! How could one set up canvas and easel, lay out one's palette quickly enough, to capture just that dramatic play of light? How swiftly did everything change in the constant shifting of the sun!

When he turned onto the Hurley Mountain Road, the Esopus Creek winding its way alongside through the rich, loamy Flats on his left, he watched the light glinting off the surface of the creek, here flickering as the water passed over stony beds, there lying in flat glaring sheets that almost blinded the eyes as it wended its course toward the Hudson River. Water, he was discovering, was one of the most difficult things to paint, its many manifestations in pools, swiftly moving streams, cascades, and slowly moving rivers, each presenting the artist with its own complex and separate set of problems.

As he had expected, he reached Old Hurley about an hour before noon and quickly found the house he was to work at. The owner, a man from New York City, was waiting for him out in front of the solidly built old stone house. A hearty, friendly sort, he offered Jake a tall glass of cider and, without small talk or delay, quickly showed him into the house and made his wishes clear in a concise, business-like way.

"I want the attic cleared out of whatever is in there. I'm not interested in any of it, and you can use, sell, or toss out whatever and however you see fit. I have some business to attend to in Kingston, so I'll leave you to your work. If you get done before I get back, kindly lock up the front door." Taking back the empty glass from Jake's hand, he reached into his breast pocket, removed a wallet, paid Jake the already agreed upon price, and, after giving him a firm hand-shake, was on his way.

A narrow flight of steps led up to the attic from one of the upper bedrooms. Jake found the gabled room to be rather full, but not too disorderly, things seemingly stored with some thought, if not always with care. Immediately at hand were several pieces of broken furniture, most with missing parts, apparently hastily put there by the previous owners until a time — which apparently never came — when they would be brought down and mended.

A cursory glance told him that it appeared to be the usual litter that ordinarily accumulated in the lives of most families.

The steeply sloped roof confining the space eventually proved to contain a hodge-podge of densely packed household items: chairs missing arm rests, backs, or legs; tables with split tops or wobbly supports; lanterns without glass; stacks of folded quilts that were either stored with ratty edges or made so by the work of field mice; some badly rusted tools; many bundles of newspapers; old toys and dolls, most of them broken; and assorted bric-a-brac. Off in one corner stood a large old chest.

Moving the stuff down the narrow stairway, through the upper rooms and, finally, out the front door to load onto the wagon was slow, laborious work. As he carried the various objects to the wagon, Jake made a mental note of which pieces he intended to keep and which he would deposit at the town dump at the end of Dug Hill Road, trying as best he could to keep them in separate piles as he loaded them in the wagon.

He decided straight off that the many tied-up bundles of magazines and newspapers would surely be discarded and, for the most part, the furniture, since almost all of it appeared to be beyond repair. Even those few pieces that might be fixed did not seem worth the trouble. Some of the quilts looked salvageable — but he would let Aunt Birgit be the judge about them, and also about several of the other household items that merely needed minor repair and cleaning. Many of the tools he found were still serviceable, needing only a bit of elbow grease to remove the rust. He figured he could easily make them look like new in no time at all once he got them home.

He saved the chest until last, having already hefted its weight when he began clearing out the attic. He manhandled it down the narrow steps, wondering how — and who — might have lugged such a burden up the narrow flight of steps in the first place. When he got the thing outside and onto the rear of the wagon, he opened it to see what made it so heavy. He found it to be full of carefully packed books.

Well that explains it — he thought — *Nobody brought that thing up full. They merely added books to it as the years went by.*

Jake began to do what he should have done while the chest was still in the attic: he took the books out to look them over. If he had done that in the beginning, he could have brought them down in separate stacks, making the job that much easier.

Books were somewhat of a novelty to Jake, his home in Brooklyn largely bare of them, an unused dictionary the only one he could ever recall seeing. He'd never seen anyone refer to it during all the years he lived with his parents. He and Freddie had textbooks in school, of course, but the only reading matter that was ever a part of his home life consisted solely of the daily newspapers, the *Brooklyn Eagle* and *Journal American* standing out in his memory since it was from their comic sections that he had copied his early drawings.

Uncle Hans had his few books about fossils that he had brought with him from Germany, but other than looking at the pictures, they had no particular attraction for Jake — besides, they were written in German and he couldn't read them if he'd wanted to. Books, for the most part, held somewhat of an exotic place in Jake's scheme of things, a commodity that went beyond his means, his capabilities, and his place in life. He had never owned a book, feeling that such things were the special province of highly cultivated people — at least of people not like himself.

As he turned them over to look at titles, he handled each book reverently, hesitant even to open their covers to look inside to see what they might contain. He quickly saw that several were individual books of a set, some of the sets containing only a few volumes, while others were more extensive. He placed them in stacks, keeping sets together, spreading the others out over the tailgate of his wagon. Some, he could ascertain, were clearly textbooks, similar to the history or geography books he had used in school. Others were obviously novels: he saw names such as Thackeray, Scott, Dickens, Eliot, Hardy. Some of these books contained pic-

171

tures but, as he hastily leafed through them, he could not readily tell what the stories might be about.

A set of gold-embossed and leather-bound books that consisted of the "compleat" works of William Shakespeare struck him as especially beautiful, and he very carefully set them one atop the other. A handsome set of books had labels that defined them as "Classics" while yet another almost brand-new leather-bound set of twenty-six volumes were identified as the "Complete Works of Joseph Conrad." A set of twenty-seven volumes contained a name he had often heard artists speak about — John Ruskin. He opened the cover of Volume I and read that he held in his hand "No. 238 of the 'St. Mark's Edition' limited to One Thousand Copies." According to the first page, it was published in 1898 by the Dana Estes & Company publishers in Boston.

Amazed at such treasures, Jake decided that the owner of the house had not meant for them to be taken away and, slowly packing them back into the chest, set it aside until his return.

He had not long to wait.

"Done, I see," said the owner as he came up to Jake. "Good. I'm planning to move my family up from Philadelphia later this week."

"I think you ought to look at these," said Jake pointing to the chest. "There seem to be some valuable books here."

"Nope," said the man definitively. "Take 'em away. If you don't want 'em, dump — or sell 'em, if you can."

"But..." protested Jake.

"Look," the man said. "I don't want the books. My womenfolk have enough of their own. I already took a look through that chest and I know what's there. They're yours if you want 'em," and, raising his hands with a, "If not, well..." turned to go into the house.

"Okay," said Jake. "Thank you ... thank you very much."

"Let me just check upstairs," said the man, "and then you can be on your way."

When he returned, Jake had the chest carefully placed under the seat next to him.

"Thanks again for the books," he said

"Thank *you* for a job well done," said the man, and closed the door on Jake.

Jake could hardly contain his excitement as he drove the horses out of Old Hurley and headed up the long, steep incline of the Dug Hill Road. So taken by his new possessions, he very nearly forgot to stop at the dump to unload the things he knew he didn't want. He unloaded the trash as quickly as possible, anxious to get back home before nightfall.

As he drove along the road atop the earthen dike that held back the lower basin of the newly dug Ashokan Reservoir, his mind was so preoccupied with the prospect of examining the chest of books more closely that he barely took notice of the lovely purplish hues streaking the sky as the sun descended on its westward course. On any other day, such a view of the Catskills looking moodily mysterious as the sun slid behind their clearly etched silhouettes would have stopped him in his tracks. In his excitement over his newly found "library," however, the view barely made an impression on his consciousness.

A single refrain played over and over in his mind.

I own a library! Me, Jake Forscher, has his own library!

26

That winter, though he had built them so many times for others, Jake could not believe that he was actually putting up a bookcase in his own studio.

A heavy snow had fallen during the night and he had beaten a path from the house to his studio so that he could use the day to work on his shelving. The books had been taken from the chest, some left in the house so that he could read them at bedtime, those he wanted with him in the studio lined neatly against the wall, waiting for the shelves to be completed. Even after having the books in his possession for weeks now, he continued to treat them with respect and awe, handling them as if they were made of glass. He still could not believe that they were *his*.

The sets he had brought to the studio — especially the Shakespeare and the Ruskin — he had carefully covered with an old bed sheet so as to prevent their becoming soiled. Of those he had left in the house, he had already begun reading the first volumes of Conrad, finding that writer's stories perfect for bedtime reading. Among the books he had found no interest in were some cookbooks that Aunt Birgit had gladly taken charge of. Though it was doubtful that she would ever refer to them, she proudly displayed them on her kitchen counter and was as pleased to have them, as she was the quilts, which she had already mended, washed, and put to use.

One of the books Jake found particularly interesting was a small, leather-bound translation of the meditations of Marcus Aurelius. Once he had opened it and had gotten past the strangeness of the sentence structure, he found it extremely absorbing and could not help picking it up time and again. He enjoyed randomly dipping into its pages and began carrying it around with him, handily available in his pocket, tool, or paint box for ready reference. Though he knew nothing of this ancient Roman — had really little inkling of when or where he lived — he quickly felt a strong kinship with Aurelius's ideas and observations about life, about character, and about proper conduct. More than once, he wished that he had had the opportunity to know this man, to have had the chance to sit and speak with him. Somehow, he felt that his own ideas — strange-sounding even to himself at times — would have found a sympathetic and understanding ear in that of the Roman Emperor.

Two other two-volume sets, the *Dialogues of Plato* and George Henry Lewes's *The History of Philosophy,* Jake peeked into, but felt their contents to be far beyond his comprehension. He resolved to keep them, however, hopeful that he might at some time be able to read and understand them.

He had chosen the rear wall of his studio, opposite the windows, to "build in" his bookcase. With the money he had made from the sale of those usable items he did not want from the Hurley attic, he purchased the finest pine boards he could find, traveling all the way into Kingston where he knew he would find a greater variety of materials from which to choose. He picked only the straightest of boards, carefully loading and unloading each piece of lumber onto and off his wagon. Ranging them along the sidewall of his studio, each piece had already been measured, cut, and sanded, all in readiness to be put together and then varnished. Jake had chosen a dark varnish, knowing that the end result would be a richly finished bookcase worthy of the books it would eventually hold.

He completed the job one early Sunday evening, the finished product everything he had envisioned. Now all he had to do was wait for the varnish to dry to a hard finish before he could arrange his books along the shelves in the way he wanted. He could already see that he had more shelf space than he needed to contain the books he chose for his studio, but figured that, as the years went by, he would be able to add to his "collection" — hopefully, with some art books. So far, however, the high cost of good art books, as important as they might be in his progress as a painter, were far beyond his present means.

In spite of its status as an art colony, art books were somewhat of a scarce commodity in and around Woodstock, and even the public libraries in nearby Saugerties and Kingston had barely enough to fill a single shelf. The only art books that Jake had a chance to look through, therefore, were those he had seen and admired at either Birge Harrison's or at several of the other artist's studios at which he had occasion to work.

He'd heard about the extensive library that Ralph Radcliffe Whitehead had accumulated for his Byrdcliffe residents, but had not been back to that place since he had returned from the war. He had no idea if there was still a strong feeling in the colony against the German people, and was not at all sure he would have been welcomed had he attempted a visit. However, a bittersweet and chance encounter the previous fall with Sarah and Calvin Steele had re-opened a door to Byrdcliffe that might give him access to Whitehead's library and, though he had done nothing about it at the time, having his own library persuaded him that he ought to take advantage of the opportunity sometime in the near future.

He had run into the couple during the final days of October when Woodstock had already been emptied out of its summer residents, and the town and its people were busily girding themselves for the coming winter. He had just left the Old Woodstock Inn and another close study of Birge Harrison's work when he saw Sarah and Calvin on the Village Green. They had seen each other simultaneously, Sarah, then Calvin, waving Jake over.

"Hello, Jake," said Sarah cheerily. "We've just spent the day house-hunting, and we were waiting here for the stage to take us to the railroad station in West Hurley. You've probably heard," she continued, nodding toward Calvin, "that we'd gotten married this summer."

"No," said Jake. He turned to Calvin Steele and extended his hand. "Congratulations," he said, then, to Sarah, "I hope you both are very happy."

Though the announcement took Jake by surprise, the finality of it somehow made it easier for him to carry on the conversation.

"Have you been successful in your hunting?" he asked them.

"Yes," said Calvin. "We found a delightful old farmhouse over in Willow, close enough to town, but still far enough away for privacy."

"Cal is an artist," explained Sarah. "I think I told you that when you two first met."

Jake nodded his assent.

"Anyway, the house has an outbuilding that has already been fitted out as a studio — just perfect for Cal. And I just love the house! It's so charming!"

To Calvin, Jake said, "Double lucky man," and turning back to Sarah, "I'm happy to hear you are so pleased. When are you moving in?"

"We'll winter in New York," said Calvin, "and move in permanently next spring. This way I can finish up my business affairs in the city and feel free to 'go native' when we move in."

"Yes," added Sarah, "Cal is represented by a dealer in Manhattan and we have to make sure that we don't lose contact."

"That, and my affiliation with several clubs," added Calvin. "I serve on the board of the National Arts Club — just busy stuff, of course, but it does keep me in contact with important people. Many dealers and patrons are members, as are the more successful artists." He grinned at Sarah. "One has to keep a foot in, you know."

"Of course," said Jake — though he was not exactly clear what "keeping a foot in" might entail, and it was only through hearsay that he knew how important a New York City connection might have for an artist. He turned to Sarah.

"How about your pottery? Are you still working over in Byrdcliffe?"

"Actually, I've gotten somewhat away from making them," Sarah said with a wistful smile. "I do miss it, though. My dream is that once Cal gets settled in and has his career firmly established, I might have a little studio myself." She turned to look at Cal. "We have the space to do it," she said.

Calvin nodded noncommittally.

"How are things up in Byrdcliffe?" asked Jake. "I haven't been over there for quite a spell." He refrained from adding that Whitehead had not seen it necessary to call him for any jobs since before the War.

"Oh, you ought to go — just for a visit. I'm sure they'd love to see you. We drop in quite often as a matter of fact. They have a wonderful library, you know, and we — Cal and I — have often found it better than what we've found in the city — at least as far as art books go."

Jake found this bit of news enticing. "Can anyone use it?" he asked.

"Oh, yes. Mr. Whitehead's very generous like that. In fact, a great many artists in Woodstock use it — whether they are connected with Byrdcliffe or not. Everyone knows about it."

"Yes," said Jake. "Now that I think about it, I'm sure I've heard some of the artists talking about using it." Heartened by the information, he intended to avail himself of the invitation as soon as— and if —he could.

Just then, Saxe's stage pulled alongside the Green and, making hasty goodbyes and promises to see Jake in the spring, Mr. and Mrs. Calvin Steele departed for New York City.

Other than a coldness around the heart, Jake had found the encounter with Sarah less trying than he would have supposed. He actually was pleased for them, and the absence of that electric thrill he once experienced in her presence made him feel that perhaps the longing he had felt for her was finally put to rest.

27

Overlook Mountain still had its winter cap of snow, but the promise of spring had already been swelling the creeks with swiftly gushing water flowing into the Woodstock Valley. The sugar maples were putting forth their red flowers, and the willows already sported a barely discernible light greenish haze.

Jake was sitting in his studio early one morning, not feeling like he wanted to paint, but also not focused enough to pick up one of his books to read. He'd been meaning to seriously try his hand at Shakespeare, but each time he had gingerly opened the pages of one of the books, he felt immediately overwhelmed by the odd language. He knew, of course, Shakespeare's reputation as a playwright of some note, but had little knowledge of what his plays were about.

If only the language didn't sound so much like the Bible!

Sitting there undecided as to where to devote his energies, his glance absently took in Sarah's cup sitting on the shelf. He had not thought about Sarah very much since their chance meeting on the village green last fall and stood up to take the cup down.

He was taken aback to find that its initial contact with his hands had very nearly caused him to drop it. Then, as he slowly turned it over in his hands — much as he had done on the day she had given it to him — he felt that familiar sensation in the pit of his stomach, a physical pain that made him feel as if someone had struck him beneath his ribs. A sharp intake of breath caused him to sit back down suddenly.

Where had all that come from?

The feeling passed after a few moments and he carefully replaced the cup on its shelf. He was perplexed at the response and, snatching up his easel and paint box, strode out the door, intent on taking a walk to see what he might find to paint or sketch. Maybe if his hands were busy, he might better clear his head.

He hadn't far to walk before he was at one of his favorite spots for studying Overlook. Not yet ready to attempt one more sketch, he sat on a large rock and studied the light falling over the craggy face of the mountain's defining ledge. The sun, still low in the spring sky, raked across Overlook's face, revealing ever-new ridges and slopes as it climbed the sky. As his focus wandered, Jake found his thoughts drifting back to that day he had wandered into St. Barbara's.

As he so often did with the mountain, he had looked at the church on that day in an altered light, had looked at the building — and its art — with different, adult eyes. He again found himself surprised that he had missed so much of its beauty when he was a boy. Why had he never noticed the art before?

Gazing absently up at Overlook, he tried to imagine the artists and artisans who made the paintings, the stained glass windows, and the statues at the church. Who were the men who carved the wooden pulpit, the huge stone baptismal font, the marble altar? What were they like? Had they learned their trade here, in America, or had they brought it with them from Europe?

What kinship — if any — had he, Jake Forscher, with these men? To *all* men who made art? And not only to those artists in the past — but also to those of today? Setting aside the fact that, unlike many of the artists he knew around Woodstock, he had made his living from a trade, what did he have in common with them?

His eyes traveled over Overlook's silhouette.

Do artists all *see* alike?

Known at one time only to those Native Americans who inhabited the region, Overlook Mountain had probably not changed much over the centuries. Yet, for all its enduring solidity, it was likely that Overlook had also presented a different face each hour, each day, each season, to the Esopus Indian who might have sat in this exact same spot.

Jake supposed that the mountain must have presented the same deceptive minute-by-minute transformations — if they stopped their labors long enough to notice — to the Dutch settlers who had come to displace the local tribes and tame the wilderness to make it habitable for themselves. But other than these visual tricks, had Overlook Mountain *really* changed that much? Looking across the densely wooded area that abutted the field in which he sat, Jake doubted if the Dutchmen, for all their busy labor, had actually put much of a dent in the surrounding landscape.

Whatever lasting impact they might have made in the New World, to those Dutch settlers, the upstate wilderness of New York must have looked nothing like the Dutch landscape they had left behind, nothing like the neat and compact little scenes that they so lovingly depicted in their warm, sepia-toned paintings.

And how had those Dutch painters actually *seen* their world? Could sunlight be so much different than it was here? His repressed memories of his time in war-torn Europe allowed for no comparison of what the light might have looked like in France. Jake wondered how much of those golden-toned hues he found in picture books were the result of what those artists perceived, and how much was simply the result of the passage of time and the aging of paint?

Were the same pigments available to painters of the past as those Jake could buy today? How constrained *was* the painter back then by the materials available to him? How freer, for that matter?

So much I don't know!

He'd been painting long enough to have purposely selected the colors to include in the box that lay beside him. In Birge Harrison's words, he had "chosen his palette," and he had settled on these specific colors even before he set out to paint a particular view in a particular light. As tubes were emptied, squeezed until the last globule of paint was forced through their necks, he would purchase new ones, always making sure that the next time he went out to paint that he would have them at the ready. It was comforting not to have to even think about replacing them with other colors, to be able to concentrate solely on the work.

How did such habit affect a painter's way of seeing?

Though he had not consciously set out to do so, Jake, in spite of his having a chosen set of colors, had usually arranged them on his palette in haphazard fashion. If he continued to carefully arrange his colors in both his studio and in his traveling box, he felt he was doing so for practical rather than artistic reasons. One simply laid out one's tools in an orderly fashion for the sake of an economic and practical use of one's time. Every craftsman knew the wisdom of keeping tools in order.

It was different, however, once one decided upon the job. Many things other than the right tools and the right materials went into the making of a good bookcase, and one had to keep a disciplined but open mind to deal with the unexpected, the fortuitous, the play of chance — all or any of which might improve the original design.

Thus, it was Jake's practice to lay out his palette in his usual, higgledy-piggledy way. He would begin by first squeezing out a hefty splotch of zinc white somewhere in the center and surrounding it, in no particular order, with dabs of yellow ocher, raw sienna, alizarin crimson, cerulean, and ultramarine blue, and, off to the side, a touch of lamp black. Then, dragging them with the knife into each other — sometimes on the palette, sometimes on the canvas itself — his painting would slowly build and take shape. If unorthodox — and he wasn't sure whether it was or not — it worked for him.

Enforced and rigid order, Jake told himself as he squeezed out his paints, might be proper for a country like Holland or for the church — the first because it was constantly on guard against a threatening sea, the second because it was constantly on guard against the chaos of sin.

Order may now characterize Overlook's apparent solidity and keep it in place — but he was sure that the apparent stability had little to do with its creation.

Well, let's see what you tell me this *time.*

Jake took out a small canvas after he had laid out the colors on his palette and placed it on the easel. Then, after looking for a long moment at Overlook's silhouette, he stabbed his knife into the cerulean blue and began quickly laying in the cloudless sky that so brilliantly shed its light on the mountain before him.

He figured that one more little oil sketch from this same location wouldn't hurt.

28

Ever since his return from Europe, Jake had been bumping into Joe Bundy, the freckle-faced young man that Ted Deavers had introduced him to at Mrs. Cooper's boarding house just before he went into the army. Deavers, completing his summer studies at Woodstock, had moved on, but Bundy, Jake had learned, like many of the League students still interested in landscape painting, had moved permanently into town, making do with an old outbuilding as both studio and home.

In the beginning, such meetings with Bundy were unplanned encounters and their conversation desultory, but Woodstock was a small town and it was inevitable that their paths would often cross. After time, they would stop to share a few minutes in conversation and Jake soon grew to like this young man for his no-nonsense and straightforward manner. Though he hadn't seemed to age much — still retaining his boyish looks — Bundy had certainly matured in his knowledge of painting.

Whenever they met, their talk invariably turned on something that the painter had learned from John Carlson and it was as much because Jake admired Carlson's work, as it was a need for the occasional companionship that made him keep his eye out for Bundy whenever he was in town. Before long, Jake was making definite appointments to meet with him over a sandwich or a cup of coffee rather than trusting to chance so that they might extend their talks about art.

Their friendship had deepened to the point where Jake had even gone so far as inviting Joe over to see his studio if he ever had occasion to be in West Hurley. Shortly thereafter, after a visit to the Maverick one afternoon, Joe had taken him up on the invite and dropped in on Jake unexpectedly.

Taken off guard, it took some moments for Jake to get used to the idea of having a stranger in his space, but he soon warmed to Bundy's obvious appreciation of what he was seeing.

"Some digs!" Joe had said approvingly as his eyes took in Jake's studio. "Looks like the real thing to me."

"Well," Jake said a bit shyly, "the paintings I make will have to decide whether it's the *real* thing or not."

Joe was still walking around the studio, his artist's eye appreciating the carefully laid out space. "It's really professional, you know? I mean the way you're set up in here."

Jake, inwardly pleased with Joe's assessment, merely mumbled a "Thanks — thanks a lot."

"God! I wish I had my own space. If I had the dough to move out of Schmidt's old barn, I'd do it in a minute! Every time I run into him, he talks about raising my rent — can you imagine? For a corner of his smelly old barn? He oughtta pay *me* for cleaning the old place out when I moved my stuff in!"

Jake laughed, but he commiserated with Joe. He knew that some of the locals had no compunction about gouging the artists whenever they had the opportunity to do so. They didn't approve of these "bohemians" in the first place, so making a few dollars off them left the townsfolk with clear consciences. They thought they were putting one over on these "city slickers," but in most cases the artists were only too pleased to find farmers willing to rent out an outbuilding or shed to them.

Housing had long been a problem for the artists coming to town during the summer. The League, before it had closed down its Woodstock facility, had attempted to ease the situation by building a dormitory for their students just off Rock City Road, but it was always filled to capacity and latecomers had to fend for themselves. Though many had boarded at the public houses — or at private homes if they could find lodging — they still needed a place to paint, and some old unused chicken coop or shed was perfect for a makeshift studio during the summer months.

Many of the farmers, however, refused to let the artists even come on their property to paint since some of the more careless ones had discarded oily rags in fields which, when chewed on by milk cows, sickened or killed them. On the other hand, just as many profited by renting out space to artists and, in more ways than one. Not only did they collect rent for the season, but artists would often set about improving their "home" by fixing roofs, whitewashing walls, or plugging up drafty cracks, allowing the owners to charge even more from the next summer's boarder.

"I've taken most of my ideas for setting up here from the studios of others, you know," Jake explained. "I've worked in a good many of 'em over the years in and around Woodstock. And, I've had a few years putting it all together. Then, of course, there's the matter of my Aunt and Uncle letting me take over this building, so, all things considered, I guess I'm pretty lucky."

"You sure are," said Joe.

"But, like I said, now I have to make paintings that'll make having a studio worthwhile." He took in the studio with a swing of his head, and added, "This part was easy. The painting part seems to be taking a bit longer."

"That'll come," murmured Joe as he took a closer look at Jake's easel. "Where did you get this?" he asked. "It's a beauty."

"I made it," said Jake. "Copied it from the one Birge Harrison has in his studio."

"Whoa! You really *are* a carpenter, aren't you?"

"Well, I know how to whittle a bit."

"Come on! That's fine work — and I *know*, old boy. My father's a cabinet-maker."

"Really?" said Jake. "How did you decide to become an artist?"

"Don't tell me *your* old man was an artist," said Joe. "Did you just follow in his footsteps?"

"Far from it," Jake replied. "My father's a butcher. A very practical tradesman. He never did accept that I wanted to be an artist." Jake laughed. "He wanted me to learn an *honest* trade."

"An old story, I guess," said Joe. "You hear it all the time. You can't believe how many art students claim — *brag* about it sometimes — that they were disowned by disapproving parents. My old man was supportive, though. In fact, he considered himself to be something of an artist — and I guess he was. He and Mom were pleased to help me out financially when I told them I wanted to take instruction at the Art Students League."

"And here you are," said Jake. "How did you decide on studying with Carlson?"

"Well, we get to pick and choose our instructors at the League, you know. If there's room, we usually get the teacher we want — and I'd wanted John Carlson ever since I first saw his work. Did you know that he studied with Harrison?"

"Yep," said Jake. "Mr. Harrison often spoke about him when I did odd jobs for him over at his studio in Shady." Jake scratched his head. "It's funny though. Other than the fact that they both seem to prefer painting landscape, I don't think their painting is much alike."

"Doesn't have to be," said Joe. "*Shouldn't* be, if the teacher is worth his salt. That's what I liked about Carlson — he urged us all to follow our own instincts — and I guess he learned *that* from Harrison."

"Then why have a teacher?" asked Jake.

"Oh, Carlson'd come around and point out things in your painting that he thought didn't work — and most times, he was right on the money. But no one — least of all John Carlson — ever told you that you have to *make* the change. A teacher is there to share his know-how, not to turn out duplications of himself. With Carlson, it was never just what brush to use or how to mix color. He spent a lot of time just talking about nature — and how he felt about it — you know, kind of philosophizing about life and things. He made me see and he made me *think.*"

"Well, he sure is a fine painter," said Jake. "And I wouldn't mind being able to make the pictures he does."

"It'll come, Jake. And when it does, you better hope that you are able to make the pictures *you* want to make. That's what it's all about, you know. Being satisfied with yourself and your work."

"Can't argue with that," said Jake. "But I still have a ways to go before I'm satisfied with either myself or my work."

Joe motioned toward a few canvases turned against the wall. "Mind if I take a peek?"

Jake was a bit uneasy, but he merely shrugged his shoulders and nodded an assent in answer.

Joe studied a few paintings for some moments, lingering over a study of Overlook. "I'm no expert, Jake, but from what I can see, you seem to be coming along. There's a roughness to your work that I sort of like — a little bit like that Dutchman — you know, Vincent van Gogh. He had a way of slathering on the paint that made you think he might have been angry with the world." He bent to peer a bit closer. "I don't see the anger here, though." Then he stood up and added, "But you sure do lay it on. What are you using here, a knife?"

"Yes," said Jake. "Sometimes I get impatient with brushes. I can't always make the darn things do what I'd like 'em to do. So, when I get frustrated enough with an un-obliging brush, I grab the knife."

"Even *sounds* like van Gogh. He was plenty frustrated! But I still don't see any anger in your work — more of a free-flowing spontaneity."

"Well, like I said, I'm still working at it."

Joe straightened up. "That's not a negative criticism — spontaneity is a *good* thing. Anyway, after all is said and done, Jake, all you have to do is please yourself. Carlson told us that all the time — and I'm just passing it along to you — free of charge. Just please yourself."

After Bundy left, Jake wondered just how long it might be before he started "pleasing himself," but was, as often happened after talking with Joe Bundy, heartened and encouraged by the young man's comments.

Being pleased with one's work, Jake knew, had something to do with putting one's mark on it. Though he still didn't sign either his paintings or his carpentry jobs, he relished the pleasure of knowing when he had done his best. Even when he finished a bookcase — whether it was the one he built for himself or the many he had built for others, he had to feel that it represented his best work.

But how could he tell when a painting was his "best"? How might he know when he ought to be "pleased"? Was an artist ever fully satisfied with a painting? Can he ever say, "There! Now that's the *best* I'll ever do"?

He had, of course, built bookcases that he had thought were just fine, but found that every once in a while a customer might ask for some changes. He — Jake — might have been pleased with the work, but the customer who commissioned it was not, and he was compelled to make the changes.

How did this apply to painting? Might one be *compelled* to make changes to a painting in accordance to someone else's wishes? Though he had as yet to sell a painting let alone been commissioned to paint one, Jake wondered what he might do if he were told to make changes in a painting that he, himself, was satisfied with. Did such things occur? How did artists handle such a situation?

He'd make it a point to ask Joe Bundy the next time he saw him.

29

His growing friendship with Joe Bundy had been gradually open-ing Jake up to others. Part of this was because he found that his painting progress depended on learning from those who knew more about it than he, and partly because he simply found that he was growing less awkward around people. Ever more frequently he found himself a bit less reserved with artists when he was in town, sitting with them singly or in small groups as they shared a cup of coffee or a sandwich at either of the two boarding houses that catered to them or at one of the several new cafés that were cropping up around town.

Though he now was sitting less on edge during conversations with artists, he continued to be uncomfortable when the selling of art came up — and selling their work seemed to be cropping up more and more. Whereas in the past artists appeared to be concerned about being "seen," now many seemed increasingly obsessed by whether or not they could "sell." The main topic of conversation in earlier days — when they were not talking about painting itself — was who got into which national show; now the topic was more often about who got into what gallery and whose work was bringing in the highest prices.

A part of him could understand the shift. There were, Jake knew, few galleries that showed the works of contemporary Ameri-can painters. The successful artists — the Coles, the Churches, the Bierstadts — sold because their work reflected European styles and techniques — and even they at times had to resort to display-ing their works in restaurants to get any public notice. The hand-ful of successful galleries in New York City almost exclusively sold European art — or art that was produced by American painters who studied in Europe at the Royal Academies of Munich, Düsseldorf, or Paris and who continued to emulate their European instructors.

American artists *as* American artists were still trying to find their own voice, still trying to produce an art that was distinctly and unmistakably "American." Patrons, however, the moneyed elite who spent their dollars on art, still preferred to invest in the established European masters. The bias also held true for the major American Museums that also tended to buy and exhibit only European art. Being accepted then, was a subject hotly discussed whenever artists got together, and now one way of determining that acceptance was through the measurement of an artist's sales.

Fortunately, the post-war boom was making it possible for a greater number of people to be flush with money and, in a spirit of new nationalism, many of them were beginning to be more open to the idea of "buying American." Galleries that exhibited and sold American-made art, though still not numerous, were beginning to pop up in Manhattan to satisfy this new market. Museums soon followed suit, and the soon-to-be-opened Whitney Museum of American Art in New York City and old, established institutions such as the Corcoran in Washington D.C., began to furnish exhibiting space for present-day American artists. Getting one's work into either a New York City gallery or into a Whitney or Corcoran national juried exhibition was a sure-fire way for an up-and-coming artist to make his mark — and his money.

Woodstock, in its ever-growing status as a world-renowned art colony, thus became for many young artists the first step towards a major career in the art world. That the colony already attracted such upcoming notables as Robert Henri, George Bellows, and Eugene Speicher, only enhanced one's chances of becoming known on a national, if not international stage. Having one's work hang alongside some of these rising stars at the Woodstock Artists Association afforded the up-and-coming artist a foot up, the cachet of being exhibited alongside a John Carlson, a Birge Harrison, or a George Bellows, of inestimable value.

When Juliana Force, a major power behind the Manhattan artscene, began visiting during summers and Herman Moore, Director of the Whitney, bought a summer home in Woodstock, their very presence put Woodstock artists in a still more enviable position of "moving up" toward recognition.

Still, "Did you hear how much so-and-so got for his latest painting?" more often than not opened each discussion about art, and Jake found the shift in emphasis disconcerting. Slowly but surely the distinction between being recognized as an accomplished artist and being a "saleable" one was becoming blurred — as if the one automatically implied the other.

After one such conversation that was dominated by the subject of selling at the "Knife and Fork," a new café in town, Jake turned to Joe and asked, "How does this constant emphasis on selling square with what you told me about having to please myself?"

"Meaning what?" Joe asked.

"Well, if you judge a work successful because it sells, am I to conclude that the artist was necessarily 'pleased' with his painting?"

"He'd be pleased with the check," another artist chimed in.

Jake turned to him. "I suppose that's so." Turning back to Joe, he continued, "But I guess I didn't know that the purpose of painting was to make a living."

"Well, why shouldn't it?" the newcomer rejoined. Like many new faces around town, Jake only knew his first name, Bart. Artists seemed to come and go so quickly nowadays — often staying in Woodstock for a single summer session — that he often found it difficult to keep track of them. Bart continued: "After all, we *do* have to eat, don't we? And pay these outlandish prices for some abandoned old shack to work in."

"I don't argue with that," said Jake. "I know what it means to make a living — I've been at it for some time myself."

"So," said Bart, "if you've been making a living from your work, then what's the problem?"

"I make a living from doing odd jobs," answered Jake. "I earn my money as a carpenter, a handyman."

"And a darn good carpenter, I'll tell you," Joe broke in. He turned to Jake. "But things are changing, my friend. The *world* is changing."

Jake flashed back in his mind to the Armory Show. "But how does this affect art," he asked. "I'm aware that a man has to make a living — has to earn his bread. But if he paints for the purpose of selling — of pleasing a customer — then I come back to what you once told me — or told me that John Carlson told *you*. You said that *he* said that painting is about pleasing yourself."

"Aye, there's the rub," interjected another artist. Jake had seen him around town, but did not know his name.

"But why should it change?" Jake insisted. "Not the world — the *purpose* of painting?"

"Simple," said Bart. "Because what pleases me may not please a buyer — and selling is what it's all about. The thing is, is that you've got to get known. That's why I've been applying for membership in the Salmagundi Club in the city — once you get hobnobbing with the big-shots, you've got a fighting chance to make a living."

"And, whether we like it or not," Joe added, "unless you're independently wealthy, you really have no choice."

The men nodded in agreement and Jake, unable to counter Joe's pronouncement, took his leave with a silent shake of his head as they went their various ways.

Jake walked over to the Old Woodstock Inn to put some finishing touches on a set of shelves he had just completed that morning in Mr. Ayres's pantry and, after packing up his tool kit, called it a day.

As he walked the few miles home, the noontime conversation continued to play back in his mind. He could understand the practicality of the argument, but still could not reconcile what he thought painting was about and what these young men were telling him it had come to. How could the making of art be reduced so quickly to *only* being a business?

He knew from his discussions with artists that the old masters had been paid for their work. Many in the past had patrons — either in the church or the royal courts — that had given the artists money and shelter — even, in some cases, fame. But from the little he knew, the idea of creating art simply for the purpose of being fed and housed did not seem to be their prime motivation for making art.

Hadn't Birge Harrison told him that *why* he painted would determine the *kind* of painter he would become? If an artist painted merely to sell, then how could that not influence the way he painted? Was it possible to please oneself, to paint because one *must* paint, while keeping an eye on the market?

And, if one merely painted to sell, then how did that make him different from any other artisan? Different from a handyman, for instance? Didn't the title of artist distinguish him from being a simple maker of stuff to sell? The baker made pies to sell. The shoemaker made shoes to sell. *He* hired out his hands and his skill for pay. But was the *artist* supposed to make things that sold?

When he reached his home, he first went to his studio to sit alone and think. The same questions swirled in Jake's head, and he could find no satisfactory answers arising from sifting the comments of the young artists. None of what they were saying seemed to have any bearing on why he, Jake, painted — nor could he find the words to try and explain his own ideas. As so often happened, he became tongue-tied when faced by anyone glib enough to "talk him down." Until he could learn more — perhaps from the library over in Byrdcliffe — he would have to leave such considerations aside. He resolved to make the visit to Whitehead's library as soon as possible.

So much to know, so much to figure out.

The mystery of what had taken place so many years ago when that steamer turned the bend in the Hudson still haunted him, and still eluded his ability to put into every-day words the meaning of the transformation in his view of the world that had occurred at that time. He knew that that experience held the mystery of the *why* of his own painting. And, though he might not be able to express it properly, he remained convinced that there was no way of putting a dollar amount on that "why."

30

The weekend promised to be fair and, other than a few chores he had to attend to for Aunt Birgit, Jake anticipated some uninterrupted time for painting. He had done several oil sketches of Overlook from different vantage points over the past week or so, and was anxious to transform the more promising ones into a larger, composite canvas.

Though he continued to make smaller studies of plants or rocks or cloud formations with his pencil, he had found that making oil sketches on watercolor paper allowed for an easier transition to the canvas. Broad strokes denoting color and shape could be accomplished in a short time, allowing him to get down some fleeting impression of light and shadow for later use. The oil was quickly absorbed into the porous paper, leaving a matte finish and a serviceable sketch that could be tucked away as easily as a pencil drawing into his tool or paint box. Whatever details were lost in the quickly executed oil study could be supplied from either his growing store of pencil drawings or from his expanding visual vocabulary once he returned to his studio.

He would tack up these small-scale studies — both pencil and oil — on his studio walls when he returned from a day's work, letting their combined impressions "work" on his mind throughout the following days. If the growing commercial aspects of painting continued to be problematic for him — if he could no longer discern a clear — or, to his mind, "higher" — purpose for the craft in others— the making of his own paintings was nevertheless slowly becoming less of a game of chance and more of a clearly regulated and defined activity. His knowledge of color mixing and his growing expertise with his tools had increasingly allowed him to more fully realize on canvas the images that he held in his head.

Not every time, of course.

This was partly true because at times the image in his mind's eye would often shift while, in other instances, the act of painting itself would lead him into new possibilities. He soon discovered that each painting, like nature itself, persisted in its right to continue as a "becoming" rather than settling into a "being," a definitive thing. And, since Jake could not be quite sure if the finished painting was ever *exactly* as he visualized it ought to look, then he was left with the frustrating feeling that each one of his paintings — no matter how he or others might momentarily perceive it — represented a failure of sorts.

His ingrained frugality made him continue to scrape clean or to paint over those canvases he was convinced had "failed," so there were never more than a half-dozen "finished" canvases in his studio at one time. Maintaining a critical eye even as he progressed, he determinedly continued the practice of recycling those canvases he felt had been least successful in conveying his intent. Besides, he had now enough sketches and small studies from which he might gauge his progress.

More importantly, Jake was beginning to understand that there existed some essential gap between the act of painting and the conceived work — some unbridgeable breach between the process and the product. Somehow, even if the process were faultless, the end product seemed destined to be flawed — or, if not flawed, then at least not quite what he had initially had in mind to paint. And further, though he still could not put it into coherent speech, he instinctively felt that, though the product might be faulty — that is, a "failure" — *how* that product was viewed and treated — by others as well as himself — would eventually influence the process of creating a new painting.

At his present stage, however, neither the process nor the product was under his control — not like, say, his building of a bookcase, which might be measured, cut, and built to exact specifications — so he had no sure way of sorting out the puzzle. Thinking about such things — like trying to keep up his end in discussions about art — merely frustrated him. It gave him a headache.

Worse, it sometimes got in the way of his painting. "Thinking" through a painting was like trying to "think" how one ought to breathe — it merely got in the way of the process. If he had to think through each swing of his scythe or axe, for instance, he would get little grass or wood cut. One needed only watch a toddler learning to walk to see how an adult, attempting in the same way as the child to "think" out each step, might periodically fall face forward. The painter who had to think through each pass of the brush or knife would suffer just as many "falls."

Meanwhile, the collection of new sketches he had tacked up on the wall would already be pulling him to the next canvas and, putting his thoughts aside, he'd lean his chair back against the studio wall and allow his eyes to take in their seductive "call" to a new effort.

Jake looked forward to these moments in his studio, alone with his familiar surroundings, alone with whatever it was that would suddenly take hold of him, and prompt him to begin the next canvas.

He'd learned the trick of having primed canvases on hand — something that Joe Bundy had suggested — ready to capture whatever fleeting images began to form and seek outlet in paint. Most of his ready canvases were either primed or painted over in earth tones — siennas, ochers, sometimes one or the other "salted" with ultramarine — ready to accept the latest landscape Jake needed to get out of his head.

With the exception of Overlook Mountain, which he painted as closely to the "real" thing as he could, his landscapes were now more suggestive than realistic, more a combination of impressions than a representation of a particular place or specific time of day. And though Overlook presented a more explicit challenge for Jake — packaged, as it were, in an ongoing relationship that often resembled a confrontational "battle" — he had resigned himself to the fact that no landscape, no matter how familiar it might be to him, was ever the same from moment to moment. It was always a becoming, always a shift in color and values — even in shape, as growth or wind would alter the position of leaf and branch. Why, then, attempt to paint a *specific* scene? In reality, there never *was* such a thing.

When the moment arrived to begin a new canvas, he would generally squeeze out a glob of ultramarine blue with a drop of lamp black onto his palette, then stabbing his knife into the yielding substance, lay in his darkest passages. From this beginning, he would build his "landscape," squeezing out various colors as the picture dictated, blending, and either brushing in or spreading with the knife each new hue so as to suggest form and shadow, shape and light.

Most often, he would begin his canvas at the top, 'back' toward the horizon, then work his way downward, or "forward', into the foreground. As far as possible, he strove to leave method out of his action — attempting at all costs to avoid — as Harrison had taught him — the use of "formula" — at times not even allowing himself to lay out his palette beforehand to avoid any possibility of habit-forming practices. As the natural light in his studio faded, Jake would finally step back from what was destined to become one of the "keepers" or one of the "failures" — the final judgment taking, at most, a day or two to decide.

Though he had tried his best not to show it at the time, he was secretly pleased when Joe Bundy had noted his spontaneity of paint application. If anything, it meant that he had not given into the lure of a pattern, the all-dreaded "formula" that was the bane of all serious painters. Bundy's mention of Vincent van Gogh caused him to make a special effort to study that artist's works the next chance he got — a chance that arose not long after Jake had finally settled upon making his long delayed visit to Byrdcliffe a reality.

Somewhat apprehensive after staying away for so long, he was pleased to find that Mr. Whitehead readily welcomed him when he knocked on the door of White Pines. He spoke admiringly about Jake's handiwork around the colony, and as they walked the grounds, even offered him some new projects to consider.

Jake noted a weariness in Whitehead's step and demeanor, a kind of hangdog look that he'd never noticed before. The man was aging, but some of the heaviness Jake detected seemed not to come from the passage of years, but rather from a growing disappointment in his venture. Though Byrdcliffe still looked prosperous, there were certainly less people to be seen around the place. To simply stay afloat, the colony had lately been designing, manufacturing, and selling their own furniture, but barely holding their own in a world that was growing increasingly addicted to cheaper, mass-produced products.

As they strolled, Whitehead pointing out some of the work he had in mind, Jake casually asked him if he might see the library.

"Of course," said Whitehead. "We've built up a fine collection, and a good many of the artists in town like to drop in to browse."

As he led Jake back into the main house to show him the collection of art books, he proudly waved his arm to take in the several shelves of books. "All we ask is that you do your reading here. I've made it a practice not to lend out our books, since several have never found their way back."

Jake nodded his understanding as his eyes took in the vast array of titles.

"I wasn't aware that you were a reader, Jake," said Whitehead. "Does art interest you?"

"Kind of," Jake replied. "I've been attempting to master the craft of painting in between jobs."

"Yes. Yes," said Whitehead thoughtfully. "I seem to recall being told by some of our residents that they had seen you sketching during your lunch breaks. How long have you been painting?"

"Well, that's a bit hard to say." Jake smiled. "I guess it sort of depends on what you mean by painting."

Whitehead answered with his own smile. "I didn't mean the kind you did around here."

"No ... no," said Jake. "I know what you meant. The thing is, there's painting, then there's *painting.*"

"Just so," said Whitehead. "Something that Birge Harrison — while he still worked here — had often tried to make clear to his students."

"Not so easy to do," agreed Jake.

"Especially now with all this rage for 'modernity'," said Whitehead. "That crowd down in Rock City have so many believing that being able to splash a few colors on a canvas is 'painting', that it is difficult to get our young people serious about it." He shook his head. "The problem is that they seem to be succeeding — only too well, I might point out. It's shocking, really."

"More of a shame, I'd say." said Jake. "I mean, painting — I think — has somewhat of a special mission. Nowadays it often seems as if some of the artists treat it as if it were something of a job. Or worse, a lark — something to do — or not do — as one pleased. As if becoming an artist was no different from being a hat maker."

"Sadly, art is fast becoming just one more form of commerce," said Whitehead. "Even here we've had to resort to selling our furniture — our crafts — in an effort to make ends meet — though we've always tried to keep our Byrdcliffe here kind of pure — more in line with the concept of a utopian community where artists and artisans could be immune from viewing their work as a mere commodity." He turned to look thoughtfully out the large window overlooking the Woodstock Valley. "A lost cause, I'm afraid."

Jake didn't reply — but he surely knew what Whitehead meant.

"Well — the world is changing, I guess," said Whitehead quietly, and taking his leave of Jake, added, "Please feel free to make use of our library here whenever you wish."

"Thank you, Mr. Whitehead," Jake said. "I will certainly take you up on your offer."

Whitehead stopped in mid-stride and said over his shoulder, "And Jake — please stop and see the foreman — that is, if you have not completely abandoned your carpentry for your painting."

Jake chuckled. "Not at all, Mr. Whitehead. I'm still a handyman — always will be, I guess." Then he added, "That is, if I want to eat."

"Yes," said Whitehead. "That's the thing, isn't it? Even in Utopia, we have to eat," then shook his head as he left Jake standing in the library.

Jake turned to the shelves — shelves he had built, incidentally — and noticed that the books were arranged either by period or alphabetically by artist, and he quickly found what he was looking for — a book about Vincent van Gogh.

He leafed through the pages and though he only gave the work a cursory glance, intending to come back at a future time to look more closely, he did not find much similarity between van Gogh's work and that of his own. What he did see, however, was not, as Joe Bundy put it, "anger," but, instead, passion — an overwhelming abundance of passion, and he felt himself strangely drawn to it.

This man has seen the mountain — Jake thought.

Of more interest to Jake for the present was a brief introduction in which the writer mentioned that Vincent van Gogh had sold only one painting during his lifetime.

31

Whatever prosperity and the chase after the dollar might be doing to painters, it surely wasn't hurting the businessman. America was riding high, the people were beginning to expand their interests beyond the home, the "Roaring Twenties" not only making folks feel better about themselves, but also to begin seriously calling into question almost all of the old values.

Though none of the larger issues that were bringing about change in the world directly influenced Jake, the ripple effect was certainly being felt in the little hamlet of Woodstock. In terms of art, the Woodstock Colony was still almost a perfect microcosm of New York City. The connection between the metropolis and the village was now solidly in place, and that link continued to bring prominent personalities in the art world to the little town nestled in the Catskills. Whether they liked it or not, even the most provincial of the locals were being dragged into a modern world where old-time mores, traditions, and beliefs were constantly being called into question.

It was for many indeed a topsy-turvy time.

"Newfangled" ideas were steadily creeping not only into Woodstock, but into neighboring villages as well, Jake finding them even at his home in nearby West Hurley. He watched Aunt Birgit as she sat at the kitchen table one day, leafing through one of the latest department store catalogues. From time to time she would pause and exclaim, "Ach, ach. So many things! So many new things that they sell nowadays."

Jake peeked over his aunt's shoulder, and saw a page featuring women in various dress, many wearing some kind of undergarments that resembled armor made of silk. Both he and his aunt blushed as she looked up at him and their eyes met.

Jake quickly moved away from the table and busied himself at the wood stove, lifting the lids as if checking whether it was ready for refilling — a task that was almost entirely in Aunt Birgit's province. He glanced down at the supply stacked alongside the stove and said, "I'll just go out and bring in a little more wood, Aunt Birgit."

As he walked back to the woodshed, Jake could not for a moment imagine Aunt Birgit in any of the get-ups he had seen in the catalogue. But he could understand her desire to make some changes in the house. For years, she had been complaining of the smell of the kerosene lamps, the oily residue seemingly saturating the curtains and wallpaper over the years. There had been times when he actually imagined he could *taste* it in his food. But now, Jake was beginning to hear her giving voice to new complaints. Most recent was the mess the wood made in her kitchen and, for the past several weeks, the unevenness of heat when she tried to bake.

Aunt Birgit was getting on in years, and Jake could not fault her for trying to lessen her daily workload. He had seen her look longingly at the new cooking ranges in the appliance section of the catalogue, envying her sister-in-law, Hannelore, who already had one installed in her Halsey Street home down in Brooklyn. Her brother had long ago switched from gas lighting to electricity, so Hanni had not been plagued by the smell of kerosene in her house for years.

Ach, the butcher business must be good — she thought *— People always have to eat, no matter what. Poor Hans! He had brought home many loads of bluestone to lay the lovely paths around her gardens, but they could not put stones on the dinner table. Ja, Ja. Hanni was lucky.*

Not only did she not yet have electricity, she also had no running water in the house, the old hand pump on the kitchen sink the only way she could bring water — *cold* water, at that — into her home. Each time she needed hot water it meant pumping it into a kettle then heating it over the stove so that even the simple chore of cleaning up the dishes stretched out into a time-consuming activity.

Of course, no running water meant having an out-house — and she was definitely getting too old to trudge outside on a cold winter's day to relieve herself.

All of which, Jake, for some time now, had keenly felt. As he unloaded an armful of wood into the box alongside the kitchen stove, Jake said, "You know, Aunt Birgit, we could use a few improvements around here. Maybe one of the first things we ought to think about is drilling a well. Having running water and an inside bathroom would make things a lot easier for you."

"*Ja*, but from where will the money come? Since Uncle Hans's death, we've been lucky to have what we need — but a luxury like that?" Aunt Birgit heaved a sigh. "I've lived with such things all my life, Jake — and remember, back in the old country it was even worse. We used to have to bring the water to the house from the stream." She motioned to the hand pump on the sink. "At least here it comes directly into the kitchen without carrying it in pails."

"That's true, Aunt Birgit, but you're not getting any younger. And besides, with so much work coming my way, I can hardly keep up. It seems that an awful lot of these city people have money to throw away."

"You had to bring up my age?" said Aunt Birgit archly. Then more seriously, "But, Jake, you already give me most of your earnings now. I see how you scrimp and save just to buy your paints."

"Well, I'll ask around anyway — just to get an idea on how much drilling a well might cost. Anyway, I could use a sink in my studio. Cleaning my brushes here in the kitchen only leaves you with more mess to clean up."

"Ach, it's nothing. I have to clean the sink anyway, so what's a few more rubs with the rag?"

"Still, it wouldn't hurt to have a few conveniences around here. Even some of the summer residents in Woodstock have been putting in running water and electricity — and they're only here for a couple of months. Sooner or later, everyone will have electricity in the area, and it won't be so expensive."

"Well, Jake, I leave it up to you. Since Uncle Hans is gone, you have been the man around the house — and you know better about these things."

"I might be the 'man around the house', Aunt Birgit, but you're the one who spends most of your time here — and if I can make it a little easier for you, I will. After all, you've taken care of me since I've been a boy, and it's the least I can do."

Aunt Birgit merely smiled.

"And besides, don't you think that I also get a little tired of cutting and stacking wood — and dragging it in here and down into the cellar? And that's another thing — that old wood furnace. It eats up an awful lot of wood for all the heat we get out of it. The registers in the floor just don't distribute the heat through the house very well."

Jake thought about the spare room upstairs, so cold in the winter that Aunt Birgit used the room to store meat. "We ought to look into heating the house with oil."

"So, all of a sudden we're the Astors?"

Jake laughed. "Well, not quite, I guess. But we ought to look ahead a bit — especially if this boom continues. There's more and more money coming into our little towns, and I intend to see that I work for my share of it."

"Well," said Aunt Birgit. "We'll see. I like our home just as it is – you keep the outside looking so pretty and neat. Uncle Hans would be proud of you!" Then with a sigh, she added, "He always was, you know."

"Your flower gardens make it pretty, Aunt Birgit. All I do is cut the grass."

"And paint the buildings, and shovel the snow, and cut the wood…"

"Ahh, come on, Aunt Birgit. I'm a handyman. That's what I do. That's who I am."

"You're more than that Jake — you always were. It has always made your Uncle sad that your own father never saw that. Me too, Jake. It's too bad that my brother is so … so …"

"*Dick?*" said Jake.

"*Ja, ja!* And now you sound like my Hans," and, with a tear in her eye, she gave him a hug.

32

Having ready access to the Byrdcliffe library opened a new world to Jake and he was glad that he'd followed Sarah's advice to make the trip to the colony up on Guardian Mountain. The simple act of turning over the pages of illustrated art books gave him great pleasure, and he felt privileged to have been given access to them by Mr. Whitehead. He still tended to handle books as if they were fragile and, though he now took down and opened a book a bit more confidently, for Jake, books continued to retain their special status as precious objects.

After 'breaking the ice' with Mr. Whitehead with that first visit, he'd been coming more often to White Pines and, after browsing the shelves, soon grew proficient in choosing those books that would best help him to find answers to the growing number of questions that came up in his steady progression of learning about the craft of painting. He now took the time to read introductions more carefully and learning how to scan the tables of contents and indexes to more quickly find what he was looking for. He noted that some of the books concentrated on the work of individual artists, while others covered specific periods or "schools." He was especially pleased to discover that Whitehead's library contained several books on technique, and these he had found especially helpful. He was still loathe to aggressively pursue an unclear point when in conversation with artists, and such books often gave him a clearer understanding of the sometime cryptic comments they would make about the nuts and bolts of the craft.

Books, he was discovering, vastly extended a person's range, allowing a solitary human being not only to reach beyond one's physical location, but also back into time. He began to put artists into proper chronological periods, saw how earlier painters influenced those who came later, and how the techniques and practices of one age developed and grew into the next. He began to see and understand the long chain of artistic endeavor, and how each new artist was connected to a confraternity of past explorers into the mysteries of their craft. In his own work, he saw the imprint of the hands of Birge Harrison, John Carlson — and other Woodstock artists — and how each of them, in turn, felt the hands of the past on their shoulders as secrets and methods were passed down from generation to generation.

And as his knowledge and understanding of the world of art steadily grew, a greater desire to explore those books in his own library took possession of him. Finding that his hands could now handle a book as easily as they could an axe or a hammer — even a paint brush or palette knife — Jake found ever more ease and confidence in settling back in his studio to open those formidable-looking volumes that had at one time so intimidated him.

He could now count himself a willing and adept traveler into the world of Joseph Conrad, delighted to discover that that author's books contained not only a story, but also a host of new ideas which he had to absorb, and with which he had to contend. He had already gone through a full third of the twenty-six-volume set of Conrad's books, always eager to begin the next as he retired to his bed for the night.

He also dipped into the books by Thackeray, Dickens and other British writers, but found his favorite English storyteller to be Thomas Hardy. Hardy wrote about people Jake could identify with — farmers, country people who worked with their hands, regular people like the townsfolk in Woodstock and West Hurley — and, as far as he could determine, had a sympathetic and sensitive understanding of nature that seemed to crop up in almost every one of his books. Thomas Hardy was a man of the soil, and Jake took great pleasure in his descriptions of rural England.

Jake could see, however, that Hardy was not just simply in tune with nature and her cycles, but also had insight into the human psyche. Like Conrad, he had the ability to penetrate into the workings of the human mind and heart, but unlike Conrad, who often dealt with exotic characters and places, the English author wrote about people not unlike Jake and his fellow workmen. Hardy's intricate plots of what might entangle an ordinary person helped Jake to better understand his own awkwardness amongst people, especially those of a different class and from a different walk of life.

Jake was also finding it easier to dip into the more difficult books that he had on his shelf — books like Lewes's *The History of Philosophy,* the *Dialogues of Plato,* and even the works of William Shakespeare.

Slowly but surely, he was getting past the strangeness of Elizabethan English, finding to his delight that William Shakespeare also delved into the workings of the human mind. He was beginning to especially favor the tragedies, finding such characters as King Lear, Othello, Macbeth, and Hamlet riveting personalities, amazed to find that even the "high and mighty" had serious flaws that brought disaster and pain not only down upon themselves, but also often on those that surrounded them. The meaning of many of the words still escaped him, but he plodded on and found that he could at least follow the thread of the story. Time and again, he would put down his brushes and open one of those tragedies, re-reading the major speeches, inwardly thrilling to the depth and breadth of the playwright's mind.

And although the intent and import of the *Dialogues of Plato* continued to elude him, he disciplined himself to periodically pick through the two-volume set to see if he could glean the wisdom he was sure they contained. Philosophy, he had come to know, meant a love of truth, and how could a thinking man shirk the responsibility of such a love? Marcus Aurelius had already made that point for him. Still, the words, though easier to read than those found in Shakespeare, were yet set in contexts that were far beyond his comprehension. Much of what he read seemed to assume some prior knowledge, some previous familiarity with terms and ideas that were foreign to him.

More easily grasped was Lewes's *The History of Philosophy.* Here, Jake was able to follow the progress of mankind's exploration of his world. Gradually, he could see how the chain of ideas grew out of former discoveries, how new concepts had been built upon and expanded as man explored and conquered his universe. The evolution of ideas, Jake came to see, was not so different from what he was learning in his reading about art — the past was a repository from which we might learn and grow, the philosopher, like the artist, nourishing himself on those who cleared the way for further discovery. If he was still not able to comprehend many of the concepts revealed in these books, he was yet coming to a clearer knowledge that he did not stand alone in his questioning — or in the world. Perhaps of even greater consequence, he had come to the realization that change — the upheaval of old ideas to make way for the new — was not just a sign of his own times, but had characterized the world since the beginning.

Of all the books on his shelves, however, it was the St. Mark's Edition containing the works of John Ruskin that was increasingly claiming his time and attention. He was particularly proud of this set. Ruskin had been viewed as something of a demigod over at Byrdcliffe, and here, right in his own studio, his shelves contained the man's collected works — a good sight more than the Byrdcliffe library had held which only boasted a handful of works written by and about their mentor. It was the writings of John Ruskin, after all, that brought about the founding of the Byrdcliffe Colony on the outskirts of Woodstock. Hervey White and Bolton Brown, armed with his description of the ideal location for an art colony, had, after traveling a good part of the country, decided that the side of Guardian Mountain perfectly fit Ruskin's bill.

They had gleaned their information from Ruskin's *Modern Painters,* a rambling compendium filled with that writer's ruminations on the craft of art, but especially rich with his observations of nature. He had heard from Birge Harrison that it was a combination of Ruskin's work on nature and William Morris's socialism that had served as the foundation for Whitehead's colony. Whitehead had studied with both Ruskin and Morris, bringing back from England their thoughts and philosophies, heroically trying to transplant their ideas on American soil.

"Design," Ruskin had written, "is not the offspring of idle fancy but the studied result of accumulative observation and delightful habit. Without observation and experience, no design — without peace and pleasureableness in occupation, no design — and all the lecturings, and teachings, and prizes, and principles of art, in the world, are of no use, so long as you don't surround your men with happy influences and beautiful things. It is impossible for them to have right ideas about color, unless they see lovely colors in nature unspoiled; impossible for them to supply beautiful incident and action in their ornament unless they see beautiful incident and action in the world about them. Inform their minds, refine their habits, and you form and refine their designs..." Such was Ralph Radcliffe Whitehead's firm belief and such was the ruling ideal behind his beloved Byrdcliffe Colony.

Jake was more than pleasantly surprised, then, to discover that part of his treasure trove of books contained *Modern Painters*, this portion of Ruskin's writings forming a four-volume section of his St. Mark's Edition. It was the first part of Ruskin's writings that he therefore undertook to read and to digest, finding the Englishman's observations on nature very close to his own — paying particular attention whenever the subject of mountains came up. Ruskin, whose earliest recorded memories are of a trip with his parents through the mountains of Switzerland in 1833, had a fondness for them that continually cropped up in his writings. Mountains, he had written, were "the beginning of all my own right art work" and laid claim as "the ruling passion of my life."

Jake could well find himself in sympathy with such thoughts and, whenever he came across a particularly compelling observation, would carefully copy out the passage and pin it up on his wall alongside his drawings. Directly over his door, he had prominently displayed one of his favorite quotes:

Herein is the chief practical difference between the higher and lower artists — All great men see what they paint before they paint it — see it in a perfectly passive manner — cannot help seeing it if they would; whether in their mind's eye, or in bodily fact, does not matter; very often the mental vision is, I believe, in men of imagination, clearer than the bodily one; but vision it is...

This quote represented for Jake the clearest description of his ongoing relationship with Overlook Mountain that he had as yet come across — and his glance never failed to take in the words whenever he left with his paintbox and easel for another bout with his own beloved mountain.

Though the solitary side of his nature found little sympathy with the socialistic leanings of John Ruskin — he would never have been comfortable with joining such a colony as Byrdcliffe — Jake found that, over the years, he would spend ever more time in browsing that writer's works. There was much wisdom embedded in his philosophy and, along with much of that Englishman's high-blown fancies, one could find nuggets of hard-won and practical observation.

As he would sit in his studio turning the pages of Ruskin, Shakespeare, or Lewes, Jake would stop his reading from time to time to take stock. During such times he would hardly recognize himself in this new role as reader and student. He'd shake his head and chuckle aloud.

Well, here I am — a bookish handyman.

He would look down at his rough hands, marveling at how easily they had adapted from tool to brush to page. What, then, was this "poor, forked animal" not capable of?

He would close the book lying on his lap and, carefully replacing it in its proper slot, run his eye lovingly over *his* library.

One book that was never left on the shelf was the little volume of Marcus Aurelius's *Meditations*. Of all his books, it was this one that rarely left his person. Much thumbed through and crammed with his scribbled notes, it was his constant companion, his silent confidant and mentor, always tucked into either his paint or his toolbox when he was away from home. It went where he went, and when he needed a bucking up for his flagging spirit or troubled mind, the thoughts of this ancient Roman never seemed to fail him.

33

The opening reception at The Mountainside Kiln was well attended, the outdoor sculpture exhibit spread over about a half-acre of manicured lawn and carefully planted gardens. A small stream, trickling from the mountainside that served as a back wall for the space, cut through the grounds, a miniature Japanese-type bridge joining the bisected parcels of land. A handsome indoor gallery complemented the grounds wherein one might find smaller pieces of sculpture or ceramics.

The gallery, owned and directed by a sculptor-potter, featured alternating exhibits of paintings and pottery during the winter and sculpture and pottery during the summer. Lenora, the owner, had a refined and discriminating taste and always insisted on curating her own shows. She would appear at her openings — always elegant social affairs — in loose and flowing robes, her long gray-streaked hair never confined by ribbons or bows or hairpins, warmly greeting her guests, her softly modulated voice always gentle, her conversation with her visitors scrupulously skirting the crass discourse of open commercialism.

The work was, of course, for sale — and none of it cheaply priced. Lenora, a one-time resident of Byrdcliffe, had an eye for quality and her stable of artists warranted appropriate compensation. Many of the artists she featured were nationally known, commanding high prices wherever they were exhibited. If one wanted to inquire about prices, one was discreetly led to a back room for discussion, far from the hearing of guests who were enjoying the work as they strolled through the pleasant grounds.

Situated just a short distance outside of Woodstock, The Mountainside Kiln, in addition to the public gallery and grounds, housed a working studio and kiln — hence, the name — exclusively used by Lenora for her own work. Though her pottery was also for sale, one never found it displayed during her gallery shows, and if a visitor was interested in purchasing an original "Lenora," one had to return after the public receptions were over. Many did.

Jake, uncomfortable in a new suit of "Sunday" clothes, had come to the reception at the special request of Sarah. She had sent him a printed invitation — the first he had ever received — or seen, for that matter — with block letters across its face announcing "Sarah Steele: Ceramist," with the place, date and time of the reception printed inside. Tucked within, Sarah had placed a handwritten note requesting that he come to help her celebrate the special occasion of her first public exhibition.

Ordinarily, he'd avoided opening receptions — now a regular occurrence at the Woodstock Artists Association — preferring to view the artwork without the usual press of people that were always present at such events. Largely social affairs, Jake found the small talk and wine and cheese buffets a bit much for him. People seemed to go to these affairs to be seen rather than to see and, though he appreciated their necessity for the exhibiting artists — many of the visitors, after all, were potential buyers — most of his artist friends readily admitted that they were just as uncomfortable as he would have been had he come to their opening.

To Jake such affairs were too obviously a part of the growing commercialism of art — and being forced, as it were, to view the work as just one more commodity on display, the work being viewed as much as merchandise as it was art — continued to be problematic for him. Since paintings were now arranged along a wall as if they were products along a shelf in a department store, he would not be surprised if, in the future, pictures of artwork would soon be printed in catalogues like those Aunt Birgit got from Sears and Roebuck or Montgomery Ward. He tried to picture Aunt Birgit turning the pages of just such a book, deciding which picture to pick for her living room. The idea was just too absurd for serious thought.

Although he was glad to spend a few moments speaking with Sarah after his arrival at The Mountainside Kiln, he found that newcomers were constantly besieging her as they came up to praise her work or to offer their congratulations on her first public showing. As much as possible, he kept to himself, finding a small bench in a corner of the garden a perfect place to observe Sarah, and to stay out of the way.

The invitation had come as something of a surprise since he had not seen much of Sarah since her marriage to Calvin Steele. The Steeles divided their time between New York City and Woodstock, usually spending their summers upstate and wintering in their Manhattan apartment, although Calvin often had occasion to go down to the city during the summer for overnight stays to attend meetings at his various clubs. The few times that Jake had seen them around town since their announcement of seeking a Woodstock residence were usually brief but cordial, Sarah always warm and friendly with Calvin — "Cal" — his usual aloof self.

Jake had little to criticize in the aloofness of Calvin Steele — after all, he himself was not a very open person — but the cordiality of Sarah often gave him pause for thought. She was essentially the same woman who gave him that cup — still warm, friendly, and quick to smile — and, though he knew that she was now the wife of another man, he could not entirely disregard the effect she continued to have on him. There was still that electric thrill, for instance, when she grasped his hand in greeting or, if in casual conversation, lightly and negligently placed her hand on his arm.

His eyes rarely left her as he watched her gracefully make her way through the crowd of people, confident and poised in her movements, always displaying a relaxed and easy manner that he knew could never be his own. He also noted that "Cal" was equally aloof to any and all who stopped to greet him — so he knew that whatever face he might have put on it, it was not a personal thing for Sarah's husband to be a bit standoffish with him.

He especially noted the cool demeanor of Calvin Steele as he spoke with Sarah. He wondered if Cal experienced the same kind of thrill when Sarah touched him. Even though Sarah's work was the occasion of the show, Cal appeared to have little interest in his wife's exhibit, nodding or smiling from time to time, but affecting the air of one who found little to commend in a "pottery show."

At one point, when Sarah came over to sit next to him for a moment, Jake asked her, "Is Cal proud of you?"

She seemed a bit taken aback by the question, then after glancing away from his stare, said, "Ceramics is not Cal's thing, you know. He really doesn't think it's an art."

She was almost forcibly drawn back to look at him as he quietly said, "*I'm* proud of you." He pointedly looked directly into her eyes and added, "And I'm honored to own one of your pieces."

"Well, thank you, Mr. Jake Forscher," she said. Then, with a smile that sent that shiver through him, "I'm honored to be in your collection."

"Well, I'm glad you *are*," replied Jake with a grin. "I've seen the prices on some of the work here, and I don't think Lenore's is a place that I can afford to shop in."

Sarah laughed out loud. "Oh, that's Lenore! She believes that if you don't put a high enough price on the work, people will not think it's worthy."

"Hmmm," said Jake. "I'd sure like to explore that line of reasoning with you some day. I still don't know how one can put a price tag on a work of art."

"Well, like I said, Cal doesn't believe a pot is a work of art anyway, so there's no problem there."

Jake didn't reply.

"But if you're serious about that talk some day, why don't you come visit some time? I do have my own little studio now — just a shed off the kitchen, really. It's all the room I need, though — I only have a kick wheel and a plaster wedge table there, but I'd love to show it off. I'd be glad to offer you a cup of tea or coffee in exchange for your time."

"My time?" said Jake. "It's *me* who's asking *you* for the time."

"Well, with Cal in New York so often, I sort of find a lot of time on my hands. You can come anytime — watch me work on the wheel, if you like."

"I'd like that very much," he said, "But would that be all right with your husband?"

"Of course, silly! Why should he mind? We both have visitors all the time — not always the same people, and not always at the same time. So promise me you'll come."

Jake was still unsure but replied, "I promise."

A small group of Byrdcliffers then descended on them, and Jake was relieved that Sarah was whisked away before she had the opportunity to make him commit to a definite date to come to her home.

He stole away when the crowd seemed to be densest, hoping that the crush of people would hide his departure.

On the way home, he found that old unpleasant feeling once again visiting his solar plexus.

God! — he thought — *I thought that nonsense was all over.*

The idea of visiting Sarah, however, teased at his mind but, with an impatient shrug of his shoulders, and a firmer stride, he pushed the idea out of his head.

What's the point. Sarah's married and me...well...

Jake's hand brushed the scar along the inside of his leg.

— *Well ... I'm me.*

34

Jake and Joe Bundy stood leaning against the rail of the old red bridge in Zena, both wrapped in their own silence as the Sawkill Creek flowed beneath them. An early morning fog had steadily been lifting since daybreak, curling tendrils of misty air still clinging stubbornly to the creek's surface. A few yards away, their easels had been set up side by side along the side of the road, both facing a clearing that opened toward Overlook Mountain. Everything was in readiness: canvases already set up on their easels, paint boxes and materials handily set out.

A fish suddenly leapt out of the water to snatch a hovering insect, breaking the silence.

"Beautiful," murmured Joe.

Jake nodded.

Another fish broke the surface of the creek. "We should've brought a line and pole."

Jake merely smiled.

"But it really is beautiful," Joe persisted. "I don't see how so many artists could ever go back to live in the city after they've spent a summer here."

"Maybe they don't like the cold," Jake offered.

"It's just as cold in New York," Joe replied. "Maybe even colder when the wind comes off the rivers down those cross streets."

"Well, that's true," agreed Jake. "Winter or summer, I couldn't live down there. Too many people for me."

Joe turned to look at his friend. "You *are* a loner, aren't you?"

Jake shrugged.

"I mean, you were born down there — in Brooklyn, right? So it's not like you're one of these provincials here who only get as far as Kingston a couple of times a year to buy supplies." He laughed.

"You know the locals call Kingston the 'city' up here — the '*big city*' means Manhattan."

"Been here permanent since I turned fourteen," Jake said. He looked over toward Overlook, the fog between them and the mountain beginning to dissipate. "I sometimes feel that I've *always* been here — that I *belong* here."

Joe turned back to watching the stream. "I can't blame you for that, I guess. Though I don't mind a trip back and forth to the city periodically, I know I could settle in here permanently myself." He glanced around. "I don't think I'll ever run out of things to paint."

Jake nodded. "How is it, you think, that not everybody can see that? I mean some of these fellows come here to paint, and they might just as well've stayed at home. What they put on canvas doesn't look like anything I've ever seen in these parts."

"Poetic license, I guess," said Joe.

Jake shrugged.

"Yeah," continued Joe. "But it is kind of strange how we look at the world."

Jake looked over at him. "Meaning?"

"Well, an artist just doesn't *see* the world as ordinary folks do."

Jake waited.

"I remember a teacher I had at the League — not Carlson. This was before him, this was when I was still down in New York — well, he said that when people — ordinary people, not artists — looked at a painting, that they tended to look at it *wrong.*"

"How so," said Jake.

"He explained it this way. He said a person, say, walks into a museum. As he walks along, he suddenly feels compelled to stop in front of a picture. He steps up to the painting, and begins to look closely. He sees that it is a picture of a lake, say, with a small boat in the foreground and trees in the background. Now, according to that teacher, as soon as that guy began noticing the water, picking out the boat, and admiring the trees, he *stopped* looking at the painting."

Jake looked dubious.

"What he explained was that what first catches our attention are shapes and colors. Somehow the human responds to them on some basic level. They — the shapes and colors — 'speak' to a part of us somewhere below our conscious minds, and for whatever reason — probably something from our past — or maybe even something we inherited from our primitive ancestors — we react. Some people react to some colors and shapes, while others respond to different ones."

He turned to Jake. "You still with me?"

Jake gave a tentative nod.

"Anyway, *that's* why the guy walking through the museum stopped in the first place. Something inside him was attracted by the colors and shapes in the painting — or so this instructor claims. Anyway, when the guy tries to figure out what halted him in his tracks — when he starts to look at what the painting is *about* — the subject, in other words — he stops looking at the painting. *He doesn't see what the artist has actually done.* All he sees are trees, water and a boat."

"I think I follow that," said Jake.

"Of course you do," said Joe. "I mean when we look down — you and I — into this water running under this old iron bridge, we are responding to shapes and colors. We don't say to ourselves, 'Oh, I have to paint the Sawkill as it flows under that bridge'. We say something more like, 'I'd like to catch how the light reflects off that. If I could only get that color!' In other words, we, the artists, don't look at *things,* but how things impress our eyes — and *that's* what we are painting, not water and bridges."

"So, the artist has eyes that work differently from those of others?"

"You could say that," said Joe. "But it's more like he *trains* himself to do it — or is predisposed to do it, maybe. Whatever — we just don't look at the world the way the ordinary person does and, when we paint, we try to share that view of ours with others. Unfortunately, they get caught up in what they *know* — boats, trees, flowers — and miss the *art.*"

Jake thought about his first look at modern art in the Armory Show. He was guilty of the same thing. He was trying to understand what the pictures *said* — he was looking for what he *knew* — and missed the art — or what *passed* for art, anyway. To his way of thinking, the jury was still out on that one.

They moved over to their easels, and both stood squinting at Overlook in the distance.

"Now even here," said Joe as he started laying out his palette, "we're going to paint side by side again and, when we're done, my Overlook is not going to look like *your* Overlook. Even artists don't all see alike."

Jake had to agree. They had painted together several times over the past year and no one — not even those least knowledgeable about art — would confuse their paintings.

"I get your point," said Jake, "but there is still a part of me that has trouble with what *some* artists see — or claim to see. I'm not convinced that some of 'em actually see blue trees and green faces. A lot of that modern stuff leaves me cold."

"Well, me too," said Joe. "But who's to say that they *can't* paint like that? If other people don't like what they paint, they can always walk away from it. No one makes them buy such pictures and take them home."

"But they sure *do*," said Jake. "Look how many can't wait to take such stuff off the walls at the Association's shows. I just don't see how someone could walk past a Carlson or a Cochran or a Chase to buy some garish smear of colors. I wouldn't want such stuff hanging in *my* home — least of all *pay* for it! I just don't get it."

"Maybe it's not for us to *get*," said Joe. "A good bit of it is ignorance, you know. At least according to some. Like I said before, the ordinary person doesn't know how to look at art in the first place. He can't evaluate what an artist has done. So, if he doesn't know what he likes, he buys what he believes he *ought* to buy — usually the latest fad. Like the average person's taste in everything — they feel they ought to be up to date, in the know. Most of them are afraid to say, 'Hey! I don't like that — I like *this*'. Somebody standing next to them might make fun of their old-fashioned taste."

"So much the worse for them," said Jake, and began knifing on some cerulean blue heavily laced with white.

"Sky's almost gray," he muttered to himself as much as to his companion.

They worked on in silence for some time, each periodically stepping back to survey his work, touching up their canvases here or there in an effort to make their pictures conform to their impressions of the scene that lay before them.

The sun was strengthening, and both had already shed their topcoats.

218

Joe was the first to break the silence.

"For a loner, you know, you're beginning to be a regular social butterfly."

"Huh?"

"You," Joe smiled, "you're breaking out of your cocoon."

Jake laid his knife down. "What's that supposed to mean?" he asked.

"Well, here we are," said Joe, "This is — what? — the third or fourth time we've been out painting together. There was a time not so long ago when I couldn't get you to stop for anything longer than a short conversation when I saw you around town."

"Didn't have much to say," said Jake.

"And," Joe added with a grin, "I hear tell that the mysterious Jake Forscher has been showing up at receptions."

"Once," said Jake. "I attended an opening reception up at the Mountain Side Kiln. One time. And I went because I was invited by a friend."

"I've heard that you're also showing up more often at the WAA."

"Not at receptions. I go so that I can see what others are doing. I go so that I can learn."

"Well, that's true. I never see you at the openings."

"Too many people. Too much talking."

They continued with their painting for some minutes when Joe again broke the silence.

"Who was the 'friend'?"

"What?"

"Who was the 'friend' who invited you to a reception."

"Sarah Winters — er — Sarah Steele, I mean."

"Is that Calvin Steele's wife? The potter?"

Jake nodded, and studiously squinted at Overlook.

"Didn't know you had a lady friend."

Jake reddened.

"Didn't know you knew *any* ladies."

Jake concentrated on Overlook.

"How do you know Cal's wife?"

"Are we going to paint or talk all morning," said Jake, letting out a heavy breath of air.

"Touchy, touchy."

"I'm not 'touchy'. I'm trying to paint here." He glared at Overlook.

"Just asked a question."

"She's not my 'lady friend'. She's just a friend."

Joe waited until he simmered down.

"All I asked was how you knew her."

Jake laid his palette knife down and wiped his hands on a rag.

"Now, this is just one of the reasons I'm a loner," he said. "People just can't resist talking — asking about anything and everything."

"Look who's talking," Joe laughed. "Aren't you the one who goes about town putting questions to every artist he sees? That's how I met you, isn't it? If my memory serves me right, Ted Deavers introduced us one day, and practically the first thing out of your mouth was a question."

"Well – that's different. I was asking about painting — not about personal things."

"Hey, I'm not getting 'personal' here, Jake. All I asked you was how you became a friend of Calvin Steele's wife, that's all. If that's too 'personal' for you, then forget I asked."

Embarrassed by his reaction, Jake took a breath and said, "I met Sarah one day while I was working up at Byrdcliffe many years ago — before the war — some time before she became Mrs. Steele, in fact."

"Now that wasn't so hard, was it?"

Joe had no idea just *how* hard it was. Sarah Winters — Steele — still occupied an unsettled place in Jake's heart and mind and, as much as possible, he avoided dwelling on thoughts about her. He was afraid that in his awkward handling of Joe's innocent question, he had already revealed too much — at least more than he was willing to reveal even to himself. He merely grunted in response and returned to his painting.

They painted on in silence, Joe sensitive enough to Jake's mood to avoid continuing with his questioning about Sarah Steele. Still, he was seeing a change in Jake — a change, that for the most part, he felt was a good thing. Self-reliance was admirable to be sure — it was, in fact, a characteristic of Jake's that had first attracted him to the taciturn handyman who showed up on that day at Mrs. Cooper's so long ago. But everyone needed someone from time to time — and whatever Jake's true feeling was for him, Joe was glad to call him his friend.

They stopped shortly before noon, the bright sunlight already so different from the pearly luminescence of daybreak that neither of them could continue with their painting.

Packing up their things, they set out on their separate ways, Joe to his studio in Woodstock, Jake back home to see what chores Aunt Birgit needed done before he could call it a day.

One more attempt at capturing you, old-timer — Jake thought. — *One more time and I'm still no closer to painting that Overlook that I know you really are. How long…how long?*

35

Jake was in his room packing his things, unsure of what and how much he ought to bring with him to Brooklyn. He counted on taking an early train to New York City since he knew that they would be staying for at least as long as the weekend, but felt that the visit may be extended. It all depended upon just how ill his father was.

Aunt Birgit had given him the news the day before, almost as soon as he walked in the door after putting in a long workday over at the Maverick. Once again, Jake was hiring out his carpentering skills to Dayton Shultis. He was taken on by Shultis to help in the building of Hervey White's latest project, a new theater to accommodate the colony's sudden interest in this particular artform. White's open-air Quarry Theater had served him well in the past, but was quickly proving to be sorely inadequate to serve the sudden outburst of enthusiasm people were showing for drama.

Theater had become big business in Woodstock, and, throughout the 20's, not only Hervey White but others as well would begin to capitalize on the growing interest. Byrdcliffe had already followed suit by catering to this new appeal in staging plays and, by the close of the 20's, when construction began on the brand-new Woodstock Playhouse over on the Woodstock-Saugerties Turnpike, it was clear that the art colony had undergone a permanent change in its creative mix, and that everyone was trying to keep up with the trend. Now, a growing contingent of theater people added their luster to the older groups of artists and artisans that hitherto had peopled — and plagued — the village locals.

"Your father is not well," Aunt Birgit had told Jake when he sat down to face her at the kitchen table. "Both your Mama and your brother think that we ought to go down to Brooklyn." She implied, but did not add the words "before it's too late." She did, however, tell him that they believed his father had diabetes.

Spring had already asserted itself, the odor of lilacs and the blinding yellow of forsythia filling his nostrils and eyes as he and Aunt Birgit walked the short distance to the West Hurley train station. Only four weeks ago his aunt's flower garden had been sending up crocuses and daffodils. How quickly things changed!

If he had to leave his beloved mountains, this was probably the best time for him to go since he never felt he could artistically compete with nature's wild springtime profligacy in its use of color. Just as the blaze of reds and golds maddeningly challenged painters at the height of autumn, the months of April and May made most artists despair of ever matching palettes with Mother Nature. She had been at it for too long, and just had too many tricks up her sleeve. Attempts to apply to canvas the same colors nature used, only resulted in a garish outrage that out-rivaled the most flamboyant and dedicated of fauves.

Not that some of them don't do just that — he thought.

As was his usual habit, Jake took the aisle seat when they changed trains at Kingston's Union Station, not caring to view the bland and sordid landscape through which the West Shore Rail Line passed. Aunt Birgit, lost in her own thoughts, silently gazed out the window. He had brought along with him his little book on Marcus Aurelius, slowly reading and turning over in his mind the views and observations of that early philosopher as the train carried him to Weehawken.

He liked the clean manliness of the Roman's thoughts, feeling that, though put into words that he might not have used himself, Aurelius's ideas must have grown out of his dealings and impressions of life. As he did quite often whenever he opened the little book, he wished that this man could be alive today. He would've liked to work alongside him, to have walked and talked with him about nature and life and the duties of man. He wondered if this Marcus Aurelius had been able to hold true to his beliefs as he grew old, and if he, like Jake, found himself in a world that seemed largely indifferent to notions of how a man ought to live his life.

Jake opened the book once again to its first page to read: "From the reputation and remembrance of my father, modesty and a manly character."

To have such a father, and to have learned such things from him!

He glanced over at his aunt, wondering what thoughts she was having about her brother and his illness.

He turned back to his book. A bit further on, he read: "And you will give yourself relief, if you do every act of your life as if it were the last…"

He turned the words over in his mind. Did this man work with his hands? Did he spend time with men who opposed his ideas? Did he prefer to spend most of his time alone? He must have, for another passage read: "… for it is in your power, whenever you shall choose, to retire into yourself. For nowhere with more quiet or more freedom from trouble does a man retire than into his own soul…"

Had he felt he belonged in the world in which he found himself?

What did Marcus Aurelius think of art and the people who made it?

Jake continued to leaf through the pages of the book, seeking out those many dog-eared pages that he had turned down to mark a particular passage or a favorite thought.

He was abruptly awakened to the fact that they were already pulling into Weehawken, and that they had to hurry to get their bags and catch the ferry over to Manhattan. How quickly went time when one got lost in one's thoughts!

Freddie was waiting at the subway station when they arrived in Brooklyn.

"I wanted to catch you before you got to the house," explained Freddie as he took his aunt's arm. "Papa is in the hospital and Mama's home … Konnie's with her."

Jake nodded.

"He's in pretty bad shape," Freddie continued. "The doctors don't hold out much hope. Poor Mama is at her wit's end. She seems so lost without Papa."

Jake didn't say, but thought: *Papa's not telling her what to do — and when to do it.*

"Of course, she would be," he said aloud.

Aunt Birgit, trying her best to keep up the pace with her two nephews, kept her own counsel.

As they walked, Freddie had instinctively put his other arm around Jake's shoulder, but feeling uncomfortable doing so out on the street, soon took it away.

"Papa's pretty much out of it," he said. "Mama needs us now more than he does."

"Are we going to the house," asked Jake, "or to the hospital?" He could not bring himself to call his parent's residence on Halsey Street "home."

"Let's go see Mama first. You need to get rid of your bags — Mama has your rooms ready — and, like I said, she needs us now more than he does." He looked at his aunt. "I was with him during visiting hours this morning — he didn't even know I was there."

When they got to the house on Halsey Street, they found Konstanze trying to get their mother to drink some tea at the kitchen table.

Obviously distraught, a handkerchief crushed against her mouth, Hannelore Forscher merely sobbed and shook her head, pushing away Konstanze's hand with the cup.

"Please, Mama," Konstanze was saying. "It will do you good." When she saw Freddie coming into the kitchen, she said to him plaintively, "She hasn't eaten anything all day."

"Come on Mama," urged Freddie. "Listen to Konnie. She's only trying to help. Drink some tea."

"Let me help," said Aunt Birgit as she sat next to her sister-in-law. "We don't need both of you sick, Hanni. You need to be strong — especially now."

His mother quickly glanced up, a look of surprise on her face. "Birgit … and Jacob! Jacob! Ach, it is good you are here." She broke down into heavy sobs, her thin shoulders moving up and down uncontrollably.

"Of course I'm here," he said quietly. "Aunt Birgit told me how serious Papa is and," he turned to Freddie, "Freddie has been filling us in on the way over from the subway."

"*Ja, ja!* You must see him before he goes. Only yesterday he was asking if you and Aunt Birgit were coming down from the country."

"We came as soon as we heard, Mama"

The whole family went to the hospital during evening visiting hours, first Mama and Aunt Birgit, then Freddie and Konstanze going into the hospital room. Jake stood by the door.

While he had waited for them to finish, Jake could tell that his father was not responding to any of their words, and wondered what each had found to say to the man lying on the bed. From across the room, awaiting his turn at bedside, he looked at his father's profile, noting that Papa's nose, hawk-like, pointed up towards the ceiling as if sniffing for prey.

When he finally approached his father's side, Papa's face looked even thinner, even more like that of a bird of prey, his hair stringy and uncombed. Jake wondered why none of the women had smoothed back his father's hair, and bent over to do it himself. He knew how much his father disliked looking unkempt. His bluish-colored jowls sagged limply from his face, moving in and out at intervals as his mouth opened and closed. Jake noticed that his father's breathing was shallow, sporadic, labored.

He was surprised to feel tears springing to his eyes. He blinked them away and scanned his father's face more closely. Papa *looked* unhealthy. His skin was parchment-like, with dry flakes clinging to the corners of his eyes and mouth. Someone had shaved him — badly. A number of gray hairs standing as stiffly upright as a copse of saplings were visible under his lower lip, another patch of stubble high up on his left cheek. The once well cared-for mustache was straggly and ill trimmed. Jake saw that long hairs protruded from his nose and ears. Closer inspection revealed Papa's nose to be heavily veined, and wondered how much his father's drinking had contributed to the disease's progress.

Finally, he said, "Hello, Papa."

He received no answer.

A little louder, he said, "It's Jacob." The eyes remained closed as if the crusted flakes in their corners rendered the task of opening them too difficult to undertake.

Jake allowed his eyes to travel up and down the length of his father's body, astounded that the covering sheet had hardly registered a body beneath it. How frail the man looked! With hardly any effort at all, Jake could easily have lifted him off of the bed with one hand. What happened to all that flesh that was once Friedrich Forscher? Where had the dandy gone? He wondered if the nurses here at the hospital had a chance to be charmed by his father's smile.

He looked again at his father's face. Why had he so feared this man? Wherein lay the power he had so firmly held over him? Surely it was not visible in this wasted body.

"Good bye, Papa," he said at last.

He received no response.

His father died several days later, never having gained full consciousness during his time in the hospital. Because he appeared so ill, Jake and Aunt Birgit had decided to extend their visit, feeling it their duty to stay by Hannelore's side. She did not really need them, their presence more of an extra burden than a comfort. She was obviously in good hands with Konstanze, and seemed oblivious to both her son and sister-in-law's attention. Freddie, meanwhile, in a businesslike and efficient manner, appeared to have all the details and arrangements for any and all possible contingents under control.

The funeral took place on a radiant May morning, the cemetery air filled with the odors of blooming lilac. As they lowered his father into the open grave, Jake thought — *a beautiful day to paint, Papa. It's too bad you never could appreciate such beauty.*

He spent the next few days at the house greeting the few friends and some distant relatives who came to his mother's home to pay their respects. When confinement in the house stifled him, he walked the streets or visited Freddie at the butcher shop on Gates Avenue.

Life in the neighborhood did not seem to change much since he had left Brooklyn. He recognized many of the same customers who had been coming to the shop since he was a boy. He half-heartedly helped out when Freddie asked him, taking over Konstanze's place at the counter when she stayed home with Aunt Birgit to look after her mother-in-law. He smiled to himself as he watched Freddie go through the same washing ritual that his father used to perform in the back of the shop at the end of the day. Freddie, however, was not so particular about getting all the blood off his hands, as was Papa. He did seem to know his business, however, and Jake felt assured that the Forscher butcher shop on Gates Avenue would have a long and successful life.

He was pleasantly surprised when he stopped in at Raphael Cohn's candy store on the corner of Linden Avenue and Evergreen Street to find that the old shopkeeper still remembered him. Cohn's was just around the corner from the butcher shop, and Jake smiled to himself as he recalled the days of running in to buy candy with the penny he had earned for sweeping up and spreading new sawdust on the floor of his father's shop.

He had dinner once or twice at the home of his brother and sister-in-law, but found the atmosphere and conversation too much like the ones he remembered as a boy growing up on Halsey Street. Other evenings, he spent with Aunt Birgit and his mother, allowing them both to vent their feelings about the loss of Friedrich, patiently listening to their stories about "the old country." When he and Aunt Birgit left to return upstate, he would have no qualms about his mother's well-being, knowing that Freddie and Konstanze would see to it that her life would continue on as before.

He and Aunt Birgit traveled back together, a well-wrapped string of weisswurst links packed in ice — a parting gift of Freddie's that he had insisted on their taking — sitting between them on the train seat.

"Ach, how we all loved weisswurst back in Bavaria," said Aunt Birgit as Freddie had handed her the bundle. "Only in the spring we could get it," she said to Jake, "when the right herbs were in season." She turned back to Freddie. "It's nice to see that your Papa brought this tradition to America."

Jake merely nodded. He knew that she was only remembering her brother in her own way — and that, as his passing signified, the final spring awaited them all.

As they rode the West Shore Railroad upstate, both once again kept their own counsel. Whatever thoughts occupied Aunt Birgit, for Jake, he felt only a sense of relief that during his stay in Brooklyn, no one had brought up his painting.

36

Lindbergh's first solo flight across the Atlantic, as exciting as it was, could not dispel the spreading sense of foreboding that hung over America during the latter half of the '20s. The year 1927 ended not only the optimism of the Roaring Twenties, but appeared for many to be a sign that it was the effective end of an era of well-being and prosperity as well. New murmurings were coming out of Germany, and the news that a man who called himself Adolf Hitler had published a book called *Mein Kampf* two years earlier caused many German-Americans to dread another bout of anti-German sentiment on American soil.

The Great Crash two years later merely confirmed people's suspicions. Hard times and hard realities were already presaged, and for all intents and purposes the remaining days of the twenties were lost ones, better put out of mind and forgotten as soon as possible.

Culturally, the old guard began to see the handwriting on the wall. James Joyce had already shocked the literary establishment with the publication of his *Ulysses* in 1922 and, in 1929, the Museum of Modern Art had opened its doors in New York City. Neither the U.S. Post Office's burning of 500 copies of Joyce's book nor the outbursts of outrage by traditional critics at the concept of a museum dedicated to "modernism" could stem the tide. In some circles, Albert Einstein's paper on the unified field theory, proposed to the world in 1929, ominously foretold that the world would never again be the same.

Change was here to stay — and not all of it looked good.

Though still resistant to what was happening in the world of art, for Jake, the dire warnings that were heard almost daily of a coming Depression caused no considerable adjustments in either his life or his habits. He neither needed nor desired little more than what he already had. He was only glad that, before things got too bad, he had found enough work to have a well dug behind the house, and to have brought running water and electricity into Aunt Birgit's home. Most of the houses in West Hurley had now been "electrified," and the improvements were still novel enough to have Aunt Birgit hug Jake if he happened to be around to share in her childlike delight each time she turned on the tap or pulled down on the chain of one of her new lamps.

The decade also brought other endings for Jake. The late '20s had not only brought the death of his father, but also saw the passing of Ralph Radcliffe Whitehead and Rosie Magee — two people far apart in Woodstock's social stratum, yet both of them sharing a special place in Jake's memories. Even more significantly for him, however, was when, two years after burying his father, he had learned of the death of his friend and mentor, Birge Harrison. Death, though long touted as the great leveler, still affected the lives of the living differently, a fact brought home to Jake each time he reflected on his reactions to the passing of Friedrich Forscher and Birge Harrison.

Though he had not attended Harrison's funeral, he did go to the memorial service held for him by the members of the Woodstock Artist's Association in 1929. As was their practice when one of their members passed away, chairs had been set up for the occasion in the Association's main gallery. The latest show, "The Erogenous Zone," a group exhibit that featured the work of its members, looked down from the walls on the gathering of people. When the exhibit had opened the previous weekend — without the chairs filling the space in formal rows as they did today — it had drawn a much larger and noisier crowd than had come to honor Harrison.

As friends silently filed in, they sedately dispersed themselves around the room. Each row of unfolded metal chairs had its fair share of empty spaces, as people, coming in singly and in pairs, bunched together or spread discretely apart as they settled themselves on the hard seats. Throughout the large room, silent waves of a hand were occasionally punctuated by somber greetings conducted in hoarse stage whispers. A few of the men feigned a hearty

230

nonchalance as they smiled or joked, but their eyes betrayed their thoughts of the day when it would be their turn to be the guest of honor at just such a service.

Some found the erotic pictures in bad taste, considering that such an exhibit was unseemly for the solemn occasion of a memorial service for an artist that had been a beloved teacher and friend to many. Had they come to the opening reception the week before, they might have felt the same uneasiness at seeing the show — but that was another matter. One of the older women — dressed in such a hodge-podge of garishly colored items of clothing in 19th century bohemian fashion that one just *had* to know that she was an *artiste* — suggested in a louder-than-necessary whisper that the work should have been taken down or turned to the wall — or at the very least covered from view.

"Especially *this* junk!" she said with a snort. "It's not even good pornography!" grandly dismissing it all with a wave of her hand.

Those who paid attention to her merely raised their eyebrows, one man turning slightly away to hide a smile as he found himself a seat.

Jake found an empty chair near the door, a corner seat — his usual place of choice at most social gatherings. He had overheard the *artiste's* suggestion and did not find it overly inappropriate. They were, after all, gathering for the purpose of the artist's version of a traditional wake — a memorial service for a recently departed member of the artistic community.

Most of those present found the show immaterial to the proceedings. The Association, after all, had seen on its walls not only an entire range of American art, from representational to abstract with all variations in between, but had also regularly played host to such memorial services for those of its members who had passed on.

Holding such a gathering at which friends — and even enemies — aesthetic as well as actual — alternately rose from their seats to relate anecdotes or share memories of the eternally departed, was an old tradition among artists. For many, it served in place of going to wakes and burials, events that were considered to be reserved for immediate family and blood relations. An artist's *real* family gathered at a memorial service, a time-honored tradition that the Woodstock Artists Association had adopted soon after it had been founded and, for most of its members, what was on the walls was irrelevant — at least for that day. They held their counsel — much as they would have done at any exhibit. Judgments, after all, were for critics — and, as any artist would readily proclaim, what did critics know?

The room gradually settled down, and after a few minutes of muted conversation, people began in no particular order to rise sporadically to say a few words about Birge Harrison. From time to time, long uncomfortable pauses between speakers occurred. At one point, two men arose simultaneously, and a silent Alphonse and Gaston show ensued, the unintended mime show easing the generally somber mood. Most, however, sat with their own thoughts, content to let others speak their minds.

Jake had nothing to say publicly. Whatever he needed to communicate to or about Birge Harrison, he believed in his heart that it all had been accomplished when that man was still alive.

Instead, Jake sat silently while others stood one after another to speak their piece, his thoughts revolving around how long he had known Harrison, and of how many hours they had spent together. He could not help but let his mind dwell on their conversations about art.

He also thought about the conversations about art that he had never had with his father.

Both of these men — his father and his friend — had exerted an impact on his life. One, Jake thought, was for the good. The other? Well, who really knew?

Had he ever really known either man?

What made anyone think that they ever *knew* anyone? Least of all, themselves? If it could be said that he knew anything at all, it was that he was dimly aware of the illusion of reality within which lives were played out. And, especially in the presence of death, we all seemed to become children — children who have barely begun to realize that they existed as separate beings. Jake found himself no different in that respect.

What, after all, was "real" in his own life?

Had that evening with Irina at the Maverick Festival so many years ago been "real?" Had those lost years during the war "really" happened?

If he was sure of anything, it was that all of nature was a becoming, that nothing — no thing — that exists in this world was a "something" once and for all. Why should he expect that a Birge Harrison or a Friedrich Forscher could be any different from an Overlook Mountain?

Can the mystery surrounding Overlook be any different from that which surrounds people?

Still, if he'd been at the problem of trying to figure out how to capture the essence of what Overlook represented for him for the past twenty-one years — and not getting one step closer — how could he even begin to understand his father whom he'd known all his life?

Jake glanced around at the scattering of people in the Association's gallery. He saw Joe Bundy sitting up near the front and stared at the back of his head.

The odd thing was to look at someone, to interact with that someone, all the time never really considering that that someone will, at one time, disappear, will some day die.

People did not even seem to realize that they were disappearing while they were still here, while they were still interacting with each other. Did they realize that, from moment to moment, they were never really the *same* person? How many "I's" can a person be in the course of a normal life span?

Is there not an "I" that I know I once was, and an "I" that Papa had defined — and an "I" that I now am? A "me" that Birge Harrison had also helped to define? Or re-define?

And how many "theys" were present in those people he knew — or thought he knew? Who was his father? Who was Harrison? Who was Irina? Sarah? Had he ever really known any of them? He had lived with Aunt Birgit and Uncle Hans for years — but had he ever really *known* them? Or was he moving too quickly or too slowly through his own lifetime to see them properly? Were people — like himself and the mountain — "becoming" at different speeds, unable to have their separate existences truly intersect?

Had he not gone from boy to man? Had he not been trying to go from handyman to artist? His father knew the boy; Sarah and Irina knew the man; Harrison knew the budding painter. There were even those lost in the fields and trenches of France that knew him as a bringer of death.

How could anyone truly *know* him?

How can I know myself?

Mired in a sea of indecision and gloom, Jake quietly slipped out of the memorial service.

He had heard enough about what others had to say about Birge Harrison.

BOOK FOUR

1935 — 1941

37

THOUGH THEY HAD taken their toll on the nation, the years following the "Great Crash" of October 1929 proved on the whole not to be too onerous for the creative members of the Woodstock Colony. True, that since the League had closed its doors and the New York City artworld had temporarily turned its eyes from Woodstock things had slowed down somewhat but artists, long used to struggling against difficult odds, found ways to ameliorate their circumstances. Some artists opened their own schools in town, meeting their expenses by taking on students; all relieved their flagging spirits by keeping their minds and brushes working, often seeking new forms of camaraderie in an effort to keep creatively alert.

At times, small groups would meet at the studios and homes of friends, sharing an evening of banter and parlor games. A favorite pastime was for the artists to gather in someone's living room, seat themselves in a circle, and each armed with a pencil and a sheet of paper, compete in a contest of wit and skill. Someone, usually the host, would call out a topic which each had to depict in their sketchpads as quickly as possible.

"Picture an artist holding his own," the host might say, and thus would follow much broad humor and hearty laughter as the more audacious would not fail to render the double entendre in the most risqué manner imaginable. The level of hilarity would rise as the liquor flowed, more ingenious titles were devised, and contestants ever more daring in their depictions.

Eventually, such informal gatherings developed into more elaborate affairs, and it was not long before hosting a "dinner party" became fashionable amongst artists — though, with times being what they were, "dinner" would often consist of only crackers and cheese. As the "dinner party" gained in popularity, what to serve and whom to invite, however, often became more important than the original purpose behind coming together — namely, camaraderie and mutual support in tough times. In any event, having a get-together always had its advantages in that it helped relieve the nagging feeling that one was alone in the creative struggle and besides, having one of the Woodstock "stars" show up for the evening, didn't hurt.

Because of Joe's persistent attempts at "socializing" him, Jake soon found himself on the receiving end — and even sometimes accepting — invites to such evening events. After accompanying Joe to several of these gatherings, he was surprised to discover that he was being treated as a fellow painter by some of the established artists in town.

Inwardly pleased at his being perceived as an artist, he nevertheless became somewhat alarmed when invitations to dinners or gatherings began coming with increasing frequency. Though, when pressured, he usually went with Joe, from time to time he felt confident enough to go alone. Never, however, would he show up at such affairs on a regular basis. Had he accepted all invitations, Jake calculated that he'd never have to go to the same place twice over a six-month period. However, he chose not to and paced his socializing to fit his own needs and desires.

Generally, other than the chance encounter in town, he avoided any daytime commitments, almost always declining any afternoon get-togethers, whether planned for the weekend or not. If he were free from work, he preferred to use his daylight hours for either going out on sketching trips or for painting in his studio. He had still not taken Sarah up on her invitation to visit her studio, the thought of spending any extended time with her a daunting prospect. From time to time, if he found himself at some gathering on the same evening that she and Cal happened to be present, Sarah would repeat the invite, but he still had not found the courage to take her up on her offer of "coming over for a chat."

Yet, for the most part, he found that spending an evening amongst artists was not only a means of learning more about art, but could also be enjoyable. On the other hand, sitting down to a dinner with others — no matter how informal — was still a trying experience for him. As often as possible, therefore, he would time his visits accordingly, politely turning down a meal on some pretext of other commitment, while accepting an evening of after-dinner discussion. Though he both enjoyed and learned much from these evening gatherings, his ingrained shyness often pre-vailed and, preferring his own company, would spend long hours either in his study or hiking to his familiar haunts to "keep up" his sketching.

Jake's interest in reading had been growing, and there was hardly a time when he felt an hour or so with his favorite authors was ever a waste of time. A good deal of the talk that passed for polite conversation at the various artist's soirees was just too much for Jake at times — too often full of politics, and the "social con-dition," and the threat of another war in Europe — topics that hardly touched his interest or attention. For a while, the repeal of Prohibition in 1933 dominated some of the discussion, but this also held little interest for Jake.

Though he shared an occasional beer or two with Joe Bundy, he preferred the homemade root and birch beers that Aunt Birgit put up when she could get the ingredients and had the energy to put them together. It was one of the few occasions when she would let him help out in the kitchen, and it was his job to cap the bottles with the old hand-held press after she carefully ladled them full with the foamy liquid. On hot summer nights, both he and Aunt Birgit would be awakened at times by one of the bottles exploding during its fermentation, and he'd have to rush down into the cel-lar to see if he might salvage a drop or two.

Those nights when the two of them got up from bed to meet in the kitchen to partake of these unexpected treats became spe-cial events for both of them. At such times they would relax their usual reserve and speak of personal things. Aunt Birgit would of-ten speak of Uncle Hans, and Jake loved her stories about the "old country," or about how she had met Hans in America at Papa's shop. He sometimes shared his own thoughts about life, about painting, about his love of nature. Sometimes, Aunt Birgit, taking stock of her nephew now in his forties, would gently question him about "lady-friends," but he would always manage to change the subject. Thoughts of Sarah still troubled him, and he had yet to find anyone else who interested him.

Such intimate discussions were rare for Jake, however, since most of his conversations with others were regularly impersonal and about other things. Too often, for Jake's part, most conversations were about everything but what he wanted to talk about — art. The endless speculation about almost everything under the sun was one of the reasons he also avoided the daily newspapers. When arguments and defended opinions got too heated during his evenings at some artist's home — the more heated, in his estimation, the less it actually impinged on their day-to-day lives — he would make his good-byes, preferring to spend his time alone in his studio.

If he did not use the time to sketch or paint or prepare new canvases, he would settle back to re-read one of Shakespeare's tragedies, or savor some favorite passage in Aurelius or Ruskin. More often than not, a single line from any one of these writers would exercise his mind to a greater degree — and certainly to greater profit — than would reading through an entire newspaper or spending three hours of "discussion" at one of those evening sessions of hot air that artists seemed to never tire of blowing off. Still, he continued to accept an occasional invitation to some artist's home or studio for an evening of discussion if only for the few nuggets about art that he might come home with — and they *did* crop up in conversation from time to time. As his socializing increased, he eventually became more discerning, and he soon had his favorites, making it a point to accept only those invitations to gatherings that promised to enlighten him.

To his surprise — and secret delight — he soon discovered that the home of Sarah and Calvin Steele was just such a place, and he rarely failed to take advantage of their invitations.

38

It was not without considerable apprehension that Jake had accepted his first invitation to the Steele's for dinner in the spring of 1935. To his great relief, he discovered that his emotions did not betray him when Sarah greeted him at the door and, though that familiar electric thrill still flowed through his body at her touch, the hollow feeling at the pit of his stomach had hardly made itself felt during the course of the evening. It was, in fact, an altogether pleasurable experience — as comfortable as it might have been at home eating with Aunt Birgit — and, at evening's end, he readily accepted Sarah's invitation to come again.

Whether it was for dinner or for an evening soirée — or both — Jake increasingly found himself at ease at the Steele's. Although Sarah had made it a point to show him her small "playroom" one day where she turned her pots, he had still not felt easy in accepting her invitation to 'visit and chat' as she worked. Cal, in spite of his occasional abrasive ways, was mostly cordial to Jake, and he and Sarah never seemed to fail to come up with interesting guests. Jake had met Sarah's parents at one of their gatherings, the evening an especially pleasant one for him.

Cyrus and Mae Winters, Jake learned, lived in Bayshore, Long Island, and usually spent a few weeks during the summer with Sarah and Cal. They were the first archaeologists he had ever met and spoken with — and found their discussions of foreign travel, accounts of their participation in various "digs," and their wide knowledge of ancient civilizations, a constant source of wonderment.

On subsequent visits, Cyrus Winters — urbane, soft-spoken, and amiable — would spirit Jake off to a corner, regaling him with tale after tale of his trips and discoveries. It was not difficult for Jake to see which of her parents Sarah took after. Sarah was particularly pleased that her father had found such a willing listener in him, and never failed to give Jake ample notice as to her parents' impending visits.

He'd also met Morris Iskowitz at Sarah and Cal's, an excitable and contentious Russian Jew who seemed to Jake to have only two topics of discussion at his command: modern art and socialism. Though Jake found little to recommend in either subject, he had grown to like Morris, a broad-chested, burly man who resembled a longshoreman more than he did an artist. A sculptor and summer resident at Hervey White's Maverick, he lived in New York's Greenwich Village where he maintained a small studio. Jake would learn later that Iskowitz and his wife Myra had undergone terrible hardships in Europe — hardships that he'd never spoken of to Jake, but of which Sarah and Cal had informed him when they were alone.

Jake, though he rarely took part, was content to listen to Cal and Morris endlessly discuss the virtues of modernism, both passionately convinced that it was the only means of salvation for the future of art. Cal had been "converted" to the cause of modernism during his studies in Paris, and was, like Morris, never reluctant to discourse on the subject.

Jake recognized the names of many of the artists they would talk about, several, in fact, that had made considerable impact at the 1913 Armory Show. According to Iskowitz — and roundly seconded by Cal — it was Cézanne who broke the "fetters of academicism," and Picasso and Matisse who had then carried the torch forward. They wondered, however, if Duchamp had not perhaps carried it a bit too far. Jake remembered this name particularly since that artist's "Nude descending a staircase" had caused quite a disturbance during the Armory Show, and had been described by someone as looking like "an explosion in a shingle factory" — a description that Jake still considered both humorous and fitting.

During such discussions, Cal would often turn his glance pointedly at Jake, as if to tell him that if he also did not see the handwriting on the wall, then — well, he would have to suffer whatever misfortune was sure to befall the traditionalists. Jake, however, never rose to the bait, content to stand aside and watch and listen to the excited volubility flow from Morris's mouth, amazed that anyone could talk for so long — and so loud — without ever seeming to stop for breath.

There were others that he had met at Sarah and Cal's, of course, but many came and went after a single visit, transients that Jake would never see again. He and Joe Bundy became "regulars," often coming together, but in spite of who might show up, Jake usually found that the evenings were generally pleasurable. The Steeles were lavish in their entertainment, and it was a rare evening when he would come home without some new information about art.

Such evenings of ample food and drink made it seem as if the ravages that the Depression had been wreaking in densely populated metropolitan areas were non-existent and, truth be told, the Woodstock Colony had probably fared better than most small towns in the hard years following the Crash of 1929. Life in a good deal of rural America was certainly not quite as horrific as it was in crowded urban areas where breadlines and the homeless were constantly on view. The rural folk of America tended to fall back on their Yankee ingenuity, finding scores of ways to increase their income by a few pennies and supplementing their food supply by doing a few more chores to make better use of their land and livestock.

Jake had discovered a particularly agreeable way to bring in a few extra dollars by turning his carpentry skills to the making of picture frames for fellow artists. He had long been doing it for himself, and he soon found a steady stream of customers for his handiwork, a corner of his studio now set aside as his workshop. When his frames started showing up on the Woodstock Artists Association's walls, Joe couldn't resist teasing him with a, "Well, that's a start."

Like most of the locals, Jake and Aunt Birgit just added to their poultry flock and the number of residents in their pigsty. Their table was never really wanting, their ordinarily frugal tastes amply supplied with fresh vegetables from their extended garden. When things appeared to be getting tougher, Jake had simply spaded up more of the yard, giving over sections of the lawn to larger rows of beans, tomatoes, squash, and greens.

What they did not eat when in season, Aunt Birgit either traded with neighbors or preserved for winter use, eking out meals with jams of huckle- and blueberries that she had hunted down and picked herself. Jake's rifle and fishing gear had been hauled out of the back room and, after due cleaning and mending, was put back into use. Venison and pork became common staples and, though he still had no great love for fishing, Jake had to admit that there were few things sweeter on one's plate than freshly caught brook trout from the nearby Esopus Creek.

Of late, when Jake and Joe hiked up the Esopus to Shokan or beyond for their painting excursions, Jake always brought along a pole, and was sure to tuck lures and hooks into his paint box, rarely returning home without something to add to an evening meal. He and Joe would share their catch at the end of the day or, if Joe preferred — which he often did — would come along with Jake to share a meal at Aunt Birgit's table.

In spite of the hard times, the automobile was fast displacing horse-drawn conveyances, and Jake had been much impressed when he saw the first new Model-T pickup truck in the village. Motorized vehicles had become so prevalent in the town, that by 1931 Woodstock had to deputize its first policeman in an effort to keep order in the flow of traffic on its narrow streets and, as far as Jake could see, the horse-drawn vehicle on public roads seemed headed for extinction. When the stagecoach to Woodstock had been replaced with a motorbus, Jake began seriously thinking about "upgrading" his means of transportation by getting one of those motor trucks himself some day.

With things the way they were, however, he could still not see his way clear toward making such a purchase, seeking other ways to make do for the present. He had already sold his uncle's heavier, bluestone-carting wagon, and had purchased a smaller cart for the hauling jobs that came his way. The smaller vehicle needed only one horse to pull it, and by getting rid of one of the horses he recognized a substantial savings in outlay. And though he largely depended on his feet to get him around, he had also purchased a small two-seated gig for both his and his aunt's use. Jake used it only for traveling longer distances, but Aunt Birgit, who could handle a horse as well as Jake, found it very handy for her monthly trips for supplies at Dominica's general store and bakery over on the Plank Road.

All things considered, Jake found little to complain of in his circumstances. He was healthy and resourceful and faced no real insurmountable problems. With a roof over their heads, three meals a day, and a few dollars coming in every day or so, by his reckoning he and Aunt Birgit were well off in comparison to many others. Neither of them wanted for anything essential, both content to ride out whatever the circumstances brought.

When, in 1932 he had heard about the Bonus Marches being formed by fellow veterans in an effort to force the Government to release funds to them, he talked it over with Aunt Birgit. They both agreed that they might well do without the handout, and so he ignored the call to join them. When he had heard later about the disastrous results of the March, he was glad that he had chosen to stay at home.

As for the Depression and its general effects on the artist, most had been long used to a frugal fare in any event, and only those most vocal about "making a living" from their art seemed to feel the pinch — real or otherwise — and to make their displeasure felt. Jake had little sympathy for them, his long years of earning his way by other means too much of an ingrained habit for him to waste much time feeling sorry for anyone too proud to perform manual labor for their bread. By this time, he had imbibed enough of the stoicism of Marcus Aurelius for it to become for him a mark of the self-reliant man.

Some American artists, however, stirred by new ideas of socialism coming from Europe by those fleeing what seemed sure to be another World War, supported whatever cause promised to improve their lot. Much to Jake's irritation, many artists, though never stooping to such measures as actually *performing* hard labor, eagerly embraced the idea of identifying with the "worker." Many became as vocal as any union leader in condemning "big business" and the "government" — rather than their own laziness and poor skills — for keeping them down by depriving them of earning a living. If he admired their desire to protest inequality and injustice, he nevertheless deplored their dishonesty in affectedly posing as "one of the downtrodden."

Overnight, it seemed to Jake, landscape and still life and portrait painters in New York City became "Social Realists," turning their talents to depicting the plight of the disenfranchised and the exploited. Many artists began dressing like workmen, eager to show their solidarity in deed as well as in picture. They haunted union halls and hung on the fringes of demonstrations, scoured the slums and eyed the breadlines in search of suitable motifs of governmental suppression and grinding poverty, scurrying back to their studios after such a "hard day's work" to put brush to canvas to show that they also "bled" like the common man.

Woodstock, always a reflecting mirror of what was happening on the larger scene, of course followed suit, and though more difficult to find such heart-rending subjects in fields and country lanes, sympathizing artists were not hard to find around town. Discussions and arguments about their "plight" cropped up more and more at gatherings, and it would not be long before government assistance in the form of newly elected President Roosevelt's programs began to be clamored for — and eventually received — by some of the Woodstock artists.

The Woodstock Artists Association was still going strong, serving as a powerful vocal proponent of what was becoming known around the world as "The Woodstock School" of painting, and many of their members meant to have their portion of government funds. Such programs as the Public Works of Art Project — "PWAP" to the initiated — the Fine Arts Project — "FAP" — and others like them were brought to the Colony to mete out commissions and funds to artists — often to the loudest if not always to the more talented or the most needy. And though these government handouts undoubtedly helped put food on the table for a great many deserving artists, in the end it had the far more disastrous effect of only bringing an unhealthy competition and divisiveness to the once closely-knit artistic community.

At times, artists were pitted against each other in a grim game of one-upmanship. Politics, rather than actual merit, often was the deciding factor in who got what. Commissions to paint murals for public buildings — one of the more publicly visible programs of giving work to artists — were eagerly sought and aggressively fought for. Resultant hurt feelings and outrage at being overlooked caused life-long rifts between many of the Woodstock artists, leaving scars that never fully healed even long after the Depression was over. What once had been a confraternity of artists in search of the "perfect painting," had become a surly group of sniping and combative men and women in search of the "perfect society" that guaranteed their survival.

Of the more salutary effects of governmental help for the town were the funds which came out of the National Youth Administration that went into the building of the Resident Youth Center on the newly paved and widened Woodstock-Saugerties Turnpike, a short distance outside of the village. Its cornerstone laid by Eleanor Roosevelt in 1939, the handsome stone building served to teach many idle young people such employable skills as masonry and carpentry. Built of local field and bluestone, the Center served as a focal point for the community, and stood as a solid example of what the wise disbursements of governmental largesse might accomplish.

While some visual artists were shamelessly squabbling about who ought to get what, it would largely be the theater people who were keeping Woodstock alive as a viable art colony. There were five working theaters in Woodstock during the years following the Depression, and though none could be considered great financial successes, they did serve to keep the community together.

Without some cohesive influence, the fiercely individual nature of creative personalities oftened threatened such communities, making them always in danger of completely falling apart. Byrdcliffe, largely confining its activities to the manufacture of furniture, had already been fading as a cultural force in the colony, and Hervey White and his Maverick were not faring much better. August of 1931 saw the last of Maverick's famous August Festivals, and one of the biggest draws to Woodstock had sadly come to an end.

To their credit, some of the members of the Woodstock Artists Association tried to ameliorate the hard times by doing something for themselves. A small group formed the "Friends of Art" and did what they could to help deserving artists by purchasing their work and, when they needed to supplement their funds to do that, even ran an Artists' Carnival in 1932 to raise money. Such self-help efforts as these — and the few who opened their own studio-schools — managed to keep Woodstock's reputation intact, and though nowhere like it had done in the '20s, managed to attract a steady but small trickle of new artists to the colony.

Jake could not help but be aware of what was going on, the subject of hard times almost always somewhere on the agenda of whoever was hosting an evening get-together. He had to smile when he heard of some artists trading their work for groceries or to pay off a dentist or doctor bill. It reminded him of his grandfather in Polling, Germany, who had run artists out of his butcher shop when they tried to pay him with pictures. Fortunately, local merchants and professionals displayed a bit more empathy — if not also a bit more culture — than did his grandfather.

Although Jake empathized with artists, he had as much if not more sympathy for his fellow workmen. He had to agree with those locals who wanted to know who was going to help *them.* If a painter or sculptor merited subsidizing, why didn't the government see fit to help out the storekeeper or the plumber or the stonecutter or carpenter? Wasn't the labor of a common workman as valuable as that of the artist?

Who was it that dug the artist's foundations, did their building and repairing, cut their firewood, and ran water pipes into their homes and studios? The old enmity that separated the townsfolk and the art community flared up anew, and not only were there bad feelings between locals and artists again, but the rising competition among artists in search of handouts also served to exacerbate the growing sense of dissension and unease.

As much as possible, Jake kept clear of contention, picking up whatever jobs were available and, when he could find none, devoting his time and energy to either his painting or to helping out with the chores at home. Better to use his time and energies on those things he could do something about. He was content to stand aside and let the weekend "philosophers" solve the bigger problems.

39

On a pleasant sunny morning, during one of his solitary jaunts up Overlook Mountain in search of new motifs, Jake came upon an old man seated on a fallen tree. A long walking-staff was resting on his shoulder, and, as far as Jake could tell, the man seemed hunched over in sleep, his eyes closed tightly beneath the bill of a tattered and once-white seaman's cap. Trying not to disturb him, Jake stepped off in a wider arc to move around behind him.

"Howdy," the old man said before Jake had taken but a few steps, and he stopped to return the greeting with a small wave.

"Cap'n Bob's the name. Yours?"

"Jake," he answered, and walked over to extend his hand to the old man. "Pleased to meet you."

"Back at you, son," and as he released Jake's hand, added, "Got a good gol-darned grip there, Jake. A working man's hand."

"I do a lick now and then," Jake said.

"What's a working man doin' with that rigmarole slung over his back? Looks like arty stuff."

"Well, it is that," said Jake with a smile. He shifted his load and propped his boot a few feet away from where the 'Cap'n' sat on the fallen tree. "I try my hand at painting now and then, too."

"A working man that paints pictures!" The old man snorted loudly, and slapped his thigh. "Wonders never will cease, I guess."

"And what's a 'cap'n' doing up here? I haven't seen one ship in all the times I've ever climbed this mountain."

The old man chuckled. "Neither have I, for that matter. Haven't *seen* a gol-darned one anywhere, in fact, for — well, let's see now — mebbe sixty years."

Jake slipped his arms out of the straps holding his painting gear and sat down alongside the old man. "You were a ship captain?"

"Hell no, boy! I shipped out as deckhand on a whaler for a year or two — worked out of Nantucket when I was a lad. The 'cap'n' handle was given me by landlubbers. Stuck ever since even though I ain't walked the deck of a gol-darned ship again. I'm a landlubber myself nowadays. My feet only know the land — and mostly this old hill here that *some* people like to call a mountain." He turned to Jake. "Hell's bells, boy, I *seen* gol-darned mountains!"

"Well," said Jake, jerking his thumb behind him. "This one suits me just fine."

"You're a mite off the gol-darned beaten track," said the Cap'n. "You come up here often? You're not lost?"

"Nope. I just prefer the quieter places."

"Yep," mused the Cap'n. "I stay off her on weekends, now. Too many gol-darned people traipsin' around." He sighed. "She suits me fine too, Jake — even if she ain't a full-fledged mountain."

Jake smiled.

Then, looking sideways up at Jake, he asked, "You married, young fella?"

Jake shook his head.

"Didn't figger you was — you don't have that hang-dog look about you." He clapped a horny hand on Jake's shoulder. "Avoid it as long as possible, boy — it's like being sentenced to parole with no chance of life, marriage is." He chuckled at his own witticism.

After a pleasant half-hour or so, Jake was captivated with the old man's store of wood lore and, after exchanging good-byes, promised to look him up at his "digs" over in Mink Hollow.

Jake held good to his promise, and as the months went by and their friendship slowly grew, Cap'n Bob proved to be a great source of new and interesting information about the Catskills — even about those places on Overlook that Jake had felt were part of his own province. The old man knew as many and a lot more of those out-of-the-way parts of the mountain that Jake had been exploring since he was a boy. Always willing to learn, Jake made it a regular practice to visit the old man from time to time at his "digs," a ramshackle, sagging building that appeared to have once served as a barn for a stately but deserted house that stood across the road.

Cap'n Bob shared the weatherworn old barn with several goats and a flock of chickens and ducks that lived on the other side of a wall separating his living quarters from the rest of the building. His "parlor" contained an old cook stove, a rickety table, one chair that looked hand-made, and a cot whose bedclothes, as many times as Jake had come to visit, never seemed to be made up — the whole affair not much above ten-foot square. Cap'n Bob appeared to have pared life down to its essentials, everything in his home within a few paces of each other and well within his reach.

If he was poor in domestic appurtenances, Cap'n Bob was rich in firepower. Jake had never seen so many and so diverse a collection of long and hand-held guns in his life. They were hanging on the walls, stacked in corners, crammed under his cot, and lying about on the few cleared spaces available.

"They all work," said Cap'n Bob. "I fire every gol-darned one of 'em at least once a year. Don't hunt much anymore — but I fire 'em to keep 'em in shape."

Though he sometimes sported a tanned goatskin across his lap on colder days, Cap'n Bob seemed not to favor trophies of his hunting prowess, and had no stuffed heads or mounted game adorning his walls.

"Got more respect for 'em than that," he said when Jake brought it up one day. "Bad enough we got to eat the gol-darned things than we should keep mementos of their killin'. Only them city slickers'd do *that*." He spat on the floor. "Stuffin' and hangin' a deer head for all to see would be just as disgustin' and uncivilized as a surgeon displayin' leftovers on his gol-darned living room wall — an arm or a leg or some gol-darned thing such as that — from his last amputation."

In fact, there was no adornment on any of Cap'n Bob's walls other than his firearms, not even a calendar or a clock, until, after Jake had visited a few times, he had given the old man one of his small oil renditions of Overlook. He had offered it as a way of saying thank you for his friendship, and for sharing his considerable lore concerning the mountain.

Cap'n Bob had accepted the gesture graciously enough and, after holding it out at arm's length, had only commented, "Well, it's *pretty* enough. But it ain't the Overlook *I* know."

Still, he deigned to hang it after Jake had left and though he never mentioned the painting again, the fact that it stood alone on the wall over his cot told Jake that he had accorded it all the proper honor he could muster.

Cap'n Bob never refused Jake entry into his modest dwelling to share in an hour or so of "palaver" or, weather permitting, of going with him from time to time on walks up Overlook. When they stayed at the "digs," the Cap'n would sometimes brew up some coffee, most often thick enough to stand one's spoon in an upright position at its dead center without its toppling over. Cap'n Bob's eating habits both fascinated and repelled Jake. When necessary, the old man would kill a goat and feed off it for as many meals — breakfast, dinner or supper — as it took to entirely devour it. Jake made the mistake of visiting Cap'n Bob the day after he had finished eating something like thirty duck and chicken eggs over the previous three meals.

"Don't have an icebox to keep the gol-darned things in," explained Cap'n Bob, "so I hafta eat 'em afore they go bad."

When the odor from Cap'n Bob's resultant flatulence got too much for Jake to manage, he suggested going out back to fire off a few of the guns. They took turns firing shots at tin cans or just simply up into the air from the armful of guns they had brought with them. Jake managed to keep the old man outdoors for as long a time as he reckoned it might take until it was safe to go back to the "digs."

In spite of such idiosyncrasies, Jake always found the old man full of homely wisdom and plain talk. As they conversed, Cap'n Bob would lay back on his cot with a pumped-up air gun that he periodically used to kill bugs, gleefully punctuating his conversation with a "Got the gol-darned pest!" if some hapless fly landed too close or an ant crawled too slowly up a wall.

Jake was especially grateful to Cap'n Bob for acquainting him with the writings of Henry David Thoreau — another woods-lover who he'd discovered had much to say about nearly everything that was close to Jake's heart.

"*Civil Disobedience* was the best gol-darned book I ever read," the Cap'n said one day. "Not that I read 'em all that much, come to think on it. Don't much care for the gol-darned things — rather go out and learn about the world for myself." He looked off into the distance as if trying to see or recall something. "As I remember, some shipboard mate lent it to me while we was shipped out for a spell. Yep. That was it. Not much to do aboard ship, you know

— and any book that said it was about disobedience got me all perked up anyhow." He smiled. "Now that Thoreau feller was a man who knew which gol-darned end was up."

It would not be long before Thoreau's slim volume of *Civil Disobedience* and his longer *Walden* found their places on Jake's bookshelves and, like his other favorites, both books were soon much thumbed through and annotated with his own notes and observations.

40

"Sooner or later you're going to have to break the ice."

Jake looked up from his cup of coffee at Joe sitting back in his seat, a lop-sided grin on his face.

Jake didn't bother to respond.

They were having lunch at Deannie's, a popular eating-place for the town regulars. Situated on Mill Hill Road, the old transformed trolley car had almost instantly attracted a faithful clientele ever since it had opened its doors. Good food, fair portions, friendly waitresses, and reasonable prices had assured its place in what Jake reckoned to be now more than two dozen new eateries that had cropped up since Woodstock's booming expansion throughout the '20s.

Joe leaned forward, setting his elbows on the table. He had an earnest look on his face.

"Well, isn't it about time?" he asked. "How long has it been, anyway? How long have you been painting?"

"I don't know," said Jake. "You want me to figure in those years that I did house painting, too?"

Joe rolled his eyes. "Come on, Jake. You've been at it for — what — twenty, twenty-five years at least?"

"Well, now that depends on what exactly you mean. Sure, I've been *at* it for a long time, but it seems to me I've got a ways to go before I'd feel comfortable styling myself a 'painter' by throwing in my lot over at the Association."

"Here we go again," said Joe.

"No, I'm serious, Joe. Granted that I've learned how to make a decent picture — at least they look as good as some of the stuff I see hanging at the Association from time to time."

"Then?"

"Well, for one thing, there's still what's in my own head that I have to consider. Wasn't it you who told me years ago that I had to please myself?"

"And?"

"Well, I still haven't gotten to that point. I still don't satisfy myself. I know in my heart that what I get down on canvas is not what I really want there."

"And just what is *that*?"

"I can't say exactly. But I know I haven't been successful yet in getting my ideas down in paint." Jake frowned and looked at his friend. "I've still got a long way to go before I start shoving my paintings into people's faces."

Joe frowned. "I'm not so sure that *any* of us can ever say that our paintings perfectly reflect what we intend," said Joe. "Do you really think that I'm happy with everything I turn out? Do you think that *any* of us are?"

"Then why do it?" asked Jake. "Why go through all the rigmarole of hanging a show, of having a reception, of inviting people to look at what you've done, if you yourself are not happy with it?"

"Well, because we have to I guess."

"*Have* to?"

"Look at it this way. A painting needs a viewer, another human being to complete the act. An unseen work of art — whether it's a poem, a book, or a painting — is an incomplete thing. In order to become 'art' it needs some kind of human response other than that of the creator. Music needs to be heard, a book has to be read, and a painting has to be *seen*."

"I see the sense in that," said Jake. "But that just brings me back to my argument. I'm not convinced that what I'm doing can yet be called 'art.' That piece of music, or book, or painting that you talk about *might* have some claim to people's hearing, reading or seeing. As far as I can tell, my canvases are still just experiments. You just admitted yourself that *you* weren't sure — that *most* of you weren't sure that your work was up to snuff — and you've been at it a good deal longer than I have."

"Well *all* art is 'experiment,' Jake. Only history can decide whether what we do can be called art."

"So maybe what you fellows are doing is advertising your failures, hanging up pictures that you know in your heart are 'experiments.' You know how long I'd be in business if I tried such a thing? I can just see me telling old man Snyder over at his boarding house, 'Well now Mr. Snyder, I've cut up and nailed together some lumber in your back room there. Why don't you come take a look and see if you can figure out what it is I made. Maybe if you like it, you'll pay me for it.'"

"It's not the same thing, Jake. You're comparing two different things."

"I'm comparing *my* work with *your* work. I don't much see the difference in that. Labor is labor."

"You're comparing art with a simple craft."

"Meaning what? Besides the fact that you just got finished telling me that half the time you weren't even *sure* you were making art, how is making pictures any different from making bookcases?"

"Oh come on, Jake! You can't tell me that you really don't see the difference between say, a painting by Rembrandt and — and — a *chair* made by one of those furniture-makers over in Byrdcliffe!"

"Of course there's a *difference*. Sometime down the line, history — according to you — decides which of the two has more value. And even though not everyone who comes along might be able to appreciate the Rembrandt, it's a pretty sure bet that every single human who attempts it, will be able to sit on that chair — and, I suppose, an equally sure bet that history will *still* decide on the Rembrandt."

Joe's head nodded emphatically. "So?"

"So — I'll bet you a dollar to a doughnut that not even Rembrandt *knew* that would happen, or knew that history would eventually come down on his side. I'll even bet that somewhere deep down, even *he* compared his occupation to that of the fellow down the street who made furniture for a living — and I guess that sometimes even he felt that he came up on the short side."

"Well, now, that's the point, isn't it Jake? We exhibit our work to measure it against our fellows, to see how the public will react. The feedback we get helps us to go back to our studios and improve on what we've done."

Jake stared into Joe's eyes. "You'd really change the way you paint because someone didn't like your work?"

256

"Well, yes, to some degree, I guess," said Joe.

Jake shook his head. "I just don't get how anyone other than me could look at one of my paintings and decide that I had failed — or succeeded, for that matter. How can they know what was in my head when I painted it?"

"They don't *have* to know, Jake. All they have to do is *appreciate* it."

"And that's it? All you care about is that someone appreciates it?"

"Well, maybe if they like it enough, they may even want to buy it, and take it home with them so that they could look at it and appreciate it whenever they darn well pleased."

"I figured that we'd get to *that* part of it sooner or later," said Jake.

"Oh, I know your line about selling, Jake. I'm not going to get into that again. Look, all I'm saying is that you ought to consider showing your work. Some of it is damn fine. That view of Overlook you gave me last year for my birthday holds a place of honor in my studio. I can't begin to tell you how many compliments it gets from my visitors. I won't mention any names, but one artist has been after me to sell it to him ever since he's seen it. But I'd never sell it! It's a gift that I really treasure — and *not* just because we're friends."

Jake took a deep breath. "Joe, listen. I don't know who said what and, to tell you the God's honest truth, I don't really care. I'll ask you again. How do *they* know what I painted — or *tried* to paint?"

"No one had any trouble recognizing that it was a painting of Overlook Mountain."

Jake shrugged. "Anyone capable of holding a Brownie box camera still for a moment can get a likeness of Overlook."

"So, how about that artist who wants to buy your painting from me? He must know *some*thing about painting?"

Jake shook his head. "And how's he any different from anyone else?"

"He's one of your *peers*," Joe said with exasperation.

"Humph!" grunted Jake. "He's not *my* peer! Not a single person has an inkling as to who I am or of what I'm trying to accomplish." He looked pointedly at Joe. "Not even you," he added with a sigh.

Not even me, *for that matter* — Jake thought.

"Well, Jake, you want to be better known — at least by artists — maybe it's time you joined the Association."

"Me?"

"Yes, you! I'm sure they'd accept you in a minute."

Jake looked down into his empty cup. "Not sure *I*'d accept it." He looked at Joe. "I belonged to a group once — we even all dressed alike." Jumbled memories of the war swam in and out of his mind. "Didn't like it then — not sure I'd like it now, being part of a group."

Joe looked into Jake's troubled eyes and decided not to push it. "Well, I know this much about you, Jake. You are as stubborn as a mule."

"*Dick,*" Jake said with a laugh.

"Dick?" said Joe with a puzzled look.

"*Dick.* Thick — a *dummkopf* —thickhead " said Jake. "My Uncle Hans would tell me that I was '*Dick*' like my father. Maybe he was right, I don't know." He shrugged. "But damn it all, Joe, who knows better than me whether my work is ready to be shown or not?"

"Well, John Carlson used to tell us that we were not always our best critics. He told us that sometimes we get stuck in our own heads, and don't really see what we're about. 'Don't paint what you're looking at,' he used to say, 'Look at what you're *painting.*'" Joe tapped his finger on the table to emphasize his point. "All I'm trying to say, Jake, is that sometimes it just takes another pair of eyes to help us see our own work."

Jake waved away Joe's argument. "Listen, you know as well as I do that the painting I gave you is only one of a long series that I've done of Overlook Mountain. And though I'm mighty pleased that you like it, to my eyes it doesn't come any nearer to what I'm trying to paint than any of the other renditions I've done."

Joe hesitated a moment before saying, "Maybe it's just fear."

Jake looked up and rubbed his chin. "You know, Joe, now that just might not be too far off the mark." He sighed. "I've thought about fear for a long time. Making pictures comes from a deep place in me. A place that's still a mystery to me — a place that Birge Harrison used to tell me holds the secret to the 'why" an artist does what he does. I might not be able to tell you outright why I want to make pictures, but I *do* know that it's not to please others or to make a living from them. As far as my father was concerned, whatever the reason a man became an artist, it was nothing more than foolishness." Jake looked down and fiddled with his napkin. "Maybe the fear is that I'll never be able to get down deep enough inside me to recognize that 'why' when I see it, or ...." He looked up at Joe. "Or maybe the truth of it is that it's just fear that my father might've been right."

Joe remained silent for a moment or two, mulling over what Jake had just said.

"Well, think about this — maybe exhibiting your work would help you overcome that fear, Jake. You know, give you some feedback from someone other than your father."

"Yes, but there's still *me*," said Jake, pointing his thumb at his chest. "Showing my work might be a way of testing my grit, but I still say that I have to please me." He looked over at Joe. "And not just because you told me so, but because *I* feel I have to — in here." He pointed at his chest again.

"You know, Jake, becoming a member of the Association doesn't mean you have to stop being *you*. All I'm saying is that it would give you a place to exhibit your work — get some feedback." He looked into his friend's eyes. "Maybe even give you a bit of confidence."

"I have plenty of confidence in my handiwork — I both accept and expect praise for my carpentry, for example. And, of course, I demand fair recompense for my labor. But how can I expect the same from doing something that I can't justify even to myself?" His mind flashed back to Crum Elbow on the Hudson. "Can't claim with a straight face that it even *comes* from me? Setting aside my argument that labor is labor, the *purpose* of making pictures is not the same thing as putting up shelves — I *know* when a shelf is needed, and when it is made correctly. I'm *hired* to make a bookcase — but no human being ever asked me to make pictures, Joe" He slapped both hands palm down on the table. "And, that my friend, is the long and short of it."

Joe threw up his hands and shoved his chair back from the table. "All I can say, Jake, is that you just might be your own worst critic. Carlson was right — we just can't judge our own work." He rose and laid his hand on Jake's shoulder. "Jake," he said earnestly, "if you can't trust the opinion of others, at least trust mine. You *are* a painter."

"I appreciate that, Joe."

Joe merely shrugged his shoulders in response.

When they stepped outside Jake said, "You have to understand, Joe, that I'm not arguing the point whether I'm a painter or not. As you say, only history can decide that. What I *am* saying is that I am not yet painting what *I* want to paint. And until that time — if it ever comes — you'll just have to put up with my stubbornness — my *Dickkopf* — my thick head."

Joe just shook his head, and left with a wave of his hand over his shoulder as they stepped outside of Deannie's to go their separate ways.

41

Afterwards, local merchants joked that it took an act of God to make the people in Washington finally spend federal money on the plight of someone other than artists in Woodstock — but while they were in the midst of it, the flood of July 1935 had been no laughing matter. No one in living memory could recall such a thing, and couldn't believe that they were actually watching over three feet of water coursing down Tinker Street, turning Mill Hill Road into a veritable rapids as the swollen Sawkill Creek sped down its long incline, rushing past its usual turn after Disch's mill and continuing on down the turnpike toward Saugerties. No one could remember such a rainstorm. No one could remember such an angry Sawkill.

Not a soul was lost, but with the resultant property damage, Jake had found more than enough work to keep him busy for the rest of that year. So much so, in fact, that for the first time since he could remember, he had not touched paint to canvas for weeks on end. Most of the first floors of homes and hotels, of stores and restaurants that had been built along the creek were water damaged, and there were months of cleaning up and re-building ahead. The federal government had released funds to repair roads and rebuild damaged bridges, and for a time at least, Woodstock laborers and carpenters enjoyed a sudden boost in employment. It took a disaster, but things looked good for a while, and housewives were happy to be able to squirrel away a few dollars from their husband's paycheck each week for the first time in many years.

West Hurley, though thoroughly soaked by the heavy downpour brought on by the rainstorm, was far enough from the Sawkill Creek to escape such damage. Outside of a flooded cellar whose waters soon subsided, Jake was pleased that he and Aunt Birgit had suffered no greater loss than having to contend with a water-logged basement. After he had sopped up and cleaned the floor and furnace, he had to admit that the old hand-dug cellar had a fresh new face. The laid-up bluestone walls and the bedrock that had been its floor were laved clean as years of dust and wood ashes had been washed away for the first time in who knew how long.

Others, however, were not so lucky — especially those whose homes or property bordered the Sawkill — and Jake felt a bitter-sweet satisfaction in making money from their misfortune. He appreciated the extra income, but felt sad that it had to be as a result of a disaster. Still, floors and walls had to be replaced, and God only knew how many new shelves he would have to build in the next year or so. So much work came his way, in fact, that he was finally able to retire his horse and purchase a second-hand pickup truck before the year was out. Life had a way of meting out the good and the bad — and Jake just turned his attention to what he knew, and to what he was able to do. When summoned, he picked up his toolbox with mixed emotions to repair or rebuild what he could.

As Jake went from job to job throughout the area, his "artist's eye" took in the changes that had transformed several familiar places. Much of the Sawkill's banks had been altered by the swiftly moving water, and he noted old sites where he had once set up his easel that were now obliterated, while new ones showed different prospects and fresh promise. He made several hasty sketches from high points in town while the water was still high, but felt ashamed in doing so when he realized that some of the people standing nearby were still watching their property float away.

When he had pulled out these sketches later that autumn, after the town had pretty much been returning to normal, he thought at first that, as a kind of memorial, he might try a painting that would show how much of the town was under water. Reflection, however, held his hand.

He recalled Joe Bundy having related to him John Carlson's dictum to avoid the bizarre, the out-of-the-ordinary, and to con-centrate on the eternal truths that surrounded us from day to day. What might such a depiction of a town in straits actually accom-plish other than his skills in doing so? Besides, he never much cared to put buildings or roads or, for that matter, anything that revealed the hand of man into his paintings. He preferred nature in her original state, always making sure, for instance, that his renditions of Overlook never included the presence of man. He tucked the drawings away, content to save them as a reminder of the event, and as a warning that even nature, with all her beauty, also had a capricious capacity for evil.

"Yessir," Cap'n Bob was saying a few weeks later as he and Jake walked beside the upper reaches of Esopus Creek. "Yessir, she is full of surprises to those who don't know how to look."

Jake waited for the story that was sure to follow.

"Now take this gol-darned creek here, for instance," began Cap'n Bob. "Wouldn't think that if you got enough of that water there in one place, that you might have a serious problem on your hands, would you?"

Jake brought up the recent flooding in Woodstock.

"I'm not talking about a gol-darned freakish thing like an inland flash flood," said Cap'n Bob. "I'm talking about the sea — the gol-darned *ocean*!" He looked up at Jake. "Ever been to sea, Jake?"

"Well, I crossed the Atlantic on a troopship during the war — across and back. Didn't much care for the experience."

"Shoot! I don't mean *visit* the gol-darned sea, boy! You was just a tourist. I mean *living* on the sea."

"Nope, I never have," said Jake. "And, I don't much ever want to, either."

"Can't fault you there, son. The gol-darned ocean has more moods than a woman. *Worse* than living with a woman, trying to live with the sea. I know, because I tried living with both. Couldn't put up with neither one, for long," he said with a shake of his head.

Jake thought about Cap'n Bob's "digs" and allowed as how a woman might have some objections of her own about sharing a life with him.

"Sea's *meaner* too, the ocean is," Cap'n Bob continued. "She's tricky and deceitful, ready to snatch away your gol-darned soul the minute you think she's your friend. They give her names, people do, but that's just a sham. The gol-darned seas have no names, you know. They're just too big to fit under such nonsense as *names*." He looked at Jake. "We do that, you know — call 'em such things as 'Atlantic' or 'Pacific' or what have you — to try and get on a more personal footin' with 'em. Pshaw! As if *that* helps! There ain't *no* name that will ever hold a sea, and there ain't never gettin' on any kind of first name basis with 'em, no matter how hard we try. I've seen her go from dead calm to fifty-foot seas in less than fifteen minutes." He shook his head. "Yessir, she's a sneaky, graspin', nasty, restless, and deceptive old witch, boy. There's no filling *her* gol-darned belly anytime soon. No wonder she harbors so many monsters in her briny bosom. I'm glad to be shed of her, Jake. You can have her, for all I care." He stamped his foot on the ground. "Give me good ol' terry firma any day!"

"Well, I can't say that I speak from any long experience," offered Jake, "but I can say that I don't disagree with you." The memory of the young man falling from the high lines of his ship into the Hudson River that he had witnessed as a boy flashed through his mind. "I surely do love these old Catskill Mountains and have no desire to ever move anywhere else."

"Shows you got *some* sense, boy." Then, glancing up at Jake, he said, "But don't go getting too squishy on these old mountains, son. Don't get too fancy-pantsy to be led astray." His eyes narrowed. "Old terry firma can be deceitful too, you know. Nature has tricks up *both* of her gol-darned sleeves, and if you look close enough and long enough, you'll find she tucks away mischief all *over* the gol-darned place."

Jake also had to agree with that as well, though he didn't bother saying it aloud. He'd seen some of nature's dark side, and knew how unforgiving she could be at times.

Cap'n Bob was never in such a dark mood as he was while speaking of the sea. Most often, Jake found him without a care, more apt to laugh out loud than to put on a frown.

He enjoyed his walks with the old man, happy to see that he, too, knew where to find the rare arbutus and the wild azalea. They soon found that their steps had often crossed on Overlook's less-traveled trails in the past, though they had not met during those times. Cap'n Bob, a serious hunter as his many firearms attested, knew how to read the tracks and spoor of wildlife much better than Jake could. He could tell where the deer runs were and whether animals had recently crossed their path, even how long ago they had done so. He read minute signs — a moved leaf, a bent or broken twig, weaving a convincing tale of just which animal had passed that way, and at times, even of where it was headed. He could detect a path through the woods that Jake could not, for the life of him, see no matter how closely he looked.

Jake was not always sure that he could believe Cap'n Bob. Often his observations seemed based on the slightest of evidence, and the old man was not above having a little fun at Jake's expense now and then.

One day they had stopped for a rest in a slight hollow deep in the woods behind the cap'n's home. The depression seemed to Jake's eye to enclose about a couple of acres, but without pacing it he couldn't tell for sure. They had been firing some of Cap'n Bob's guns throughout the afternoon, and had retired to one side of the indentation to get out of a rising wind.

"Used to be a pond here," said Cap'n Bob after they had settled on a fallen log that sat just below the rim of the depression.

Jake looked around. It seemed plausible, but he could see no obvious clues that would indicate that the hollow might once have contained water.

"A pond?"

"Yep," nodded Cap'n Bob. "Right here," and he stamped his booted foot as if the action validated his claim.

Jake looked around again. "How do you know?" he asked.

"Saw it," said Cap'n Bob. "Plenty of gol-darned times. Used to come here to meddy-tate."

Jake had some trouble picturing Cap'n Bob in 'meddy-tation,' but the old man was full of surprises, so he didn't pursue the matter. He looked closer around him. "Did you fish here?"

"Nope. No gol-darned fish. Too small, I guess."

Several moments of silence ensued.

"Well, what happened to the water?" Jake finally asked.

Cap'n Bob turned to Jake and said, "Well, now that's the interesting thing, you see. I was up here one December a few years back, and I just came to sit as I usually did." He paused. "Well, I did just that, you see, and I sat here while the day got colder and colder. Bye and bye, a flock of gol-darned geese flew in, and lit right there in front of me on that gol-darned pond." He looked over at Jake. "Guess they didn't notice me sitting there all still and all. Anyway, they gabbled and splashed around for some time not noticin' that all the time it was getting' colder and colder by the minute." He glanced at Jake. "*I* certainly noticed, I can tell you that."

Jake waited.

"Then, by golly, the gol-darndest thing happened, Jake. Right there before my very eyes, that gol-darned pond slowly froze solid, and before they knew what was happening, those geese found their feet freezing right along with it. You should've seen it, Jake. You could tell they were as surprised as I was, the way they carried on with their honking and flapping."

Cap'n Bob slowly rose from his sitting position. "Ready?" he asked Jake. "The wind's dying down so we might as well head back."

"Wait a minute, now. What happened, Cap'n Bob? What'd those geese do?"

"Why, with all that flapping going on, they just finally got it together, I guess, and darned if they didn't just up and fly away with that gol-darned pond." He turned his gaze south. "Suppose it's somewhere down in Floridy now."

Jake stood there for a moment with his mouth hanging open. "Why, you old…"

Before Jake could even begin venting his outrage, Cap'n Bob was bent over, holding his sides as the woods rang with his guffawing. He looked up at Jake with tears in his eyes. "I'm telling you, boy, you gotta watch that arty stuff. It'll take the man right outta you." He doubled over with laughter again. "Boy, I sure had you there — admit it now, Jake. You were dangling on the end of that line like a gol-darned bug-starved pickerel."

Jake just stomped on ahead of him as he tried to shut out Cap'n Bob's intermittent snorts and guffaws.

42

Jake sat looking at a reproduction of "The Fast-Day Meal," a painting done by Jean Baptiste Siméon Chardin in 1731.

He had spent the better part of a morning at the Byrdcliffe library, idly browsing through the art books looking for no specific information, but simply allowing the colored reproductions to flow past his eyes as he turned pages. He had pulled a heavy tome down from the shelf and, coming across the page containing Chardin's painting, had it lying open before him. He'd been staring at it for several moments. The book featured the works of several past masters and, of the many reproductions it contained, he was arrested by this particular still life.

He bent forward to look closer at the page.

What was Chardin thinking as he painted that picture?

What was in Chardin's mind as he painted those objects — a pestle resting in a cup, a copper pan, a skillet, a pail, a ceramic pot, two eggs, a couple of scallions, a cloth draped over the edge of the shelf, three fish hanging from a string? Were they paintings of actual objects — or did he paint them from his memory? How long did it take him to arrange these things in the order he placed them?

What was in his mind?

Why had he ranged those particular objects along the sideboard with the light falling on them from the left? Why in that particular order? Were they painted from real or imagined objects?

Considered individually, none of the objects seemed to have any special claim to significance or beauty. None of the utensils depicted appeared to be costly. He himself might have easily assembled a similar set of objects from Aunt Birgit's kitchen.

The perishable fish, the eggs, and the bunch of scallions — if not eaten when he had finished painting — had long since turned to dust. In all probability, the pans, the cloth, the crockery, and pestle no longer existed. By his reckoning, Chardin painted "The Fast-Day Meal" over 250 years ago, and even if a person could find objects today that resembled those in the picture, the chances that they were the selfsame objects were well nigh impossible.

What were Chardin's thoughts as he squeezed his prepared pigments from pig bladders, mixed them, thrust his brush into them, and applied them to canvas?

The title that the artist had given the picture — other than declaring that the fish and eggs and scallions were the usual fare during the time of fasting — told Jake nothing. Surely no one could construe the painting as some kind of religious homily, some pious admonition as to what our diets ought to consist of at a certain time. But perhaps they *did* just that — after all he was now looking at it with the eyes of a modern man. To him it was simply a painting. What did it mean to Chardin? To those who saw it then?

I see him painting that pan standing on edge, the light reflecting off its rim and bottom.

Jake thought of his many attempts of trying to paint Overlook.

Was Chardin, like me, trying to get down on canvas the essence — the "thereness"— of his subject? Was he particularly trying to depict that pan, that egg, that scallion, standing before him?

Jake flipped a few pages of the book to look at some of the other reproductions of Chardin's work, but kept returning to look once again at "The Fast-Day Meal."

What could Chardin have been thinking when he made not only this still life, but the whole series of them that were reproduced in the book? It was obvious that some of the paintings depicted the same objects in a slightly different light, in different arrangements, and from slightly altered viewpoints.

Jake bent over once again to peer more closely.

What makes me convinced that it is indeed a pan, an egg, a fish, a piece of cloth that I am seeing on this page? More — what makes me believe — yes, believe — that those objects once actually existed, once stood before Chardin in all their physicality?

* * *

"You look at them long enough," Jake said to Joe when they met at The Knife and Fork later that day, "and somehow those paintings of a few household items — stuff you find around any kitchen — seem to be pointing to something more, something beyond what they actually represent."

Joe held his silence, waiting for Jake to continue.

"I don't really know how to say it," Jake continued. "It's like you're drawn into and then *through* the painting — on to — well, I don't know what — but something *else.*"

Joe nodded to show his agreement if not his complete understanding of what Jake was attempting to express.

Jake struggled on. "In the end, I couldn't tell if it was his subject, or the way he had arranged his still lifes, or — or — if it was his technique that caught my attention. But *something* persuades you that there's more there than meets the eye. That he wasn't just painting a pot or a vegetable."

"Well," said Joe. "There's Chardin."

Jake looked up with a frown. "Meaning?"

"Meaning that *every* artist — even the bad ones — put something of themselves into their work. They can't help but doing so."

"You mean like — well, their style?"

"More than that, Jake." He screwed up his face. "More than his signature brushwork, or what we call his 'handwriting.' We — you or I — can't pass a Carlson, or a Harrison, or a Bellows hanging on the Association's walls without knowing that it *is* a Carlson or a Harrison or a Bellows. We don't have to read the tag or see their names written across the bottom of the paintings to recognize who did them." He made it a point to look directly into Jake's face. "Even though they *do* all belong to the same association."

Jake got the point, but didn't respond.

"But I mean even *more* than that, Jake. Bellows would never paint a woods scene like Carlson or Harrison might, and even Carlson and Harrison are miles apart when you're familiar with their work. And it isn't just style — the way they handle their materials. It's *more*. They also put their *minds* into their work. I don't want to sound corny, but — you know — they put their *souls* into their painting. We all do what we do because we are what we are. And, whatever that is — soul, mind, personality — whatever — it's bound to show up in our work."

Jake remembered the first time that he had seen Vincent van Gogh's work, and his thought that that artist had also — as he put it to himself back then — 'seen the mountain'. He nodded slowly and looked at Joe.

"So Chardin is also showing us himself."

"Right. Maybe even more so than he does in his famous self-portrait — the one with the rag tied around his head? We see in his still lifes not only how he *sees* the world, but also how he *feels* about it. If he was sitting here with us right now, he'd probably have the same difficulty speaking about it as we're having. It's not all that easy to put into words." He smiled. "Probably that's why we're artists and not writers."

Harrison's words came back to Jake.

Think about why *you want to paint, Jake. That will determine what kind of a painter you will become.*

"I mean," Joe went on, "who knows why I like to paint mountain streams, Bellows likes to paint boxers, and you like to paint Overlook Mountain? We paint those things because they mean something to us, because they somehow represent a world we admire or want to be a part of or — well, maybe because those things just puzzle us, tease us, keep us in wonderment. And because they do these things to us, because they hold us in thrall, so to speak, we unconsciously reveal that relationship to others when we paint them. We show people a side of us that not even *we*'re always on top of."

Jake smiled. "You make it sound like we're afflicted — like we have some kind of obsession."

"Well, don't we?"

Jake thought about the many times he had painted Overlook Mountain, and about the hundreds of drawings he had made over the years. Drawings of flowers, of trees, of rocks. Drawings of a single flower, a single leaf, a single stone.

Just like Chardin, I guess. He painted jugs, I paint pebbles.

Both drifted off into their own thoughts for several minutes, Jake recalling his earlier assessments of such Hudson River painters as Cole and Church. He'd found their depictions of the Catskills too grand, too glorious, somehow — not as ' uncultivated' as he saw them. But then, perhaps they were attempting to depict some-

270

thing 'beyond', 'something behind' what was in front of them. Wasn't he?

"Yes, I guess we all have our hobby-horse," agreed Jake.

"More like we all have our *demon*," said Joe. "And speaking of 'demons,' I better get going. I promised Andrea I'd help her pull some prints this afternoon, and she doesn't like being kept waiting."

"Then you'd better get going," laughed Jake. "I don't want her getting mad at *me* for holding you up."

Andrea Browne, a fine etcher and printmaker who had moved up to Woodstock earlier in the year, was a vivacious and strong-willed woman whose dedication to her art was almost frightening — at least to Jake. His lack of experience with women in general gave him little to go on and, in Andrea's case, he pointedly kept his opinions to himself.

He found all women somewhat mysterious, but women artists, in their tenacious dedication to their art, even more so since they often seemed to pursue it at the expense of all else. Many of them smoked cigarettes or little cigars — something he had never seen before — and were pretty free in their use of profanity. Though he got used to seeing them smoke, he never felt comfortable with hearing cuss words coming from their mouths. However intimidating he had found Andrea to be during the few times he had spoken with her — she both smoked *and* swore — it was obvious that her impact on Joe was considerable, and he had no desire to interfere in whatever kind of relationship seemed to be growing up between them.

Lately, Joe had been bringing Andrea with them to evening get-togethers, and, judging from the way Joe looked and acted around her, it was evident that it was not only their love of art that served as the binding force. Though he had no idea how it would all turn out, Jake was pretty sure that he would soon have to share his friend with a permanent partner at his side.

When he thought about it — which wasn't often — he was aware that he was usually 'odd man out.' Many of the artists he knew were married — some to other artists, but many that were not. He was often the only single person at evening soirées and, at times, teased about it, but if it bothered others, he thought little about it. There were still no women in his life, and he had never given serious thought to taking one on as a wife.

He had lived without a partner this long and, so far, was content to remain unattached. Although he had depended on Aunt Birgit over the years for preparing many of his meals, he had little doubt that, if it came right on down to it, he could easily fend for himself. In any event, when he thought about Joe and Andrea, he could not imagine what it might be like to share a house with another artist.

From the few he knew that were artists as well as husband and wife, it was the rare couple that seemed to get along peacefully. He already knew the difficulties of the highs and lows of being an artist — he could only wonder how it might be to attempt to coordinate such mood swings with a life-long partner. Most of the artist-couples he knew had separate studios, but even that did not always allow for smooth sailing. Beside the difference in medium, technique, or style that either might follow, there would be the usual clash of personalities that lay behind such divergent paths — which, as Jake well knew, could crop up at the most inopportune times and, more often than not, during an evening get-together with fellow artists.

Since it was most often that his evenings out were with the Steeles, it was between them that he had begun to sense an underlying tension that seemed to be constantly playing beneath the surface. More and more there appeared to be a strained truce keeping them in check when they were in public. He already knew Cal's opinion of "making pots," but whether their separate creative paths were at the bottom of the tension or not, Jake was sensitive enough to know that some bone of contention lay between them that was serious enough for it to sometimes show through in the presence of others.

The growing number of times that he would note sniping asides from Cal or pouting silences from Sarah was too numerous to dismiss as casual tiffs. Though he usually felt a sadness for Sarah when he witnessed these outbursts, he had little basis to assume that all the blame might be put on Cal — though that was precisely where he placed it in his mind. Neither Cal nor Sarah ever confided in him, nor would he have dared ask either of them what the trouble might be.

All he knew for sure was that he did not think that he could tolerate living under such circumstances. If ongoing frictions were a normal part of married life, he'd do well to keep clear of it. As much trouble as he was having with his painting, the last thing he needed was to share that misery with a wife.

43

It was Cap'n Bob's canny insights as much as it was Joe's persistent urging that had caused Jake to finally yield and, in the fall of 1938, he applied for and became a member of the Woodstock Artists Association. It had been a major step for Jake, and the undertaking of it fraught with self-doubt and anxiety. He was as much surprised at the Association's ready acceptance of him as a fellow artist as he was in his audacity to publicly proclaim his wish to be accepted as one.

"Now all you have to do is submit a painting for the next exhibition," Joe said with a grin as they left the Association.

Jake looked at him with panic in his eyes. He had hardly gotten over the fact that he had just filled out the forms and paid his dues for the year.

"That might take another forty years or so," said Jake woefully.

"We'll see, we'll see," was all Joe said for the time being.

Joe had in mind a double celebration for the next year — Jake's first painting hanging in an exhibit in 1939 at the annual show, and the announcement of his own engagement to Andrea. With a little finagling, both occasions could fall on the same date — or as close to each other as to seem so. For the moment, he was just pleased with his success in getting Jake to take that first step toward acknowledging himself as an artist.

Though he never told Joe, Jake had actually been prodded into the act of joining the Association after a trip up Overlook with Cap'n Bob. He and the old man decided to ferret out some old haunts, Cap'n Bob bringing one of his shotguns to see what he might bring home for dinner — or dinners, depending on how large the animal was that he brought home. He'd brought his double-barreled 12-guage loaded with both shot and slug so as to meet whatever occasion arose — and Jake toted along his painting gear.

It was late fall, but still mild enough for most of the upland trees to retain their foliage. Consequently, the woods were ablaze with the reds and golds of a typical Catskill Mountain autumn.

"You keep stoppin' to make them gol-darned pitchurs," complained Cap'n Bob, "and one of my poor goats'll have to pay the price. I'll never come across any game with you lollygaggin' along like that!"

"You go on ahead," said Jake as he laid out his materials to make a quick oil sketch. "I'll catch up to you — you ain't so hard to find in the woods with all the noise *you* make. It's a wonder you ever catch anything, the way you go barging about."

"Pshaw!" retorted the old man. "I go through the gol-darned woods quieter'n any Injun! It's *you* with that gol-darned claptrap on your back getting caught on every other branch that causes all the hullabaloo. You ought to be ashamed of yourself traipsin' around the woods like a gol-darned pantywaist cartin' all that arty stuff. Pah!" he added and stamped off in a huff up the mountainside, muttering as he climbed, "Shoot! I'm embarrassed to be even *seen* with you out here in the gol-darned woods. Sure hope we don't run into anyone we know. Probably the gol-darned deer are hiding behind the trees *laughing* at us right now! Pshaw!"

Jake caught up with Cap'n Bob some time later, drawn to his loud snoring as he lay against a log drawn up under an overhanging ledge that had served them as shelter many times in the past.

"Thought you was an old she-bear snorting up here," he said as he shook the old man awake. "I could hear you a quarter of a mile away."

"Ahh, horse feathers!" Cap'n Bob grumbled. "There ain't no gol-darned game around here anyway. I guess it's back to goat again. Or a batch of them duck eggs."

"Speaking of food, are you hungry?" asked Jake. "I got a couple of sandwiches here that my Aunt Birgit made up for us."

"Hell, yes, I'm hungry! My mouth hasn't stopped watering since my stomach thought we was going to bring something back to eat today. I've been hankerin' for some vennyson for weeks now. Hell, I'd a been happy with a gol-darned rabbit!"

As Jake joined Cap'n Bob under the protecting ledge, both men sat back to take in the scenery while they ate their lunch. The sloped hillside was heavily and variously wooded, the dark green of the conifers, tucked here and there between the hardwoods, serving as a foil for the gaudy colors of their neighbors.

"Gawd, but it's pretty up here," Cap'n Bob mused.

Jake nodded his assent.

Looking up at Jake out of the corner of his eye, Cap'n Bob said softly, "I can see why you want to paint her, Jake. Nature sure is a sight to see."

Another nod from Jake.

"But still," the old man said a bit louder, "I'd rather see her in person, so to speak, than to meet her second-hand like, in a gol-darned pitchure." He took another bite of his sandwich. "Kind of feel sorry for the people who only know nature through pitchures. It just ain't right."

Jake leaned back and heaved a sigh. "I guess I have to agree with you, there. Pictures just can't tell the whole story. You got to *feel* nature and *smell* her to get the full impact. I don't think *any-body* can do justice to old Mother Nature in pictures — least of all me."

"Then why try?" Cap'n Bob mumbled around a mouthful of sandwich.

Jake took another deep breath, "Can't help it, I guess. It's just something I have to do."

Cap'n Bob seemed to take his time to digest both the words and the food. "Like an obligation?" he finally asked.

"Yes — yes, I suppose it is," said Jake.

Cap'n Bob nodded. "Good sammitches, them. Your Aunt takes good care of you." He looked over at Jake. "Old lady?"

Jake found the question a bit forward and wasn't sure of the reason the old man had brought it up. "Sixty-ish, I guess," Jake said after a moment or so. Was Cap'n Bob looking for a mate? He had no idea of the old man's age — he could have been anywhere from forty to eighty. It was hard to tell, though he remembered that Cap'n Bob had told him he went whaling "mebbe sixty years" ago. Then again, he never *was* sure when the old man was giving him a straight story. "Yes, I guess she will soon turn seventy."

"Figures," Cap'n Bob said. "Takes age to know how to do things proper."

Jake was relieved when he saw that the subject of Aunt Birgit was confined to her 'sammitch' making and had apparently been dropped. Oddly, he also felt, if not relieved, then without his usual discomfort, when Cap'n Bob next asked, "How long you been making them pitchers, Jake?"

"Since I was kid back in Brooklyn," Jake answered. "Well, drawings, anyway. I started painting when I was about eighteen, nineteen, I guess."

Cap'n Bob thought about that for a moment or so. "Long time," he finally said. He looked over at Jake. "And you still don't think you got it right?"

Now it was Jake's turn to consider. "Well, I think I know how to *paint*. Thing is, like I said before, I'm not sure anybody can really paint *this*," and he swept his arm around to indicate the scene before them.

"I like my pitchure well enough."

It was the first time he had commented on the painting that Jake had given to him since his initial assessment of its being "pretty."

"Oh, it's passable enough — or else I wouldn't have given it to you as a gift. But, like you said back then, 'It isn't *your* Overlook.' Well, I'll tell you Cap'n Bob, it ain't *mine* either."

"Don't know as I follow that."

Jake paused to frame his thoughts. He wasn't sure why, but he felt for some reason that he had to get it properly said to this old man. "It's not my Overlook because I *know* that this old mountain cannot be summed up in a picture — not in a drawing and not in a painting and not even in a photograph. I might not know all her secrets — not near as many as you do — but I know I have yet to make a painting that even comes close to what I want to say about her."

Cap'n Bob finished off his sandwich and leaned back. "And that might be?"

Jake drew in a long breath. "I think I'm not trying to paint Overlook so much as I'm trying to paint what I *feel* about her. I want to show how she awes me, how she pleases me, how she angers me. I want to show her magic, her aloofness, her contrariness." Jake took another breath, surprised that he could share with this old man what he was never able to share with another. "I want to paint what she does to me," he laid his hand on his breast, "in *here*."

"Tall order."

"I suppose it is," said Jake. He felt as if a weight had been taken from his shoulders.

"The obligation?"

Jake nodded. "The first time I truly saw this old mountain, I was a kid coming up the Hudson on a Day Liner. I'm not sure I can tell you what it was like seeing the Catskills from thirty, forty miles away like that, but to me it was a magical thing. I never forgot that sight or the feeling I had back then — I *still* feel it even though I haven't seen Overlook from that distance for quite a while now."

Cap'n Bob nodded. "I think I know the feelin' — but with me it was the first time I saw the sea." His eyes looked off into the distance. "But I've learned to *hate* her," he said with some vehemence. "She played too fast and loose with some of my mates." He patted the earth. "Not like this ol' gol-darned mountain, now."

"Well, I've never come to hate Overlook — or *any* of the Catskills, for that matter — but old Overlook can sure exasperate me from time to time. At any rate, it's that feeling I got back then — when I was, oh, 13 or 14 — that I'm really trying to paint — that I'm trying to share with others."

Cap'n Bob thought about that for a while. "Kind of like trying to paint love or honor or — well — hate, ain't it?"

Jake spread out his hands in a gesture of helplessness.

"Terrible burden to place on a young lad's back."

Jake just shrugged.

"Probably ain't possible."

"Maybe," Jake agreed. "But I still have to keep trying."

"The obligation."

"Yep, the obligation."

"Terrible burden."

They sat in silence for several minutes, each lost in his own thoughts.

"See that sugar maple over there?" Cap'n Bob finally said.

"Which one?" asked Jake "There's a bunch of 'em."

Cap'n Bob pointed. "The one with the gold on one side and red on t'other."

"Yeah, I see it. Beautiful."

"Wonder why she's two-toned like that. You know, all yaller on one side, and blazin' red on the opposite."

"Maybe the way frost hits it or something. The red side there faces north — maybe that has something to do with it."

"Mebbe yes, mebbe no," Cap'n Bob mused. "Suppose she looked like that last year? The same colorin'?"

"Hard to tell," said Jake with another shrug of his shoulders.

"And the year before that?"

"We'd have to come each year to find out, I guess," said Jake.

Cap'n Bob turned his head this way and that. "I don't reckon it's the same from year to year. Never noticed such a thing with the maples back at the digs. *They* sure ain't the same each year."

Jake nodded. "You might just be right — but to tell you the truth, I just never noticed. I mean, I see them change every year — can't help but notice that, can you? But I never kept track of a special tree."

Cap'n Bob looked over at Jake. "Well, I have Jake, and I can tell you they're *never* the same from year to year." He punctuated the statement with a quick shake of his head. "Nope — never."

Jake wondered if he was in store for another of Cap'n Bob's tales and decided he would not rise to the bait.

"Why do you reckon Mother Nature can't get it right?" Cap'n Bob finally said.

"Can't get what right?" asked Jake with a puzzled look.

"That maple. This mountain. Every gol-darned thing, when you get right on down to it. Keeps on a-changin' as if it don't really know *what* it oughtta be. I mean, an oak is always an oak and a maple a maple. And rocks don't change into water, or dirt into air. But none of them gol-darned things is ever the same in themselves from year to year. You think mebbe Mother Nature don't know what she's about?"

Jake was taken back somewhat by the question. "But that's part of her beauty – her *nature*, isn't it?"

Cap'n Bob looked at Jake shrewdly. "You don't hold her to account for that?"

"For what? For being herself?" Jake answered with some exasperation.

"Well, boy, if *she* can't get it right, what makes you think it's *your* job to get it right?"

Jake was stuck for a response.

"She keeps turnin' those gol-darned leaves out year in and year out — never the same shape, never the same color, never the same *any* gol-darned thing. But she keeps on a-doin' it for all to see and, I suspect, for all to enjoy, if they've a mind to."

The light was beginning to dawn for Jake.

"Sure seems like a never-endin' struggle," said Cap'n Bob. "But *she* don't seem to mind. *She* don't sit around complainin'. *She* don't keep us from enjoyin' the spectacle." He looked at Jake. "Mebbe that's *her* obligation."

Jake smiled, and leaned back once again to take in the beauty that surrounded them.

"Mebbe it's the gol-darned *struggle* that's important, Jake." He looked up at the sky. "Mebbe *that's* your obligation — to show others the struggle."

He got up slowly and leaned on his shotgun.

"Looks like rain comin'. Guess we better head back. Want to stay over at the gol-darned digs for grub this evenin'? Pay you back somewhat for the lunch."

Jake didn't have to think about it for long. "Nope, but thanks for the offer. I have a few chores to do around the house for Aunt Birgit."

"Well, best get to 'em," said Cap'n Bob. "Got to keep an old lady like that happy." He gave Jake a sly sidelong look. "Never can tell how long any one of us'll be around to pay her proper respect."

44

Sarah Steele — probably through Joe Bundy who, much to Jake's embarrassment, had been spreading it about town — had gotten wind of Jake's first showing at the Woodstock Artist's Association's Spring Exhibit in 1939 and, in honor of the occasion, had invited a few guests for a small dinner party at her home on the Wednesday evening before the event.

Though Jake had no intention of attending the opening — scheduled on the Saturday of the same weekend that Joe and Andrea were getting married — he did agree to serve as best man for Joe on Sunday, and had happily accepted Sarah's invitation. To also appear at the opening reception of the Spring Exhibit, however, was far more than he thought he could handle.

As they sat down to dinner at a large table set out for their guests — Cal and Sarah joined not only by her parents Mae and Cyrus but, along with Andrea, Joe, and Jake, the Iskowitzes and a new couple, Catherine and Edward Fielding, she, an art historian and he a noted mural painter — the evening's conversation inevitably centered on discussions of art.

"I'd be a wreck," Jake was telling Andrea as they took seats at the Steele's dinner table.

"And I'm not?" Joe joked as he put his arm around his intended bride. "How do you think I'm going to survive on Sunday when I have to go up to the altar to tell this lady that 'I do'?"

"Oh, you'll survive," said Jake as Andrea playfully poked Joe in the ribs with her elbow.

"He'd better!" she said with a laugh. "We've got a ton of things to do in the next few days."

Joe and Andrea had decided to combine their two separate

studios inside a large barn that stood behind an old farmhouse they'd purchased over on Zena Road. The barn was large enough to divide into a painting and printing studio, and with an overhead hayloft that Joe planned to convert into a storage area, it promised to give them plenty of space. After so many years of getting along in Schmidt's outbuilding, Joe was in his glory, and with the extra bonus of a small stream running through the property, he could not have been more pleased.

"Even with Andrea's new press, we still have enough room to hold a square dance in the middle of the floor," Joe had joked earlier.

Andrea had added the making of woodcuts to her already extensive work in etching, and began excitedly telling Sarah and Cal how the new process allowed her a dramatic starkness she had not previously achieved.

"You might get more nuance, more delicate detail in an etching," she was explaining, "but with the woodcut, its very coarseness allows for a stronger statement. The early Germans really knew how to exploit the medium, using bold lines in a very expressive way. Dürer, for example, was a master with the woodcut — though even he got so skilled at it that some of his later woodcuts began to look more and more like etchings."

Jake leaned back in his seat and smiled as he watched the animated couple as they encouraged and interrupted each other in conversation. He envied them their unabashed display of mutual affection, both of them hardly able to stand even a moment without some physical contact occurring between them. He was genuinely happy for their discovery of each other, barely cognizant during the course of the evening of the old familiar attraction he felt for Sarah. He knew it was there, of course — he doubted if it would ever abate — but managed to keep it even further from his thoughts in deference to his friend's happiness.

The meal over and the dishes cleared away, desultory conversation quickly faded as Morris Iskowitz, returning to a subject he had brought up earlier, began steering the after-dinner discussion by proclaiming loudly, "As if artists don't have enough to be anxious about, now they have to worry about being hounded by these meshugganehs down in Washington with their 'red scare' nonsense." He glared around the table. "Now we are bandits and traitors because some of us expose the evils of capitalism? Pah! And they have the nerve to call this a free country!"

"Well, now Morris," his wife cut in. "You know how it was in Russia. We've had a good life since we've come to America."

"That's neither here nor there," Iskowitz snorted. "In America we are *supposed* to be free to pursue life, liberty and happiness. How can an artist do his work if he has to look over his shoulder? If he has to worry about every red-baiter lurking around the corner like some government spy waiting to report him to the authorities?"

"He has a point, Myra," the muralist, Edward Fielding, said to Iskowitz's wife. "Artists ought to be free to paint what they choose or to speak out without the fear of reprisals. Look what happened to Diego Rivera's 'Man at the Crossroads.' His mural at the Rockefeller Center was destroyed just because he put Lenin's face in the picture. This Red Scare has so roiled up the country that no one feels safe anymore — our Government ought to be protecting artists instead of persecuting them."

"Oh, Ed," protested Fielding's wife. "How many artists do you know who've been *persecuted*?"

"Surely, even one is too many?" Cal said as he turned to Catherine Fielding.

"I don't see why the government ought to be concerned with a person's politics," said Cyrus Winters. "What does it matter how an artist votes if his work is artistically acceptable?"

"Well, the artists have brought it on themselves by painting political subjects," said Joe. He turned to Iskowitz. "As well as getting *involved* personally in politics."

Iskowitz dismissively waved his hand. "It's not just politics — it's xenophobia! They are prejudiced against modern art because it's from Europe — to them, it's 'un-American' — and therefore suspect!"

"That's partly because we've been trying so long to *have* an 'American' art,'" said Catherine Fielding. "Artists have been plagued by European influence since day one. In the beginning, all our artists were trained in the old country, and they painted in old world style — whatever old country they came from or studied in. We've been searching for a purely 'American' art ever since."

"What about the Hudson River School?" asked Jake. "Didn't they paint American subjects?"

"Yes — but in a European fashion," said Catherine. "Look at Bierstadt — right out of the Düsseldorf Academy! And Cole or Church – try to separate the influence of the Royal or French Academies from anything you might call 'American' in their paintings."

"I see what you mean," said Jake.

"Anyway, that's neither here nor there," said Iskowitz. "The point is, just because you bring back ideas from Russia or Paris doesn't mean that you are a communist!"

"Well, so far such things haven't touched us here," said Sarah as she smiled at her guests. "Why don't we turn to more pleasant topics?"

"Not *yet*, they haven't happened here," said Iskowitz, unwilling to be sidetracked. "Not yet. But who knows? You mark my words — you give the government an inch and they'll take a lot more than a foot! How many expected such a thing as Kristallnacht in Germany? The most cultured country in Europe?" He glanced at his wife. "Oy, how many of our family fled Russia to go to Germany because they thought it was a civilized country?"

"That was a shocking thing," said Cyrus Winters. He turned to his wife. "How many times have we been on archaeology digs with German scientists?" He turned back to the others. "Why, Mae and I have met many cultured Germans that we have long considered as friends." He shook his head. "How could such an intelligent people turn to such savagery?"

Sarah again tried to lighten the conversation. "Well, enough of shocking things for now." She turned to her father. "You know how upset you get when you are agitated, Daddy. Let's just digest our meal in a calm and pleasant manner."

Jake, relieved to have the subject of Germany dropped, said, "Yes! We are here to celebrate Andrea and Joe's upcoming marriage, aren't we?"

"And your baptism of fire, too!" said Joe with a laugh.

"Yes," said Cal. "Jake here will have his first taste of standing naked before the public." He turned to Jake. "Well, old man, you're probably smart to avoid the reception — I don't know of any artist who actually *enjoys* such torture."

"Here, here," said Fielding as he raised his glass. "A toast to Jake and a double toast to Andrea and Joe."

Jake held up his hand. "Well, don't expect me to sell off my tools just because I'll have a picture hanging in a gallery. In fact, I've got some pretty steady work right now with that new Playhouse being built in town."

"Yes," said Sarah. "Let's also toast the new Woodstock Playhouse."

"To the theatre!" said Catherine Fielding. "Woodstock isn't dead yet!"

The shift in conversation lightened the mood and soon the group moved from the dinner table to find places in the Steele's living room.

Sarah noticed that her father was trying to steer Jake off into a corner, but Sarah cut him short with a, "Now Daddy, no private conversations. Tonight we have to share our guests of honor with everyone."

"All right, all right," said Cyrus to his daughter. Then, turning to Jake, he said, "But I reserve the right to ask for some time later this week. The Missus and I are staying until next weekend and I'd like to speak with you about cave paintings."

Although Jake had no idea what Mr. Winters was referring to, he promised he would return in the middle of the coming week, turning to Sarah to see if that was all right. "It's a date. Wednesday afternoon," she said and, taking them by the arms, pulled them both into the midst of the ongoing discussion.

"It was an amazing experience," Fielding was saying. "I had seen his 'Guernica' while we were in Europe, and for several weeks after, I couldn't touch a brush."

"An amazing man, that Picasso," said Cal. "Between him and Matisse, they have almost single-handedly rescued what was fast becoming a moribund pastime of man."

"Absolutely," agreed Iskowitz. "They saved us from that nonsense of 'impressionism', which was only prolonging the already worn-out love affair that artists had been having with realism since Adam."

"Well," said Catherine Fielding, "it's true that I don't think I could tolerate one more of Renoir's big, red, rubbery nudes, but to declare realism 'worn-out' might be a bit extreme."

"So spake the historian," intoned Iskowitz.

"Well, to get back to Picasso's 'Guernica' again," said Fielding, "I remember feeling that I had just witnessed some terrific benchmark in art, some major turning-point that he had accomplished with that painting. It was such a total statement — I mean, it summed up all the elements of great art in one grand gesture — color, composition, movement, and, above all, *meaning*. What else might an artist say? I remember thinking to myself, 'Well, old man, that's the end of *your* painting. This fellow's said it all!'"

The room was silent for a moment or two, each digesting what they had just heard, but before anyone could speak their own thoughts, Fielding continued.

"I literally couldn't bring myself to start another canvas for weeks. I mean, I was paralyzed! Then, almost by chance, some time later, I happened to see a newsreel of the bombing of Guernica — the very same Guernica that Picasso had depicted in his painting." He looked around the room to insure he had their attention. "Let me tell you, seeing that film was like a revelation, and turned me right around once more. It was so graphic, so *real*, that all I could think of was that Picasso's painting, for all its power, was really just another piece of decorative art. That film showed it and *said it all!* Visually and aurally — you could see it *and* hear it. It was almost like experiencing the real thing! It made me think that not only was Picasso passé, but the whole business of painting as well." His eyes swept the room. "Painting is finished! I mean, how can the painter compete with the camera?"

"Whoa, whoa," cut in Joe. "You can't be serious about that!"

"Yes I am," said Fielding. "The photographer is already well on the way to making us painters obsolete. He can do in an instant what takes us weeks to accomplish."

"*Realist* painters obsolete – maybe," said Cal. "That's why Morris and I think that our only real salvation is modern, non-figurative art. The day of the still life and genre picture may be over, but there is still much more that the artist can express."

"Wait, wait," broke in Joe again. He turned to Fielding. "Let me get this straight. You say that the camera trumps the brush, right?"

"Right," said Fielding.

"Well, let me ask you this. Suppose — just suppose for the sake of argument here — that Vincent van Gogh had a camera. And let's suppose that, instead of *painting* his self-portrait, he had set up a camera on a tripod and took his own picture. Do you really think that we wouldn't have lost something here? I mean think about it. A handful of snapshots instead of the several paintings he had done of himself." He looked around the room triumphantly. "Why, the camera will *never* replace the human eye."

"He's got a point," said Catherine Fielding. "The camera can only report — the artist can interpret. Maybe I'd better not start weeding out my research library just yet, Morris."

"Well of *course* the camera will never replace the artist," said Iskowitz. "But let me tell you — it will surely put the brakes on artists getting away with the same, tired old still life or landscape. Who needs another painting of an apple or another tree?"

Jake surprised himself by blurting out, "Did *you* ever try to paint a tree, Morris?"

Iskowitz threw up his hands. "I'm a sculptor, not a painter. But what's the difference? All I'm saying is that the world doesn't need another painting of a tree — or of a hill or a field. It's been done — and done to death! Such paintings no longer have any relevance." He threw out his arms, palms up, and appealed to the group. "That's all I'm saying."

"But that's what I'm getting at." Jake, unable to stop himself, forged ahead. "It's easy to say that we don't have to paint another tree if you've never painted one yourself."

"*Now* you stirred him up," said Joe with a grin. He had never heard Jake speak up like this in any of their evening gatherings before, and he sat back to take in the show.

"Seriously," continued Jake. "Who can say that any painter has exhausted the way *any* object might be painted. I know from my own experience that I still haven't gotten a single tree right yet. But that's beside the point. That might just be my inadequacy as a painter." He faced Iskowitz. "But suppose someone were to tell you that the last thing the world needs is another chunk of twisted steel or carved rock that signifies nothing. Doesn't nature carve stone indiscriminately or war twist steel into fantastic shapes? What 'relevance' is there in art that only repeats what any inanimate force can do?"

Iskowitz held up his hands and fell back in his seat in mock horror. "I've awakened a tiger!" he exclaimed.

It was true that those who had known Jake had never heard

such impassioned speech coming from his mouth, and they all looked on in wonder.

Catherine Fielding broke the silent tension with a, "Hear, hear! Well spoken, Jake."

Everyone burst into laughter as Jake blushed furiously. Cal patted him on the back, saying, "That's the spirit! After all, that's what these get-togethers are all about."

"Right," said Myra Iskowitz. "This is a free country," she paused to look pointedly at her husband. "And we all have a right to our opinion."

"No matter how wrong it might be," added Iskowitz, his palms stretched out and upward once again.

"I'm not so sure how 'wrong' it is," said Catherine Fielding. "After all, the thing that has kept art alive for all these years is the fact that it keeps changing, keeps looking back as well as looking ahead. The pendulum swings. All styles and subjects come and go, what is in favor this year, goes out the next — and so on. Who can say that anyone has the final answer? Even the most cursory glance at art in the world today will show a wide range of work — and each proponent of a style or a movement or a particular subject — if he's serious about his work — will fight as passionately as Jake has just done for us here. It's what makes my job as an art historian so interesting — and so necessary."

"And another speech-maker heard from," Iskowitz said in a mock moan. "What artist has a chance when it comes to the art mavens?"

"Or the critics!" exclaimed Joe.

"The *worst* art mavens of all," said Iskowitz as he threw up his hands again. "Don't get me started!"

The party broke up shortly after, Joe and Andrea wanting to get going early to make their preparations for the upcoming wedding festivities.

As Jake took his leave, he promised Cyrus Winters that he would come back to visit on Wednesday afternoon.

Walking home in the crisp coldness of the early spring evening, he felt rather pleased with himself, but not so confident after all that he had said anything worthwhile.

How easy to sound like you know *what you're talking about* — he thought.

45

The following Wednesday proved to be one of those exceptionally warm April days that had a way of fooling people into thinking that they were finally seeing the last of the cold weather.

Jake and Cyrus Winters sat on spacious Adirondack chairs out in the back of Sarah and Cal's home, heads thrown back and enjoying the warmth of the sun falling on their faces. The Steeles had put in a small flagstone patio situated halfway between the house and Cal's studio, a handsome building that stood in the shelter of the encroaching woods. Jake had stepped into the studio long enough for a brief look with Joe Bundy when Cal extended the invitation before one of their evening get-togethers but, feeling that he was intruding, stayed for only a few moments. The quick glance was enough for him to see that it looked no different from most studios he had been in.

The patio, shaded by surrounding trees, served as a secluded haven that the Steeles often used for quiet moments. Jake and Cyrus had retired there after a light lunch prepared by Sarah and her mother.

Handing each a cup of coffee, Mae Winters told Jake how lovely she thought the Bundy wedding had been, and turned to leave them in privacy.

"I'll be sure to tell them how much you enjoyed it, Mrs. Winters," Jake said as she walked toward the house.

"Charming couple, the newlyweds," Cyrus Winters was saying. "The missus and I were quite pleased to have been invited to their wedding on Sunday. Mr. Bundy, I take it, is an old acquaintance of yours?"

"Yes," said Jake. "I met Joe before the war, but it was not until after I had returned that we became closer friends. He and I go out once in awhile to paint on site."

"Yes, yes. Sarah and Cal took us to the Association's opening last Saturday, you know. She was quite excited about your picture. The missus wanted to buy it, but Sarah told her that it wasn't for sale. I rather liked it myself. Had a strong quality about it. I don't know much about painting, mind you — not my field, you know — but it seemed to exert a rather forceful impact on the viewer. Yes, yes — I rather liked it very much."

"Thank you," said Jake, a bit uneasy with the praise though pleased to hear about Sarah's reaction to his painting. One of his recent renditions of Overlook Mountain, it had, for Jake, still something lacking to allow him to call it 'finished' — though he could usually say that about all of his paintings.

Eager to change the subject, Jake said, "So, Mr. Winters, you mentioned something about 'cave paintings' the other night?"

"Indeed — those found in Altamira — that's in Spain, you know. They've discovered some important stone-age drawings there — found them sometime back in the last century — and the missus and I have been speaking about traveling there to see them. Quite well preserved, from what we hear."

Jake's interest was immediately quickened. "Stone-age drawings? I didn't know that such things existed. Sarah has told me about pottery — that some ancient pots and vessels have been unearthed, but I didn't know that prehistoric people made pictures as well."

"Oh yes," said Cyrus Winters. "These particular drawings are believed to have been made by Cro-Magnon man, but we've already found a great deal of evidence of man's early attempts at image-making — when I say 'we' I don't mean the Missus and I, of course, but scientists and archaeologists from around the world. Many of the artifacts have been unearthed in old tombs — such as those found in the pyramids of Egypt — but they've long been discovering markings and carvings etched into rock faces and standing stones around the world."

"That's amazing," said Jake. "I had no idea that the making of art had such a long history."

"Well, whether we can call it 'art' or not, is not all that clear. That's rather a modern term — relatively speaking. But the making of images — like those found on the walls in the Altamira caves — had evidently been a custom of man for many thousands of years. In fact, the making of such marks and symbols appears to have occurred long before man's invention of writing — perhaps even of speech. We still have much to learn about pre-historic practices, but the fact of their existence leaves no doubt that early man made images. They've been found around the world — even right here in America."

"What kinds of images were found in the caves in Spain?" asked Jake.

"From the articles I've read, there seems to be a depiction of some kind of hunt. There are bison — handsomely represented, I must say from the reproductions I've seen — and human-like stick figures, which seem to be holding what look like primitive spears. Interspersed with these recognizable images are also abstract markings, which have not yet been deciphered. Mae and I are anxious to go to Spain to have a first-hand look."

Jake shook his head. "And these come from the Stone Age?"

"As far as we can determine, yes."

"That's amazing. How were the drawings made, Mr. Winters?"

"Again, from what I've read, it appears that they used pulverized earth for their color — great-great-grand-daddies, I presume, of your modern day paint pigments. They also seemed to have used an early type of pencil in the form of sticks burnt at one end — much like your charcoal sticks, I should imagine. The whole affair is remarkably well preserved — like many of the digs that the Missus and I have been on in Egypt. The dry air, you know."

Jake was dumbfounded. "And it goes back that far! They were drawing bison on their cave walls!"

Cyrus Winters nodded.

"And in Egypt? They were doing the same thing?"

"Not precisely," explained Winters. "The Egyptians were a civilized people — not Stone-Age men whom we might barely call 'human.' The Egyptian images — and hieroglyphics — their earlier form of writing — were different, their animals and figures more stylized and less realistic. But like the earlier examples we find, there was also an admixture of literal and abstract images being made."

"Abstract — do you mean like what the modern artist means

when he calls his art 'abstract'?"

"Now, I am no expert on painting, Jake, and I am not very familiar with all your modern-day terms and techniques. Literally speaking, *all* art is abstract — even the most representative. However, by 'abstract' images I simply mean markings that seem to bear no resemblance to any object. These kinds of markings, in fact, seem to be much older than either the Cro-Magnon bison or Egyptian hieroglyphic. We've found them the world over, not only in the East, but in such places as on the rocks in Ireland that were probably left by early Celts, and in South America where the Incan people once lived. Whatever they mean to us — and so far, they do not mean much — they undoubtedly held some meaning for our ancient forebears."

"Might we ever find out?" asked Jake after a moment of thought.

"There are theories, of course. Otto Rank, a noted German psychologist, has done some extremely interesting research on the subject. A book of his — *Art and Artist* — was translated into English a few years ago, put out, I think, by the publishing house of Alfred Knopf. You might want to look up a copy sometime, Jake. In any event, Rank believes that such early abstract markings indicate the dawn of man's inklings — his first expressions — of something beyond himself, beyond even what he could see and touch. Rank goes so far as to assume such activity to be a form of ancient aspiration for the unknown — a primitive search for spirituality." He paused to search for words. "You might say it was an early form of religious activity, if you will."

"I'm not sure I follow that," said Jake.

"Well, it's all very speculative, of course," said Winters. "But since the images pre-date the rise of language, Rank thinks it represents a primitive kind of reverent expression. Religion, as we know it, does not come into full flower until a language can be used in which it may be codified." He noted Jake's frown of puzzlement and continued, "A religion as we understand that term, you see, needs a dogma, a set of beliefs, which its founders deem necessary for its adherents to learn and to follow. Rules are proposed — like the Ten Commandments — and then, as man evolves, elaborate emendations and rituals follow. But in order to create such a system — an agreed upon set of symbols that can be identified as a particular 'religion' — a common language must be in place so as to be able to disseminate the dogma." He paused to see if Jake was following him. "But what could man do before he invented such systems of language? Otto Rank feels that whatever instinctive spiritual yearnings — if we can call them even that — our ancestors had, they tried to express them in the strange and incomprehensible images that they left behind on rocks and cave walls. Presumably, as he evolved, he translated these early urgings into spoken and written languages that, in turn, developed eventually into full-blown religious systems."

"There's a lot to digest there," mused Jake.

"Well, think of it like this, Jake. Early man seems to have regularly placed their markings on upended stones — quite often placed at the top of some natural rise. We assume that they paid homage in some way — perhaps by kneeling or lying prostrate in front of it. In any event, today that simple stone has become Saint Peter's Basilica in Rome or Notre Dame in Paris. Such beautiful edifices are simply elaborations of that original marker — but, presumably, the initial, primitive impulse that moved man in the beginning remains the same." He reflected for a moment. "Unfortunately, many today *only* see the edifice. We've become so skillful with our words and art that we've lost sight of that ancient impulse." He sighed, and added, "Perhaps we've elaborated *too* much."

Their conversation was interrupted by raised voices coming from inside the house. A few moments later Mae Winters appeared, and opening a book, took a seat a little distance from them. She and her husband exchanged glances, but no words passed between them.

Jake broke the uneasy silence. "Then these early artists were priests or something?"

"I don't know as we can make that leap, Jake. We have no way of knowing anything about the people who made these images. We don't know what his peers thought of either such images or of those who made them. All we know, if Rank is correct in his assumptions, is that these early people were responding to some inner urge or need to express themselves in the manner that they did. What we *do* know for sure is that they hunted, that they made primitive tools and vessels — as you already know from Sarah — and that some, it appears, made images."

"So, from what I understand of what you're telling me, this early image making — this 'art' — came about from some impulse within them. Some urge they felt but had no way of expressing — they couldn't speak, they couldn't write, so they made marks?"

"Something very like that," agreed Winters. "We do not know when man turned to making representational images — like the bison on the caves of Altamira. But obviously, as he learned how to control his tools, how to use the earth to make his colors, he began turning his eye toward the world around him in search of subjects to draw."

A light came on in Jake's head. "So the making of pictures — of making things that he could *see* in the world around him — came later?"

"It appears that way, Jake. From all indications, our first artists had a much more elemental reason for creating his symbols than that of simply replicating his world through picture making. You might say, as Otto Rank infers, that he was originally trying to paint God — or at least his conception of something beyond himself — and when he found that beyond his capabilities — which he most likely often did — he turned to painting the things in his world."

Their conversation was again interrupted by what appeared to be some kind of altercation going on in the house.

Mae Winters looked up from her book. "Calvin has come back from the city in somewhat of a foul mood," she said quietly to her husband and returned to her reading.

Jake's head was spinning with ideas. Before he could properly digest what he had just heard or even frame his response, however, they were again disturbed by another outburst from inside the house, followed by the slamming of the front door. A moment later, Sarah, red-eyed and obviously upset, came out through the back door and walked towards them.

"I just made some fresh coffee," she said. "Would anyone like a little cake?"

Jake could see that she was struggling to keep her emotions in check and, avoiding her eyes, said, "Oh, no. I really have to be going." He turned to Mr. Winters. "Thank you again, Mr. Winters. I've learned a great deal today and look forward to continuing our conversation."

"Why not this coming Friday, before we leave on Saturday?"

294

said Cyrus Winters. He glanced over at Sarah.

"Oh, absolutely," she said. "Friday would be fine. Cal is spending a long weekend in the city and ..." She stopped suddenly and, after a moment, said. "Friday's fine, Jake. It'll give Dad something to do while Mom is packing." She smiled at her father and ruffled his hair. "Jake can keep you out from underfoot and out of Mom's way."

Jake thanked Mr. Winters again, and bowing slightly to Sarah and her mother, promised to return Friday afternoon.

46

Jake spent almost the whole of the next day in his studio, mulling over Cyrus Winters' words, idly looking from painting to painting as he tried to make sense of all that he had learned. Most of what Cyrus had told him made sense — what escaped him, he chalked up to his own ignorance, his unfamiliarity with such theoretical discussions. A practical man all his life, Jake had grown to rely on physical things — what he could heft in his hands and re-work with his tools. In this respect, he was not unlike his father "who only knew meat," as Uncle Hans liked to say. At bottom, he knew that he approached his painting in the same manner — light on theory and heavy on hands-on 'doing'.

Still, what he did manage to come away with from Cyrus Winters' comments seemed to give him a better understanding of what he now only referred to as his 'why'. In his browsing in Whitehead's library, he did not remember coming across any books that dealt with the origins of art — most being monographs of either individuals or periods. Although he'd given a great deal of thought to how *his* art began, he knew relatively little about how man came to making art in the first place. Could he view his own development from child to man as a sketch of a more complete work — a compressed version of man's evolution from stone-age days?

Friday turned out to be a typical April day, the weather again seasonably cold. As he drove over to the Steele's, he continued to mull over what he had learned, still finding the ideas too abstract for him to grasp and sort out to his satisfaction. Pushing them back in his mind, he turned his attention to negotiating the pickup down the twisting road only to find that, no sooner had he put Cyrus Winters' ideas out of his head, thoughts of Sarah flooded in to take their place.

What was all that business between her and Cal?

"Nope," he said aloud. "Leave it alone." He hunched over the steering wheel. "You're having enough to think about right now," he growled, as he made a show of increasing his concentration on the road.

Too cold to sit out on the patio, Sarah had settled them in the living room, two cups of steaming coffee and a dish of cookies within reach on a small table between their chairs.

"Go to it, gentlemen," she said. "I'm going upstairs to help Mom pack."

Cyrus needed no prompting to launch into his subject.

"Are you familiar with the writings of Plato, Jake?"

"I have his *Dialogues* in my studio," said Jake, "but, to tell the truth, I've had little success in getting very far in my reading."

"Well, it *is* rather heavy going," admitted Winters. "Especially for the uninitiated. Have you ever taken any philosophy courses?"

Jake reddened. "I've been out of school since I was fourteen, Mr. Winters."

"Really?" said Winters as if surprised. "Well — if I am not being too presumptuous, I'll sum up his main idea since I think it germane to our discussion of the other day."

"Please do," said Jake. "I'd be much obliged if you did."

"Well, now, I don't mean to set myself up as a professor of philosophy, you understand. It is just that I know that trying to glean what is important from the bulk of Plato's work can be intimidating to the beginner, to say the least. But if we compare some of his thoughts to what Rank had to say about the prehistoric artist … you recall what I'd said of his *Art and Artist* on Wednesday?" Noting Jake's nod, he continued. "Well, when we compare the ideas of Plato and Rank, we arrive at some interesting propositions." He paused to gather his thoughts. "Briefly, Plato believed that this world we live in," he waved his hand to take in the surrounding area, "is in constant flux, always in a state of change."

Jake nodded. "Yes, I can follow that."

"Now over and beyond this world — up in 'heaven' so to speak – is what he called the ideal. It is a place of pure ideas that never change. In other words, these things around us — chairs, table, the trees, the mountains — us — is a world of becoming, and there," he pointed upward, "is a world of being. This world — our world — is only a reflection of that other world." He pointed at the floor. "This is illusion." He again pointed upward. "*That,* according to Plato, is reality."

Cyrus Winters looked questioningly at Jake to determine if he was following his explanation and, after Jake's nod, continued.

"Our world, according to Plato's philosophy, the world we live in, is always striving toward that ideal world — but, because of the nature of existence, nothing in this world can ever attain it. If it did, it would cease to exist as a thing in this world."

Jake frowned.

Cyrus pointed outside to a tree. "Over there is a tree — an oak, I believe."

Jake looked and nodded his assent.

"It is trying to be an ideal oak tree — just as the pine or maple or elm is trying to become its perfect self — its *ideal* self. It is the same for everything that exists in this world. A cat is trying to be an ideal cat, a human is striving to be an ideal human. If that oak or a cat had finally attained perfection — had finally become the *ideal* tree or cat — then it would no longer have to go through these worldly transformations. It will have ceased 'becoming' and will have 'become.' In Christian terms, it would "go to Heaven.' However, to the ancient Greek of Plato's time, there were no such concepts as "good" and "evil" in the Christian sense. A man striving for the ideal was simply doing what he ought — to avoid doing so simply indicated that he was uneducated, ignorant. To *purposely* avoid striving for the ideal, then, was not so much an act of evil to the ancient Greek as it was one of stupidity."

Jake nodded thoughtfully.

"I don't mean to be pedantic here, Jake, but our word 'educate,' though from the Latin, is derived from this Greek concept. It literally means to 'lead one out of oneself' — to be an 'educator' in Plato's time meant to train a person how to bring himself forth into his true being — in short, to realize or bring into actuality, his ideal self. Ideally, then, to be educated ought to mean that one has learned how to live the virtuous life — the only life worthy of an intelligent human being." He paused for a moment. "Language is such a difficult thing — so difficult to explain things when we are hampered by words." He looked at Jake. "For example, I've just said that the Greek thought that one ought to live a virtuous life

— but one must really understand what they meant by 'virtuous' — an English word, incidentally, that hardly describes what the ancient Greek meant by the term. We've gotten it second-hand from the Latin — which they called 'virtu'." He spelled it for Jake. "We have no literal translation of it in our language. Our word, 'virtue' — with an 'e' at the end — is rather a watered down version of the original. Again, we must go to Latin to get a clue to what was meant by 'living a virtuous life' — they translated it as 'excellence.' But here again we get somewhat diverted from the Greek intent." He furrowed his brow in thought. "Perhaps the closest I can come to it is our word 'rectitude,' which implies living a good life by *choice*. To the Greek, the educated person was one who learned his true self, and who then chooses to rigorously live up to that self."

The Meditations of Marcus Aurelius came immediately to Jake's mind. "Not that I've had any extensive schooling to go by," he said, "but judging from what you're saying, I'd say that I've never really had an *educator* for a teacher while I was still in school. "

"Yes," said Cyrus. "A sign of our times, I'm afraid. We've come to use the word quite loosely, that's for certain. I doubt if you can find more than a handful of teachers today who know the true meaning of the word — or of the serious import of their profession. More often than not, a student today simply goes to a teacher to learn a specific subject — since, more than likely, that is all a teacher has to offer. Even worse, those who think they have some comprehension of what it means to 'educate,' merely lead their charges toward a superficial understanding of their individual idiosyncrasies — their *personalities* — as if the incidental opinions, beliefs, attitudes, and so forth, that one learns from parents, or haphazardly picks up from one's peers, are identical to what one *is*. This, I'm afraid, is not education, but unmitigated indulgence, pure and simple." He sighed. "Mankind will come to rue the day that we chose such an easy path in the instruction of our children, Jake. However, we've run far afield. So, to come back to our subject of art, we find Plato had very strong ideas about the artist, which he spells out in the last book of his *Republic*. Again, I will sum up if I may."

"Please do," said Jake. "This is fascinating."

"Well — Plato's argument runs thus: Since this world is a world of illusion, a world not of permanency — a *symbolic* world, so to speak — the artist who merely copies nature is doing his fellows a disservice since he can only lead others away from the ideal. In a sense — a *real* sense in Plato's mind — the artist who paints a tree — say that oak tree outside — is merely making a symbol of what is *already* a symbol. And, no matter how well he makes a painting of that tree, he accomplishes nothing other than confusing the uneducated man who is already ignorant of the true nature of the world. Therefore, the artist is banned from Plato's ideal republic because, in the end, he leads man *away* from truth through his propensity to simply replicate the illusion. The artist compounds the lie — he creates illusion on top of illusion. Because his final work of art is necessarily in stasis, he gives the impression that the *world* is in stasis — that it is not constantly in flux, forever changing, forever striving towards the ideal." He looked at Jake. "Are you still with me?"

"Oh yes! Yes, I am," said Jake.

"Now, if we set these ideas of Plato alongside of what Rank says about early man, we see an interesting correlation. If early man began with abstract images — non-figurative markings — and only later came to depict the world around him, then perhaps we may conclude that he was once closer to his true nature — ironically, closer to Plato's ideal man. Such an artist — if we may call him that — may perhaps not have been banned from the Republic. It is only when man begins to *believe* in this world — believe enough in it, that is to say, to *emulate* it — that he begins to lose his initial and primal connection to that *other* world, the world of abstraction, the world of pure idea dissociated from the physical universe. In effect, he steps away from God and into the world."

A memory of one of the parables Sister Celine used whenever she caught him gazing out the window instead of paying attention — which was often — swam up in his memory. "Remember, Jacob," she would admonish with her finger pointed upward. "Jesus tells us that 'He who loves this world, loses the next.'"

"Have I lost you?"

"No, no," said Jake. "No … it's all sinking in."

"So, to put it another way, we can say that Rank's early image-makers stopped making symbols and started making pictures — started covering his cave walls with bison and the like. Perhaps *that* is the moment when 'art' steps into man's history."

Feeling as if he had been holding his breath under water, Jake leaned forward and audibly expelled the air from his lungs.

"Whew!"

"Too much?" asked Cyrus Winters. "Am I loading you down with too much theory?"

"I don't know right at the moment if it's too much or too little," said Jake with a shake of his head. "I can promise you that I'll tackle those dialogues of Plato again as soon as I can. But, I do know this — you've gone a long way in clearing up my own thinking about painting and art — at least about *my* painting."

"Then it's a good time to stop." He turned his head, as he heard Sarah and Mae coming down the stairs. "Besides, here are the womenfolk, right on cue."

Jake rose to meet them.

Sarah looked at the two full cups of cold coffee and the untouched dish of cookies.

"You guys are easy," she said with a smile. "Want these hottened up?"

"Uh, uh," said Jake. He raised his hand to his brows. "Not me. I'm full up to here."

Sarah laughed. "Dad can do that to you — I know."

"He *does* love to talk," said Mae as she affectionately put her arm around her husband. Then, looking up at him, she said, "Well, dear. We're all packed and ready to go in the morning."

"And I'm heading back to my studio to do some reading," said Jake, smiling at Cyrus Winters. "I've got some homework to get to."

He said good-bye to them, bowing to Mae while warmly gripping Cyrus's hands.

"Let me get you your coat," said Sarah, and walked him to the kitchen.

Thanking her "for everything," Jake avoided her eyes as he hastily opened the door and stepped outside into the bracing air. Taking a deep breath, he hoped that the cranky heater in his truck would cooperate.

A few weeks later, after the Spring Exhibition had been taken down at the Woodstock Artists Association, Jake brought his painting over to the Steeles and asked Sarah to give it to her parents the next time she saw them as his way of saying thanks.

47

In an effort to breathe new life into the declining popularity of the Byrdcliffe colony, Dr. Martin Schutz, founder of the newly established Woodstock Historical Society and an active member of Woodstock's intelligentsia, suggested to Mrs. Whitehead that they invite a number of notables to come to Byrdcliffe to speak on the various arts. This way, at least on weekends, the buildings and grounds might effectively be utilized and, if successful, might once again put the little colony back in the center of Woodstock's cultural scene. Mrs. Whitehead was amenable to Dr. Schutz's suggestion, and thus was born the series of weekend lectures, discussions, and poetry readings that would become known as the "Byrdcliffe Afternoons."

In mid July, Jake, along with the Bundys and the Steeles, decided to attend on the afternoon at which several painters were going to speak. Scheduled to appear that weekend were Joseph Pollet, Henry Billings, George Biddle, and Carl Eric Lindin. Although Jake was not familiar with the other three, he had encountered Lindin from time to time while that artist had still been teaching at Byrdcliffe and, knowing a bit about his work, was looking forward to hearing him speak.

Unused to attending formal lectures, Jake was apprehensive when he saw Sarah and Andrea take out notebooks and pencils after they had found seats. Never having attended college, the idea of taking notes had never occurred to him. When he noted that neither Joe nor Cal had followed suit, however, he figured that he had not committed any serious blunder.

As soon as the first speaker, Joseph Pollet, began to speak, he almost immediately put any unease about the matter out of his mind. He was always a listener, and found little difficulty in keeping up with Pollet's arguments on the individuality of the artist and of art's importance to society. It was the same when Billings and Biddle followed with their presentations. He listened attentively and had little trouble in following their lines of reasoning or in picking out their main points.

Lindin, the final speaker, began by sharing Hans Wahlin's twenty-five theses on "What is Human in Art," followed by a few of his own observations on the Swedish artist's philosophy. Though he had learned something from all of the speakers, Jake was most interested in Lindin's idea that creative energy was essentially "ethical," and, in his concluding remarks, had asserted "the road to culture and art still runs through Plato and Christ."

Lindin's words had taken root in his mind and, as they sat around discussing the lectures at Deannie's later that afternoon, Jake said to Sarah, "When Lindin concluded that the path to art runs through Plato, I couldn't help thinking of the last discussion I had with your father."

"Is that what you two were talking about? I know you had your heads together for quite a piece of time." Sarah smiled. "Mama told Daddy that he was in his element after you left — a captive audience and no one to interrupt him. I do hope that he didn't talk you to death."

"Well," interjected Cal, "you know how your father can go on — and on — and on." He glanced around the table to see how his joke had been received.

Sarah ignored the jibe and kept her eyes on Jake.

"Not at all," said Jake. "Yes, we were talking about Plato — and much more. I have to admit that some of what he had to say went over my head, but there was a great deal that had hit home for me." He glanced over at Cal. "I look forward to his next visit," he said pointedly. "I could listen to him any time. He certainly has a wide range of knowledge, and I appreciate his taking the time to share it with me."

"Lindin also said that the path was through Christ," put in Joe, "but I don't know about that. All of that religious stuff sounds a bit airy-fairy to me."

"Oh?" said Andrea. "And I suppose we ought to just discount all of that 'airy-fairy' art that came out of the Renaissance?"

Joe rolled his eyes upward. "All I'm saying is that I try to keep that pious stuff out of my painting. Carlson told us that Birge Harrison taught him to 'See big and grab the essential.' That's good enough for me."

"He's not all that wrong," said Cal, "though you wouldn't catch me applying it to painting landscapes!" He turned to Andrea. "No matter how great the Italian Masters were, they might have been even better had they not been hamstrung by the Church. Religion has no part in art." He turned to Jake. "Neither does philosophy, for that matter. Art ought to be about art, and doesn't need an outside subject to make it important."

"Art for art's sake, you mean," said Andrea.

Cal nodded. "Exactly."

Jake frowned. "Then how about plumbing for plumbing's sake? Or carpentry for carpentry's sake? Or *anything* for its own sake?"

"Your point?" said Cal.

"Well, let me ask you. Suppose you hire me to build you a bookcase, and I just come over and cut a lot of boards and nail them together however I wish. Or a plumber ran pipes higgledy-piggledy and didn't care whether it brought clean water into your house or carried out dirty water from it? Would that be all right with you?"

Cal snorted. "You're lumping things together. Fine art has nothing to do with the trades."

"I don't see how that affects your argument," said Jake. "You're saying that art is an end in itself — that it shouldn't be involved in anything other than itself. Can anything really be an end in itself and still be of value?"

Sarah looked at her husband. "Well?" she said.

"Oh this is ridiculous!" said Cal. "All of you are just so outmoded in your thinking! You're all in a rut — Lindin and the whole lot of old fuddy-duddies in this town — you're hanging on to old ideas that no longer have any validity in this day and age. The days of art being tied to telling stories or — or *selling* religion, is over! Art has its *own* meanings, its *own* validity. It *is* its own end. And whether you agree or not, it need not serve any other master other than to follow its own dictates."

"Well! There goes Ben Shahn, Jack Levine, Isabel Bishop, Philip Reisman, and that crowd," said Andrea. "First the Renaissance goes out the window, and now the Social Realists!"

"Tying their art to politics is no better than tying it to religion," said Cal. "Besides, they're still stuck in the dead-end of representational art too, so, in a sense, they're no different from the Renaissance painter or sculptor being patronized by the Pope. Michelangelo and Raphael and the rest of them might just as well have been making rosary beads as paintings. And the Social Realists are no different — they're not making art, they're making propaganda. They're just serving a different master."

"Oh, if Morris Iskowitz could hear you now!" said Andrea. Calvin Steele's dismissal of the Social Realists — and political art in general — touched a sensitive nerve. Andrea had been devoting much of her work to the cause of ameliorating social ills, and took offense with Cal's high-handedness.

"Morris, for all his political posturing, still keeps his ideology out of his art," retorted Cal. "His heart may bleed for the social outcast, but his art is pure. He, at least, knows the difference between making art and making speeches."

"Well, 'pure' art may be fine for *you*," said Andrea, "but for the poor man on the street, he has to know that we are on his side. He can't afford a decent meal let alone a work of 'pure' art. That's why I've turned to printmaking. With a small press and a clear message we can make affordable art, and get the word out to a far greater number of people. Our art has a *purpose* and that purpose is to make the world a better place."

"And that's very admirable," said Cal. "But that doesn't make what you run off your press *art*. 'Pure" art, as you put it so dismissively, also has a purpose — it is to raise us above the savage. Since time immemorial 'pure' art has been leading man out of the caves and into civilization — but it has done so on its *own* terms. Oh, it may get sidetracked now and then and put in harness by the church or politics or whatever new 'cause' the bleeding hearts choose to espouse — but it always manages to get free again. Social ills have been around for as long as we've had societies — but they come and go just like the present ones will. 'Pure' art, my dear, will endure — shall *always* endure."

Calvin Steele's polemic effectively put a damper on further discussion, and they soon broke up to go their separate ways.

Jake found that the afternoon had offered up many new ideas — Cal's included — and they teased his mind as he puttered around in his studio that evening.

Again, as abrasive as Calvin Steele always seemed to be — at least to Jake — what he had said about art not serving other 'masters' had something to it, especially when those other masters were worldly masters. Art, if Otto Rank was correct, might have originally served another end, but it was not anything that existed on earth — at least not until later. And even then, according to Sarah's father, abstract symbols continued to be made alongside the representational drawings. However, if Rank's theory was right, the making of images originally served an unseen, otherworldly, master. A spiritual one, as Cyrus Winters put it, and not necessarily the Christian interpretation of spirituality that Cal had been railing at. He wasn't sure, but he supposed that in other cultures there might be art that served Buddhist, Hebrew, or Islamic religions. He'd have to ask Cyrus Winters about that the next time he had the opportunity to speak with him.

Still, when Jake thought of the art of Calvin Steele or Morris Iskowitz — in fact, *most* of the modern art that he had seen since the Armory Show — he could find nothing 'spiritual' in it. Shapeless sculptures of pure form or seemingly random splotches of color held no attraction for him at all. Though such works of art certainly represented nothing that *he* had seen on earth, neither did they suggest anything of a 'higher' or 'spiritual' nature — at least it did not do so to him. How could such stuff — 'pure' or not — "lead us out of the caves" as Cal put it?

When he thought of the work he had seen at the Armory Show, he still tended to think that Uncle Hans and Aunt Birgit were right in regarding the confusion of images he had seen as no more than reactions against a hostile world. In that sense, they were more in line with the kind of art that Andrea Bundy had been defending. On the whole, however, Jake had sloughed off much of what he had seen at the Armory as self-indulgent excesses— simple outbursts much like the child's angry smears of paint on the living room walls in reaction to a parent's scolding.

Jake's sense that it was only self-indulgence on the part of the artists was reinforced by the discussions of the Rock City Group that he used to overhear when he returned to Woodstock after seeing the Armory Show back in 1913. Much of the talk back then centered on "freedom" — though, other than a release from traditional rules of draftsmanship or subjects such as landscape, Jake could not always determine what they sought freedom *from*. To them, anything that smacked of the academy was automatically suspect and irrelevant. 'Who needs to learn how to draw when I only want to paint?' was a constant refrain. Such arguments puzzled Jake. How could you tell the artist who *couldn't* draw from the one who chose *not* to draw? Surely it was difficult to make such a determination from much of what he saw at the Armory Show.

As to art for its own sake, it appeared very often to be much more a matter of art for the *artist's* sake. It seemed to Jake — contrary to Cal's argument that art should serve no master — that the artist who subscribed to that theory had only tricked himself into believing that he was actually free of restraint when he was now simply under the power of his own whims. '*I* want to paint like this.' '*I* don't want to take the time to learn how to draw.' '*I* am my own person.' How was this not simple self-indulgence? In his lecture, Lindin had mentioned the importance of ethics in the making of art — how did that mesh with Calvin Steele's belief that art ought to civilize us? Wasn't bringing man out of the cave just another form of ethics?

He would have liked to have Cyrus Winters there with him in his study as he pondered these matters. Jake liked the way the older man explained things, and wished that he were there to help him sort out these puzzles. Calvin — and Joe and Andrea, for that matter — were too close to their work to see beyond their own interests. Cyrus Winters had a broader perspective — had no vested interest in the subject of art. Even Cap'n Bob, for all his lack of sympathy for art and artists, offered a wider point of view than he might get from Cal or Joe or Andrea.

Until he might see Mr. Winters or the Cap'n, however, he contented himself with struggling once again with Plato's *Dialogues*, figuring that if he read more closely he might discover some clarification to the ideas crowding his head. He pulled Volume One down off the shelf and, leaning the back of his chair against the wall, settled in for a few hours of reading.

When the effort to make any headway eventually proved too daunting, he took the *Meditations* down from his bookshelf, and browsed though the Roman emperor's stoical observations of life, hoping in the end to gain strength if not wisdom.

48

It was still early September, but Jake could already see the beginnings of color starting to tinge the trees up on Overlook's higher reaches. He'd set up his easel in one of his favorite places, the open field owned by the High Woods chicken farmer who for many years had allowed him ready access to the view. Jake arrived shortly after dawn, impervious to the slightly damp chill that permeated the air as he went about his business of setting up his canvas and laying out his paints.

The clucking of waking hens in the large coop behind him did not disturb his thoughts as he stood quietly in the middle of the field gazing up at Overlook. He was aware in the back of his mind that the farmer would soon be out to feed his flock, but also knew that the kindly old man would not disturb him, would wait until Jake had folded up his easel and stop to say hello and thanks at his back door.

Jake continued his gaze. Bits of yellow and gold shone like jewels near Overlook's peak in the first rays of sunlight. A lush green — from this distance appearing as one homogenous hue — covered her lower flanks.

The blanket of green covering the land during the autumn season was different from that of the spring — it appeared more forceful, darker, more "green." It looked so unlike the delicate yellow-greens that appeared in March and April that one might have thought that the very trees had been replaced. Variations in hue were readily perceptible in the spring, the different trees each sporting their own choice of pastel raiment. Slowly, however, those subtle nuances would disappear and eventually level out to the uniform green of summer.

Jake knew that the homogeneity was an illusion, that on closer inspection, there were as many different "greens" in summer as there were in spring. Yet the illusion was compelling. Had he tried to paint what he saw from the field in which he stood, he would have used the same green for the entire mountain, mixing in only bits of blue or yellow here and there to suggest light and shadow on the larger masses.

Jake never tired of the changes. He loved his mountain in all seasons, eager each day to see what "face" she might present to him. Coyly hiding her flanks in morning mist? Sporting a multi-colored coat in autumn? Showing off her new cap of gleaming white after a snowfall? Or just glaring at him in bright sunlight — as she threatened to do today — daring him to set up his easel to try and paint *this*!

He wondered how a landscape painter could confine himself to painting in the studio. Yet, so many of the younger ones seemed to be doing just that. In recent years, he rarely ran into them out in the fields or woods in spite of the fact that they continued to bring landscapes into the Association's exhibits. He often heard some of the newcomers complain of the fickle weather or of the bugs or of the shifting light.

Still, how could they paint what they didn't even know? To his eyes, many of their landscapes look "posed" — almost as if the trees and fields had come into their studios and had sat for their portraits. He had long given up trying to figure out why some of the younger "moderns" felt it necessary to paint in unrealistic col-or and stylized forms, but many of these were realists — or at least *claimed* they were. Yet, as technically proficient as their paintings might look, to Jake their landscapes often seemed flat, sterile, too "manicured" to be convincing. You could *feel* that their paintings were not done out in the open air.

More troubling to him of late was the fact that since his mar-riage to Andrea, it was even getting difficult to get Joe Bundy to come out with him for a hike and an on-site sketch. Though he still painted out-of-doors, Joe was content to stay close to home, finding, as he put it, "a million new things to paint every day right on my own property." Apparently he had taken John Carlson's les-sons to "look out your back door" to heart. True, Joe's landscapes still had the stirring vitality that was the hallmark of the outdoor painter, but Jake missed their daylong or overnight jaunts up Overlook in search of new motifs. To his mind, nature had too much to teach the landscape painter for him to confine himself to one place — least of all a studio!

He turned to his palette and began lightening a glob of cerulean blue with white, trying as best he could to duplicate the delicate hue of pearly gray that filled the morning sky over Overlook. Cloudless. He filled the upper third of his canvas with swift passes of the knife.

Wiping the blade of the knife clean with a rag, Jake paused to lower his eyes from the sky to the scene before him. He knew that the confidence he felt when he painted the sky was now to be sorely tried. Capturing Overlook's swiftly shifting colors would not be so quickly accomplished as the uniformly flat, blue sky.

Birge Harrison had once spoken to him about the nature of color and how it affected the landscape painter. He'd been comparing it to music at the time and Jake, having no frame of reference for such a comparison, had comprehended little of what Harrison had been saying. He had gotten the point that a landscape painter's *only* place was outside of the studio, but it was only in later years that bits and pieces of what Harrison had tried to convey to him had not only come back, but had begun to make sense.

He could still recall that afternoon in Harrison's studio and, though it was years ago, still remembered the gist of the "lesson." Harrison tried to teach him that the color humans see was the result of vibrations — that color did not exist as a thing, but only as a sensation.

"The tree exists," he said, "But its color is only the result of our perception."

What would Sarah's father say about that? What might have Harrison thought of Plato's idea that not even the *tree* existed — and that *all* was a matter of perception?

"Color," he remembered Harrison saying. "The most important thing to a painter, doesn't even exist! Not only that, but the colors we *do* perceive are only half of the story. There are colors above and below our range of seeing, but they are still out there. Some of those color vibrations come to us as heat or sound. We can't see them, but we *feel* and *hear* them — they are there and they are affecting us as we stand outdoors. So the landscape painter who tries to paint nature from his studio is just not going to be able to paint a convincing landscape. It's not enough to make a tree *look* like a tree. You have to make it *feel* like a tree, *smell* like a tree. And the only way to do that is to allow that tree to affect all of your senses — even the ones you are not aware of — before you can ever succeed in painting it. You need to get not only the tree into your work, but you have to get *you* into your work, the *total* you — the conscious and the unconscious you. The French impressionists even got *sand* into their paintings when they painted beach scenes — you can still see it stuck in the pigment if you look close enough. But it takes a lifetime, Jake. It takes a lifetime of being *in* nature before you ever get it right — and even then you're going to fall short. Believe me, I know, Jake — I'm *still* learning."

At the time, a good deal of this was lost on Jake since he had all he could do to keep track of the basic concepts Harrison was firing at him. But now, after so many years of working with pigment, of struggling to master the distinction between line and mass, the lessons came back to him, and he was beginning to have an inkling of what the old master was attempting to teach him. He'd come a long way from learning about the mixing of primaries. He now knew how complementaries worked, about how 'warm' and 'cool' colors interacted, how colors seemed to come forward and recede, about aerial perspective, and a lot more technical stuff. But technique, he was beginning to find out, was not even the half of it. When you got right down to it, there was your blank canvas, some colored sticky stuff that you applied in blobs and smears, and what you saw — or *thought* you saw — out in front of you. Not very different from a kid with a sheet of paper, a handful of crayons, and an image in his head that only he can see.

He squinted at Overlook.

One more time, old girl.

49

"We'll go down to see the new Empire State Building and find a nice restaurant to eat at," said Jake. "Then we'll go to Brooklyn and visit the family. You haven't been down for years, and the trip will do you good."

Aunt Birgit, always intimidated by the largeness of New York City, did not appear eager to make the trip, so Jake continued to push. "We can spend a day or so with Mama and go visit Freddie and Konnie and their two children at their home. I'm sure little Freddie Jr. and Kirstin will be happy to see their great aunt. Come on, Aunt Birgit, we'll make a little holiday of it!"

The idea of seeing the children sparked her interest and Aunt Birgit seemed ready to relent — but she still would not commit. Even when she lived with her brother in Brooklyn, the thought of a trip to Manhattan filled her with dread. Moving upstate to the little town of West Hurley with Hans was one of the happiest decisions of her life.

She loved her home and was always reluctant to leave it. Nowadays even shopping trips held no interest for her, and she had fallen into the habit of depending upon Jake to bring in whatever supplies she needed. With the running water, the new propane-gas kitchen stove, the electricity, an oil furnace to heat the house, and an inside toilet, she had everything she needed, and had no desire to leave the privacy — and security — of her own domain. She and Hans had always loved their home, and even if Jake had not insisted on the improvements, she'd *still* love it. Compared to what she'd grown up with as a young girl back in Germany, the inconveniences of a water-pump, kerosene lamps, and wood stoves had never felt like real hardships. And though she had to admit that heating the house with oil certainly made life easier and the house cleaner, she was glad that neither Jake nor she was willing to give up the hours of quiet pleasure that having a wood-burning fireplace in the parlor had given them over the years. Working out in her flower and vegetable gardens was as far away from her home that Birgit Wolff ever wanted to go.

For his part, Jake had no great wish to make the trip either, but felt that the advancing ages of both Aunt Birgit and his mother made the visit to Brooklyn a must. Who knew how many years either of them had left? Though New York City did not hold the same dread for Jake as it did for his aunt, he had really no great desire to visit the family in Brooklyn. Even with his father gone, visiting his old home remained a trying experience for him.

More selfishly, he was further inclined to take the trip since he knew that the hard years of the '30s had also taken its toll on steamboat travel along the Hudson. With business falling off, fewer trips on the Day Liner to New York City and back were scheduled, and he wanted to take advantage of its services before they stopped running altogether.

After further persuasion on Jake's part and much deliberation and planning, they decided to make the excursion in the spring of 1940, at a time when Aunt Birgit would not be inconvenienced by the heat.

"I never liked the city in the summer or the winter," she said. "Too hot or too cold — not pleasant like up here. Must be all that cement."

Jake agreed with a nod, knowing that her reluctance had more than the weather behind it. Still, he couldn't disagree with her. He also preferred the spring or autumn to visit the city, and on the rare times he made the trip alone he always tried to schedule it just after or shortly before the Day Liners began and ended their seasonal journeys up and down the river.

Once they decided on a date, Aunt Birgit's level of excitement rose as the day approached. She had enlisted the help of her adjoining neighbors to "keep an eye out" on her house and, when the day finally arrived, Jake prevailed upon the young postal clerk who lived across the lane to run them over to the train station in his new motorcar.

"Ach," exclaimed Aunt Birgit as she climbed into the back seat.

"I never dreamed I'd be in one of these things." She turned to Jake. "Is it safe?"

Jake smiled as he settled her in with their bags tucked on the seat beside her. For as long as he'd had his pickup, he never once could get her to take a ride in it with him. "As safe as our gig used to be," he said. "Maybe even safer when you consider that this contraption doesn't bite when it gets contrary."

Gary, the postal clerk, chimed in with, "Don't worry Mrs. Wolff. I drive over to the post office every day and I guarantee you're in good hands." He patted his hand on the dashboard as if he were patting a horse. "We'll get you to the station safe and sound!"

"Well, it sure is neighborly of you to do this," she said.

"No problem at all, Mrs. Wolff. The train station is practically right on my way to work anyway. So just don't think that you're putting me out any. It's the least I can do after all those fresh vegetables you bring over to Mom every summer — and those cookies for me! This way I can pay you back, sort of."

"Well, we thank you anyway, Gary, and appreciate your kindness," said Jake.

Their arrival at the train depot in Gary's motorcar allowed for Aunt Birgit to make a grand entry, and Jake was amused to watch his aunt as she stepped out onto the platform with her head held high like some highborn lady. He could see little of her former reluctance to visit the city as she stood rigidly erect while waiting for the train to come.

Jake, however, saw that even the excitement of the short train trip to Kingston and then down to the Rondout to catch the morning steamer had already been wearing on Aunt Birgit's energies. When he got her settled up on the observation deck of the steamer, he noted how fragile she was. She had always been such a robust and capable woman that he hadn't noticed the slow deterioration over the years. He felt a little guilty about insisting on the trip, but when he also thought of both her and his mother's age, he satisfied himself that he was doing the right thing. He felt confident that it would be good for both of them.

"You just sit back and enjoy the scenery, Aunt Birgit," he said. "I'm going to stroll around a bit." When she turned to him with an uneasy glance he added, "But don't worry. I'll check up on you from time to time. Can I get you anything? A warm drink?"

"No, no," she answered. She patted her large handbag. "I have everything I need here."

Jake knew that she had packed several sandwiches to "tide them over" in spite of the fact the he had told her several times that they might purchase anything they needed during the trip down river. He thought that a look into the sumptuously appointed dining room when they first boarded might change her mind, but she merely glanced around and headed for the door, content to remain outside.

"You're sure now?" he asked again.

"This trip is expensive enough," she had retorted. "I'm not sure why you're willing to waste money like this anyway."

And again he reminded her of how much fun it would be to see the changes in New York City, of how nice it would be visiting Mama and Freddie, and especially of how exciting it would be for Freddie, Jr. and Kirstin to see and spend some time with her. Thoughts of the children brought her around once more, but Jake could still hear her muttering about the "expense" as he left her sitting on deck.

Satisfied that she was all right and would have a good view during the trip, Jake hurried to find a place along the starboard railing. They had already left the landing and had pulled out into the middle of the river, as Jake turned toward the stern to watch his beloved mountains slowly recede. The sight still stirred him. The early morning sun was already high and warming, the entire eastern face of the Catskill range lit up like the backdrop of a stage setting.

Jake divided his time during the trip between checking up on Aunt Birgit and in keeping his eye on the receding silhouette of the Catskills until they rounded the bend at Crum Elbow. Once the mountains were out of sight, Jake settled himself alongside his aunt, and as they ate their sandwiches, allowed his eyes to take in the landscape closer to the river.

There were many changes since his voyage upriver as a boy. More homes appeared along the river's banks, and he noticed less activity as they stopped at the various landings along the river route. Railroads and motor vehicles had been gradually replacing the barges and steamers as a means of transporting goods or people. Everyone seemed in more of a hurry now, wanting to get both their goods and themselves to and from places in less time.

The few hours in the City quickly took their toll on Aunt Birgit. Jake could tell that it was as much the bustle and noise as it was the getting to the Empire State Building that had sapped her energies and, fter a short time looking over the city from the building's observation deck, they left for Brooklyn.

Chagrined that he had insisted on the short stopover in Manhattan, Jake salved his conscience by satisfying himself that at least the trip to Brooklyn was necessary if only that it gave his aunt and his mother an opportunity for what might be there last time together.

* * *

Change had almost been the only topic of conversation after they had settled in at his mother's home on Halsey Street. Aunt Birgit had visibly shown the strains of travel, and Konnie was quick to note and tend to it, offering her a cup of tea almost before she had gotten out of her coat.

Aunt Birgit breathed a heavy sigh of relief as she finally extricated herself from the children and sank back into a seat at the kitchen table, the cup of tea that Konnie had handed her already up to her lips before she was seated.

"Be careful *Tante* Birgit. It's very hot," said Konnie. She turned her attention to her children. "And Freddie! — Kirstin! — you let your *Tante* Birgit catch her breath! You'll have plenty of time to play with her after she gets settled. Now go to your room and play."

Jake was pleased by his sister-in-law's ministrations to Aunt Birgit, something she had undoubtedly been accustomed to in attending to her mother-in-law. Both Aunt Birgit and Hannelore Forscher were well into their seventies and, seeing them together, the two sisters-in-law almost seemed like sisters so similar were they in their manners and expressions.

As the ladies settled around the kitchen table to exchange gossip and catch up on news, his brother led Jake into the parlor where they could talk. Jake was amazed at how much his brother resembled Papa. Freddie, in spite of his getting rid of the mustache in deference to the latest fashion for the "clean-shaven look," was the spitting image of their father. As usual, he even *sounded* like Papa.

316

"You're looking fit, little brother," said Freddie.

"And *you're* looking prosperous." Jake patted his brother's stomach. He appraised Freddie's growing bulk — so much like papa! — and realized that he was looking down into his older brother's eyes. "Though I'm not so sure that I'm the *little* brother anymore."

Freddie sprawled into a sofa. "Well, yes, business is good — and, being in the butcher business, we never go hungry, that's for sure."

Jake remained standing. "How's Mama? She's looking frailer than ever."

"Not so good — not so good. Konnie and I are thinking about moving in with her here. That way Konnie can keep a closer eye on her. Besides, this house is getting to be too much for her."

"She all right with that?" Jake asked. "You're moving in?"

"Oh, yes," said Freddie. "We've been talking it over with her for quite some time now, and she seems eager for us to make the move. We figure on bringing our stuff over, and setting her up in her own apartment upstairs. As it is, Konnie is over here almost every day to help keep things in order. This way, we can combine our energies — and, of course, save on rent."

"It makes sense," agreed Jake. "You know, Freddie, I've never really thanked you for looking out for Mama. It's good that you're here to help her."

"Well, once she got past Papa's death, she was really not much trouble. She and Konnie get along first rate, and Mama seems to love having the kids around even though the little devils quickly tire her out." He smiled fondly. "She certainly tends to spoil them, that's for sure."

Jake wondered if his mother's change of heart came about after his father's death. As far as he could recall, Mama was never very demonstrative with her affections when he and Freddie were children.

"Well, that's fine, Freddie," said Jake. "I'm glad to hear that all is going well for you — and Mama. And the kids look great!"

"Yes," said Freddie as he rapped his knuckles on the wooden arm of the sofa. "Knock on wood — we've got nothing to complain of." He looked up at Jake who had remained standing. "And you, Jake? How are things with you? Aunt Birgit seems to be taking care of you all right."

"Oh, she's always done that. Sometimes a bit of a fussbudget but we've always gotten along fine."

Freddie frowned. "Never found a line that suited you, eh Jake? It's too bad you never settled into a steady trade."

Here we go again Jake thought.

"I've never wanted for work, Fred. We're not going hungry either, Aunt Birgit and I."

"Well, yes — if you want to call being a handyman 'work.'"

"Seems a lot like work when I'm doing it," said Jake as he took a seat across from his brother.

"Oh, you know what I mean. It's not a *real* trade — a business. You need to have an occupation that people look up to."

"You mean like a butcher?"

"Well, yes — I happen to be looked up to in this neighborhood. I'm known as a solid citizen, a person who can be depended on. Now that the kids are attending St. Barbara's, Konnie and I have become active in the church. The community looks up to people like us Jake — we give the neighborhood stability."

It was hard for Jake to see West Hurley as anything *but* stable — and, for that matter, his occupation as anything but acceptable. But, long used to this line of reasoning from his father, he chose to ignore arguing with his brother.

"So the kids go to St. Barbara's?"

"Yes. Konnie, you know, was brought up a very strict Catholic, so sending the kids to St. Barbara's was pretty much of a sensible thing to do."

Sensible. A by-word of the Forscher household. "Do they like it?" Jake asked.

"Well, I suppose they do." He looked at Jake. "What's their 'liking' it have anything to do with it? They go to school to learn — not because they *like* it."

Jake shrugged.

"It's an odd question," said Freddie. "Maybe not having children of your own has something to do with it." He laughed. "How would you know how kids are anyway?"

"True," said Jake.

Freddie hesitated a moment before asking, "How come you never got married Jake?"

Jake settled himself back into his seat. "Lots of reasons, I guess.

318

For one, I never found a woman that I *wanted* to marry."

Freddie shook his head. "You never fell in love, Jake?"

The conversation was leading him into areas that he did not want to go and only said, "I'm not sure — I'm not even sure that I know what 'love' really is, Freddie. But for now, I'm fine the way I am."

Before Freddie could pursue the matter, Konnie came in to tell them that supper was on the table.

Jake quickly jumped up and said, "Good! I'm starving!" and followed Konnie into the kitchen where — at least to his way of thinking — a sumptuous feast was carefully laid out on the table.

"Wow!" he said. "You expecting more company?"

Konnie had outdone herself.

"My, my," said Aunt Birgit. "There's enough here for several meals."

Jake was already helping himself to the various wursts that they had brought home from the shop and, heaping his plate with piles of sauerkraut, pickled potatoes, and beets along with a large chunk of freshly-baked bread, immediately fell to filling his mouth.

"Dig in," said Freddie with a beaming smile, pleased that his wife could show just how prosperous they were.

Eventually, the discussion came around to world events and, particularly, to what was transpiring in the "old country."

The news of Germany's aggression and the threat of a new World War deeply troubled Aunt Birgit and Mama, both of them deploring what might once again happen to family members who still lived there.

"This Hitler sounds like a fanatic," Aunt Birgit was saying to Hannelore. "And now with this marching of troops into Austria, who knows what might happen?"

"I don't know that he's a fanatic," interrupted Freddie. "After all, it's been too long that we've let the world put the whole blame on Germany for what happened in 1914. No one had clean hands back then. And, even now, the Munich Pact that he's made with Britain, France, and Italy, shows that they all agreed to the partitioning of Czechoslovakia. Annexing Austria was the logical next step — after all, they are all Germans, *nicht wahr?* He is only doing what is best for his country."

Jake glanced over at his brother. He could never remember

hearing him speak German before.

"That's true," said Mama looking over at her sister-in-law. "We know how much the rabble-rousing extremists have been fomenting trouble since the end of the big war. We've gotten letters from family that are heartbreaking to read." She held out her hands, and turned toward her eldest son. "He's only trying to help our people, isn't he Freddie?"

"Of course, Mama! He is a good leader. Look how he has brought prosperity back to Germany!"

"But what about what they are doing to the Jews?" said Konnie hesitantly. "This can do no good."

Freddie waved her remark away with disdain. Looking at Jake, he said, "What do women know about politics?"

Jake kept his counsel, but Aunt Birgit pushed on with, "And that Kristallnacht? Such a shameful thing! How could such terrible destruction like that help our people?"

"Ahh, the Jews," said Freddie with another wave of his hand, but did not contradict his aunt.

"It certainly is not helping our people in *this* country," said Konnie a bit more confidently. "The children come home from school in tears because the other children taunt them."

"What?" said Freddie. "How come I was not told about this? Who taunted them? Why were they crying?"

Konnie looked from her husband to her children. "Tell Papa what they do," she said.

"They call us 'kraut' and 'Nazi'," said Freddie Jr. He looked up at his grandmother. "What is a 'Nazi,' Grandma?"

"*Du lieber Gott*, all over again," said Aunt Birgit, as Hannelore Forscher passed her hand over her eyes.

"It's nothing," said Freddie, glaring at his son. "And I don't want to hear that they made you cry again, young man!" He slammed his hand on the table. "Next time you fight them back when they call you foolish names."

Kirstin's eyes filled with tears at her father's growing anger.

Jake pushed himself away from the table as his brother roared, "*More* tears!"

What price prosperity? Jake thought.

* * *

Both he and Aunt Birgit felt a sense of relief when they left Brooklyn to cross over to Manhattan three days later.

Jake thought about making a visit to the Metropolitan Museum of Art, but knew that Aunt Birgit had had enough and was more than ready to get back home.

"Care for another jaunt around the big city before we head back upstate?" Jake teased.

"Ach! You get me on that steamship as quick as you can! I miss my home!" she replied crankily.

They caught the morning boat, and, thankfully, the warm and sunny weather held. He might have been mistaken, but he thought he detected a visible lightening of her spirits and a more youthful spring to her step as they sailed upriver.

Jake knew the feeling.

50

"It's all about light, isn't it?" said Jake.

Joe, staring at the flowing water of the brook, was locked in thought, and did not answer right away. "Hmm," he finally offered.

Jake took that for a 'yes.'

They had their easels set up a few yards apart, Joe's facing the brook behind his house, Jake's turned in the opposite direction, facing Overlook Mountain. He could just see its peak over the trees that lined the road across from the Bundy's home. Puffy little summer cumulous drifted overhead, strung out in a row as if coming from the smokestack of some faraway locomotive.

It was a bright sunny morning, and one of the rare occasions that he and Joe had recently been finding time to paint together. They both always enjoyed sharing the experience of painting and talking but, for one reason or another, never seemed to find the right time. Either the weather was bad, or one or the other had prior commitments to attend to during the daylight hours.

For Joe, it was the duties of a husband that most often kept him away, while for Jake, it was his day work.

Although he no longer did handyman work — scything or swinging his axe — his prime source of income continued to be his carpentry, a skill for which he was regularly sought out by both townspeople and artists. Nearly all of the farmer's outbuildings that had once served as temporary "studios" were no longer available, most already converted into full-time working studios or made over into homes. Like the once popular boarding houses of Mrs. Magee and Mrs. Cooper, inexpensive and ready accommodations were now a thing of the past. Living in and around Woodstock was beginning to be a pricey undertaking as land taxes increased and boarding and rental fees rose accordingly. The steadily growing population demanded new homes, and slowly but surely the farms disappeared as more and more artists took up permanent residence in and around Woodstock and Jake found no lack of jobs coming his way.

He diligently pursued his painting, but attempted fewer canvases now, taking more time to compose his thoughts and his compositions, tackling each new landscape with more deliberation and less impetuousness. He continued to use the knife more often than the brush, feeling that it gave a less fussy finish to his work. There were still times when he fell into his old habit of wanting to 'draw' his picture when he had a brush in his hand, and the result was almost always disappointing.

He had long taken Harrison's "squinting lessons" to heart and, when he came upon a new view that showed possibilities, deliberately ignored details to better concentrate his attention on values and masses. Jake's years of drawing had so conditioned him to seeing only line, that making the transition to painting still meant that he had to unlearn this ingrained habit, and to consciously force his eye to see mass. He had to constantly be on his guard to overlook "edges" and instead to note how shapes interlocked and worked both against and with each other. Slowly, he was learning how value — qualities of light and dark — affected perception, how it made things seem to advance and recede on both the canvas and in actuality.

And though he had become highly proficient in the mixing of his oils, he was still learning and discovering how the application of color complicated the process. Finally, on top of all that, he was becoming ever more aware that, in spite of what appeared to be 'out there,' his own state of mind remained of paramount importance: how *he* felt at that moment since it was ultimately *his* perception that carried the day. It had been an important revelation to discover that his vacillating state of mind was just as important — if not more so — than the ever-changing tricks of nature.

The puffs of cumulous marching across the sky increased as the morning warmed. Jake ignored them, refraining from including them in his painting. Clouds were never easy — especially these lacy cotton-balls. Whenever he attempted to put them in a painting, they never "sat" right on the canvas, always looking as if they were added as an afterthought. He preferred the more dramatic stratus clouds — streaks of wispy vapor that could be suggested in quick, sweeping slashes of his knife.

"I guess," Joe suddenly said, interrupting Jake's train of thought.

"Guess what?" asked Jake.

Another long pause as Jake waited for an answer.

"What you just said — that it's all about light," He leaned his head to one side, studying his canvas. "But sometimes I'm not so sure." He laid his brushes down and stepped away from his easel.

Jake followed suit and they met somewhere between their set-ups, each averting his gaze from the other's easel in respect for the unspoken law of not looking at an unfinished canvas unless invited to do so.

"I mean there's the light," continued Joe. He looked up at the sun. "Yes, the goddamned, ever-shifting light!" He turned his eyes toward the brook he was painting — for how many times? A hundred? A thousand? — and said, "But then there's the brook. The goddamned brook!"

Jake shook his head and laughed.

"It's not funny," said Joe. "It's maddening! Yeah, sure, it's the light. Every instructor I ever had always said, 'It's the light, boy'. But what light? The light that shone on that goddamned brook an hour ago? Twenty minutes ago? Two *seconds* ago? How am I supposed to know *which* light I'm supposed to pay attention to? I've painted this brook from the exact same spot I don't know how many times — in early morning, noontime, mid-afternoon, late afternoon — Hell, I've sat out here when it was almost dark trying to get it right."

Jake nodded. "I know what you mean." He looked toward Over-look. "My Uncle Hans used to talk about the 'blue hour' — you know, that time between sundown and darkness — what we'd call twilight, I guess. I've never seen any artist that ever caught *that* light just right."

"The 'blue hour'," said Joe. "I like that."

"My uncle said that they always called it that in the old country. I know exactly what he means — the world does look blue, kind of, at that time of day."

"Maybe Inness — at times," said Joe. "He could sometimes get that bluish color in his landscapes. But, you're right. Maybe we Americans just don't see that 'blue hour.'"

"Funny that they saw it like that — I mean different from the way we do." He scratched his head. "I wonder if the light's different over there."

Joe shrugged. "What I've been saying ... light is light is light."

After awhile, by silent and mutual consent they decided to call it quits and began cleaning and packing up their brushes. After the assenting nod had been acknowledged, each had wandered over to the other's easel to look.

"Where's my house?" asked Joe after a few moments.

"I sold it," said Jake. He glanced back at his own painting. "It didn't really belong there, anyway."

Joe bent to look closer at Jake's painting of the row of trees and distant field that lay across the road from his front porch. "Nice," he said. "Your usual strong statement." He straightened up. "But I still miss my house." He turned to look over at Jake who was peering intently at his painting of the brook. "What's *wrong* with my house? Don't you like it?"

"I like it well enough — especially when Andrea's cooked up something good to eat inside." He jabbed his thumb in the direction of Overlook. "But that view was there long before somebody decided to plop a house right down in the middle of it. I prefer seeing it the way it was before."

"Hmmm," murmured Joe. "Do you think you'll ever put buildings in your paintings, Jake?"

"I don't know." He pointed to Joe's painting. "I like this — especially the way you've handled the shade on that opposite bank." He turned to Joe. "Do you think you'll ever get this brook just the way you want it?"

Joe threw up his hands. "*Which* brook? The one that was there two hours ago? One hour ago? Five minutes ago? Or the one that's there now? Just like the light, it changes all day long. Hell, I don't even want to think about the business of seasons here — and all that involves. That Greek — what was his name? — Heraclitus — once said that you can't step into the same river twice. Boy, was he ever on target!" Joe snorted. "Must have been a painter as well as a philosopher."

"So, I guess what you're saying is that it's not just the light, but how it falls on your subject."

"To tell you the truth, Jake, I'm not sure *what* I'm saying. Like I said a few minutes ago, art instructors are always harping on light. 'Look where it's coming from.' 'See how it casts shadows.' 'See how it affects color.' And so on, and so on. But I haven't met a teacher yet who didn't contradict himself at one time or another. About all you can actually say, I guess, is that there are no hard and fast rules — that's why all the experts eventually contradict themselves. True, we need light to *see* — but I'm not always sure just what it is we're supposed to be seeing."

Jake pondered that while he folded up his easel. He looked up at Overlook's peak.

So, are you really there? Or are you just a trick?

"I mean," Joe continued, "there's that brook. I see it every day, but I'm not exactly positive what it *is*. I'm not sure I'm making sense here, but the thing I'm trying to say is that the light is falling on objects the nature of which we are hardly aware. Talk to some scientist, and he'll tell you that this tree here or that rock over there is not really as solid as we like to think. It's made up of molecules, atoms — whatever — but things we really can't see that are not only in constant movement, but sometimes not there at all." He threw up his hands again. "So, what we're seeing is not *really* what we're *seeing*. Now make sense out of *that*."

"It sort of makes sense," said Jake. "There are times when I think that I can see Overlook Mountain better in the dark — when I *can't* see it — than when it's in full sunlight. I mean *really* see it — like in my mind's eye." He looked over at Joe. "You know what I mean?"

"Yeah, kinda," agreed Joe. "It happens sometimes to me when I'm with Andrea. Like, we'll be sitting in the dark, no lights on in the house, and just sitting there talking to each other in the living room. Sometimes I get the strange feeling that I can *hear* her better — and, I suppose, *see* her better — when I can't see her. Or, at any rate, can't see that image that passes for her." He frowned. "Ahh, it's all illusion, the whole thing. Those Hin-doos got it right. And the light just makes the whole picture-show play out before us — just as if we were sitting in a theatre watching a moving picture. Turn off the projector light and all we're left with is a blank screen."

326

Jake nodded. "I've read or heard somewhere that when we look up at the sun, we can only see it as it was about eleven minutes ago because it takes that long for the light to travel to the earth. That's kind of eerie when you think about it."

"And when it *does* get here," added Joe, "it simply bounces off whatever it strikes, and it's that bouncing that our eyeballs see — it's what makes perception happen." He shrugged. "Aaah, it's *all* eerie, if you ask me."

"I *did* ask you," he said with a smile. "So, in a sense, we never *really* see what we're looking at — only the light that's reflected off it."

"Whatever '*it*' is," said Joe. "Whatever the Hell that brook is over there that I keep trying to paint." He looked at his painting and frowned again. "Geez! The last thing Andrea needs is another one of my brook paintings added to the collection."

"But they usually sell at the Association exhibits, don't they?"

"Yeah — one every month or so for every *three* I make each week."

They headed toward the house.

"Coming in for a bit?" asked Joe.

"Nope. Got a few chores to do for Aunt Birgit before the day's out." He put his paintbox on the front seat of his pickup.

"She's getting on in years, isn't she," said Joe.

"Yep — but still going strong. She'll probably outlive me."

Jake glanced up at Overlook once again.

So whose trick are you? Mine — or God's?

He climbed into his truck and before driving off, said, "Like I said, Joe. It's all about the light, isn't it?"

"Get the Hell out of here," said Joe as he waved him off. "And say hello to Aunt Birgit for us," he yelled as Jake pulled out of his driveway.

51

A little over twenty years after Jake had come home from the "war to end all wars," World War II broke out, and once again Europe was in turmoil and conflict. Hitler's invasion of Poland on September 1, 1939, precipitated a declaration of war against Germany two days later by France and Great Britain. To the consternation of many Americans, their country would once more find herself involved in the affairs of foreign nations when, just a bit over two years later, after an attack by the Japanese on its territories at Pearl Harbor on December 7, 1941, the United States joined in the action the following day.

America's entering the war did not come altogether as a surprise to those who kept abreast of events. Germany's actions preceding its invasion of Poland seemed designed to provoke negative world opinion and, although most Americans were reluctant to once again be involved in Europe's affairs, December 7th put an end to all arguments against our participation. For Jake the only bright spot on the horizon was that he was too old to participate in the coming carnage.

Though neither he nor Aunt Birgit suffered any of the anti-German feelings that had once beset Uncle Hans and that were now being experienced by Freddie and Konnie's children, such sentiment did crop up again in Woodstock. This time, the bugaboos of imagined spies turned some people unreasonable while it merely brought fear to others. German spies were seen everywhere by the alarmists even, to Jake's amusement, spotted sending "messages" to God knows where from Overlook's peak. For his part, Jake went on as before, avoiding political discussion and going on about his work.

His frame-making "business" had become so successful that he soon found it possible to spend less time on outside projects and more in his studio. At forty-seven, he was not sorry to take on fewer jobs. His years of hard work had begun to tell, his ability to bend and twist not as easy as it used to be, and the light labor involved in frame-making suited him just fine.

His frames were prized not only for their rusticity — a great favorite with the landscape artists — but also for their fine workmanship, and it was not long before many of the Woodstock artists — landscape painters or not — sought him out. He slowly built up a stock of various moldings for just this purpose, and had even begun looking forward to the short visits of artists who came to his studio to choose whatever style suited their subjects or tastes. Always a patient listener, Jake carefully heard out his customers, and there were few that were ever dissatisfied with a "Forscher Frame."

Jake, meanwhile, was learning a great deal about the framing of pictures, supplementing what he learned from artists with what he could find in books. Artists of the past, he had discovered, had often chosen to make their own frames, unwilling to trust anyone else to make the proper "match" for their work. The framing of a picture, he soon discovered, was almost as much a fine art as was the painting of it. A frame had to "fit" — not only in size, which was obvious — but also in its suitability to the work being so enclosed within its border. A frame ought not "fight" with a picture and it was generally felt by most artists that the best kind of frame was one that you did not notice when looking at a painting. The frame should enhance but not overpower. The days of the ornate and gilded baroque frame, so suitable for palace walls, were gone — how many lived in palaces today?

A corollary to this lesson about framing pictures was that of arranging pictures in an exhibition. He had long heard about the hazards of "hanging a show" — both by those who did the hanging, and by those whose work was hung. Few artists are ever quite satisfied with the positioning of their work in an exhibition, but most were incensed by having their work hanging above or below the "line." The line — or the eye-level position — was most often the privileged position of the senior members of any organization. A hard-and-fast but unwritten rule, the general feeling was that, no matter the quality or subject matter of the work, older members had "earned" the right of preferential treatment and thus have their paintings properly seen. Newcomers had to be content with having their work either "skyed" — that is, hung above eye-level — or placed so low that the viewer had to uncomfortably crouch to clearly see it. To any artist, however, any position other than on the line was unsatisfactory since the work could only be improperly viewed when it was not.

But Jake had also learned that there were even more subtle problems to deal with in this business of hanging a show. There were pitfalls facing the person responsible for setting up an exhibition that were less obvious than placing a picture above or below an arbitrary but well-established sight line. To hang a show with some skill meant paying close attention not only to position, but also with an educated eye toward picture content — and even, at times, to the frames themselves. Artists and knowledgeable museum and gallery visitors had long known that pictures "speak" to each other, as well as to the viewers gazing upon them. Some paintings can "out-shout" their neighbors simply by virtue of their strong compositions or colors or frames. Moving a painting from one location to another where it has different "neighbors" can often strongly influence its impact on the eye. Woe to the picture hanger who ignored such things! An irate artist was sure to be in the near future of the miscreant to set matters right.

Jake had even noticed this phenomenon in his own studio when he took down one painting to replace it with another. All of a sudden, a picture could look "better" or "worse" than it did previously when it hung alongside of another — or no painting at all. This realization would be further reinforced on his rare visits to a museum like the Metropolitan Museum of Art in New York City to see his favorite pictures, only to find that the directors had moved them to other walls or rooms. The change in his perception of the paintings in their new positions was often startling, so altered would they appear in different locations.

Since the hanging of their work was often beyond their control — or worse, under the direction of people who may never have painted a picture themselves — artists had become necessarily wary over the years of how and where their work was to be seen. Though he had no extensive experience of having his work shown in a gallery, Jake turned a sympathetic ear to his long-suffering and long-complaining customers. He welcomed their comments and suggestions, often picking up new tips and ideas during their visits, constantly astonished at how many things an artist had to worry about in addition to the difficult task of plying his trade of image-making.

Along with such finer points as to the framing and hanging of artwork, Jake was also steadily improving in evaluating his own development as a painter. If he was still not as confident as he might wish to be, he had definitely come a long way since his fumbling attempts during his early years of groping his way toward mastering the skill. Though he often felt handicapped by having to learn largely on his own, he had only in recent years come to appreciate Birge Harrison's repeated counsel that such a method was perhaps the best after all.

In retrospect, he could see that Harrison was wise enough to give him ideas rather than lessons. By having to find his own way, Jake was beholden to no teacher and, more importantly, had no lessons to unlearn in the search for his own vision. All too often he had seen younger artists attempting to imitate their instructors, turning out poor copies rather than original works. What Jake painted was his alone — and whether good or bad, could only be laid at his door. He still stubbornly refused to put anything but his initials — always using the same-sized small block letters, no matter the size of the painting — in the lower right hand corner of his canvases. Titling his paintings became increasingly more difficult over the years since so many had Overlook as its major feature. If his work was persistently realistic, his titles became increasingly more abstract as he resorted ever more often to such general designations as "Summer," "Fall," "Vista," "Early Morning," "Mist," or simply, "View." The only other identifying mark his paintings contained was a date on the back — a habit he continued more for his own use than for the convenience of others.

No longer a stranger to the Woodstock Artists Association's gallery walls, he was still as thrilled as he was dumbfounded whenever a painting of his was accepted for exhibition. Equally disconcerting was to be seen and acknowledged by locals as well as artists, not as a carpenter, but ever more frequently as an artist. At one of the few times he attended an opening reception, he heard some people excitedly speaking about one of the paintings and, upon turning to see which painting they were looking at, was amazed to learn that it was *his*.

On another occasion while he was visiting the Association on a Saturday afternoon, he overheard a young man speaking about one of his most recent renditions of Overlook to a woman beside him.

"Very powerful," he was saying. "Strong brushwork — or is that projecting ridge of paint there the result of a knife-edge? Step closer and see how the painter builds up the pigment so that it not only *suggests* the bark of a tree, but actually *looks* like it! The texture is almost overwhelming in its impact. Yet, step back a few paces and look how it all melds together in a seamless depiction of nature. Surely a fine painter!"

When the gallery attendant pointed out to the speaker that Jake was the painter, the young man strode over and introduced himself as "David Lehrer from New York City," making the announcement as if Jake undoubtedly already knew — or ought to have known — who he was. Vigorously shaking his hand, "David Lehrer from New York City" immediately launched into a series of comments and questions before Jake had a chance to respond any further than giving his name.

Taken off guard by the suddenness of the encounter, Jake could only flush and stammer, unable to intelligently answer the questions that were so rapidly being thrown at him. Anxious to avoid the man's pointed questioning, Jake protested a pressing commitment and quickly made his escape. He had never felt easy talking about his painting to strangers and, for reasons just such as this, had customarily avoided the Association on weekends when there were more visitors coming in.

Even more unnerving, however, was the first time some youngster came up to ask *him* for advice! Blunt at first — perhaps *too* blunt — he had slowly warmed to the idea of sharing some of his ideas with a younger artist, remembering his own need for such conversation when he had first started out. He could see himself in their faltering approach, their hesitant questions, and their obvious pleasure when he took the time to pay attention and answer them.

Selling his work was still problematic for Jake and, in spite of the Association members' urging, he continued to put a not-for-sale or "NFS" sticker alongside his paintings whenever they appeared in exhibitions. The Association Board, not unreasonably, expected their members to sell their art since a percentage of each sale went into their treasury. As it was, not many artists were selling their work now with the apprehensions and fears of what a new war might do to the economy. Though he was more willing to discuss his feelings about selling his art — often quoting Henry David Thoreau's admonition that "trade curses everything it handles… and though you trade in messages from heaven, the whole curse of trade attaches to the business" — he had still not reconciled himself to the practicality of putting a price tag on his paintings. Notwithstanding the usual argument that it was the "product" and not the artist's creative "soul" that was being sold, Jake still felt strongly that, at bottom, the making of art was precisely those "messages of heaven" that Thoreau spoke of, and that turning the making of art into a trade could only sully it.

Having his foot more firmly planted in Woodstock's creative community made him more sensitive to the inner workings and machinations of the various Woodstock cliques that had been continuously forming and reforming since the art colony's inception. Ever since the infighting about funds in the '20s had caused so many rifts and hard feelings, many of the artists had been aligning themselves along new lines of interest that did not always coincide with those of the past. Whereas at one time the Colony had been broadly separated into the several groups at Byrdcliffe, the Art Students League, the Maverick, and Rock City, nowadays the groups tended to be smaller, splintered off from what had been formerly centered on conservative, moderate, or modern predilections.

With Byrdcliffe now almost entirely out of the mix insofar as the visual arts were concerned, modernists, traditional landscape painters, and those in-between, tended to band together in like-minded political and social groups that to Jake's mind were often divisive and self-defeating. The Association, once proudly proclaiming its inclusiveness, was beset with in-house squabbles that periodically resulted in member resignations and defections. Coupled with the slowly tightening economy, this pervasive alienation between what was once a close-knit confraternity of artists with one aim — to make and exhibit art — caused the Association to completely cease the practice of holding exhibitions throughout the entire year of 1941. Cohesiveness among artists was slowly disintegrating in the Colony and, for Jake, none of these shifts in focus and attitude boded well.

When, on December 8th of 1941 the United States entered the war, it seemed to be a moot question if the once flourishing art colony would ever regain its former glory.

BOOK FIVE

1947 — 1954

52

IN THE SUMMER of 1947, the Art Students League of New York returned to Woodstock and once more offered summer sessions outside of its facility in New York City. Though some of the instructors had been taking their classes out to Central Park to experience on-site painting from time to time, the costs of running a full-scale operation outside of its walls on 57th Street were too forbidding during the war years — they had neither the enrollment nor the available funds to justify it. Painting *en plein air* had become somewhat passé in any case, and the number of students registering for landscape painting classes had been accordingly dwindling. The resumption of their summer classes in Woodstock, however, was as much a matter of necessity as of policy.

The simple fact was that the school had been unexpectedly flooded with so many applications for classes — for year-long as well as for the summer season instruction — that they had no other recourse but to resurrect their summer season in Woodstock to accommodate the sudden increase in enrollment. After so many years of barely-filled classes during the depression and on into the war years, the Board of Control was both pleased and astonished to discover that their building on West 57th Street in New York City, in spite of its size — and almost overnight, so to speak — was simply full to overflowing.

Most of these new students were veterans just returned from the war, newly discharged from the military and ready to rejoin America's work force. Their time in the service had exposed them not only to new experiences, but also to new ideas, new lifestyles, and — perhaps even more important — to new horizons. They sought broader opportunities, and for many, a fresh start in a different career seemed the shortest path to attain them.

Although the war had brought many hardships to America in the form of food or gas rationings, the abrupt production of quickly needed military hardware had also brought about a new and burgeoning economy to its people. Those too young or too old for active service had fared relatively well back home during the years their armed compatriots had given their time and lives to their country who, upon their release from duty, were eager to share in the prosperity they helped to create and to protect.

Not content to come back to small-town employment, over-worked farms, or the drudgery of menial, low-paying jobs, many turned to the government they had served for compensation, and they sought it in the form of direction, jobs, and opportunities. They wanted not only a hero's welcome, but also a chance to start anew; they wanted to become not only productive members of society — but to become more *affluent* members of that society.

It was estimated that after the war the US Army was shipping GIs home at the rate of one million a month, so the difficulty of satisfying all demands was a considerable one for the government. Whatever the bureaucrats in Washington could and would do, however, they were fortunately not alone in seeking ways to face the situation. Some of the homecoming veterans had their own entrepreneurial ideas of how to better their situations.

One 38-year old US Navy veteran, William J. Levitt, for instance, fell back on his past experience as a builder and, coupled with a new vision inspired by the mass production methods of Henry Ford, saw an efficient way to put up quickly-constructed, afford-able homes for his fellow veterans. Thus, was "Levittown" born on New York's Long Island. At the rate of 30 new homes a day, Levitt not only made his own fortune, but also made it possible for many of his compatriots to find inexpensive housing as well.

Bold and daring in its conception — by comparison, during the depression years, builders were happy to put up *two* houses a year — William Levitt's idea was considerably more newsworthy than the more modest steps taken by the government. When mea-sured against Levitt's ingenious contribution to the problem, the $50.00 given to veterans upon separation from active duty seemed to many to be small potatoes indeed.

The $50.00 mustering-out pay, of course, was not the only effort

338

the government made to rehabilitate their homecoming veterans. The Serviceman's Readjustment Act of 1944 — more popularly referred to as the "GI Bill" — went a long way toward alleviating the problem. In addition to the building of veterans' hospitals, offering low interest mortgage loans, and disbursing some four billion dollars in the form of unemployment benefits between 1944 and 1949 to some nine million vets still out of work, the government provided stipends and low-interest loans for those who wanted to attend college or trade schools.

Nearly ten million far-sighted men and women took advantage of such incentives to further their education or to better their vocational skills. One particularly innovative aid provided by the government — one that would prove especially auspicious for the Art Students League — was the making of "career films" designed and produced to offer guidance upon reentering the working force. This rather simple device proved invaluable for those who chose to take advantage of the service, coming home as they did to a job market that, for most, had greatly changed during their years away on active service.

One such film, which carefully outlined the steps a person might take if a career in commercial or fine art might seem a desirable path for them to pursue, was made in collaboration with the Art Students League of New York. The storyline of the film followed a young man on a visit to the League's facility in New York City, showing his careful choosing of instructors, his eventual registration, and then a brief overview of his attending several classes. The short film included a visit to Woodstock and a look at the League's summer facilities and its courses of instruction at that site. If a career in art had never before entered the mind of a GI, this brief peek into the makings of an artist had not only a tremendous effect on many of the veterans, but also, as it transpired, on the League and its future as well.

No one had envisioned that such a large number of people would opt to take this particular path to a "better" future. However, a career as a commercial artist seemed not only "cushy" but, after months in muddy trenches and the prospect of more dirt back home on the farm, it looked like a nice, clean way to make a decent living as well. If the little film the Government had made for the US Army proved to be a major windfall for the League, the impact on Woodstock, featured as it was in the film, would be equally dramatic. The little town, just like the near-empty studios of the League, was suddenly being filled with many new faces.

The reopening of the League's summer sessions thus caused an abrupt increase in Woodstock's population. In general, the town had already been slowly growing over the years, augmented by ever more artists taking up permanent residency in the picturesque little town. From less than 2000 residents before the war, however, the mid-forties saw Woodstock's population double in size. As a result, the little village would undergo many changes — changes that, though appreciated by many, would not be universally welcomed.

Many of the native old-timers, who had only grudgingly begun accepting the artists in their midst, now found their once quiet little hamlet beginning to take on all too many citified ways. Bad enough that once gas rationing had ended in 1945, summer tourist traffic was increasingly becoming more noisome and intrusive, but now favorite little lanes and byways were beginning to sport "official" street names — just like nearby Kingston or in any other big city.

Some of this "citifying" had been brought about by the more "pushy" of the creative community that — according to many of the old-timers — had been gradually "taking over." Always conservative and mostly Republican, native Woodstockers had been content to allow their town to be run by those elders who conformed to a trusted and timeworn pattern of tradition. Ever since the '30s, however — some traced it back to when those "reds" began showing up over at the Maverick —artists, not willing to remain on the sidelines, had been gradually seeking more involvement in the town's policies. More often than not, however, the town's fathers routinely ignored their voices, and things had gone along as they had since time immemorial. To the growing frustration of those who sought change, the usual townsfolk retort, "It worked before, so why fix what ain't broke?" stymied and infuriated them.

The older contingent of the creative community was delighted to be suddenly reinforced by this new stream of artists, musicians, actors, and writers that had come from not only a wider area of the United States, but also came armed with a slew of fresh ideas on how the "new" America ought to be organized.

Artists from the West, from the South — from all points of the compass — descended on Woodstock, a great many of these newcomers coming away from the war with a strong desire for change, and who felt no compunctions about shouldering their way not only into town, but also into town politics. Their ever-growing presence gradually eroded the hold of the far right which had for so long held sway in the control and managing of town affairs. Though the locals had readily accepted "outside" money, "outside" *ideas* had always been less attractive, and this new population appeared aggressively determined to upset their hidebound resistance to change.

Whereas the creative community had once been satisfied to remain aloof from the locals and their issues, those that had become residents of Woodstock now began quietly registering to vote, some even thinking about running for office. When John Pike, a watercolorist and a Woodstock artist of some national note had actually done so — *and* won a seat on the town board — it sent shock waves through the entire community, creative as well as that of the townsfolk.

53

With their increase in numbers, it had become the fashion for the several artists' groups to meet at each other's homes on different nights of the week so that a greater mix of ideas and joint participation could take place. The Steeles had settled on the third Thursday of the month for their evening get-togethers and, with the exception of the Iskowitzes, the "usuals", including Sarah's parents when they were up for a visit, were present at their latest gathering. Pike's election to the town board almost immediately dominated the discussion.

"Well, Morris would have been pleased," Edward Fielding was saying as he put down his drink.

"I'm not so sure about that," said Cal. "As politically opinionated as he was on social issues, he always felt that the political arena was no place for an artist. Like John Sloan, he eventually saw the pitfalls in over-involvement for the artist, and kept all traces of politics out of his work."

"Anyway, I would have liked to hear his comments about Pike's election. He would have had some choice things to say, I'll bet," said Catherine Fielding.

"Yes," said Sarah, then added with a sigh. "It's not the same without Morris. He always added a bit of spice to whatever topic we were discussing — political or otherwise."

"Rather shocking the way he went," said Fielding.

"And sad," said Cal. "They were so happy with their new loft down in SoHo. Morris went on and on about all the room he had."

"It certainly made Myra happy — at least in the beginning," said Sarah. "Their little studio apartment in Greenwich Village had become impossible for her — no room to move around with all of Morris's sculptures cluttering up every room."

"'Cluttering up'," said Andrea Bundy. "Not a very flattering way to speak of his art, is it?"

"Well, you know what I mean," said Sarah defensively. "It was even difficult to go to the toilet — you had to practically fight your way in, for heaven's sake."

"It is a little difficult when you're a sculptor," said Joe. "I mean, each new piece needs its own space. At least with paintings you can stack them against a wall somewhere out of the way." He turned to his wife. "And with your prints, no problem — you can store them away in drawers."

"That's true," said Cal. "Sculpture presents its own problems to the artist — and space for its storage is not the least of it. As if artists don't have enough to worry about, finding buyers who are also willing to give up space for their art purchases has always been a handicap for sculptors — especially for those who make large constructions like Morris did. Institutions, of course, have the room for such purchases, but individual patrons need not only money but ample space in their homes to accommodate most pieces of sculpture." A wistful look passed over his face as he added, "And, to tell the truth, Morris's sculptures were not selling all that well anyway."

"So, the 'clutter' had to be a problem," Joe said, and then added, "for both of them."

Jake remained silent throughout these comments on Morris's work, never having much warmth for it in spite of his liking for the man. He was one who would certainly not have made room for one of Morris's steel concoctions in *his* home or studio.

"I also miss Myra," said Catherine Fielding. "I always enjoyed her bon mots of wisdom which she could so slyly interject when Morris 'took off' on one of his verbal flights of fancy footwork."

"Yes," said Jake now that he found an opening where he might contribute. "She was a tempering influence on him — sort of a safety-valve that could draw off his flashes of rising steam."

"It's sad that she doesn't come up to Woodstock anymore," said Sarah. "We've tried — often — to get her to come up from the city and spend some time with us." She shook her head. "But, she always begs off. Says it wouldn't be the same without Morris."

"I suppose that not being an artist herself never gave her any real connection to the Woodstock coterie," said Catherine. "She came here each summer because Morris did — and that was that."

"He was brilliant, though," said Cyrus Winters. "He knew what he was talking about — and he knew so much. I always enjoyed our conversations — although I must admit, when it came to his passion about art, he often left me far behind." He looked off into the distance. "But when it came to world politics, he was extremely well informed. I learned a great deal from him."

"That's true," said Cal. "He was well read about a great many things. Myra once told me that as a young man he had almost become a rabbi. Something of a family tradition for their first-born sons, I seem to recall. But somewhere along the line, Morris had rebelled..." Cal paused to glance around the room. "No great surprise there, I guess." He waited until the chuckling subsided. "Anyway, in defiance of his father, he had gone off to become an artist."

Turning to Joe, Jake smiled and said, "Maybe *that*'s why I liked him."

At Sarah's questioning glance, Jake explained, "Defying his father. I once shared my own early experiences with Joe — about how my father tried to steer me into a practical trade when I was still a boy."

"Seems to go with the territory," said Catherine. "You'd be surprised how many artists were opposed by well-meaning parents." Then, after a moment, she added. "And rightly so in some cases, I should think. I can easily come up with a great many so-called 'artists' who should've listened to their parents."

Her observation met with no dissents from the group.

"Birge Harrison once spoke to me about family opposition years ago," said Jake. "He said that he thought it was God's way of preparing an artist for life's ups and downs. He believed it just made them better artists."

"And what does that say for those who grew up in a nurturing environment?" mused Sarah's mother.

No one answered, but Jake had noticed Sarah direct a covert glance at Cal when Mae Winters broached the question.

"In any event, let's hope that the conflict with his father helped prepare poor Morris for the life he had to face," said Cyrus. "He and Myra certainly had to contend with some terrible things during their lifetimes. It's probably a blessing that he had found such consolation in his art."

"But always so excitable," said Joe, shaking his head. "I always thought that he'd die of a heart attack some day during one of his tirades."

"But to fall down an elevator shaft, of all things," said Mae Winters. "I mean, how bizarre!"

"Awful," said Sarah. "Myra was just beside herself when she told us the news. 'It's this damned new loft,' she called to tell me. 'Who knew where the hell that elevator was half the time? And Morris — it being all new to him, and his head, as usual, on his next sculpture rather than where he was going — just stepped through the gate. Oh, I can still hear his shout as he fell. And all because of his damn sculptures! *That*'s why we moved and *that*'s why he died!'" Sarah looked around at the group. "It was just awful to hear her go on like that."

"Hard to see what Myra will do," said Cal. "I mean, as far as all of Morris's sculptures are concerned. What is she going to do with that loft full of work?" He shook his head. "He hadn't sold a piece for some time."

Sarah sighed. "She calls his work her 'millstone,' you know," and shook her head sadly.

"How awful," said Mae Winters.

They were silent for a while, each wrapped within their own thoughts.

"Anyway," said Andrea Bundy breaking the silence. "Getting back to John Pike and the town board. I, for one, think that it's just great. Artists *ought* to be involved — not only in this backward little town, but in national politics as well. I think that this new idea of a union that some of the artists are talking about would be a great first step."

"You mean this 'Artists' Equity' business?" asked Cal.

"Yes," said Andrea. "I think it would be a fine thing if we could learn to pull together. At least with something like the Equity, we'd have a voice."

"Strength in numbers," said Cyrus.

"Right. Strength in numbers," repeated Andrea. "As a union we'd have our own political body, a solid platform from which we can act and gain power."

Catherine Fielding shook her head. "I guess it's been done before." She stopped to look at each of their faces. "I'm thinking of the old guilds," she explained, then added, "But a union? If you mean in the modern sense, I just don't see how it would work. Unions have power today because of their ability to strike." She looked around once again. "Who'd *really* care if an artist went on strike?"

"That's exactly right," said Cal. "If I decide to put my brushes down for a month, I doubt if I'd appreciably upset anyone's applecart."

"Well," said Andrea, "art has always served a social and political purpose, and there is no reason why the artist as well as his art shouldn't to be out there on the line. At least the Artists' Equity is *trying* to do something, trying to get artists to *think* of themselves as a unified political force."

"I'm not so sure that it has *always* served such ends," said Joe. "What political purpose did Rembrandt's art serve? Or Renoir's? Or a whole bunch of others for that matter?" He turned to Catherine. "You're the art historian — what do you say?"

"It's difficult to read motives into the artists of the past, of course," she answered. "I would assume, however, that there are as many motives to turn to art as there are artists. As in all professions, we are bound to find persons engaging in various activities for any number of reasons, and there is no cause to think that artists are any different in that respect. One can, though, point to some artists whose political intentions are rather obvious — Goya for example — or Daumier — or even Hogarth. And under some circumstances, even the non-political artist can be drawn into the arena."

"Like Picasso and his Guernica," interrupted her husband.

"Yes, like him. Sometimes an event can be so overwhelming in its impact on an artist's life that even the least political personality can become momentarily involved. Picasso was certainly moved to make some statement about the attack on his native Spain, but then he was never entirely unpolitical during his lifetime. There was his brief involvement with the communists, for example. He even became one of their showpieces while traveling to Russia at their behest to attend some party function or other."

"Well, I don't know about Picasso, but for me, getting involved with politics would be too much of a distraction," said Joe. He looked over at his wife. "Me and Andrea have gotten into this discussion before. She views art as some kind of reforming agent that can cure the ills of the world." He shrugged, and then added. "As if making a thousand prints depicting the latest horror perpetrated by the government is going to persuade those Washington types to mend their ways."

"It may not persuade the government," said Cyrus, "but by reaching the hands of a thousand activists those prints might sway a vote here or there. Art often reflects life, and there is no reason that the artist cannot be affected by — or effective in — his social milieu. The artist has as much right to have his voice heard as anyone else, I should think."

"That's what I've been telling him," said Andrea. "We need to educate the public, and one way of doing that is through art."

"Maybe so, maybe so," said Joe. "But all too often the process merely cheapens art and coarsens the artist. It puts art on the same level as the broadsheet or the daily newspaper. Art ought to uplift, ought to enlighten. *That*'s education, too, and the real artist has been doing that a lot longer than he's been out stumping for this or that political party."

"I have to agree with Joe," said Cal. "You all know my position on the matter. I've long maintained that art ought not serve any other master than itself. The artist who allows his talent to be used in the service of political propaganda is no better off than poor Michelangelo dancing to the Pope's tune."

"Right," agreed Ed. "Just think of what sculptures he might've left the world if he hadn't been coerced into painting that blasted Sistine Chapel! He wanted to carve — Julius made him paint! How was he — or art — served?"

"Kee-rect!" said Joe. "The artist ought to avoid being a reporter *or* a politico. He oughtta be an *artist.*"

"Yes!" said Andrea angrily. "And slowly starve to death!"

As soon as he said it, Joe knew he was on thin ice, and reddened at Andrea's retort. They *had* had this conversation before in the privacy of their home, and he was only too well aware that it was Andrea's brisk sale of her prints that had often made it possible for them to put food on the table. Few people were buying paintings during the war years, and his pride could barely live with the growing number of canvases that remained unsold.

The others could not help but notice the brief flare-up, and all averted eye contact with the Bundys for some moments.

"Fresh drinks?" said Cal, suddenly rising to his feet.

Cyrus took out his pocket watch and announced, "Not for me, thanks. I think I'll just turn in."

Mae Winters started to follow him, then stopped to turn to her daughter. "Would you like a hand in cleaning up, dear?"

"You go along, Mrs. Winters. I'll give Sarah a hand," said Andrea.

"Me too," said Catherine.

The straightening up quickly done, the gathering soon broke up.

"Until next month," sang out Sarah as her company went their several ways.

54

Whatever opinions artists might have had about John Pike's election to the town board, it was not long before Jake discovered what some of the townspeople thought.

It was a hot, sticky afternoon and Jake had no desire to continue work that day. He had spent the morning putting up canning shelves in a basement at the home of one of his regular customers, and coming up from its damp coolness into the stifling heat of the noontime sun quickly convinced him then and there to call it a day.

He was planning to go back home to do a little painting, but knew that the trapped heat under the low ceiling of his studio would make it too uncomfortable to work.

Hard enough to get a painting right without having this heat working against you.

Putting his tools into the back of his pickup, he decided to head over to Deannie's for lunch, hoping that the afternoon would bring relief — and perhaps a short sketching hike before supper.

No longer housed in the old trolley, Deannies' increasing popularity had allowed its owners to transform the place into a proper eating emporium, its brand new face proudly taking its place alongside the growing number of other business establishments on Woodstock's Mill Hill Road. Though it kept its long counter at which the town's workmen preferred to eat, Deannies now included two "dining rooms" with small, individual tables and chairs scattered throughout the rooms. Plainly decorated, the restaurant continued to appeal to locals and tourists, its non-assuming décor and "home-style" fare still good, and still moderately priced.

Jake had come in the back door, and noting that the tables — as usual — were all occupied, headed toward the counter with its familiar row of well-worn stools. The restaurant had continued to be a favorite hangout for Woodstockers, and many would linger for hours over a cup of coffee and a chat, a common ritual that the owners never discouraged. Cash-strapped art students or out of work locals could always find shelter and mutual commiseration with their fellows at Deannies. Since room always seemed to be found for the latecomer, no one complained of how long they took up space or of how endlessly they managed to stretch out their last dime or quarter.

Jake took an empty stool at the end of the counter closest to the cash register. He nodded to three locals who sat a few stools away down at the other end. He knew them casually, having worked with two of them at one time or another on various jobs.

He could not recall their names, but this would not have been out of the ordinary. It was not unusual to spend a morning or afternoon working on a day-job alongside men without proper introductions taking place. A simple nod or an occasional "Hand me that, Bud," or some such interchange would suffice in most cases. You were there to work and not to socialize. Collecting or remembering names was an uncalled-for bother that one could well do without. Getting the job done and your pay at the end of it was all that needed to be accomplished.

He greeted the waitress when she came over with her pad and pencil in hand and ordered his usual cheeseburger and coffee. A pleasant, well-rounded woman, he never found her impatient or curt, always quick to return a smile or a friendly jest whether she had a roomful of people to wait on or not.

When she brought his food, he smiled and said, "Still the best cheeseburgers around, Joannie."

"You keep on telling folks that, Jake," she replied. "The more they order, the more we'll make."

After their brief greeting to Jake, the men at the other end of the counter had ignored him and resumed their conversation.

"Well, it was enough to make a dog laugh," the eldest, who sat in the middle of the trio, was saying. Then, doing a poor imitation of a woman's voice, he continued. "'I live over on Bellows Lane.'" He turned his head back and forth to make sure both of his listeners heard him. "Bellows Lane! Can you imagine that?" he guffawed. "I swear to God, that's just what she said!"

Both of his companions snickered.

"Now just where might *that* be, I asks her," continued the storyteller. Then, trying to mimic her voice once again, he continued, "'Oh,' she says. 'Right off Lower Byrdcliffe Road. I'm the last house in.'"

The snickering increased.

The speaker shook his head. "'Course, she meant that little jog off of the shortcut from Rock City Road that runs on up to that artsy-fartsy crowd on Guardian Mountain — you know, on the left there." His left arm shot up over the head of the man beside him, emphasizing the direction.

"Yeah, yeah, we know," his friends chorused.

"Bellows Lane! Humpf!" He swiveled his head once more to look at his stoolmates. "You know who started *that* tomfoolery, don't you? It's that Pike feller on the town board. He's took to giving the names of *artists* to our roads and lanes here."

"Now ain't that a caution," said the man on his right.

"Hell's bell's boy, it's more'n that!" said the older man. "It's a goddang shame the way those people are taking over! It's gettin' so a man can't find his way around his own town anymore." He swallowed the rest of his coffee. "*Bellows* Lane!" he snorted once more.

One of his companions glanced up at the clock behind the counter. "Shoot!" he exploded. "Going on twelve-thirty! I'd best be going."

"Where you off to?" asked the older man.

"Got a little job up in Bearsville," he said. "A little brush clearin', is all."

"What time you gotta be there?" asked the third.

"Supposed to be there at eleven," he answered.

"It's goin' on one!" the eldest laughed, as he pointed his gnarled thumb up at the clock.

"Right," said the other as he clapped on his hat to go.

Jake smiled to himself.

Woodstock time — I'll never get used to it. I guess my always being on time is another thing I inherited from my German ancestors — along with my 'dick' head.

The two remaining continued their conversation as Jake sat quietly and ate his lunch.

"You lookin' for some work?" the older man was saying.

"I suppose," came the answer. "You got somethin' in mind?"

"Got a pretty big job comin' up next week," he said. "Could use a hand."

"Doin' what?"

"Clearin' stumps over on the near side of Ohayo Mountain. Some city feller buildin' a house up there."

The other shook his head. "What the hell they want to build on the side of a mountain for, anyway? Ain't we got enough flat land around here?"

"Who the sam hill knows!" He snorted. "Has to put a road in, too." Another snort. "Probably gonna give it some other artist's name when it's done."

"How long you figger the job'll take?"

"I dunno — A week, mebbe. A little more — less." He paused to lift off his cap and scratch his head. "Depends on that finicky old bulldozer of mine."

"You still got that old Caterpillar?"

"Yep. Gettin' as tetchy as an old woman, that sonuvabitch. Never do know how it'll act once I get her fired up nowadays."

The young man bobbed his head.

"Last time I used 'er, she kept on a-sputterin' and fartin' like she wanted to up and die. Kept losin' power. Got to where the goldurned thing couldn't pull a sick woman off a piss-pot." He shook his head again. "Then the old bugger would get a second breath and go to beat all hell again, all rip-snortin' and full of pepper." He slapped both hands on the counter. "I'll tell you, boy, one of these days I'm gonna trade that old 'dozer in on a yeller dog and then shoot the blamed thing!"

He stood up and the other followed suit.

"Anyways, you want the work or not?"

"Sure, why not," the younger man said. "I can always use an extra dollar or so."

Jake nodded to them as they left.

On his way home, Jake played over in his mind the conversation of the workmen at the diner.

Woodstock had been changing, that's for sure — but then it had been doing so for as long as could remember. He thought about the new house going up on Ohayo Mountain that the older man had spoken about, and how frequently this was happening in and around Woodstock. There were hardly any farms left, many already cut up into lots with new houses built on them. Maybe building on the side of a mountain was the only alternative left open to the city-dweller who wanted a place in the country.

I wonder how long Overlook will keep her wilderness intact? — he thought.

And there was no doubt that the artists had brought change to the town over the years. Mostly, the townspeople had either resisted or ignored — as best they could — these "outlanders," continuing to graspingly accept those changes that brought money into their pockets while vocally up in arms about those that did not.

The reason for a good part of the ill feeling, however, could also be laid at the door of the artists themselves. By and large, they had long gone their own way, ignoring the local populace as country bumpkins, viewing local residents and tradesmen as beneath their notice and not even worthy of their contempt. They stuck together in their communities, Byrdcliffers, Mavericks, Leaguers, and Rock City Moderns alike in fraternizing with their own, only interacting with townspeople when they needed work to be done or necessities replenished.

Of late, however, he noticed that a good deal of that aloofness on the part of artists had been slowly breaking down. If the face of the town had changed, well, so also was the face of the creative community. Some of the newer artists, themselves from small towns across America, mixed more freely with the locals, showing up at local watering-places and drinking elbow to elbow with the workmen who stopped in for relaxation after a hard day's work. Their tongues loosened by spirits, it was not long before artist and laborer — or town storekeeper — would be sharing jokes and manly banter. It was no longer so unusual to witness neighborly interchanges at places like Deannies, artists and locals bellying up to the counter or only a table-breadth away, exchanging near-friendly nods and words of greeting.

Some of these relationships developed even further in that some of the old Woodstockers would pose for certain artists who wanted to include some 'local color' in their work. Woodstock itself, now that it could lay claim to its own fame, became, as did its landscape in former years, a paintable "subject." Nowadays, recognizable homesteads and familiar local characters were beginning to appear in paintings exhibited at the Association and, every so often, one might spy an old-timer furtively slipping into the gallery to see a rendition of his house or weather-lined visage hanging on one of the walls.

Yes, indeed. No matter how you looked at it, Woodstock had been changing.

55

"When we consider," said the slight, bespectacled man as he raised finger after finger for emphasis, "that curators, docents, ticket takers, publicity staff, guards — even janitors — are paid, then it seems reasonable that we, the artists, ought to be treated equably."

The speaker, Yasuo Kuniyoshi, a League instructor and one of the driving forces behind the formation of Artists Equity, saw that he had the attention of the crowd of over 300 persons seated and standing around the room.

"After all," he went on, "no art museum or gallery could exist without us. Doesn't it seem unfair that artists — who have to pay for their materials, pay for their matting, pay for their framing, pay for crating and shipping — even, in most cases, paying an entry fee for the 'privilege' ..." he wiggled his fingers in the air to indicate quotation marks ... "are not being compensated like all the others?"

Andrea Bundy, flanked by Jake and her husband, swiveled her neck to vehemently nod her head to both.

They, along with other artists, gallery directors, dealers, curators, art historians, critics, and museum directors, were attending the first "Woodstock Art Conference" being held at the Art Students League summer facility on the Woodstock-Saugerties Turnpike — now officially designated "Route 212" by the State — in late August of 1947.

Kuniyoshi — "Yas" to his friends — was an inspiring speaker, his oratory honed and his enthusiasm fired by years of political activism. One of the older-generation Woodstock artists, he'd been living in the Colony since the '20s, struggling along with them through the hard economical times of the '30s and, since the post-war economic boom had come to town, been urging his fellow artists to seek ways of reaping some of the benefits.

A Japanese-American, "Yas" Kuniyoshi's activism was further fueled by a more personal sense of inequality. Shortly after December 7, 1941, he was declared an "enemy alien" despite the fact that he'd already been writing broadcast speeches and designing anti-Axis posters for the Office of War Information. Deeply humiliated by the experience, Kuniyoshi thus felt the thrust of inequality both as an artist and as a man.

Enlisting the aid and support of the Woodstock Artists Association, Kuniyoshi and his co-workers had worked hard to make the Conference a success, giving it the title "Artist and his World" with the hopes that it would be the first of a long series of annual discussion sessions designed to motivate artists to action. He'd been delighted and heartened by the large crowd that had come to Woodstock from New York City and beyond for the occasion, eager to share with his audience the outline of Equity's platform that he and his friends had been hammering out over the past several months.

"Our first move," Kuniyoshi told his audience, "will be to charge the exhibiting institution a rental fee for the use of our work."

A small but important step, this was the main bargaining chip Equity had in its arsenal, and he allowed for a brief pause for his words to sink in.

"Any organization," he continued, "that refuses to pay this rental fee, will be blackballed by the artists."

After another pause for emphasis, Kuniyoshi then went on to outline for his listeners the rest of their "15-point" plan.

Of all the issues that Kuniyoshi had brought up during the Conference, it was the baldly stated threat of "blackballing" that had lingered in the minds of his listeners — and not only of those present who were representing the exhibiting institutions he was referring to.

The new breed of artists that came to Woodstock after the war ended was not only more inclined to get involved in local affairs, but differed from their older colleagues in other ways as well. They were less clique-y, and other than joining the Association for a convenient place to exhibit their work, were less willing to affiliate with a group any larger than a small circle of friends. Though the

356

legends of communities such as Byrdcliffe, the Maverick, and the Rock City Moderns were still reverently passed on to all newcomers, the younger artists preferred to form their own coteries, some even going out of their way to avoid those places where the older members of the Woodstock creative community tended to congregate.

Whereas the majority of the older artists heartily endorsed and were willing to try the blackballing tactic, many of the younger ones only saw a windfall of unexpected opportunities suddenly coming their way. If their more recognized fellows chose to stand aloof, what was to prevent them from stepping in and taking their place? Deliberately turning a deaf ear to the efforts of Equity members trying to persuade them to become part of a cohesive group with common interests, many — including the second-rate as well as the up-and-coming — quickly stepped in to fill the gap. After all, how long might it be before they would again have the chance of showing at such prestigious venues as those institutions that were being considered for blackballing?

Jake, for one, was not really surprised. Though the "scabs" that maneuvered behind the backs of their fellow artists to curry favor with the museums were roundly criticized and duly snubbed, Equity's leaders had simply not taken into account one of the fundamental truths concerning the very people they were attempting to serve. They had forgotten the fact that, by nature and by necessity, artists were, first and foremost, individuals. Affiliations with clubs and the like notwithstanding, when alone in their studios, most artists tried to follow their own visions and, as far as possible, were committed to going their own way. Hadn't this been the very hallmark of the creative individual since time immemorial? Hadn't every one of them heard at least one story of the artist who flew in the face of common sense, who had defied family — had gone against even his own interests — in order to "follow his own star"? To envision a "union" of such individuals seemed to Jake to be doomed from the outset and, in spite of the idealism of Kuniyoshi and his followers was, as far as he could see, destined to remain an illusive dream.

And, although he had come to it for different reasons, Joe Bundy's conclusion was no less absolute than Jake's — a fact that they had discussed between them a few days later.

For their part, knowing full well that the average visitor was not as aesthetically discerning as might be hoped, the museum directors immediately saw that they could fill their walls and galleries as easily as before — albeit with the work of unrecognized or less qualified artists — and blithely chose to ignore the threat. Some clever publicist had come up with the term "Emerging artist," which soon became a favored and much-used description in the titles of upcoming exhibits.

The only tool that might have made Artists Equity an equally viable force in the arts partnership, therefore, was undermined almost before it had a chance to be fully tested.

The three Woodstock Art Conferences that followed were more sparsely attended, the final one petering out in internal squabbles that even many of the artists eventually lost interest in. The older — and wiser —members that had witnessed the undermining of their only ace-in-the-hole by less scrupulous climbers, had already drifted away. Many others soon followed, bitterly disappointed that their grand idea of a forceful union had degenerated into just one more "social club" which, without teeth, merely offered its members a new place to exhibit and the usual balm of camaraderie.

56

Jake stepped back from his easel.

How many times have I done that? Stepped back?

He wiped his palette knife on a rag, then walked across the room to sit in his chair.

He sat looking at his painting for some moments then, standing up suddenly, walked back to his easel. Bending over, he peered at different sections, his eyes inches from the canvas. Again, he backed away several steps.

Stepping back. Will I ever go forward?

Straightening himself, he tentatively raised his hand, knife hovering over the canvas, then suddenly dropped his arm and walked back to his seat once again.

Ironic, that people often tell me that they feel as if they can step into *my paintings.*

He sat looking at the painting for several more moments.

In recent years, he had discovered that the process of painting was becoming as absorbing as choosing a new view of Overlook — which, it seemed, was becoming less and less of an issue for him.

Not that Overlook no longer challenged him — far from it. The definitive depiction of the mountain — if there ever could be such a thing — continued to elude him, still managed to slip out from under brush or knife, and still boldly faced him each dawning day with a smug look on its face, still confident in its solid massiveness that it would never be conquered by the likes of Jake Forscher.

No, there were still paintings of Overlook he had to make.

But whether it was because of desperation or the sheer novelty of doing it, he had been spending more time in painting other subjects as well. Rifling through his boxes of drawings, he would sometimes choose a particular one and pin it to the top of his easel. After first checking the date on the back, he would try to recall the place and day that he had made the drawing as he prepared his palette. Then, when the mood seemed right, he would begin.

As he varied his subjects and became less intent on "seeing" Overlook appear on his canvas, he gradually paid more attention to the act of painting, becoming more engrossed in the sensual preparations of mixing and spreading the paint. He more consciously monitored his thoughts as he chose a subject, or tried to methodically reconstruct the particular day a drawing he had chosen to paint had been made. He tried to watch his hands, deliberately slowing down his movements as he blended and applied his paints. He began noticing the tension he felt in his arms and shoulders as he worked, became aware of the furrowing of his brow.

It had slowed him down, of course — had even ruined a painting or two when he became overly observant of himself instead of paying attention to the picture arising from the canvas. But being cognizant — however briefly — of that application — of not only the application, but of its effect on both the canvas and on his body, was oddly liberating — even exhilarating. He seemed somehow outside of himself when he allowed his participation in the process to come to the surface, to be experienced as fully as it could. At such times, it was as if he were stepping back not only from his easel, but from himself, observing not only what he was painting, but *how* he was painting.

Jake was vaguely aware that — at times — the act of creation could also be an act of liberation from his usual, ordinary, day-to-day self. He knew — hadn't he experienced it? — when all went well, that creating could be an uplifting disconnection of self from the physical body. And, though he could not state it in any coherent form, he sensed that, at bottom, it was — as Birge Harrison, Cyrus Winters, Joe Bundy — even Cap'n Bob, had put it — all in their own ways — the process and not the product that was of paramount significance.

Rising from his seat once again, he decided that the painting was done, and had just begun cleaning up and putting his things away when he heard a soft knock at his studio door.

Startled, since no one ever came to his studio without his invitation, he walked over and opened the door to find Aunt Birgit standing there in an obviously distressed state.

"Aunt Birgit?"

"It's your mama," she said in a quiet voice.

Jake took her arm and led her over to the house. When they got inside he immediately took her to the nearest chair at the kitchen table and sat down opposite her.

"I got a letter from Freddie. That nice man Gary brought it over from the post office." She took it from her apron pocket and handed it to him with shaking hands.

Jake quickly read through its contents. Customarily brief as were the few letters from Freddie he had received over the years, it simply told of how quickly the end came. He read: *She had been feeling poorly for a day or so, and without warning died suddenly.* Jake read on. *Konnie heard her fall, and by the time she ran upstairs to see what had happened, Mama was already gone.*

Gently placing the letter on the table, he passed his hand over his face. He experienced little emotional impact from the news. Nothing like how it affected his Aunt, at any rate, and he got up from his seat and walked over to lay his hand on her shoulder.

"Why don't you lie down for awhile," he said. "You're shaking all over."

Aunt Birgit pulled herself up to an upright sitting position.

"I'm really all right, Jacob. Just thinking about poor Hannie — your Mama …" She heaved a sigh. "To go so quickly like that!"

Jake looked down at her to see if she truly was all right.

"The funeral is tomorrow," she said as tears welled up in her eyes.

Jake had already read that in Freddie's letter.

"Well, you know, Aunt Birgit — with the mail so slow, and all."

"We should be there," she said sadly. "We shouldn't miss poor Hannie's funeral."

Jake knew that his Aunt's grief was deepened by the fact that they had received the news in such an untimely fashion. He had been urging her for some time to let him have a telephone put in, but she had vehemently resisted this latest innovation.

"Ach," she would say whenever he brought it up. "Who needs such an intrusion in the house? If anyone has to get ahold of me, they can either knock at my door or write me a letter. Hearing one of those contraptions ringing in the middle of the night would frighten me out of my wits!"

Well, someone did have to get "ahold" of her, and unfortunately it was for the kind of thing that brooked no dallying. His Aunt was merely adding a feeling of guilt to her sorrow because of her stubborn refusal of installing a telephone. And who knew how much of her distress was simply the confronting of her own looming mortality? Close in age to her slightly older sister-in-law, she could hardly have ignored the fact that her own death could not be all that far in the future.

Jake looked down at her hands twisting a handkerchief in her lap. He always had seen them as strong, capable, constantly busy at whatever task needed to be done. "Idle hands …" she used to say, leaving the rest of the old adage unsaid. Jake saw the bluish network of veins on the backs of her hands through her translucent skin. They seemed frail and unfamiliar to him as they aimlessly twisted the daintily embroidered piece of cloth.

"Well, there's nothing to be done about it now," soothed Jake. "I'll leave right away — take the next train down." He looked down at her bent head. "There's no need for you to make the trip, Aunt Birgit. It'll be too much for you."

His Aunt did not demur, but merely nodded to her nephew. "I'd only be in the way, anyway," she said, bravely trying to put on a smile.

"Oh, you'd never be in the way, Aunt Birgit. Freddie and Konnie — and especially the kids — would love to see you — you know that."

"Yes," she agreed, her eyes lighting up a bit. "It would be nice to see them — but not now. No, not now." Her eyes clouded over. "Oh, but we both should be there for the funeral, Jacob. I owe her that much."

Jake was silent, his hand gently massaging her thin shoulder as she once again took up the spasmodic twisting of her handkerchief.

He knew that she was not up to the ordeal of both the hasty trip and the graveside service and, after she had composed herself, again gently persuaded her that her presence at her sister-in-law's funeral would be an unnecessary burden that neither he nor his brother would impose upon her.

* * *

Jake did not stay to visit with Konnie and Freddie after the funeral, returning upstate the next day on the morning train out of Wee-hawken.

A small quiet affair, he shared the few details of his mother's burial with Aunt Birgit, bringing back hellos and hugs from Konnie and the children

As the weeks passed, images of his mother would creep into his thoughts, surprising to Jake since, when she was alive, he rarely dwelt on the quiet, self-effacing woman that had married his father and gave birth to him and Freddie.

At those moments she came to mind, Jake would lay down brush or tool and stop what he was doing to stare off into space.

Mama ... I hardly knew you.

57

Morris Iskowitz's warning that Woodstock artists would eventually hear from the "red-baiters" came to pass even before Equity's Fourth and Final Woodstock Art Conference was convened. George A. Dondero, the Republican Representative from Michigan, had Artists Equity officially read into the 1952 Congressional Record as a Communist "front" organization. Although Dondero allowed that the organization might have innocent 'dupes' included in its membership, he insisted that many of its leaders were either card-carrying communists or fellow travelers, and he did not hesitate to so register them in the Record.

Yasuo Kuniyoshi's name figured prominently on the list, and his dream of an artists' union was irrevocably branded as a "red" organization with damning finality when the United States Congress affixed their official seal to the document.

As interest in the grand idea of a union waned amongst Woodstock artists, Andrea reluctantly drifted away from the Equity group. Although she and a few others would always stay in sympathy with their platform, she had finally acknowledged to Joe her loss of faith in their power to affect policy. Long convinced that politics had no place in art, he was tactful enough not to blurt out a "told you so" to her.

In general, the close-knit Woodstock artist community was beginning to unravel as the newer generation of artists seemed increasingly less inclined to group together, less apt to espouse one single style, technique, or genre. They were open to anything that promised them advancement in their careers and, when Equity seemed a lost cause, they sought success elsewhere.

"Success," of course, usually meant "sales" and, much to Jake's consternation, the selling of their work seemed of paramount importance to most of this newer generation. Much more so, at any rate, than when the idea of a painting being "good" only if it sold began coming up back in the post-war years of the '20s. Though he could admire the independence of the younger artists, he could not accept their obsessive preoccupation with "fame" and money. If Jake had found it distasteful in the past, the commercialization of art had come back in spades after World War II.

From what he could gather, much of the problem seemed to center on what Birge Harrison used to call the "why" of painting. Harrison had argued that the kind of an artist a person became depended in large part on why he became one in the first place — and Jake had pretty much adopted the idea as his own over the years. He knew that in his own case, his reason for painting continued to be an answer — of sorts — to that original impulse arising on that day when he first glimpsed the Catskill Mountains from the deck of the *Hendrik Hudson.* Whether he willed it or not, it was in response to *this* urge — and not that of making money — that drove him back to the easel day after day.

If any of the current crop of artists had chosen art from some inner compulsion, from some real or perceived need to paint or carve, he saw or heard little indication of it. Many, after seeing the film made by the League and the U.S. Army, readily admitted that they had "gotten into this racket" to make money in the field of commercial art, and only a handful, comparatively speaking, were "converted" by influential instructors to seek a career in fine art. However, to those making the transition, making art at an easel rather than at a drafting table didn't necessarily mean that you still couldn't make money. This prevailing attitude of art being a means rather than an end, did not sit well with many of the League's older instructors or students who resented their classes being diverted from the finer points of becoming serious artists.

Whatever discussions on art that Jake chanced to sit in on or overhear around town these days all seemed to be directed outward — away from the "why" of painting and aimed at what the other fellow was doing, and how much attention who or what was getting. It was about "getting ink" — getting one's name in the papers — and once you got "written up" it meant getting wider recognition. Everyone knew what had happened to Jackson Pollock after an article about him appeared in *Life* Magazine. Hadn't *he* turned into an overnight celebrity, transformed from a struggling artist into a best-selling one just by getting his name in a magazine? How could you argue with that?

Since the end of the war, the idea of art as a commodity was now almost universally accepted in the creative community. As newspapers, magazines, radio —and now, television — gave art and artists "more ink" and air space, businessmen started to look at art as just one more new product to invest in. This sudden interest by entrepreneurs was given a further boost by the advent of advertising. It was soon evident that *how* one sold was as important as *what* one sold, and press agentry became a new profession for the quick talker. It sold snake oil in the past — why should the selling of art prove to be any different? Now that New York City had wrested the title of "art capital" from Paris, new art galleries began to proliferate, and few dealers were reluctant to avail themselves of the effectiveness of an "ad campaign." Never before had artists seemed to have so many opportunities of showing and selling their work.

"All you have to do is get into a gallery," was a refrain Jake heard over and over. "Once you're in, you got it made," went the new gospel. "The dealer does all the work for you."

Yes — Jake thought — *Then, since he knows what sells — even though he might have been selling cars or shoes or real estate in the past and knows nothing about art — all you have to do is paint whatever your dealer tells you to paint.*

Ironically, many of these dealers and gallery owners had their business acumen honed by Artists' Equity, the very organization that sought protection from a grasping world that cared little and knew less about art and artists. To the chagrin of many artists, those dealers that attended the Woodstock Art Conference held in 1947 came away with a far keener insight into how the system "worked" than did they. Though Kuniyoshi could not sell his idea of a union to his fellow artists, the dealers had clearly gotten the message and soon after formed the American Dealers Association — or "ADA" as it came to be commonly known. If artists could not see the handwriting on the wall, the merchants could. The more astute dealers took especial note of how artists could not — or would not – act in unison. Consequently, in their own bonding for a common cause, they found artists — who practically flaunted their own divisiveness — to be easy marks and ripe for the taking. Art Museums, also managed by shrewd businesspeople, would not be far behind in getting in on the bandwagon of commercialism, seeking ways of increasing their popularity while increasing their "gate" by often turning deaf ears and blind eyes to talent and taste in the hectic process of scrambling for the latest "blockbuster" show.

The spread of commercialism in New York City was echoed in Woodstock as privately-owned art galleries began opening up in town. Before the War, the Association and a few local establishments such as Mr. Ayres's Woodstock Inn had been the only places for Woodstock artists to show their work locally. Now, with some of the New York City dealers opening up "branch" galleries in town in an effort to cash in on America's growing prosperity and sudden interest in the purchase of art, Woodstock artists found new venues — and new markets — for their work. It would not be long before both private and corporate buyers —— in hopes of finding a better bargain by shopping "upstate" in search of their art — added yet another element to the weekend mix of tourists coming into the little village.

Yessir, the town of Woodstock was surely changing, and Jake could find himself in sympathy with the workers he had overheard at Deannie's a little while back. They were not the only ones who couldn't "find their way around town" these days. Many of the old guard also began to feel like they were in a "new" town. Painters who had continued to carry on Woodstock's former glory as a world-famous mecca of landscape painting now found themselves on the fringe and, much to their annoyance, had to put up with the disrespectful wags of the new breed referring to them as "The Woodstock School of Outhouse Painting."

Some members of that "school" — like Jake and Joe Bundy — were content to simply step back and avoid the new crush. Jake had been regularly — if sporadically — showing his work at the Association ever since Joe had helped him "break the ice," and both found their representation there enough to satisfy their needs.

Still, no matter which faction you were a part of or what personal opinion you might hold on where you thought the town was heading, to the unaffiliated and unconcerned tourist, Woodstock continued to be an exciting place to visit. If they were only vaguely aware of the larger distinction of art as either "modern" or "academic," they were in any event blithely uninterested in the finer points of internal dissension or nuance. They were content in seeing and enjoying the quaint little village in the Catskills as a viable and vibrant art colony where, if they kept a sharp eye out, they might be lucky enough to pick up a "bargain".

58

None of their close friends were surprised at the Steele's separation and eventual divorce, though, for Jake, it took some getting used to. It, of course, reopened a side of his life that he had thought permanently buried. True, being in her presence had never lost any of its electric thrill for him, but he had been habituated for such a long time in seeing her as Cal's wife, that he had managed to keep whatever emotions she brought out in him well below conscious levels. And, although he knew that she was always pleased to see him, always openly grateful for his respect and friendship for her parents, he had scrupulously avoided allowing his speculations to probe the possibility of any deeper feelings between Sarah and himself.

Sarah had announced the separation at one of her Thursday evening soirees in the winter of 1953, calmly explaining her husband's absence at his usual place at the head of the table as she filled the wine carafe.

"Cal moved out this week," she said off-handedly.

Though most of the group non-committedly kept their silence — it was obvious that Mae and Cyrus Winters had already known — Jake's head had snapped up at the casual announcement.

Catherine Fielding broke the silence. "Is everything all right for you, dear?"

"Oh yes," Sarah said airily. Then, more soberly, "It's been a long time coming and, to tell the truth, I feel very much relieved."

Jake still sat as if transfixed, while Cyrus Winters had an 'it's about time' look on his face.

Joe, in an effort to cover his friend's stricken look, said, "Well, I guess we all kind of thought it might happen, didn't we?" and nudged Jake gently who, oblivious to Joe's urging, continued to sit as if struck dumb. Quickly turning to Sarah, Joe added, "Not that it makes it any easier for you, of course."

"Of course it doesn't," said Andrea. "These things always take their toll." She looked closely at Sarah. "No matter how we might think we're prepared for them."

"Well, Andrea," said Sarah, "you can rest assured that there will be no great toll taken here. Cal had alienated his affections long ago, and I've long gotten used to thinking of him as just one other guest in the house." She smiled at her company and then looked at her mother. "Not that he's been here all that much — even as a guest."

"He has been spending a good deal of time in New York," said Mae Winters.

"Not that we've missed him," Cyrus said quietly.

Sarah ignored her father's remark and continued. "He's been so wrapped up in his work that he's been spending most of his time staying in the City so that he could be in closer contact with his gallery." She looked around the table. "He's been doing quite well," she added somewhat absently.

"So, what are you going to do?" asked Catherine.

"Do?"

"I mean, with your work — your self — will you be moving out?"

"Oh, no," said Sarah. "Cal has agreed that when the divorce comes through, I shall keep this house." She shrugged. "He never really liked it up here." She turned to Joe. "He never showed his work at the Association, as you know. After he joined it when we first moved up here, he just let his membership lapse. He thought Woodstock too provincial, too backwoodsy for an artist to get ahead. He felt that being outside New York City — unless it was to move to Paris — dulled an artist's senses, made them too set in their ways to ever get ahead." She paused to sip her wine. "No. I'll stay here and he'll move down to the City — he's all but done so already, in fact. He's got an eye on a studio somewhere along 8th Avenue, and as soon as he can get it, he'll move out of his parent's apartment."

"Too 'backwoodsy'!" exploded Joe. "I guess he hasn't been around town lately, has he? From what I see, the work being produced up here is just as much 'up to date' as the stuff you can find down at the galleries in Manhattan." He turned to Jake. "Maybe Jake and I are a bit 'backwoodsy' — still hammering away at our landscapes. But if Cal thinks that Woodstock is still Birge Harrison's "best landscape school in the world" — well he's got another thought coming. There's enough new styles cropping up on the Association's walls each month to make your head spin. And some of these new artists in town are real up-and-comers — making as good a living as they might make down there."

"And living a whole lot cheaper, I daresay," said Edward Fielding.

"Yes," Sarah said absently. Then looking up, "Cal did mention some fearful amount that they wanted for renting the studio he has his eye on."

"I'm sure it'll be worth it," said Cyrus Winters, leaving his remark to be interpreted however his listeners wished.

Jake finally found his voice. "And you?" He reddened. "Uh — your pottery work?"

"Oh, I'll surely continue with that," said Sarah avoiding his eyes. She gave a nervous little laugh. "I'll have to earn my keep somehow, won't I?"

"Will you convert Cal's studio?" asked Andrea.

"I don't know," answered Sarah. " I don't need much room for my wheel, and Lenora has been kind enough to allow me to use her firing facilities at The Mountainside Kiln. For the past several years she has set aside time for a few of the local women to take advantage of her equipment, and I've been taking her up on her generous offer. I'll just have to see what the future brings. But, for now anyway, I don't intend to do anything with Cal's studio after he removes the rest of his things."

Mae Winters suddenly got up from the table. "Well, let's get this food on the table before it gets cold."

Sarah quickly stood and joined her. "Yes! Our friends must be starving! Here we invite them for our usual good conversation, and we sit around as if we were at a wake." She placed a plate in front of Jake. "Your favorite," she said. Then, continuing to distribute the full plates as her mother handed them to her, she cheerily exclaimed, "Now don't disappoint me by picking at it."

For the next two months Jake had avoided Sarah's gatherings, unsure of just how her new status as a semi-divorced woman might affect him. He kept to himself, going to and from whatever jobs came his way without stopping in town, even evading Aunt Birgit when he was at home by spending long hours in his studio. At each of the times the third Thursday of the month drew near, he would put off the Bundy's queries with some hastily cobbled excuse that he had to attend to other matters, not caring if they were plausible or not.

Although he had surmised the reason behind Jake's decision to forego the visits, Joe approached his friend's actions obliquely, preferring not to send him into one of his deep silences when prodded on personal matters. He had come to Jake's studio on the pretense of discussing some new frames he was planning to buy, and as he was looking over Jake's stock he casually said over his shoulder, "You been sick?"

Jake glanced in his direction. "Nope."

"Haven't seen you in awhile."

Jake shrugged as he set the canvas he had been stretching up on his easel.

"We missed you at Sarah's the last couple of Thursday nights."

"Figured that's why you came over," said Jake. "You've been using the same frames for the past ten years." He grunted. "Didn't suppose you came over to check out my stock."

"Well, if you haven't been sick, then where've you been?"

"Here — there. What's the difference? I keep busy."

"Yeah," said Joe. "I see a new canvas or two over there against the wall." He glanced over at Jake. "So you've been painting evenings now? Always thought you preferred to work in natural light."

Jake gave a look of annoyance. "*No*, I haven't been painting *evenings.*" He busied himself at arranging his colors. "Aunt Birgit likes me home nights — makes her feel safer."

" Right," Joe snorted. He walked over to Jake's side and grabbed his wrist. "Those colors don't need arranging — you've kept them in the same order for as long as I've known you. They don't move around by themselves, you know. Now look at me and tell me why you're not coming to Sarah's dinner gatherings."

Wrenching his wrist free, Jake whirled on him angrily. "What's it *your* business anyway?" he growled. Then he lurched away and sat down heavily in his chair. Chagrined at his outburst, he looked up at Joe with a miserable look on his face. "Darn it, Joe, you know full well why."

Joe looked at him with genuine sympathy. "We *all* know Jake." He said gently. "But avoiding her won't solve anything."

"It'll stop me from making a complete fool of myself," said Jake.

Joe looked at his friend. "I'm not so sure about that," he said.

"What am I going to do?" groaned Jake.

"Well," said Joe. "You might try coming over this Thursday and see what happens. No matter what comes up, Sarah isn't going to throw you out, you know — and besides, the rest of us really miss you. It's just not the same not having you there."

Jake looked up at Joe with a wry look on his face. "Oh, of course — I'm just such a great conversationalist."

Joe laughed. The tension now gone between them, he walked up to Jake and patted his back. "Yep! Guess I'll stick to the frames I've been using. Thanks for letting me look, though."

"No problem," said Jake. "Now get out of here … I've got things to do."

"Think about it," Joe said as he went out the door.

Jake studiously stepped back from the fresh canvas he had placed on the easel, and as he squinted at it, let out a noncommittal, "Hmmm."

59

Icy wind blew down from the direction of Overlook. Mercifully, the graveside service was brief.

Jake, Joe, Edward Fielding and Cyrus Winters, leaning heavily on a stout wooden cane, stood stiffly on one side of the open grave. On the opposite side, Andrea, Mae, Catherine and Sarah, huddled together arm-in-arm, their bodies hunched against the cold wind. Konnie stood at the foot of the grave, Kirstin on her right side, and Freddie Jr. standing on her left. A handful of neighbors stood several paces away.

The day was sunny, but it was early April and warm weather was a long time away.

The minister ended his monologue and, closing his book and nodding to the group, quickly walked over to his warm and waiting car.

Jake, standing tall and looking down at the coffin that contained his Aunt, turned to Joe standing at his right.

"She left the house to me," Jake said in a strained voice. "Isn't that — something?" The last word caught in his throat before he completely broke down. A strangled sob involuntarily escaped from somewhere deep within and, for the first time that he could remember, he broke down into tears.

Joe and Ed quickly came to his side, each grasping an arm as Jake's knees gave way and he began slumping to the ground.

Jake, recovering his balance, looked up at Ed and said once again in a choked voice, "My aunt gave the house to me. Isn't that something?"

The women, joined by Konnie and Kirstin, had hurriedly walked around the open grave to offer whatever comfort they might give him.

"C'mon, old man," said Joe as put his arm across Jake's shoulders, "Get in my car. I'll take you home."

Jake, embarrassed and unable to halt the rasping sobs that broke from his throat, kept his head down and let himself be led a few steps towards Joe's car.

Sarah stepped forward and said firmly, "No, Joe. You go home with Andrea." She took Jake by the arm and, leading him to the rider's side of his pickup, said to the others, "I'll take him home."

Once she got him to the house and seated at the kitchen table, Sarah quickly found the coffee and set about brewing a pot-full.

"Like it strong?" she asked.

Jake nodded.

His shoulders were convulsively heaving every few minutes or so and he did not trust his voice. He hadn't been able to say a word as Sarah drove him home from the cemetery. Each time he attempted to speak, his voice would break, and another sob would be wrenched from his body.

Sarah would simply reach over to put her hand on his shoulder in an effort to calm him, and to prevent him from even attempting to talk. She did the same as he sat at the table, patting him gently on the back or shoulder whenever he would seem to be trying to speak. Her touch was enough to halt his attempts.

She found two mugs and, when the coffee was done, filled them both.

"Milk or sugar?" she asked.

Jake shook his head.

She glanced around the tidy kitchen. "Can you tell me where I might find the sugar?"

He pointed to a cabinet over her head.

As she added milk and sugar to her coffee, she quietly said, "Drink, Jake."

He docilely obeyed, and took a long draught of the liquid.

"Good?" she asked.

"Perfect," he managed to croak.

"Don't try to talk, Jake. Not yet. There's plenty of time." She settled herself back against the high-backed chair. "I'm not going anywhere just yet."

When they finished their coffee, Jake stood up and motioned towards the living room.

"Shall I give you a refill?" she asked. "I certainly could use another cup."

Jake nodded and walked through the dining room into the living room, silently taking his usual seat by the fireplace. He stared into its cold, darkened opening.

Sarah came in a few moments later and handed him a fresh cup of coffee. She looked around and Jake motioned her to take the rocker sitting cater-corner to his.

After a few moments, he pointed to the fireplace and gave her a questioning look.

"Yes," she said. "A fire would be nice. I think we all got quite a chill out there. April is always so iffy when it comes to the weather."

The kindling and firewood were already there, the job of seeing that "the makin's" were always ready for Aunt Birgit his responsibility since he was a boy. Jake, carefully placing his cup on the table that sat between their chairs, got down on his knees and busied himself at the chore of lighting the wadded paper on the hearth.

As his hands worked at the task, Sarah noted that the convulsive shakes of his shoulders had almost ceased.

Once back in his seat, he took a deep breath and took up his coffee cup. "That's better," he said in a somewhat steadier voice.

Sarah wasn't sure if he was referring to the fire, which was already blazing happily away, or to himself. She just said, "Yes. It is."

Quietly sipping from his cup, he said after some moments, "Good coffee — just like my Uncle used to like it."

Sarah just smiled.

"This used to be his chair," said Jake, patting the arms of the rocker he was sitting in. "Aunt Birgit had to almost take a frying pan to my head before I got up the nerve to use it after he — he …" Jake inhaled deeply in an effort to prevent another sob from escaping.

Sarah remained silent.

"Anyway …," said Jake after he regained control, "and the rocker you're sitting in was Aunt Birgit's"

Sarah looked alarmed and was on the verge of getting up when Jake said, "No, no. Please, Sarah, stay sitting. Who better — since you already know how to make coffee like she did?" Jake smiled slightly, the first Sarah had seen all day. "All you need is some knitting in your hand," he said before he lapsed into silence once again.

They sat through the long afternoon and evening, Jake getting up occasionally to feed the fire, Sarah to go back to the kitchen to get more coffee. When the first pot ran out, she automatically began a second. And, a third.

Afterwards, Jake couldn't remember all that he had talked about with Sarah that day. But he knew that he had gone on for what seemed like hours — long after it darkened outside, and the day had come to a close.

Sarah, quietly rocking back and forth in her companion rocking chair, rarely interrupted as bits and pieces of Jake's life were laid out before her. She took in each revelation without comment, silently noting how these various parts of his life fitted into the man she had known — and was just beginning to know.

At first, the words came out of Jake sporadically and in no discernible order; at times, during long, silent pauses, Sarah would lose the thread and could not tell exactly where he was in the chronicling of his life.

She knew, of course, when he was referring to his boyhood and his relationship with his parents — especially with his father. She sat quietly as he told her of his memories of Brooklyn, of the parochial school he attended and of his visit to the Church, of the nuns and their strict instruction, of the family butcher shop, and the candy store around the corner. He said little of his mother. He told her of the slow alienation from his brother.

"He didn't come today," he said, "because he still hasn't forgiven Aunt Birgit for missing Mama's funeral." Jake looked off into space. "We haven't communicated since." He sighed. "Not that it bothered me so much, but Aunt Birgit was hurt."

Sarah simply nodded.

"Freddie — my brother — was so much like Papa," Jake said softly. "So much ..."

Another long silence, as he seemed to concentrate on the curling flames.

"His wife and children seem nice," she offered.

Jake nodded without turning his head towards her.

"Your niece — Kirstin, is it? — is the spitting image of you, Jake."

He shrugged and raised his eyebrows.

"Her mother — Konstanze — told me that she wants to be an artist."

Jake looked up at the ceiling. "That ought to make Fred real happy."

They sat quietly for some minutes, each, wrapped in thought, staring into the fireplace.

Then, leaning forward in his rocker, Jake suddenly opened up, words spilling from his mouth as if released from an abruptly opened floodgate.

He spoke of the days he used to lie on the parlor floor in his father's home copying pictures from the "funny sheets," and of the times the nuns would punish him for drawing in his textbooks. He told her how his father would cuff him when he drew pictures at the butcher shop, or how his mother rarely showed affection.

He shared with her his dread of the sea and of his love of thunderstorms with their rumbling of rolling noise and cracks of streaking lightning.

"Supposed to be the best thunder-boomers in the world," he told her. "An old friend of mine — Cap'n Bob — told me that the two places that had the worst thunder storms in the whole world were around Cape Horn and right here in the Catskills."

After so many words, he paused for some minutes, and then told her about his friendship with Cap'n Bob, the "only close friend he had next to Joe."

He told her of that boat trip up the Hudson, and the first time he had seen the Catskills *en masse*. He even attempted to describe his feelings as the steamboat swung around Crum's Elbow, but found that he still was not able to put it into words.

Sarah just smiled as he spoke of those moments on the ship's deck, her thoughts wandering to Jake's paintings.

Stymied for some minutes by his inability to share precisely with Sarah just what that day on the river had meant to him — how whatever had occurred within himself that day had become the driving force in his life — he lapsed again into a long silence.

Both sat listening to the occasional crackling of the fire.

Then, shaking his head as if coming out of a sound sleep, he would continue on his monologue.

"My mother and I were never very close," he said. Then he

378

spoke of Uncle Hans and Aunt Birgit, of his respect for his Uncle and of the love he felt for his Aunt. Of how his Uncle encouraged his painting, and of how Aunt Birgit saw to his daily needs.

"I'll miss her," he said simply.

He spoke to Sarah of his work as a carpenter, and of his constant struggle with painting. Then he told her of his talks with Birge Harrison, of his meeting Joe Bundy, and of their eventual friendship. He told her of all the things he had learned from artists as they came and left the area.

He even touched on his days in the war — something he had never spoken about to anyone. Once started, he found it easier to recall those horrible times, unaware as he spoke of them how they were affecting Sarah.

Still, she let him go on, instinctively knowing that all these things had to be said, needed to be released from their imprisonment in order for him to get past this day of his Aunt Birgit's burial.

Eventually, he got to the day she had given him the cup. She heard him struggling to find the words to let her know just how much that had meant to him. Then found him struggling even harder to tell her how she had never really been out of his mind.

"Even when you got married to Cal," he said softly. "I know it was wrong, but I just couldn't get that day you gave me the cup out of my head." He looked over at her shyly. "It was never very easy for me to visit you two, you know."

Sarah sat silently, her eyes on her lap.

"I still have it, you know," he said.

She looked up at him questioningly.

"The cup — it's over in my studio."

She smiled. "And I still have the drawing you gave me."

In later years, neither could recall how they had ended that evening of talk, nor of how they had come to share Jake's bed.

Jake lovingly traced the features of her face as she lay next to him. Then, rising on her elbow, Sarah pushed the covers down to the foot of the bed.

She ran her hands over the hardness of his body, silently marveling at how strong he seemed. She noted the muscled arms and flat belly. She pointed to the scar on his leg. "The war?"

"Yes."

She ran her fingers down its length. "Does it ever bother you?"

"Nope." He twisted his head to look into her eyes. "Just means I can't have any children."

"Who needs them?" said Sarah. "I've been living with a child ever since I married Cal. I certainly don't need one at this stage of my life."

"I'm too old anyway," said Jake. "Couldn't tolerate 'em."

"By the way," said Sarah, "how old are you?"

"Starting to crowd sixty — and you?"

"None of your business!" she said, and giggled.

Jake reached over to tousle her hair as her giggle changed into a deep belly laugh. Then, caught up in her infectious joy, he also gave in to deep chuckling until both fell back on their pillows in helpless spasms of laughter. As he lay next to Sarah, he felt as if gravity had been suspended, and that great weights had been removed from his body.

When they awakened the next morning, there was no embarrassment, no superfluous talk.

Although a word or two might have been passed behind closed doors between their West Hurley neighbors, no one in Woodstock raised an eyebrow when, after her divorce from Cal had been finalized, Sarah moved in with Jake.

60

If townsman and artist had been noting changes — either in alarm or in pleasure — in the town, Woodstock was merely reflecting what was happening throughout the region — and beyond.

The Ulster/Delaware railroad line leading into the Catskills from Kingston had been discontinued in 1954 with the West Shore Railroad along the Hudson River following suit shortly thereafter. The automobile was now the favored mode of transportation and, since traveling time was no longer a major factor, people had no need to rely on resort living when they made their trips up and downstate. The quick weekend trip to the mountains had now replaced the lengthy summer stay, and overnight motels began taking the place of the grand old resorts that once catered to tourists.

Over the years, the Catskill Mountain House had been slowly falling into decay, the once famous hotel falling into disuse and disrepair as Woodstock tourists increasingly shunned her old-style accommodations. Abandoned for long periods of time, the inevitable degeneration of the stately old building had been furthered along by the pointless vandalism of heedless visitors. Some of the owners attempted to deter these vandals by closing off the road to the hotel and, though it helped to stem the problem, many of the locals — youngsters intent on mischief among them — knew alternative routes up to the abandoned building. Eventually, local lawmakers closed off all of the usual access roads up to the summit of Overlook, and Jake found that suited him just fine.

Though less often than he did in the past, Jake occasionally climbed the mountain to one or more of his old haunts, varying his site as the seasons brought more or less foliage.

"It's amazing," he said to Sarah one warm autumn day when they had climbed to the summit together, "how all traces of civilization seem to disappear when you view the world from up here. It's like Woodstock hasn't changed one bit since the first time I climbed Overlook back when I was a boy. All the hustle and bustle, all the new shops, all the traffic, are gone." He put his arm across her shoulders as they sat side by side on a fallen log. "Kind of nice when you think of it"

Sarah snuggled against his side. "Yes," she agreed. "Especially when I'm with you."

"I have to agree, you know, with many of the old-timers here. Woodstock has certainly changed a lot over the years, and not all to the good."

"Oh, I don't know," said Sarah. "Sometimes change is good," and she snuggled up against him once again.

He kissed her hair. "Yes, *some* changes."

"Did you ever come up here with anyone else?"

Jake smiled. "You mean like with another woman? Sure, plenty of times. I made a regular habit of escorting young women up here during the summer tourist season."

Sarah thrust her shoulder into him, and he laughed again.

"Nope," he finally said. "I've only been up here with Cap'n Bob — but never to this particular spot." He hugged her closer to his side. "This was *my* spot." He looked off into the distance, then added, "Although I have imagined that I shared it with some Indian who first found it long ago."

"Tell me about the Cap'n again" she said.

"Well, he was a character — a real honest to goodness character. I told you that he lived over in Mink Hollow — in a shack that seemed to always smell of goats and chickens. Anyway, I learned a lot from that old man." He looked down at Sarah. "Nothing like the things I learned from your Dad — but important things all the same. He taught me a lot of wisdom along with a good deal of woodlore." He looked off into space again. "I miss him."

"He died before Aunt Birgit, didn't he?"

"Yep, several years before. A neighbor found him near frozen, lying in his bed with his pellet gun still in his hand. He apparently died in his sleep — just like Aunt Birgit." He paused. "Kind of a nice way to go, in your sleep. I don't think either of them suffered before they went."

"That's a consolation."

"Yes," agreed Jake. "Yes, it is … and they had long productive lives. Well, I don't know what others would have thought about Cap'n Bob's 'productiveness', but I can't recall either of them ever really being sick. Aunt Birgit had worked right up to the night she died, you know. She had been busy in her garden, clearing brush and leaves away from her newly-bloomed crocuses only that afternoon." He was silent a few moments. "I found her lying in her bed, a peaceful look on her face." Another pause. "It was the first time I had ever been in her room — all those years, and I had never seen my Uncle and Aunt's bedroom."

Sarah kept her silence.

"She was always up before Uncle Hans and me, the kitchen stove already fired up and fresh coffee brewing. I always loved the smell of coffee in the morning. She never broke the habit after Uncle Hans passed away, doing the same thing for me every morning." His breath caught for a moment. "Anyway," he continued, "I got up that morning and when I didn't smell the coffee, I knew something was wrong. I knocked on her door several times, calling to her before I found the nerve to open it." He smiled at Sarah. "Old habits."

"Yes, they're hard to break."

"I guess that's certainly true. Anyway, getting back to Cap'n Bob, I never did find out the cause of his death, but I suppose like Aunt Birgit, it was just old age. I have no idea how old he was — I never did know his age — but he was a tough old bird. He had no trouble scrabbling around this mountain, that's for sure. There were times I had trouble keeping up with him." He chuckled. "Yep, he was a real character."

"You're a bit of a 'character' yourself," said Sarah.

"Me?"

"Yes, *you*," laughed Sarah. "You're a bit of Woodstock lore yourself, you know."

Jake frowned.

"Don't give me that 'Jake Forscher' look, Jake Forscher! People were talking about you as some kind of 'mystery man' ever since I laid eyes on you back in Byrdcliffe."

He looked at her incredulously.

"It's true," she insisted. "One of my friends back then used to call you the 'Gary Cooper' type — strong and silent." She looked up at him. "Haven't changed much, as far as I can tell."

"Silent!" he retorted, "Why I haven't stopped blabbing since I know you. Since I *really* know you, I mean."

"And that's all for the better," she said. "But, Jake Forscher, the carpenter-artist, has been a topic for conversation for as long as I can remember."

Jake snorted. "Gary Cooper!" He snorted again. "I sure ain't no movie star!"

"Well, you're *my* leading man," she said demurely.

"Let's get back to the Cap'n," he said gruffly. "I told you about his guns, right? And the way they even found him with one — his old pellet gun — in his hands when he died? Well, he had a slew of 'em. Handguns, shotguns, rifles — every imaginable firearm you could think of. Some you couldn't *even* think of, actually. There were antiques as well as one-of-a-kind guns, things he picked up from God only knows where. I never knew where he got the money to pay for them, but they were likely a very valuable collection, as far as I could tell."

"Was he a hunter?"

"Not really. He didn't like the idea of killing for sport, but he did often bring a shotgun or rifle along whenever he came on one of my painting hikes. Whatever he shot, he would take home to eat, that I know. But he mostly seemed to live on the goats, chickens, and ducks he raised." Jake paused. "He used to love to fire those guns, though. I had no idea where he got the ammunition for some of them, but every so often we'd go out behind his shack and have a shooting spree, blasting away at tin cans, old bottles, or just firing up into the air at nothing in particular. He loved their craftsmanship, the way they were designed and built. I guess that guns were his idea of art."

"What became of them after he died?"

"From what I hear, relatives showed up shortly after his death — a niece and nephew from the city that I don't remember him ever mentioning — and claimed whatever he had. I don't know what they did with the guns — probably sold them off — but as far as I could tell, they were the only things of value that he owned." Then he added, "Except his wisdom. Anyway, I didn't know that

Cap'n Bob had any living relatives — at least he never spoke of them to me."

"It sounds like you might have liked to have some of those guns yourself," said Sarah.

Jake shrugged. "Well, some of them were real beauties. They really *were* works of art. I wouldn't have minded having one or two to hang on my wall."

"I like seeing your paintings hanging there instead," said Sarah. "I never did like guns."

"Well, like I said, they were works of art." He shrugged. "I also don't care for guns — never was much of a hunter. Still, I'm curious about what Cap'n Bob's niece and nephew did with his collection." He looked off into the distance. "Funny thing about inheritance."

Sarah gave him a questioning look.

"Inheritance," he repeated. "The way things are passed down in families — sometimes to people who don't have an inkling of the worth or value of the things they inherit." He turned to Sarah. "There are times that I still can't believe that Aunt Birgit left the house to me." He quickly added, "I know, I know — but it still came as a complete surprise when I found out. I had to read her will several times before it really sank in."

"But it was kind of natural for her to do it, wasn't it? I mean, who better deserved it — or was more entitled to it?"

"I know all that." Then pointing to his head, he said, "I know it up here. But it still amazes me."

Sarah hugged him around the neck. "I love you," she murmured into his ear. "Even if you're *not* a movie star."

"Yup," he said in an unconvincing imitation of Gary Cooper. "And I love you, woman" He got to his feet and pulled her up from the log. "Now let's get down off this mountain. I still have time to do some measuring for those new shelves in your studio."

61

Since Sarah was in his life, Jake had become a more consistent exhibitor at the Association, entering work at almost every show unless it specified genres or styles that did not include that of landscape painting. The combined force of Sarah's gentle urging with that of Joe Bundy's long-standing campaign to "take himself seriously" gradually wore him down and he not only exhibited more often but, though he still felt not quite right about it, also began selling his paintings.

Whether or not his work was always accepted at juried exhibitions meant little to Jake, since he adamantly insisted that it was his own, and not someone else's approval that ultimately mattered to him. He remained strong in his convictions that art ought not be viewed merely as a commodity — at least that his art was not — and it remained his practice not to affix a full signature to his work. Although he would include details such as date and place on the backs of his canvases, he persisted in merely scratching his initials into the lower, right-hand side of his paintings with the point of his palette knife.

Ever since he had converted Uncle Hans's old carriage shed into an enclosed studio for Sarah, they had gotten into the habit of "visiting" each other's workplace when one or the other finished up for the day. Sarah now had her own wood-burning catenary kiln — a project that Jake found a great deal of pleasure in installing after he had put the finishing touches on her new space — and although she had attracted a number of clients on her own, she continued to sell the bulk of her work through Lenora.

Though he found Sarah's unannounced visits to his studio

while he was at work both uncomfortable and unwelcome in the beginning, her maintaining silence as he worked eventually won him over. He gradually grew to enjoy her quiet presence — even to look forward to it — and, eventually, even looking forward to hearing her comments when he put down his brushes at the end of a session. He drew the line, however, with others. Joe was one thing — and those, of course, who came to purchase frames. But his studio was his work place — his "thinking" place, and he had no intention of turning it into some kind of social hall. Though he enjoyed their coming and staying over at their house, Sarah's parents or not, not even Mae or Cyrus was offered an open invitation to come into his studio unannounced. The living room was the place for idle talk — even for his discussions with Cyrus, though now that he was getting on in years, he seemed less able to carry on the long talks that Jake had come to look forward to.

If at first Sarah tended to offer only general statements about how "good" his paintings were, as time passed her observations became more pointed, more discerning She asked intelligent questions and avoided gratuitous platitudes. One of her great pleasures was to have discovered boxes full of Jake's drawings and, when he offered no resistance to her rummaging through his sketches, she spent many quiet hours looking through them as he worked at his easel.

Sarah had also convinced him to keep his paintings on view, hanging them not only in his studio, but also in almost every room of the house instead of keeping them stacked against the walls of his studio. One day, she even suggested to him that he ought to make a selection of his drawings and make a little book of them, but when she added that they would "sell well," he abruptly changed the subject. She persisted, however, in hanging his paintings throughout the house, choosing them to suit her own taste.

"Place looks like a gallery," he would say. "A new exhibition almost every other day."

"I should think that you'd be better able to watch your progress — or lack of it — if you keep them up where you can constantly see them," she said one day.

"I guess," was all he was willing to say at the time but, as they kept appearing on new walls in each of the rooms, he had to finally admit that she was right. He *was* able to see a rough kind of evolution, a kind of progress — at least in *some* parts of *some* paintings.

"You needn't view them as masterpieces," she reasoned. "Only see them as lessons."

"Hard to look at them," he said, "when I can see what's wrong with each and every one of them."

"Well don't look at them as admonishments — look at them as ways to improve." She glanced at him sideways. "That is, if you *want* to improve."

He reached over and grabbed her around the waist. "You devil, you! How come you always have the right thing to say? Everybody else — well, Joe anyway — goes out of his way to avoid riling me by saying such things."

She gave one of her belly laughs. "How else am I going to tame you?"

"*Tame* me! You make me sound like a wild man."

"Well …" she said archly. "It sounded pretty much like you and Cap'n Bob *were* wild men. Scrabbling around the mountain and shooting guns off, and all."

This bantering between them was something new for Jake, and he loved it. He had certainly heard and contributed to such light conversation from time to time on the job, but had never dreamed that such things might go on between a man and a woman.

At other times, in her more serious moments, he found her equally delightful to be with.

One afternoon of such seriousness was still fresh in his mind, and he knew that what she'd said that day in his studio was in large part what made him accept himself as an artist — an *exhibiting* artist.

She had been carefully studying several of his latest canvases that she had lined up on his wall, waiting for him to finish up before allowing herself to speak. Each was a slightly different view of Overlook, each unmistakably distinct from the others although they were all of the same subject.

He finally wiped his hands on a cloth and sat down. Patting the seat next to him that he had brought into the studio for her convenience, he said, "OK. Sit down right here and out with it. I can see you're busting at the seams to tell me what I've done wrong," and, when he saw her grimace, added, "or right."

Sarah remained standing and slowly turning her head from one canvas to the next, said, "You know, Jake, *they* say it."

Puzzled, he asked, "Say *what?*"

She turned from the paintings to face him. "What you've been telling me — and everybody else ever since I know you — what you claim you can't say."

"You lost me, Sarah."

"That day on the boat when you came upriver as a boy — you know, at Crum's Elbow. You have always said that you couldn't put into words what you felt back then. That you couldn't explain to anyone how seeing those mountains for the first time affected you." She turned back to the paintings and pointed. "*They* say it, Jake. They say it very clearly."

He looked at the paintings and then at her.

"And just what is it that you think they're saying?"

"Well now, that's just what I'm trying to tell you, Jake. *I* can't put it into words any better than you can. But they *do* speak, if you only listen. It took living with them for some time in order for me to hear them, but they *do* talk to me." She sat down next to him. "They talk in their own language, Jake. They just don't use *words.* But it's clear to anyone who truly looks just what it is that you experienced so long ago when you were still a boy."

Jake leaned back in his chair, scanning but not really seeing the latest series of paintings of Overlook that he had done.

"Don't you see, Jake? All the time you've been telling people that you couldn't put into words just what it was that compelled you to paint Overlook, you were 'telling' them through your *paintings.*"

He didn't respond, but continued to look at the paintings.

"You always got a little tongue-tied when anyone pressed you on your paintings — you know that, Jake. Well, I think it was because the paintings were already expressing the very thing you couldn't say in words." She took in the paintings with a sweep of her arm. "They were saying the same thing over and over: 'Look at what I saw that day!' Nobody was able to make the connection — not even those of us who knew you well — because you've been sharing your paintings with others so sparingly. You never gave others a chance to see them as a group, as kind of a running narrative." She grabbed his arm. "Do you see what I mean, Jake?"

"Yes," he said slowly. "Yes, I think I do."

"Dad used to talk about pottery being the expression of a certain group — that if we only 'listened with our eyes,' we could hear ancient people speaking to us through not only their pottery, but through all their artifacts. Each tribe had its own individual way of making and designing things. It's just a different language, a different way for people to communicate with one another."

Jake stood up abruptly and began pacing the studio. "Yes," he said slowly. "I seem to remember his talking about that to me when he told me about the cave paintings." He scratched the back of his head. "He said that these pictures of animals and figures came later — that earlier images and signs were abstract — I think he used the word 'symbolic'." He stopped to scan the paintings again. "He said that if we could only interpret those symbols then we'd be able to understand what they were attempting to express."

"Exactly," said Sarah with excitement. "For instance, it took years for archaeologists to decipher some ancient scripts. Often it was only when they were able to amass a certain amount of inscribed artifacts — clay tablets, stones, papyrus, whatever — for comparison and cross reference that they could make any headway." She paused for a moment and rose from her seat. "Did Dad ever tell you about the Rosetta Stone?"

"No — no, I don't remember his telling me about that."

She stood before him to halt his pacing.

"Well, the French found this stone — this tablet — at a place called Rosetta in Egypt, and it gave them a key to unlocking the mystery to the ancient inscriptions they had been finding in tombs for years."

She turned him toward the paintings. "Now, my stone-age man, let's concentrate on these paintings here."

He raised his eyebrows, pretending to be insulted. "Stone-age man?"

"Yep. *My* stone-age man," she said with one of her belly laughs. "But seriously, Jake, think about this for a moment. How different are your pictures from those made by our ancient ancestors? I mean, *they* couldn't speak — they didn't have a language yet — at least not an articulate one, as far as we know." She looked at him. "So, *they* couldn't voice their thoughts — and neither can you." She pointed to his paintings again. "So, in a sense, these are *your*

Rosetta Stones — we just need to interpret them to get at what you are trying to communicate."

Jake rubbed his jaw then slowly sat down. Finding no words, he merely expelled a heavy breath.

"You're seeing what I'm getting at, aren't you Jake?"

He nodded.

"In a larger sense, we're still all stone-age people. I mean, there are still things that we feel, that we experience, that we *know* in here —" Sarah touched her breast, "that we can't put into words. Some people make music, others dance — and some paint." She looked intently into his eyes. "And they do it, Jake, *because there's no other way for them to express those feelings!* As sophisticated as we think we are, we still don't have a single, comprehensive language. Here we are in the middle of the 20th century and we still haven't come up with one means of expression to fit all occasions."

"I wonder if we're meant to," said Jake.

Sarah shrugged. "God only knows," she said. "But He certainly hasn't made it very easy for humans to share with others all that they can feel, or imagine, or experience. Just think how many wars could have been prevented if people were able to fully communicate with each other! How many misunderstandings would instantly clear up if we had one sure-fire way of expressing who we are and what we feel and what we want and what we mean?" She caught him by the arm and looked into his eyes. "Jake, you experienced a very profound thing that day you first saw the mountains from the boat, and I'm sure that it changed you in some very deep way. So deep, that for all these years you haven't been able to tell anyone what really happened that day. You couldn't communicate it in *words,* Jake — but you've been communicating it through your drawings and paintings ever since."

Jake took her in his arms. "I kind of like *this* way of communicating," he said and gave her a long kiss. "Now putting *that* into words wouldn't be quite as pleasurable as the real thing."

"Well, thank you my stone-age man." She disentangled herself from his arms and turned him toward the paintings of Overlook. "But seriously, Jake. You could say the same for them, you know."

Jake stood wrapped in thought for several moments. Sarah's comments brought back the conversations about pleasure that he had with Joe and Birge Harrison so long ago. Back then, they had spoken of the need for the artists to please themselves, a principle that Jake had conscientiously followed over the years. He had no scruples about painting over a canvas that displeased him, and would never let a painting leave his studio that he had not lived with for some time, keeping it out of sight until he was convinced that he could not improve it. He still remained unsure if he had ever captured Overlook from its most advantageous viewpoint or in the best light, but would content himself at times that *this* view, at any rate, came as near as possible to what he wanted to depict. In short, he demanded that each painting please *him* and, as far as he was able, remained rigorously critical of each attempt. He had for so long disciplined himself in judging his work in relation to his own pleasure, that this business of a painting having to please someone else still struck him as irrelevant.

After silently staring at his paintings for a piece of time, he turned to look at Sarah.

"Do they please you, Sarah?" he asked.

"Well of course they do, silly." She searched his face. "What a thing to ask? You *know* that I have always admired your work."

He was silent for some moments, but somehow her answer didn't satisfy him. After some more moments of silence he said, "I guess that really doesn't count." He saw her questioning look. "Your liking them, I mean."

She frowned, but before she could speak, he continued, "I don't mean that you shouldn't be pleased — or that I don't value your opinion. Of course I do. But your liking my work — finding pleasure in it — is, well, tainted..." He paused as he was met with another frown. "Well, maybe that's the wrong word — maybe I mean 'prejudiced'." Her frown remained. "Anyway, your assessment of my work is compromised — now *that's* a better word — it's compromised by your feelings for *me*."

He was pleased to see the frown finally disappear, and be replaced with a thoughtful look.

"I have to agree with that," she finally said. "Compliments are always suspect since we are often unaware of motives and intentions." She thought for a moment. "But then let's leave my pleasure aside." She looked impishly at him. "But only for the moment, and for the sake of argument, that is." Then, seriously, "What about the strangers who have walked into the Association and praised one of

392

your paintings. *They* don't know you, or have any reason to want to flatter you or make you happy. They're only concerned with their *own* happiness, their *own* pleasure. It seems to me that if someone buys one of your paintings, it's to take it home to hang up on a wall so that it could be enjoyed. Obviously they admired your painting because it *pleased* them. What about that?"

Jake had no answer.

"Well *that* counts, doesn't it?" she prodded. "Surely the adding of a bit of pleasure to someone else's life — regardless of what *you* might think of that particular painting — couldn't hurt, could it?"

Jake maintained his silence and just replied with a shrug and a smile. Having no ready rebuttal, he decided to keep his counsel.

62

With Jake happily seconding the idea, Sarah continued to host
her "Third Thursday" gatherings, the switch from her house in
Willow — which she was now renting out — to their home in West
Hurley, a transition that was barely noticed or commented upon.
The absence of Morris and Cal had been since filled in by Myra
Iskowitz, who was now coming back to Woodstock — at least dur-
ing the summer months — and some newcomers, David Lehrer
and his wife.

In his late 40s and an established art critic, Lehrer was no
stranger to the Woodstock artscene, having been sent up by his
city editors to review Association shows since Woodstock's pre-
World War II heydays. An unassuming and thoughtful man who
loved his work, Lehrer, like many others, had been captivated by
Woodstock and, since early summer, he and his wife Lynn had
been renting Sarah's home with an option to buy. Jake, who had
a slight recollection of meeting the younger man at the Association some years ago, welcomed Sarah's suggestion that she invite
her new tenants to their Thursday night gatherings. The fact that
he recalled Lehrer's having some positive things to say back then
about his work, only made it that much easier to accept him and
his wife in his home.

Had he known that Sarah had planned a special little celebration on the occasion of his sixtieth birthday for this particular
Thursday, he might not have been so open to *any*one's coming.
She had sworn all to secrecy, however, and Jake, none the wiser,
just anticipated another evening of pleasant conversation with the
added attraction of Cyrus and Mae who had been there all week,

both comfortably settled in Jake's old room which he had long since transformed into a guestroom.

Taking advantage of the opportunity to meet with Joe for one of their increasingly rare painting expeditions together, Jake, leaving Sarah and Mae in the kitchen preparing for the evening, kissed them both as he set out to leave for the afternoon.

Myra Iskowitz, who came early Thursday morning to help out, arrived just in time to meet Jake as he stepped out the door, exchanging a brief hello and an awkwardly negotiated hug around the easel slung across his back.

"Have fun," she called to his back as he strode towards his pickup.

"You've done wonders with that man, Sarah," Myra said, after embracing both her and Mae. "I've always liked Jake, but I think I like the *new* Jake a whole lot better."

"Yes, he's a keeper," Sarah said.

"He seems a lot easier with himself since you two've been together," Myra observed. "A bit more 'open' … less reserved."

Sarah watched as he pulled away. "Yes," she said thoughtfully.

Myra looked at Sarah questioningly. "He's not?"

"Well, yes," said Sarah turning to Myra. "But …"

"I certainly have to agree with Myra," chimed in Mae, busy at the sink. "At least he's not as aloof as he used to be." Then, after a slight pause. "Though not with Cyrus. Those two can spend hours talking together."

"So what's the 'but' mean?" asked Myra turning back to Sarah.

"Well, there's a closed spot in him that I just can't seem to penetrate at times … a spot that I can't touch."

"*All* men have *that*," laughed Myra.

"Of course they do," agreed Mae. "Do you think your father has shared everything with me over the years? And how about Cal? Was he always transparent?"

"Oh, I know that, Mom." She bit her lower lip. "But I don't mean a deliberate shutting out … a withholding, like Cal used to do. Jake isn't secretive or hiding anything." She shrugged. "It's just that he seems to have a place inside him that's just … well … Jake. A place that I'm not even sure that *he* can get into, at times."

"Hmmm," said Myra. "So, is it a good thing or a bad thing, then?"

"For me?" Sarah thought for a moment. "I don't know if I can call it 'good' or 'bad'. It just puzzles me ... though sometimes I wonder if it isn't a bad thing for Jake. There are times when whatever it is seems to eat at him." She threw out her hands. "Oh, I don't know! Maybe it's all in *my* head."

"Well, he sure seems a lot more happy in his skin than when Morris and I first met him at your house," Myra said, giving Sarah a hug.

"Yes," smiled Sarah. "He's a keeper, all right."

"Well, for whatever it's worth," said Mae with a sidelong glance at Myra, "Daddy and I are both glad he's in your life."

Sarah hugged her mother, then grabbed both by the arms. "So, how about we get busy and see what we have to serve for our guests tonight?"

The Lehrers were the first to arrive in the evening. After introducing David and his wife, Lynn, to Myra, Sarah led them into the living room. "Make yourself comfortable — although I should point out that the rocker on the left side of the fireplace is Jake's fiercely guarded province."

Lehrer smiled. "A man's home, et cetera." He and his wife took seats near the window and added with another smile, "I wouldn't presume to violate my host's hospitality ... least of all his castle."

"Well, are you ready to 'violate' his liquor cabinet? What can I bring you both?"

When she returned to the kitchen to fill their orders, Myra leaned close and whispered, "Oy! What would Morris have said if we had invited an art critic back in the old days!"

Sarah giggled. "What would he say if he knew *Jake* would be the host?"

Myra raised her eyes to the ceiling.

"Now, I'd better get these drinks out to Lynn and David, or they'll think I forgot about them."

The Fieldings knocked at the front door at the same moment that Mae and Cyrus came downstairs from their room.

"It's like Broadway and Forty-Second Street here!" said Ed Fielding as they all trooped together into the living room.

Lehrer leapt to his feet as Sarah made introductions.

"We've got to cure you of *that* habit in a real hurry," said Fielding as he shook hands with Lehrer. "God forbid we have to get formal here!"

"Oh yes," said Catherine. "God forbid that we have someone with manners in our presence." She took Lehrer's hand. "A pleasure," she said.

"Well, lah-di-dah," Ed said, making an exaggerated bow to his wife. Then turning to Sarah, "Where's my drink? I've been here for almost two minutes!"

"Right behind you, smarty pants," said Myra, her hands filled with a tray of drinks. She glanced to see if the Lehrers needed refills. When she noticed that they had hardly touched their drinks, she turned to the others and said, "I hope this is OK — I've brought you all your usuals."

A chorus of assents was returned as each found themselves a seat.

"Where's Jake and the Bundys?" asked Catherine.

"They should be here soon," said Sarah. "Jake and Joe went painting today, and I assume they stopped to pick up Andrea since they went in Joe's car." Glancing around to make sure that her guests were comfortable, she returned to the kitchen to bring out the trays of cheese and crackers they had prepared earlier.

No sooner had she picked up the trays from the kitchen counter when Jake and the Bundys came in.

"Are we late?" asked Jake as he kissed Sarah on the cheek. "We painted until we almost couldn't tell which colors we were using — and then we had to pick up Andrea."

"No you're not late," laughed Sarah. "Since when did we have a time schedule?"

"Oh, you know what I mean, honey," said Jake as he gave her a hug. "Joe and I get so little time to paint together, that we like to take advantage of every minute we can."

"And Andrea's been scolding us ever since we picked her up," said Joe. "Said she's been waiting for hours."

Andrea swatted him on the back of his head. "Oh, I did not." She turned to Sarah. "These guys are like kids when they get together."

"I know," said Sarah. Then with a grin, "Don't you love it?"

* * *

Dinner over, they all settled in the living room, the conversation begun over the meal rambling on in its usual fashion, sometimes involving everyone, at other times broken into smaller groups of two or three.

"I've seen several of your murals, Mr. Fielding. I especially liked the one down at Fredericksburg," David Lehrer was saying.

"Ed," said Fielding. "Call me Ed, please." He turned to his wife. "If that's all right with *you*, Miss Manners." Catherine airily waved him off, and he turned back to Lehrer. "Thank you for the compliment. Are you very familiar with muralists?"

"Well, I know of Rivera's work, of course. I wrote a piece on him some time back. But I also know the work of others — I became somewhat familiar with Tom Benton and Kenneth Hayes Miller when they were giving mural classes at the League — and Lynn and I have even met some of your fellow muralists here in Woodstock — Anton Refregier, Ethel Magafan, Wendel Jones."

"I remember your piece on Rivera," said Catherine. "I recall it being quite perceptive."

Lehrer bowed his head in her direction.

"He's too modest too admit it," said Lynn Lehrer. "But he *is* good."

"Quite a demanding process I should think," said Cyrus Winters.

"Not something *I'd* want to tackle," Joe interrupted. "Easel painting is difficult enough without taking on an entire wall. And anyway, painting to somebody else's specifications never appealed to me. Pity the poor portrait painter, having to please not only his sitter, but his whole darned family — not to mention all of his friends, to boot!" He made a dismissive motion with his hand. "Might as well paint by *numbers* for God's sake!"

"I was referring to Lehrer's *writing* about Diego Rivera," said Cyrus. "If I am correct, he was sort of the 'daddy' of mural painting, wasn't he — at least for American artists? I daresay that writing about an originator of a movement can be quite daunting."

"Well, it is easier jumping onto a familiar bandwagon, than cutting one's teeth on something new," Lehrer agreed.

"I take some exception to your comment about portrait painters, Joe," said Catherine Fielding. "What about Velázquez or Rembrandt? Or John Singer Sargent? Do you think they painted 'by numbers'?"

"Well, now, *they* were painters," Joe said with a shrug.

"Getting back to the subject," said Ed Fielding, "It would be my guess that writing about *any* art would be difficult. I sometimes doubt if many of the so-called critics I've read — and I do not make it a practice to read many — have ever attempted a painting themselves."

"Morris used to call them eunuchs," said Myra. "It was his contention that although critics might be able to give a detailed description of *how* it was done, they couldn't do it themselves."

Lehrer laughed. "Yes — an age-old complaint. I once looked up 'criticism' in Bartlett's Quotations, and found a slew of equally clever comments on what artists thought of the critic. One of my favorites is by Rodin who claimed that critics were the fungus that grows at the roots of oaks."

"Not half as bad as what some critics have written about artists," said Fielding.

Lehrer nodded. "That's certainly true."

"Well, I for one think that critics play an important role for the artist," said Joe. "Carlson — and he wasn't the only instructor who preached it — often told us that we are our own worst critics — that we *needed* an outside opinion."

"If only to keep us honest?" joked Fielding.

"Well, at least on the ball," said Joe.

"Although I hate to admit it, I think Joe has a point," said Andrea. "One doesn't necessarily have to know how to make art to tell good from bad."

"I'd have to agree with that," said Lynn Lehrer. "I have never picked up a brush in my life, but I'd like to believe that my years as a publicist for both a New York City art academy and a small art museum have given me some insights over the years into what is good and what is not."

"Hear, hear," said Catherine. "I'd like to believe that we art historians also know something about who's got promise and who's wasting our time."

"Teachers *ought* to tell us," said Joe. "But, I suppose if they need to make a living, they'll keep you in class for as long as you continue to pay. But I agree, you don't have to be an artist to have a good eye."

"Something like a boxer's trainer?" asked Cyrus. "I certainly am no expert on the art of fisticuffs, but I recall reading somewhere that John L. Sullivan's trainer never stepped into the ring with an opponent in his entire life — but that didn't prevent him from turning old John L. into a champion."

"Then, of course, there are those who attain genius without the aid of a teacher at all," said Sarah. "Like Mozart, for instance."

"Or, in *spite* of a teacher," countered Ed Fielding. "The woods are full of more artists who've been thrown off course by a poor instructor than by a poor critic."

"There's a lot to say for that," said Joe.

"Like anything else," said Sarah, "there has to be two sides to it. There are undoubtedly good and bad critics as there are good and bad artists." Nodding toward Lehrer, she continued, "I've taken the time to read a good deal of David's writing ..." she glanced around the room and said with a smile, "You know, I had to get to know my tenant before I rented the house to him" — then continued, "... and I found that he generally takes a balanced view. I've read several of his critiques aloud to Jake, and he ..." she motioned toward Jake — "agrees with me."

Jake nodded. "I find a lot of substance in what David says. It's not all gobbledy-gook like a lot of people babble on about art — artists included."

"Who are you writing for now, David?" asked Catherine.

"I've been freelancing for the past few years," said Lehrer. "I'm not sure which paper or magazine I'd like to write steadily for — I'm not so sure that *any* of them would want me on a full-time basis. So many of the newer publications have adopted a stance to which they expect their writers to adhere." He shrugged. "I can't really say that I whole-heartedly agree with many of my colleagues, so I like to keep my options open."

"Morris used to say that if you took all the adjectives out of a piece of art criticism, you ended up with bupkiss," said Myra.

"Bupkiss?" said Mae Winters, who had been sitting quietly throughout the discussion.

"Means — pardon the expression — 'goat shit'," David said. "And I'm sure that I would have liked your husband, Mrs. Iskowitz — he seems to have had a healthy respect for, what in the end, is merely opinion." He looked around the group. "That's all it boils down to, you know — opinion."

"But then there are opinions and *opinions*," said Andrea. "Not all opinions are equal."

"That's certainly true," said Lynn Lehrer. "One of the things that attracted me to David was his careful way of making judgments. I always knew I could rely on his honesty when I asked for guidance."

"Of course," said Lehrer. "There are informed opinions that, generally speaking, ought to be listened to. For example, if I feel sick, I'm going to go to a doctor and not ask advice from a plumber." He smiled at his own witticism, then continued. "Presumably, a critic is informed about his subject. But that is not to say that all critics *are* — far from it, in fact. Readers have to have some confidence in the critics they choose to listen to, and they can only do that by taking the time to check credentials."

"True," said Catherine Fielding. "There have been quack critics, just like there've been quack doctors. It's a danger to take the advice of either."

"Better to go to a good plumber than to a quack doctor maybe, right David?" said Myra.

Lehrer laughed. "Right."

"But is it really possible to write critically about art?" asked Jake. "Sarah had brought up the subject some weeks ago, and I've often spoken about it with Cyrus — that is, that art has its own language and cannot necessarily be put into words. Can anyone actually *say* what a picture means? I know that *I've* never been able to speak about my own art in any intelligent way."

"This is a real question," agreed Lehrer. "It's stymied aestheticians for ages and no one has come up with a definitive response to it yet. For example, unless you can read Japanese, you cannot legitimately say that you've read a haiku poem — only that you've read a *translation* of it, and that is manifestly not the same thing. So, if there's a problem in translation from one verbal language to another, think of the enormity of the problem when you attempt a translation from a *visual* language to that of a verbal one. Speech has its own vocabulary, but so also does art — and historically, the language of art pre-dates the verbal one by centuries."

Catherine nodded in agreement.

Lehrer continued. "Lynn deals with the problem every day. Her job of having to inform the public about what a museum has to offer — or an art academy, when she worked for them — is not as simple as writing up an advertisement for a new car or a can of soup. First, one has to believe in the product one is representing and, second, have some knowledge of that product. When it comes to criticism, the issue is further compounded by the fact that art criticism is a relatively new phenomenon in Western society. Just think of it — the first written art criticism did not appear until the Renaissance — Cennini wrote the first handbook on art in the 14th Century, and criticism *as* criticism did not appear until years later. Meanwhile, art has been created since pre-historical times, and that makes the art critic an extremely new kid on the block."

Jake, thinking about his own frustrations, asked, "Then why even attempt it? Why keep butting your head against a wall?"

"I do it because I think, Jake, that art is important — I sincerely believe that ever since the first painting was made on a cave wall, that art has been taking us *out* of that cave. I want to somehow make my readers see that." He paused. "I might ask you the same question, Jake. Why do painters continue to paint when it appears obvious that they are never quite satisfied with what they create?"

"Well, that may be true," agreed Jake. "But technically, by your own reasoning, I'm staying within one language, right? All I'm doing is translating one image — the one before me — into another on the canvas. It seems to me that your job is different, more difficult — if not as you seem to suggest, impossible."

"I have to admit that there are times when I wake up in the wee hours of the morning in a sweat because, at bottom, I *do* feel like a charlatan when I write about art. I mean, language is so ambiguous in and of itself. Words are slippery things and, in the wrong hands, can do considerable damage."

"You've got *that* right," said Myra Iskowitz. "We've gone through two world wars because language has failed miserably when it comes to true communication."

"True," said Catherine. "When you consider that you can look at a van Eyck and comprehend his meaning, listen to Mozart and hear his message, or stand in the center of St. Peter's in Rome and get a sense of eternity — without understanding a word of Flemish, German or Italian — you can see how much more effective *those* languages are, how their distinct vocabularies speak in much clearer terms to the human psyche, than does the written or spoken word. There is simply no contest."

David shrugged. "And yet, here I continue to write, continue to wrestle with the enigma — all the while feeling, as I said, like a charlatan. A trickster who can only succeed by deceiving the audience."

"I think that artists can feel the same way, at times," said Ed Fielding.

"And some bona fide tricksters among them, I'm sure," said Joe.

"Oh, I'm sure of it, too," said Lehrer. "There have indeed been some 'tricksters,' as you call them, out there. One need only read some of the comments of Picasso to see how he delighted in duping his admirers. He was well aware of the ignorance of both his buyers *and* his dealers — and he had few scruples about putting one over on them whenever he could. It's truly amazing when you read about the enormous sums that people have spent on some of his most obvious 'jokes' — simply because his name appeared at the bottom. He knew it and because they didn't, he felt they deserved to be fleeced." He turned to Jake. "Which brings me back to your assertion that you are 'making images of images.' But what of the artist who chooses to paint non-representational art? Say, for example, an abstract expressionist like Pollock who merely allows his colors to drip or splash on his canvas?"

"And then," interjected Ed, "some abstractionists claim that they are making images of their *inner* feelings — expressing their psyches, their souls. How does one go about criticizing *their* art?"

"Well, now," said Joe. "Like we said about opinions before, there's art and there's *art*. Is pouring house paint out of a can onto a flat canvas, art?"

"Now we're *really* in deep water," said Catherine. "I wouldn't touch *that* one with a ten-foot pole — even if I *am* an art historian."

"Maybe *because* you're an art historian," said Lehrer. "You just know better. The question of whether an artist of the past was 'good' or 'bad' was difficult enough for everyone to agree on. In today's art world the very question of what can or cannot be called 'art' is up for grabs. I doubt if there's a critic today who would attempt a definition of 'art'." He looked around the room. "I know that *I* wouldn't."

"But isn't that a critic's job?" asked Cyrus.

"Well, they used to think so — until the French Impressionists came along," he said.

"Why's that?" asked Jake.

"You have to sort of put yourself back into that time," said Lehrer. "Here they were, a part of and writing in a world where academic standards had been the rule for as long as they could remember. Anyone who came to the annual salons with open eyes could see what made a painting good, and anyone who had the skill, could write about what *made* them good. Everyone knew the rules — *every*one. Then along came Manet, Monet, Pissarro, Renoir — the whole bunch of impressionists — who presumed to break the rules, and when they did, the critics had a field day. They all fell over themselves to hoot the loudest, each intent on out-scorning the other when it came to describing what these poor, misguided fools were trying to pass off as 'art.' Who could predict that in less time than it took to earn your credentials as a credible critic that these 'clowns who painted with guns' would resonate with the public? The fickle, uninformed, public?"

"Right," said Catherine." Then, Manets, Monets, Pissarros, Renoirs — the whole lot — began flying out of the galleries, clamped under the sweaty armpits of the 'great unwashed' that couldn't wait to slap down their francs and carry them home."

"True," continued Lehrer. "History played a nasty trick on the critics — and it was a trick they never forgot. The hooters became the hooted, and critics have never again been the same. Once burnt, it was a brave soul who would ever again go out on a limb and proclaim to the world what was 'bad'." He shrugged. "Critics have been running scared ever since, I'm afraid. Which critic today dares to say that abstract expressionism, for instance, is nonsense when their work is finding more and more buyers? Nowadays, critics seem to bend over backwards to find something positive to say — even when they don't understand or even *like* what they're writing about. It's become somewhat of a game."

"A game, it would appear, in which everyone is a loser," said Cyrus. "How can art — whatever that means now — continue to evolve — or survive?"

"Another good question," said Ed Fielding. "Any takers?"

"Well, I have to believe that it's more than just a 'game' since I spend a good deal of time promoting it," said Lynn. "Whether we like it or not, art has become something more than a pleasant diversion for the aristocracy, and my job as a publicist means I have to convince the public that art is important to everyone."

Dejection seemed to envelop the room as each sat silently wrapped in thought.

Catherine broke the silence. "Well, it's lasted this long. I'll put my money on its survival."

"Yes," said Sarah. "As long as it continues to have the power to please people, it will survive."

"Yes," echoed Mae Winters. "A little pleasure in such a world can only be a good thing."

"A slippery slope, that," mused Cyrus.

Sarah looked over at her father for clarification.

"Using pleasure as a guiding principle," he said. "Could prove to be dangerous. Some people derive pleasure from pulling the wings off flies, or setting houses on fire."

"Or shoving people into ovens," said Myra.

"Not a very trustworthy thing to rely on then, I guess," said Joe.

"Especially when the 'relying' is being done by a growing public that, for all accounts and purposes, knows relatively little about art," said Catherine.

"A growing *buying* public," said Lehrer.

"And one with a lot of money to spend," said Lynn. "We just have to continue to show them where their money does the most good."

"Which is why we have to inform them — the critics, the publicists, *and* the artists ought to be informing the public," said Andrea. "I've been saying that for *years*."

"Not an easy task," said Lehrer. "Even the average *educated* person knows little about art. Sure, there's been an upsurge of college attendance since the end of the war — a marked increase in the number of literate people who now make up our 'buying public.' But the key word here is 'literate.' There's absolutely no denying that our population is made up of better *readers* — but how many of them are taught to read *art*? Which is why so many of them depend on what they read in the papers and books and magazines when it comes to their understanding and knowledge of it. Let's face it — looking at art *critically* is simply hard work, and the average person will depend on someone else to do his research. He'll simply *read* what the 'experts' have to say and act — or buy — accordingly."

"Hence the power of the critic," said Ed Fielding.

"And, like I say," said Lehrer. "There are just too many critics who have caved in to public opinion, and who've resigned themselves to walking on the safe side."

"They've all learned their history," said Catherine. "Look at the growing number of colleges that now offer degrees in art history for art majors."

"*Another* can of worms," said her husband. "The university-produced 'master' of arts!" He snorted in disgust. "*History* used to produce 'masters' — not history *majors*. It took *time* to discover which artist made the grade. Nowadays colleges do it in *four years*! Talk about mass production…!"

"*And* they step out into the world ready to take on jobs as curators, art historians, or …" she glanced at Lehrer, "… critics."

David Lehrer merely raised his arms with his hands palms up.

"Well *this* is certainly a depressing way to end an evening," said Andrea.

"There's only one way to fix that," announced Sarah, as she left to go into the kitchen.

She returned a few moments later with a lighted birthday cake in her hands, and walked up to Jake as choruses of 'Happy Birthdays' filled the room.

His mouth hanging open, Jake turned crimson as he struggled for words, but before he could find any, Joe yelled out, "Look at his ears! They look like exit signs!"

Whatever depression might have lingered in the room was soon dissipated in laughter.

Later that evening, when the guests had gone and her parents were off to bed, Sarah brought Jake a gaily-wrapped present.

He looked up quizzically. Then, with a frown, he asked, "What's this?"

"Open it and find out."

It contained a single copy of a limited edition she had privately published. Jake silently read the title:

CATSKILL MOUNTAIN VIEWS:
Selected Drawings by Jake Forscher

With an Introductory Essay by Catherine Fielding

"Andrea designed the cover. Do you like it?"
Jake could only look up at her through tear-filled eyes.

BOOK SIX

1961 - 1969

63

WITH WHATEVER FACTION a resident of Woodstock identified, all were unanimous in their alarm at Woodstock's latest invasion. If Ralph Whitehead and his Byrdcliffe adherents had looked disapprovingly at the bohemianism of the Maverick crowd, *every*one was appalled at the new group that began cropping up on the town's streets in the '60s.

They called themselves "hippies." Some said the name was borrowed from the "Beat Generation," a kind of proud declaration that they were even more "hip" than their predecessors had ever thought of being. Whatever they called themselves, however, the local residents had a lot more of their own colorful epithets to describe the "flower people" who were showing up on their village green. Although the few wandering "beats" that had drifted through town a few years before the hippies had raised some eyebrows, they were nothing compared to these newcomers.

Most hippies were attracted to Woodstock's long-standing fame as the "in place to be." Known for its lure to the artist, the younger generation, disgusted with the war in "Nam," with their government, with their educational institutions, and with a host of real and imagined civil wrongs, interpreted Woodstock's famed distinction as an answer to their search for a place of freedom. They had heard from their parents and grandparents of the old "roughing-it" days at the Maverick, and had now come to claim their inheritance. After the arrival of the first stragglers, others came just because *they* were there, taking for granted that it would be in Woodstock where they could find their true "brothers and sisters."

In the beginning, only a few wandered around Woodstock's

main thoroughfare, headbands holding flowing locks in place as they quietly collected on the village green, often squatting in cross-legged circles. Most of the residents figured that, like the handful of beat poets who had come during the '50s, they would soon move on. From what they had seen, these newcomers seemed a lost, penniless lot and, even if they did bring money — which was always welcome — the town could offer little for them to buy. Heaving a collected sigh at this newest manifestation of Woodstock craziness, they persuaded themselves that this, too, shall pass.

They soon had to acknowledge, however, that this was wishful thinking.

As the '60s progressed, the hippies seemed to be multiplying over-night, slowly turning the town into an extended "Maverick" by setting up makeshift camps wherever they could find space for a sleeping bag — or two, or three. They filled the village green and overflowed onto Tinker Street, making people step over them as they laid claim to ever more sidewalk space. And, when Woodstock proved too small, they spilled over into adjoining towns. The problem was getting serious, and dire predictions about the end of Woodstock steadily increased.

If anything could unite the townsman and artist in a common cause, it was the hippie. Though generically bestowed on any scruffy youngster with a battered guitar slung over one shoulder, a rucksack full of drugs over the other, a headband across the fore-head, and a flower behind the ear, there was in fact a wide range of people who comfortably accepted the title of 'hippie.' From the most radical reformer to the least involved and stoned-out lost soul, the "tuned in, turned on, and dropped out" generation included a whole gamut of ages and personalities espousing an even greater hodge-podge of social and political positions.

To the town merchant, they were already objectionable because they brought little or no money with which they might mitigate their general offensiveness. This would soon change, however, and whatever objections they had were now turned to alarm when they discovered that even hippies had their entrepreneurs. "Head shops" full of beads, tie-dyed clothing, and drug paraphernalia began appearing in town to supply their needs.

To the artist, the ubiquitous guitar began to appear ominous and could only mean that the tenor of the art colony was shifting.

Hervey White's concerts had their place, but who knew where this business of roving bands of guitarists would end up? Who knew how long it might be before visual artists were shunted into obscurity? Like the townspeople of old, artists were huddled in their groups wondering just whose town this was, anyway.

Having a common enemy created more strange bedfellows in Woodstock during the decade of the '60s than the wildest politicians could ever imagine.

By and large, the older artists kept aloof from the fray, secure — as much as any artist could ever be — in their work, ignoring this latest "fad." They viewed it as just one more incursion that the art colony would eventually absorb, confident that the "age of Aquarius" would gradually transform itself into just another example of "Woodstock-ness." If these kids had drugs, well, they had had their alcohol, didn't they? No self-respecting artist that they knew was ever a *total* stranger to the local 'package' store.

Jake generally went along with this laissez-faire attitude toward hippies, choosing to disregard them as he did anyone or anything that did not impinge on his life. Of more alarm to him was what he considered the continuing deterioration of quality in art. What he had seen at the Armory Show so many years ago was beginning to seem tame compared to what he now saw hanging on the walls at the Association's exhibits.

The topic of the latest show — latest "outrage" Joe had come to call the exhibits at the Association — would invariably come up whenever the two spent time together.

"Sometimes I feel like one of those fossils you have in your studio, Jake," Joe was saying as he took his cup of coffee from the waitress. When she was out of earshot, he leaned toward Jake and said, "I hardly feel welcome anymore here in Deannie's, the way these kids give you the once-over when you come in."

Jake sipped his coffee. "They don't even see us, Joe."

Joe shook his head. He had grown a beard over the past winter — much to Andrea's distaste — and pulled at his chin whiskers. "I remember one day back in '55 or so when Fred Saunders — you know, the fellow who spent a lot of time painting down in the Rondout — stood complaining outside the Association doors. 'Goddamn it,' he said, 'there'll come a day when they'll be hanging macramé alongside our paintings, here. What the Hell is this place coming to?'" He gazed out the window alongside the corner table they usually occupied. "Saunders didn't know just how prophetic he was."

Jake nodded. "Well, Joe," he said with a twinkle in his eye. "Maybe it *pleases* those artists to make the stuff they do."

"Oh, for God's sake, Jake! Don't throw that old line back at me — and how can you call them *artists!*" He peered into his friend's eyes. "I know damn well that it bothers you as much as it does me — it bothers *any* self-respecting artist. It's just plain nonsense! Hell, I could walk out the door right now, go into the woods, piss on four trees, say I'm doing 'my thing' and, in no time at all, I'd find some smart-aleck dealer who'd tout it as a 'happening.'"

"Sounds like it might have a chance," said Jake. "You could call it 'Territorial Rights' and they'd probably write you up in one of these slick new art magazines. Might even bring in a dollar or so." He grinned broadly. "Make you famous."

"Jesus Christ!" said Joe as he slammed his hand on the table. "How can you sit there and make jokes about it?"

"Who's joking?" asked Jake with mock seriousness. "You go out and piss on those trees and you'll be famous in no time at all." He nodded his head. "I guarantee it."

Joe began to sputter, then fell back in his chair. "You're right, Jake. It doesn't do any good going on about it."

"Remember David telling us about how the critics were betraying their profession? Well, he might've been right. It seems that no one is taking responsibility to direct our course anymore. Let's face it, Joe, we're adrift and no one knows where we're going or how to stop the ship." He sighed. "All we can do, I guess, is hold on and go along for the ride."

Joe leaned forward. "Now that ain't exactly right," he said. "The way I see it, nobody *ever* gave the critic the job — or the right — to direct traffic. Remember, Lehrer also said that the critic came *after* the artist. So that means that it's the responsibility of the *artist* to lead. *We* — you and me — have to direct the course of art."

"Yeah," said Jake wearily. "Me and you — and the macramé rope twister, and the paint splasher, and the scrap metal welder, and the — the tree-pisser — and …" He threw out his hands. "Who's to decide, my friend, *which* artist is going to do the leading?"

Joe turned his eyes upward.

414

"I'll tell you who," continued Jake. "It won't *be* the artist — it'll be the *buyer!*"

"The buyer?" Joe snorted loudly. "The buyer! — Hah! — The public! — The mob! — The great unwashed!" He took a breath.

"Run out of names yet?"

Joe waved his hand in disgust. "What the hell does the *buyer* know?"

"I agree," said Jake. "You don't have to convince *me.*" He waggled his finger at Joe. "And if you remember, my friend, I brought up the very question a hundred years ago — back when you and your fellow League students were trying to convince me that selling art was the way of measuring success."

"*One* of the ways," groused Joe.

"My recollection is that even way back in the '20s, it was one of the *most* talked about ways."

"Yeah, you're right," agreed Joe reluctantly. "But we were young — what did *we* know?" he said defensively. "How could we know that this …" He spread out his hands. " — that *this* would happen? Who knew that we'd be surrounded by uninformed buyers?"

"Well, David Lehrer for one, I suppose," said Jake. "And I suspect there were a few others who saw the handwriting on the wall."

Joe moaned. "Where were they when we needed them?"

Jake shrugged. "Who would've listened?" Draining off his cup, he added, "Who listens *now?*"

64

Some people were listening — but it wasn't to the complaints of Joe Bundy or Jake Forscher — or to any of the artists who were echoing their sentiments. People were listening to *music.*

Those artists who thought they might be pushed into the background were beginning to feel justified in their fears — the ever growing "Soundouts" — modern manifestations of the old-time "sing-along" — were drawing far bigger crowds than their exhibitions had ever done in the past. Certainly, it was the younger people who were crowding to hear the latest folk groups, but such music events were also drawing a good part of the tourist trade as well — and that was not altogether a good sign for many artists.

Ever since folk-singing became all the rage and such "stars" as Bob Dylan, Pete Seeger, and Joan Baez had either moved into or spent time in town, it was for music and music alone that a great many tourists were coming to the art colony. They came to Woodstock in the '60s to hear Jimi Hendrix, and Peter, Paul and Mary, and not to look for "art bargains."

The Woodstock Artists Association, seeing which way the wind was blowing, had tried its best to stem the tide and, in an effort to refocus attention on what made Woodstock famous in the first place, mounted an exhibit entitled "Art of the Past" in 1959. The show was a huge success, drawing a great many visitors, and, for a time at least, the artists glowed in the limelight.

Several of Jake's and Joe's paintings and a series of Andrea's prints were included in the show and, for a few brief weeks, brought a certain amount of acclaim for Joe. A local newspaper sent a reviewer to cover the event, and though the names of Jake Forscher and Andrea Bundy — along with a great many more that participated in the exhibit — were merely mentioned, Joe's work had prompted the reporter to devote a full paragraph of praise to his paintings.

The notice caught the attention of a woman reporter who regularly contributed to the social pages in the Sunday edition of Kingston's daily newspaper, *The Freeman*. She had decided to write a profile on Joe, and when she called him to arrange for an interview, he had experienced a mixture of surprise, pride, and disbelief.

Growing increasingly more fidgety as the day of the interview approached, Joe seesawed between seriousness and jocularity, at times pontificating on the rightness of the attention he was getting to outright facetiousness about the whole thing — nearly sending Andrea into distraction. When the reporter finally arrived, Joe had settled into a state of buffoonery from which he could not seem to extricate himself during the entire time the reporter was there.

After they had settled themselves in his studio, the reporter's first question was to ask Joe to what he attributed his success.

The question tickled his funny bone even more. All he could think of was how, after all the years of relative obscurity, he had suddenly gotten from one paragraph in a local newspaper to "success."

"Attrition, I guess," was his answer.

The reporter looked up from her notepad. "Attrition?"

The interview went steadily downhill from there.

When the profile appeared the following Sunday, complete with a photograph of the bearded artist standing alongside an easel with a painting of a brook prominently set up on it, Joe alternately squirmed, grunted, reddened, sputtered, hooted, and threw up his hands, as he read it.

"Curmudgeon!" he howled as he threw the paper down. "What the hell is *that* supposed to mean?" He glared at Andrea. "Shoulda known as soon as I found out that it was a *woman* who was going to write about me, that it was going to be a botch job. Probably doesn't know a *thing* about painting."

Andrea looked up at her red-faced spouse.

He saw the storm brewing and quickly said, "Well, you know what I mean. Young girl like that ..."

The look continued.

"Gosh darn it, Andrea! I mean, read what she has to *say* here!"

He bent down to pick up the newspaper and read aloud. "Funny!" "Cantankerous!" "*Curmudgeon!*" He stopped to glare. "Contentious!" "Disgruntled!" He looked at Andrea. "Well, haven't I a right to be?" He threw the paper down again. "Not a word about my *painting*. A description of my *studio* — but not one, solitary, critical comment about my *painting*!"

Andrea stood up. "Would you like a cup of coffee?"

Joe's mouth dropped open. "*Coffee?*" He flopped down on the nearest chair. "For God's sake, Andrea! *Coffee?*"

"Yes, Joseph. Would you like a cup?"

He looked at her nonplussed, then nodded.

As she handed him his cup, she said demurely, "Can't imagine where she got that 'contentious' business from."

Joe hunched down in his seat.

"It was a *profile*, Joe — not a critique of your work. And what did you expect anyway? You probably brought it on yourself by not giving her any straight answers. For God's sake, Joe, you were hopping around like you had ants in your pants the minute she showed up." Andrea giggled. "Just be thankful that she didn't portray you as a child molester."

He looked balefully over at her.

"Well, you know what they say — even a bad review is still a review." She pointed to the paper lying on the floor. "And look at all the ink you got — an entire half-page in the Sunday papers!"

When he thought about it, Andrea was right. Notice was notice and, whatever he thought about the piece, it brought attention not only to him, but also to the whole art community. In time — and after the ribbing he got at the next Thursday gathering at Jake and Sarah's — he even found some good points about the article and, when he was alone, would read it over to himself. Though he never told Andrea, he even went out and bought extra copies of the edition, and tucked them away under a pile of drawings.

She found them, of course, but never let on. She'd hold them for a time when he was particularly being a pain in the ass.

Besides, he had still been basking in the knowledge that the "Art of the Past" show had not only seen the sale of the three paintings he had entered and most of Andrea's woodcuts of local scenes, but also Jake's large "Overlook: Early Morning." Jake's painting had been purchased by a woman from Connecticut — not at the opening reception, but several days later — and no matter what Jake said about his being "*pressured* by his friends because this was such an *important* show," he knew that the sale had not altogether displeased his friend.

To Jake's great pleasure, Kirstin, his brother's daughter, came up for the opening of the exhibit and, as she put it to Jake and Sarah, "to check out the Woodstock scene." She spent a few days with them and, since Sarah's parents were staying in the guest-room, had taken over their living room, immediately settling in as if at home. When she opened her rucksack and spread its contents over the floor, Jake was relieved to see that it contained only clothes and a few painting supplies. He wasn't sure what he expected to see amongst his niece's belongings, but he knew what many youngsters had packed away into their backpacks these days, and he was somewhat apprehensive. Kirstin rolled out her sleeping bag in front of the fireplace, put her handful of toilet articles on the hearth, and seemed as comfortable as if she were staying at some luxurious resort.

It fell to Sarah and Mae to show Kirstin around town, the three of them going out arm in arm after breakfast to go "shopping." In the afternoon, Kirstin went to explore Woodstock's environs with Jake. He drove her up to California Quarry, and as they walked around he told her about her great-uncle Hans and his bluestone work. He then took her around to some of his favorite old haunts, and was pleased when she seemed able to match them up later with some of the canvases in his studio.

Kirstin also endeared herself to the Thursday night crowd who had stopped over for a brief visit on the night after the opening, practically monopolizing David's time when she found out that he was the "famous" art critic.

I didn't know you knew Mister *Lehrer*, Uncle Jake!" she enthused when he introduced them.

"Neither did we," said Joe, winking at David's wife, Lynn. "I always knew him as 'David.'" Chuckling at his own joke, he turned to Lehrer and said, "I didn't know we were supposed to call you *mister*, Mister Lehrer."

Kirstin almost immediately engaged David in discussion, both pleasing and bewildering Jake with the steady stream of new art terms that he heard flowing from his niece's mouth. He stepped away when he heard her saying something about 'less is more', David nodding sagely at her words.

He spread out his hands and looked over to Catherine.

"Don't look at *me*," she said. "I'm just as lost as you are. My studies in art history never got *this* far."

* * *

As they prepared for bed on the second night of Kirstin's stay, Jake sniffed the air and said to Sarah, "Do you smell something burning?"

"Come to bed, Jake — it's only Kirstin."

Jake looked puzzled. "Is she making a fire? It's the middle of summer …"

Sarah looked up at Jake. "It's pot, Jake. Kirstin's smoking."

"Pot? Smoking?"

"Marijuana — weed – grass," said Sarah. "Whatever they call it — she's probably smoking one of those — what do they call them? — 'joints'?"

Jake sighed and got into bed beside Sarah. "Well, at least she wears a brassiere," he said.

"Oh, she's sweet, Jake. I love the way she calls me 'Aunt Sarah' and Mom and Dad 'Grandma' and 'Grandpa.'" She snuggled next to him, then said thoughtfully, "Does she know that we aren't married?"

"Oh yes," said Jake. "She told me that her father has made it perfectly clear to Freddie and her that their Uncle Jake is 'living in sin.'"

Sarah giggled.

"She told me yesterday up on Magic Meadow that she thought our living together was 'cool' — says we're 'hippies'." He chuckled. "Claims that our generation anticipated hers by at least fifty years."

Sarah gave in to one of her belly laughs. "Oh, she's precious!" she said when she caught her breath.

"Seems like a nice girl."

"Woman, you mean," said Sarah. "I've always said she resembles you Jake. When you consider her interest in art, she *could* be your daughter, you know."

Jake chuckled. "Not when you consider her gift of gab, you

wouldn't. She sure can go on — hard to get a word in edgewise."

"Like you probably *tried* very hard," Sarah teased. "She *is* quite a nice young woman, though — a lot more level-headed than most of these young people today."

Jake reached out to turn off the table lamp beside the bed. "Yes — maybe so," he agreed. "When I took her up on Overlook, though, I'm not sure that she really understood what makes Magic Meadow *magic.*" He rolled over on his side. "Anyway, it's hard to see how she can be Fred's daughter." He sighed. "Guess you never can tell how a kid's going to turn out."

Sarah gave him a gentle poke in the back. "Look who's talking," she murmured.

* * *

After the excitement about the "Art of the Past" exhibition died down and Kirstin and Sarah's parents had left, Jake and his friends had agreed that the Association exhibit had done its job of bringing art to the forefront once again. It would not be long, however, when even this event would become drowned out, as amplifiers were increasingly turned higher.

The townspeople occasionally thought up other ways of bringing back the art trade, new ideas for rejuvenating the spirit of the old colony, but found themselves in a losing battle with the "Age of Aquarius" and its on-going love-affair with music — *loud* music. Different ideas for this "art festival" or that "craft festival" were periodically brought up and tried out — until the word "festival" became so overused that no one wanted to hear it anymore.

If an undercurrent of gloom gradually infused the old-timers once again, near panic gripped them when they got wind that some promoters were talking about bringing the Newport Jazz Festival to Woodstock as a permanent fixture.

"There goes the neighborhood," was becoming a familiar mantra whenever and wherever artists got together.

65

Ever since Sarah had opened the door a bit wider into Jake's studio, he felt more at ease having visitors 'invade his privacy' — his usual description of a visit from whoever showed up at his door. Joe Bundy, of course, had been coming over for years, but he had begun to come more often nowadays, and for longer periods of time. Since Joe increasingly disliked having their morning coffee at Deannie's — "because of the crowd" — they had fallen into the habit lately of dropping in at each other's studios to "have a 'cuppa' and chew the fat."

To Sarah's surprise — and secret delight — Jake had recently been asking David Lehrer to "stop by some day," and even more delighted when David took up his offer. She quietly encouraged the budding friendship and, when Jake seemed open to it, began bringing over pots of coffee and plates of "finger food" on the days they got their heads together in Jake's studio.

For Jake, his conversations with Lehrer were a continuation of the discussions he was used to having with Sarah's father who, in recent days, had begun to show signs of failing. Cyrus would often doze off in the middle of discussions, and his usual habit of digression would lead him off at times into directions from which he could not always find his way back. Cyrus's aimless wanderings had saddened Jake as much as it troubled Sarah and her mother. Jake had grown to look forward to the mind-stretching discussions that Cyrus had once provided, and David Lehrer stepped in to fill the growing gap.

Jake admired Lehrer's inquiring mind and, unlike Cyrus who had no problem in confidently putting forth his ideas as if they were "gospel," found David to be open to having his statements or assumptions challenged.

When Jake pointed out the difference in his conversations with Cyrus while David was visiting at his studio one afternoon, Lehrer responded simply, "Dialogue."

Jake returned an expectant look.

Lehrer pointed to Jake's bookcase. "Plato. According to him, dialectic dialogue is the only sure way to discovering truth."

"I'm listening," said Jake as he tilted the back of his chair against the wall.

"Well, most people just talk — you know, like the discussions we usually have at our Thursday night get-togethers. It might be entertaining – even informative now and again — but generally such discussions end up with most people going home no better off than when they came. They leave with the same ideas they come with."

Jake pursed his lips. "I'm still listening."

"They are not really having dialectic dialogue — at least in the Platonic sense. I should say, in the Socratic sense, since it was from him that Plato learned it. Although dialogue is more properly conducted between two people, the point here is that when people get together for discussion they are generally only voicing their opinions — and, more often than not, trying to get others to *agree* with their opinions." He shrugged. "Let's face it, Jake, people — especially when they get older — are not really interested in *learning.*"

Jake gave what Lehrer interpreted as a gesture of agreement.

"The thing is, they are not seeking any new understanding. They are not trying to arrive at any lasting truth — they are merely dispensing it – or *think* that they are. Plato — or Socrates — believed that no one actually *knew* what truth was, and that it was only through an exchange of ideas — dialectic dialogue — that we might attain it — or at any rate at least get *closer* to it since, to Plato's way of thinking, the possession of truth was not possible for humankind. Truth, Plato taught, only existed in the ideal."

Jake nodded his head more affirmatively. "I recall Cyrus trying to explain the ideal to me a long time ago," said Jake. "I sort of got it, but …" and gesturing towards the bookcase — "never really got much further in understanding Plato."

Lehrer reached over and put his hand on the box containing

Plato's two volumes of Dialogues. "Do you mind?" he asked.

"Not at all," said Jake.

Leafing through the pages of Volume One, Lehrer asked, "Your annotations?"

Jake nodded.

"Looks pretty well thumbed," he said, and looked up at Jake.

"I've been trying."

"No easy job."

"So Cyrus warned me."

Lehrer glanced over the other titles. "Nice collection — seems thoughtfully selected."

"Hardly," laughed Jake, and told him how they'd come into his possession.

"Remarkable," he said, when Jake finished his tale. Then, pointing to the other books on the shelf, he asked, "Are they all this well used?"

"Pretty much." Jake shrugged, and Lehrer raised his eyebrows. "I had a lot to learn. Anyway, tell me more about Socrates. I gathered from the books that he was Plato's mentor, but I know little else about their relationship."

"Well, he certainly was his mentor. His teaching of Plato and Plato's teaching of Aristotle was one of those wondrous coincidences of history that has never been equaled or repeated. In any event, Socrates exemplified the process of dialectic dialogue, going out and about with his students and showing that most of what people spoke was opinion and not truth. He would come upon a politician in the market place holding forth on some subject — say patriotism, for instance. Socrates and his entourage would stand by politely listening for some time, until he would break in and ask the speaker, 'What do you mean by patriotism?' 'Well, like saluting our flag,' might come the answer. 'I see — but isn't that just an *example* of patriotism? I still don't understand what you mean by patriotism,' he would say and turn with a smile to his students The speaker, annoyed, would then say something like, 'Well, it's fighting for your country, honoring its laws, Now do you understand?' Socrates would stand silently for a moment or so and then say, 'I'm still not sure. Aren't they just two more examples of patriotism? You haven't yet told us what you *mean* by patriotism.'" Lehrer waved his hand in a circular movement. "And so on, and so on. Eventually, Socrates would show his students — and the crowd who had gathered to listen — that the speaker did not actually know what he was talking about. He was just talking – giving opinion. He was not giving the people truth. This would go on from day to day, from speaker to speaker, and Socrates eventually taught his students that truth was not so easy to come by. You can imagine how this went over with the politicians. They finally had to pick him up, lock him in a cell, and eventually make him commit suicide. He was just too much of a pain in the ass — they couldn't afford to let him wander around instigating the hoi polloi to insubordination. But he left his pupils with the important lesson that those who speak do not know and that those who know do not speak." He looked at Jake. "I'm sure you've heard that before.'

Jake nodded in agreement.

"Well, that's where *we* got the expression from — from Socrates. Socrates also taught his students — and us — that he learned from an oracle that we should 'know ourselves' — and that by knowing ourselves — *truly* knowing ourselves — we will learn that we can never *know* anything." He paused. "Most of us go out into the world blandly voicing our beliefs and our opinions to others who have their *own* beliefs and opinions that they want to tell *us*. Meanwhile, here and there you *might* find two people quietly in dialogue who are actually seeking a clearer vision of truth."

"But, if as you say, it's unattainable, then why make the attempt?"

"Well, we could — as the saying implies we ought — remain silent and not show our ignorance. But I, for one, find it difficult to not at least *try*. I believe — and notice, Jake, it is my *belief*, not a truth — that one ought to try to educate oneself, and sharing in dialectic dialogue is one way of doing it." He stood up. "Let me give you an analogy — something any professor of logic knows is an irrelevant form of argument, but here it is anyway. You probably know that ancient seamen used the stars to steer their way through uncharted seas, right? Now there wasn't a sea captain alive who believed that he might ever *reach* a star, but that didn't stop him from using them for guidance. So, bad as the analogy is, you get the point. We aim high to get ahead, and educating yourself is one way of achieving it."

425

Jake smiled. "Cyrus had some choice comments about education." He chuckled. "He once told me that most people think education is like the mumps — you get it once when you're a kid and that's the end of it."

"I'll bet he did," said Lehrer. "Probably of the opinion that it hardly goes on today even with our kids. Again, notice that I said 'opinion'." He smiled. "But I think of education as kind of a cataloguing of our ignorance — and that's not such a bad thing if you understand it in that way."

"Not sure I follow you there."

"Let me use myself as an example. I took my first course in art history when I was in college. Now when I completed it, that little taste made me realize that I hadn't learned as much about art history as I did about how much I *didn't* know about it. So I took another course. The same thing happened because I now learned that there were *new* areas about which I was ignorant. So I tried again — the same result. The more I learned, the more I realized how vast the subject was, and that even if I spent the rest of my life taking courses, I *still* wouldn't know all of what there is to learn about art history. Aha! I finally said to myself — I have to *specialize!* So I decided to concentrate on the French impressionists. But after a course in *that*, I discovered that I didn't know enough about, say, Manet or Monet, to really consider myself an expert. So I took courses in Manet and *only* in Manet. Guess what? The more I learned about *him* the more I came to see how much I didn't know about his work, his life, his art, his ideas — and so on, and so on. I found that I had just been going in the opposite direction, from the general to the specific, and *still* not getting anywhere near the *truth* of anything." He sat back down. "So, Jake, that's why I say that education is a gradual unfolding of our ignorance — and for that reason alone, I think it's valuable."

"I get the point. Unfortunately," said Jake, "most people I know that have taken a course in something, try to come across as experts."

"Just like the politician speaking in the marketplace," said Lehrer. "And I agree with you. The world is full of 'experts', Jake. You just have to keep asking questions, and eventually you *and* the expert will learn how much you don't know. Obtaining an education ought to be a humbling thing. It ought to teach us that we can never stop learning. It ought to teach us that there just *aren't* any experts. I've come to a point in my life when I no longer judge people by the answers they give me, but rather by the *questions* they ask me. *Every*body has an answer, Jake. Only the wise offer another intelligent question."

66

In April of 1964, Andrea Bundy had a one-person exhibit in a New York City gallery, which, by all accounts, was a resounding success. Invited by the gallery director to participate in its planning, she and the director spent several days in choosing the works which were to be included in the month-long showing.

They had decided on the title, "Social Realism: A Look Back," in hopes that it would draw those people who could see the parallels between the present unrest and the turbulent '30s, and Andrea had a great many that represented that early period to choose from.

Some 75 prints were chosen — etchings, woodcuts, aquatints, and lithographs that, once mounted *en masse*, told a dramatic story of oppression, unrest, and poverty. The exhibit attracted large numbers of viewers, drawn from both the older generation that had lived through the Depression Era, as well as the younger, politically involved crowd and, to the gratification of both Andrea and her dealer, a great many prints were sold.

The attention that the exhibit promised to garner had also alerted the press, and several critics from newspapers and arts magazines — David Lehrer included — had come to a special preview opening to "write up" the show. As usual, the articles that appeared over the next several days ranged from superficial notices that devoted most of its print-space to the daily crowds that appeared to fill the gallery, to the more serious, critical analyses of both the work and the era it depicted.

A good many of the Woodstock artists had gone to see the show, and for a day or two at least, "Social Realism: A Look Back," was the "talk of the town". Jake and Sarah's usual Thursday night group had, of course, gone to the opening reception, all of them pleased that Myra, who "wouldn't have missed it for the world," showed up at the gallery to join them.

Kirstin had also come, her presence so delighting Jake that he almost made a pest of himself introducing her around to anyone he could buttonhole. Mae, concerned about Cyrus making the trip into the city from Long Island, reluctantly decided to stay at home to watch over him.

They had capped the evening with dinner in the Village, Myra suggesting an Italian restaurant that used to be a favorite eating place of Morris's. All of them in good spirits after such a successful reception, the evening was filled with laughter and "catching up" on news. Myra wanted to hear all the latest Woodstock gossip, eager to know "who was sleeping with whom" or what had become of "what's her name." Sarah and Andrea happily filled her in on "the latest," as Jake and Joe rolled their eyes. The Fieldings and the Lehrers tastefully avoided talking about or responding to many of these "tidbits." David, in any event, was already deep into 'art-talk' with Kirstin who had immediately staked out a seat next to him as soon as they entered the restaurant.

Myra brought them up to date on the New York City art scene, informing them that Calvin Steele had been making "quite a name" for himself lately. Then, turning to Sarah, she added, "He re-married, you know."

Sarah received this piece of news with a simple raise of her eyebrows. The rest of the group remained non-committal, no one asking for any follow-up discussion on the matter.

Myra then told them of her own "news" — a plan to try to get funding in order to turn her loft into a public museum that would feature Morris's sculptures.

"There seems to be some interest," she said. "The way they swing back and forth with trends down here, sometimes you don't know which way to turn. You have the 'cutting edge' galleries on one side, and the traditionalists on the other." She laughed. "It's hard to tell which side is more desperate. Morris would have loved being in the middle of it!"

"With the current art scene in such a state of flux," said Catherine, "it must be difficult for funding institutions to know where to put their money."

Myra nodded. "Yes … but so far, it seems promising."

"There's money out there," said Lynn Lehrer. "I'll keep an ear out for you, and if I hear of anything that looks worthwhile pursuing, I'll let you know."

"Thanks," said Myra. "You're a doll!"

*　*　*

The flush of excitement that they had all felt at the opening reception and which had carried over into their evening discussion during dinner in the Village, lingered for days after they returned upstate and, on the Thursday evening following the show's opening, Andrea's success still dominated the discussion.

Joe, beaming like some proud father of a newborn, kept saying, "Yessir! Talent always shows — *always.*" He put his arm around Andrea's shoulders. "Didn't my girl, here, show 'em?" He looked from face to face. "Well, *didn't* she? At least *some* of them fancy New York dealers know talent when they see it. Yessir! … Talent always shows, I say."

Andrea would just roll her eyes upward, delicately trying to extricate herself from Joe's periodic surrounding arm and next outburst. She was embarrassed, and tried to graciously accept the group's accolades and praises.

Eventually, Joe settled down, and the group's effusively congratulatory comments set aside for more serious discussion.

Catherine Fielding, much to Andrea's relief, deflected the laudatory statements about the success of the opening reception by turning to David and saying, "That was some piece you wrote about the show."

David held up his drink and nodded.

"Seriously, it was well done," she said.

"Yes," said Andrea. "I really want to thank you. What you said was beautiful."

David again nodded.

"Your commentary on the Social Realist painters — on the whole period, in fact — might well grace the pages of an art history book," Catherine continued. "I wish *I'd* written it."

David broke his silence. "It's difficult, you know …"

Edward Fielding broke in. "It's no easy task to write intelligently about *any* movement, but I must agree with Catherine — your

430

piece on the '30s and Andrea's work was top-drawer."

"Thank you," David said, as heads bobbed in agreement and glasses were lifted in salute around the room. "But I was going to say that it's difficult to write about a friend, about someone you know personally. There is always the problem of clouded judgment because of the association — and it's so easy to open yourself up to a charge of playing favorites." He shrugged. "A bit of a tightrope."

"And one that some of your fellow critics seem to be unable to walk," said Edward. "We won't mention any names, but there are those who've become virtual mouthpieces for their 'chosen' few."

"That's certainly true," said Catherine. "Makes you wonder if they are only protecting their own interests. From what I understand, some of these — I hesitate to call them 'critics' — maybe 'touters' is more apt — some of them appear to have the works of their 'chosen' — as Ed calls them — in their own collections. If this is true, then there seems little incentive for them *not* to be flattering in their comments about them."

"Oh, I don't see as David's done any flattering," said Joe. "Seemed pretty straightforward to me."

Andrea looked at her husband. "Not that you're *biased*, or anything."

Her comment brought a smattering of laughter from the group, followed by Jake's saying, "But it *was* straightforward. I think David concentrated on the significance of the work, and left all the unnecessary 'adjectives' out. Morris would have been real proud of him." He looked at Lehrer. "You did a good job, David."

"The black and white helps," said David, and as he saw the questioning looks passing from face to face, added, "It makes it less difficult to *see*. I've always found that it was easier to assess a person's art when you had access to their drawings or sketchbooks." He motioned toward Andrea. "And when an artist's work consists almost entirely of black and white — like Andrea's — it makes it that much easier — at least it does for *me*. It certainly doesn't make *her* job easier — just the opposite, in fact, since she can't hide any shortcomings under the cover of color. So, again, black and white is appealing to me, since it makes my job simpler."

"How so?" asked Edward.

"Well, color is so seductive — for me, anyway. And the more

successful an artist is as a colorist, the harder it is to see the underlying work. I sometimes look at a Bonnard, for example, and I can't always *see* just how good he is. His color is so lusciously rich that it distracts, takes the eye from seeing composition, line, the underpinnings of the work. In short, I guess what I'm saying is that, unless I can see *through* the color, I have difficulty seeing the work at all." He looked around. "So — with Andrea's prints, I could concentrate on what she was saying — and on how well she was saying it. In my estimation, she has added immeasurably to the body of social realist work — and it was my pleasure to write about her show."

"Well, it certainly didn't *hurt*," said Joe. He grasped Andrea's shoulders once again. "My little lady here sold a batch of prints!"

David shrugged. "Not because of my article," he said. "They sold because they were *good*."

"I know David's argument about color," said Lynn. "The fact is, though, that it is color that is precisely what the buyer seeks and wants. Most equate color with beauty, and in spite of what the pundits would have us believe, beauty still sells."

"That's because there is so little of it in our lives," said Sarah. She glanced at Jake. "I don't think you'll ever convince some artists that beauty isn't important."

"And I'm glad for that," said Lynn.

"But beauty — as has been so often said — is in the eye, et cetera," said Andrea. "Not many would claim that 'beauty' describes my work — yet, as Hogarth, another social commentator, wrote in his *The Analysis of Beauty*, beauty in art must be defined in relation to its line, its fitness, its regularity and simplicity — among other things."

"I wonder, though," said Sarah. "Would you really say that some of Schongauer's gaunt woodcut depictions of Christ are 'beautiful'?"

"It's true," said David. "Beauty needs some close looking into by the critics of today. I'm not so sure that we can easily slough off the problem." He turned to Andrea. "Not even by resorting to the old saw about its being in the eye of the beholder. Just where, exactly, do we draw the line between ugliness and beauty?"

"Perhaps ugliness *can* be beautiful," suggested Ed Fielding.

"Not to the people *I* have to convince," said Lynn. "I'm certainly not disparaging Andrea's work — far from it." She turned to Andrea. "If I didn't like it, I wouldn't have purchased those two for my collection … but I must confess that I was surprised to see the turnout for the show. In my experience, it has simply been like pulling teeth to get buyers interested in black and white art."

"And, again — there can be a lot of beauty in the well-made etching or woodcut," said Ed.

Catherine, who had been pondering David's remarks about color, asked, "I find what you're saying about black and white interesting — especially what you said about looking at sketchbooks — drawings." She frowned. "I wonder what you feel about drawing — I mean generally. It seems that today it is so discounted by the so-called experts — sloughed off as if an unnecessary bother that a painter need not tolerate."

David thought for a moment. "Yes, that's certainly true. The argument goes that an artist who wants to paint with a brush, doesn't have to waste his time learning how to use a pencil."

"That's nonsense," said Joe. "These kids today are just too lazy to learn the basics. They want to slap on paint and put 'em up for sale." He snorted. "Instant Matisses!"

"I understand your exasperation, Joe," said David. "I certainly agree that I see a growing number of canvases that ought never to have left the studio. But, you can't blame the young artist either, who hears about Matisses going at auctions for thousands and thousands of dollars. They look at an art book and figure that they can do the same thing and, if the public pays money for them, why not cash in on the trend themselves?"

"But they're going off half-cocked!" said Joe. "They don't seem to know that Matisse and Picasso and — well, *all* of them — all started out being able to draw!"

"True," said Catherine. "But seeing the connection might be beyond some of these youngsters — especially since we see drawing being neglected with more frequency today at art schools."

"Exactly," said David.

Jake broke in. "Still, I'm not so sure. For example, I don't start my canvases with a drawing." He turned to Joe. "I know, for instance, that Joe most often starts out with a charcoal outline before he begins to apply his paint — but I don't."

"It's the way I was taught," said Joe. "Carlson always had us begin with some kind of general outline — even if we didn't always follow it."

"I know," said Jake. "But I remember when I first watched Birge Harrison paint, putting paint right on a blank canvas, I asked him why he didn't begin with an under-drawing — and he told me that sometimes he did, and sometimes he didn't. Since he was only giving me a demonstration on how to mix colors and use a brush at the time, he said he didn't need one. But then he said that it was up to the painter — he told me to do whatever suited me best — that no one could tell another painter how to paint."

"Sounds like I would have liked to have met him," said David.

"Well, now, that might be true," said Joe. "I know that a lot of painters attack the canvas directly, and Jake *does* go right at it with his knife and colors — I've never seen him paint any other way." He held up his hand. "*But* — but Jake can *draw!* Anybody that takes a look into that little book that Sarah made can see *that!* I still remember Ted Deavers telling us about the time he met him sketching up on Overlook — and, the first thing I noticed when I got to know him, was how good his drawings were!" He turned to Jake. "So, you might not use them directly, but I don't care what you say — those years of making them shows up in your paintings."

David agreed. "If only for the development of hand and eye coordination, drawing is certainly helpful to the artist — and, as you say Joe, it can't help but show up in Jake's work."

"Especially in the figure painter's work," said Catherine. Then, as if in afterthought, "That is, if there *are* any figure painters any more."

"It is getting increasingly more difficult today for them to be taken seriously," agreed David. "Which, incidentally, is another reason why Andrea's show is important. It will do the younger artists a great service to see how powerful a statement can still be made by using the human figure."

"Well, it may be out of favor right at the moment," said Ed Fielding. "But I'm sure that it will never be totally abandoned. The human condition will remain with us for as long as we're human — and what better way to express that condition than through using the human form?"

"It's true," said Catherine. "The pendulum will continue to

swing whether we will it or not."

"I tend to agree with you both," said David. "But for now, at any rate, the art of draughtsmanship is getting bad press and, there's no telling when it will regain its long-held status as a necessary requirement for the artist." He turned to Jake. "Look at your niece, for example. Kirstin is presently enamored with the minimalist movement. She told me she has taken no drawing classes at the League — and saw no reason why she had to."

"She's now a Minimalist?" asked Jake.

"Yes. She believes in the idea that the less you put of yourself into your work, the more the art can convey. Kirstin seems to wholly subscribe to their dictum that 'Less is More'. At least she did when I was speaking to her at dinner the other night." He shrugged. "Who knows what she believes now? Styles and innovations move in and out so quickly with these youngsters that it is hard for anyone to keep up."

"Especially for dinosaurs like us," said Joe.

"I wonder what the next great 'truth' will be?" mused Jake.

"It's hard to say," said Catherine. "Will it slow down in the '70s? Revert in the '80s? Who can tell what the year 2000 will bring?"

"I shudder to think of it," said David. "Thankfully, I won't be around to sort it all out — or have to write about it."

67

The following summer, David and Lynn Lehrer had finally realized their long-held dream of purchasing Sarah's home in Willow. Living in the city, though it had its obvious advantages, had also many drawbacks. They both loved the Woodstock area and the peaceful solitude that country living offered, finding that the commute that both would have to occasionally make into the city well worth the time and effort for the pleasure they would derive from the change in lifestyle. Lynn loved the roomy old house, and David especially looked forward to converting Cal's studio into a library and study.

Lynn, who had left her position at the museum, had begun her own art consulting practice, her long years of networking with the upper echelons of the art world insuring a widespread and steady clientele of corporate patrons and buyers who both knew and respected her expertise. Turning Sarah's unused studio into a tidy and compact office space, she had everything she needed, the telephone serving in the place of having to actually travel back and forth.

"I certainly don't miss the hectic city life," she was telling Sarah one afternoon when she and David had come over for a visit. "For the few times a month David and I have to go down to Manhattan, we almost look forward to the trip nowadays … but I wouldn't trade my Willow haven for the world, you can count on that!"

Sarah smiled as she poured out two cups of freshly brewed tea. "I know what you mean. My parents always wanted me to take over their home down in Bayshore, but ever since my days at Byrdcliffe, I knew that my heart belonged to the area. I also loved that home up in Willow — and if it wasn't for my ex-husband, I would have loved it even more." She led Lynn into the living room. "But I *really* love it here."

"David's been singing Woodstock's praises for as long as I know him. At first I wasn't too keen on the idea of moving up here permanently, but now that I'm here, I could kick myself for putting off the move for so long."

"Well, I'm glad you're here, Lynn. Jake loves talking with David, and I can't begin to tell you how pleased I am that we've become such close friends." She looked off into the distance. "We keep losing them, you know ... friends, I mean. First Morris, and now Myra."

"I really felt badly about that. Of course, I didn't know her as well as you, but I was so happy to have finally gotten her funding to turn Morris's studio into a museum. It seems we no sooner got the word to her that she was gone."

"Yes," said Sarah in a subdued voice. "An unhappy beginning, a life of struggle with a strong-willed husband, and that final blow ... I guess life just caught up with the poor woman and finally overwhelmed her. We were told by relatives at her funeral that she had a massive stroke and never recovered."

"Such a shame ... a waste, really. Good people — good friends — are not all that easy to find."

"That's why I'm so pleased that Jake now has your David."

"Yes," said Lynn looking out the window towards Jake's studio. "They certainly get into it when they get their heads together, don't they?"

"God only knows what they're talking about today," said Sarah. "But you can bet it's something about art."

Over in Jake's studio, he and David were indeed speaking about art.

David was seated as Jake paced.

"Dialogue," said Jake. "We were talking about dialogue a while back. You were telling me about the fabulous threesome — Socrates, Plato, and Aristotle." He halted his pacing. "Mostly though, you were telling me about Plato and Socrates and of how important it was for people to have serious dialogue with one another."

"Yep."

"And Aristotle? What about him?

"Now there's a conundrum," said Lehrer. "The most influential of the celebrated trio, and my least favorite."

Jake settled into a chair. "And therein lies another tale, I am sure."

Lehrer grinned. "Now Plato, after they killed off Socrates, decided to write down what he'd learned from him — hence, the 'Dialogues.' Essentially, he compiled all the truth — or, to be more 'Platonic,' *approximate* truth — that he could glean from his master. For the modern reader, the Dialogues stand as a compendium of all the known wisdom of Plato's day."

"Quite an homage to his mentor."

"Absolutely! But Plato didn't just include in his Dialogues what he felt was knowable at the time he wrote — he also included what he *didn't* know. Like for instance, it was obvious that no one would ever come up with a conclusive definition of 'patriotism' since it was an abstraction. Socrates made that pretty clear. You could pretty well get off with having a fair grasp of what a tree was, for example, but such things as patriotism, or love, or hate, and the like, were not tangible, they were not physical things. They weren't trees that you could point to and say to your neighbor, 'There, *that*'s what I mean.' Most important for Plato was that you could never nail down the most important abstractions of all — the true, the good, and the beautiful — the three primary attributes of what he called the ideal world."

Jake nodded. "Yes, I remember something of this from my discussion with Cyrus. He spoke of this world — *our* world — being a place of 'becoming' and the other, the ideal, of a world of 'being.' He said that all things in the world strive for, but couldn't reach that ideal."

"Right, though I only *wish* that all things — especially people — actually *did* strive toward it. In any event, these abstract ideas of truth, goodness, and beauty were not definable — as we found out with beauty when the topic was brought up after Andrea Bundy's Manhattan exhibit — and Plato was forced to resort to myth whenever he attempted to write about them — and there's the rub."

As David warmed to his subject, Jake could almost feel his excitement.

"Aristotle, being Plato's pupil, had taken all this in, but — and this is one hell of a 'but' — he decided when he went off on his own to stick with what he *could* know and to disregard the rest. A brilliant mind, he chucked the myth, avoided the abstractions of the 'true', the 'good', and the 'beautiful', and concentrated on the trees. And not only the trees, Jake, but on almost every physical aspect of the world that there was. Like I said, he was brilliant — and irresistible. He simply started sorting and ordering and cataloguing things — tangible stuff — and eventually became the father of science."

"And for this you dislike him?"

"I *hate* him!" Lehrer almost shouted. "Well, not really, but for all he did in our gathering of knowledge — and make no doubt about it, Jake, if it wasn't for him we wouldn't have indoor plumbing and electric lights today, but as far as I'm concerned, Aristotle effectively and single-handedly halted the search for truth — and the good — and the beautiful. He only gave us — and granted this is a big 'only' — the world."

"Back up a bit," said Jake.

"I know, I know! Get me on Aristotle and I begin to foam at the mouth. But you see, Jake, once he turned all eyes on our physical world, he turned them away from that ideal world that Plato was so desperately trying to define. Aristotle's brilliance forever after lured every inquiring mind that came after him into defining our world — and they've been doing it ever since. Today's scientist is the most respected 'expert' that we have, Jake. It doesn't matter that every few years some great scientific 'discovery' is either improved upon or discounted, we still lay our greatest honors at the feet of Aristotle's never-ending troop of cataloguers."

He paused and stood up to begin pacing.

"Now — here's the problem, Jake. What happened to the myth? What happened to Plato's 'true', 'good', and 'beautiful'? While the greatest of our intellects have been chasing after atoms and distant galaxies, the priests and rabbis and imams and cenobites and shamans and palmers and what-have-yous — every one who fancies himself some kind of divine stand-in — have taken the myth into *their* bosoms, into *their* tabernacles, into *their* arks, and have locked it away to be worshipped as a *mystery*! They just took the true, the good, and the beautiful, and lumped them into a neat definition of 'God' — once and for all taking them out of the realm of investigation. According to them, we are not to have *dialectic dialogue* about the true, the good, *or* the beautiful since it would be 'irreligious' to do so. We must not question, but simply *believe.*"

"And belief, like opinion, may not be truth."

"Exactly! And *that's* the crime I accuse Aristotle of committing, Jake. He was just too damned convincing! Too damned brilliant! He gave us knowledge, Jake, but knowledge is not *understanding* — knowledge is not *wisdom.* Albert Einstein put it beautifully when he told the world, 'Knowledge has helped us build the atom bomb; *wisdom* will tell us what we should do with it.' Unfortunately, not many got the message. Aristotle, you see, has commandeered all of our most promising minds and turned them away from solving the *only* thing worth knowing — the wisdom of understanding just what 'beauty', 'goodness', and 'truth' are!"

At that moment, Sarah knocked on the door and she and Lynn brought in some goodies.

"Remind me not to get on his bad side, Hon," Jake said as he made room for the tray in her hands.

She and Lynn looked from one to the other, but only got stupid grins in return and, seeing that there would be no explanation from either of them, left them to their discussion.

Pouring himself a cup of coffee, Jake said, "Okay, Aristotle led us astray and took along all the brains in his wake. But how am I supposed to see Plato as a hero if he has banned artists from his Republic? That just leaves me brainless *and* homeless, doesn't it?"

Lehrer laughed. "He didn't exactly ban *all* artists — after all, *he* was one himself, as you can tell by the Dialogues. The world has long seen his writings as a major work of literature."

"OK, granted. But the painter?"

"I think we have to look closely at what he said. He objected to those artists who simply imitated nature, since he felt that they were only making copies of copies."

"Granted *again.*" Jake pointed to his paintings. "Where does that leave *me?*"

"Hold on." Lehrer held up his hands. "The way I understand him, he felt that the mere imitator was not looking into nature *deeply* enough. Many of the artists of his day were simply getting too facile, so technically proficient in their craft that they were getting glib. I tend to agree with the Italians of the Renaissance who interpreted Plato's admonition as a warning to the superficial artist. They — the Italians — saw the genuine artist as divinely inspired — literally 'breathed into' — by the gods. If obedient to that inspiration, they were doing the gods' bidding."

Jake thought back to Cyrus's explanation of Otto Rank.

"Now this, Jake, is what brought me to the study of art in the first place. I believe that the artist — and that includes the dancer, the musician — any genuinely creative person — is the only one who has picked up the thread of Plato's myth. Unlike the 'holy' man who accepts it as is, the artist is still *exploring*, still *delving* into the mystery. The artist's hand — if guided by inspiration — is participating in the divine creative act. He alone is seeking — through having dialogue with nature and his art — the 'true', the 'good', and the 'beautiful'."

Jake slowly let his eyes wander over the several paintings hanging in his studio.

After some moments of silence on the part of both men, Lehrer picked up his train of thought. "This is not to say, of course, that *all* artists are divinely inspired. Some have directed their eyes, so to speak, earthward — as Aristotle so eloquently directed — and have painted only what they can *see*. *These* are Plato's 'copiers of copies' — and *these* are the artists he banned from his ideal community."

Jake continued his silence.

"So, for *me*, Jake, the job of the critic is to separate the inspired from the copiers. It is the critic's job to discern which of the artists are, in fact, approximating the 'true,' 'good,' or 'beautiful.' We need to discover which ones are having genuine dialogue. It has become the job of the critic because, in most cases of genuine inspiration, the artist himself is unaware of what is transpiring. He *cannot* ever truly know, of course, since he is mortal. However — and this is what the Italians have contributed to Plato's conception — if one 'has eyes to see,' then the divine message can be seen in the finished work."

He paused to hold up his hand.

"Now, I know *that*'s a very big proposition. There are so many variables to consider." He held up his thumb. "There is first the artist. How faithfully has he conformed to the inspiration? How far has he intruded *himself* into his work? How glib is he? There are

— and have always been — shallow artists who have produced shallow work. But the artist in love with his own cleverness in wielding the brush or chisel, Jake, is no different from the glib priest in love with his gift of speech — both can lead you *away* from the true the good and the beautiful — away from 'God.'"

He raised his index finger alongside his thumb.

"Then, there's the viewer. How deeply is *his* vision colored by his own beliefs, opinions, and prejudices? Remember, Plato says that we are all under the influence of our individual illusions — our own particular set of beliefs and opinions. We are subject to our *personalities* rather than to our personhood — our personhood, that is, according to Plato. So, what does the *viewer* bring to the table and how does he 'color' what he sees?"

He added his middle finger to the two fingers still raised in the air.

"Finally, there is the work itself. How 'readable' is it? Does it 'speak' to us? Furthermore, *which* work of art 'speaks' more clearly to the human understanding? A painting? A piece of sculpture? A poem? A sonata? Or, how about some primitive dance?"

He dropped his arm and stopped to refill his cup.

"Now think of *this*, Jake. In today's free-for-all art world, there are increasingly conflicting opinions on the definition of what makes a person an artist, and on what makes a product a work of art. Today we accept so many 'messages' as art, that we are unable anymore to determine which of them might be the real thing. You can go out and buy books that advertise anything from the 'art' of flower arranging to the 'art' of designing automobiles. Just wading through the growing glut of candidates for the title of artist is, to say the least, daunting."

He sat down heavily.

"At least it is for me," he said quietly.

Jake sat rubbing his jaw, his head swimming with David Lehrer's words.

Then David, rising from his seat, stood in front of one of Jake's paintings.

"So, my friend, where *does* that leave you?"

68

Autumn was beginning to assert herself, the tips of sugar maples around the house just beginning to turn brilliant yellow. Soon they would turn to deeper ochers, orange, and some even to a dark red. Jake and Sarah spent a quiet morning, neither having anything special planned to do. Jake went out to his studio in mid-morning and tinkered around for a half hour or so, but felt no urge to begin anything ambitious. He glanced at his latest painting drying on the easel, not willing to judge it either finished, or in need of touching up. From puttering around his studio, he turned to puttering around the yard, absently moving a tool here or there, bending at times to pull a few weeds from the flower garden.

He sniffed the air.

Frost soon — he thought.

He went to the house to find Sarah cutting up apples.

"Apple pie?" he asked.

"Yes. I thought it would be nice to make one for supper."

Jake glanced out the window. "Good year for apples. Should make the farmers happy."

Sarah looked over at him. "Thinking about going into farming?"

Jake turned. "Huh?"

"You seem restless, Jake."

He sat at the table and ran a finger through the flour scattered across its surface. "I don't know — I guess so." He got up. "I guess maybe I am restless."

"No painting today?"

"Not in the mood." He walked to the door.

"Want to talk?"

Jake turned to Sarah and looked into her eyes. "Yes — yes, maybe I do."

"Let me finish up here," she said, "and I'll put up a pot of coffee." She pushed him out of the kitchen. "Go sit in the living room — I'll be in as soon as I get this stuff out of the way."

Jake silently obeyed, taking his usual seat alongside the fireplace. He was sitting there staring off into space when Sarah came in with the tray. She set the pot on the hearth and, after pouring them both a cup of coffee, took her seat on the opposite side. She sat quietly, waiting for him to find his words.

He sipped his coffee. "Hot."

She nodded.

"Too bad that apple pie isn't ready yet."

She sipped her own coffee, allowing him to find his own way.

"It keeps going around and around in my head, Sarah." He leaned back in his rocker. "I don't know as I'll ever straighten it all out."

She looked over at him inquiringly.

"Any of it — all of it." He put his cup down and got up on his feet. "*None* of it!"

She watched him as he paced a few steps then took a seat on the other side of the room. For a split second, she felt disoriented, never having seen him sitting in any other chair of the living room than in his usual rocker.

Jake sat for some moments looking at the wall over Sarah's head. She had hung three of his large paintings over the fireplace, a series of Overlook Mountain that she had always loved. "Overlook: Dawn," "Overlook at Noon," and "Early Evening on Overlook," ran from left to right across the wall. She always called it her "triptych" even though it was in fact three separate paintings, all done over a period of several years.

Jake dropped his eyes from the paintings and looked resignedly at Sarah from across the room. "I listen to David, I listen to Catherine — and I've been listening to Joe for as long as I can remember — and all they do is further confuse me."

He got up to get his cup and returned to other side of the room.

Sarah kept her peace.

"And darn it all, Sarah, I miss talking with your Dad!" He then added, "Not that *he* didn't confuse me, too."

Sarah's thoughts drifted to her parents as Jake sat for some mo-

444

ments in silence. She also missed their regular visits, wondering how her Mother was coping with Dad's creeping senility. They had drastically cut back on their trips upstate, the distance from their home in Bayshore too much for them to easily travel.

Jake's voice broke into her thoughts.

"I'm not any further now than when old Birge first showed me how to put paint on a canvas," he was saying. "No further at all."

Sarah got up to refill their cups.

Jake looked back at the paintings over her head when she returned to her seat, and said, "I look at them sometimes, and I'm not even sure that I painted them." He shook his head. "God only knows where they come from — or what they mean."

Sarah blew into her cup to cool down her coffee.

"Sometimes the discussions we have when the group comes over keeps me awake half the night," he said. "I keep trying to figure out what any of it really means — I mean when it comes right down to making a painting." He grunted. "'Less is more!' Now just what the hell is *that* supposed to mean?" He threw up his hands. "David can throw around so many labels — so many different 'isms' that they make my head swim. Not that I don't half-way understand what he's driving at — I usually come away with the gist of his arguments — but when I sit alone with them, they begin warring with each other in my head." He paused. "Worse — they war with *me*."

Sarah heaved a sigh.

"He never *outright* tells me, you know."

Sarah indicated her question with a look.

"About my work," said Jake. "He's never really *tells* me what he thinks of my paintings. Good? Bad? Never a word."

Sarah slowly nodded her head.

"Yet, at the same time I think he *is* telling me — you know, indirectly, like." He got up and threw his hands out in a helpless manner. "I don't know, Sarah — I really just don't know. You'd think that after all these years, I'd have some grasp of it all — some definite sense of what I'm doing. Even now, I can't point to a single one of my paintings and say, 'right! now that's a *good* one!'"

"Does it matter?" Sarah asked softly.

Jake sat back down. "What? That I don't know what the hell I've been doing all these years?"

"What David thinks."

Jake sat silent for several moments, staring at his paintings "What he *knows* matters," he said finally. "I'm not sure it matters what he thinks about my work, but what he — and Lynn, for that matter — knows about art, does. What Catherine, and Edward, and Joe, and Andrea, and *you* — and even your Mom and Dad — have to say about art, well, *all* of it matters in some way. You all seem to have pieces of a puzzle that I can't rightly see the whole picture of." He shrugged his shoulders. "I just keep trying to put all of it together, and hope that the picture I end up with is one I *want* to see."

That evening, after Sarah had gone to bed, Jake sat in the living room by himself. He again sat across the room quietly surveying his three views of Overlook Mountain.

Was I supposed *to be seeing you all these years?*

Kirstin's words rolled over and over in his mind.

Less is more! — Less is more! — Less is more!

He thought of his conversation with David about the Greeks and the Italians.

"They began to look earthward," David had said.

Right. And then they got lost — lost in the world, lost in themselves.

His mind returned to the Armory Show and the first time he had seen abstract paintings. He had thought them nonsensical at the time. They didn't make *sense* — but just what did *that* mean. David had said that Plato discounted *sensible* things precisely because, being subject to our senses, they were illusion, they were not "real." Were non-figurative artists closer to truth? Did he miss something — does he *continue* to miss something when he dismisses them so casually?

Those who have eyes, see.

All right, but what about those artists who put too much of *themselves* into a work of art. Didn't David also talk about them? About the glib artists who were carried away by their own skill? Plato rejected *them* too. And didn't he also once say that many of today's abstract artists claim that they are expressing their own inner feelings? — their own "psyches"? How much "truth" can there be in that? Even if such paintings hold any truth for the painter, what do they do for *me?*

Jake shook his head in an effort to clear his mind.

"All art is abstract," Cyrus had once said to him years ago — but just what did *that* imply?

Jake slammed his hands down on the arms of his chair.

More important, what does it imply for me?

He got up and walked over to look more closely at his paintings of Overlook.

Was I ever supposed to see you?

69

Jake's framing 'business' had been slowly dwindling since the early '50s, the demand for his hand-made frames decreasing in the same proportion as did Woodstock landscape painters. Younger artists, rightly so, preferred more "modern" frames that harmonized with their work. The local art supply store now stocked a wide variety of "ready-mades" and, for many, these served their needs perfectly well. Jake had always believed that a frame ought to "fit" the work, and he had no complaint about the loss of business. For him, it was just as well since it gave him more time to have his studio to himself — or to the visits of Sarah, or Joe, or David. He had grown used to having them there, whether it was Sarah quietly watching him paint, or David and Joe involving him in discussion — even finding himself, at times, looking forward to their visits. He did not miss the unexpected and, at times disrupting, visits of the stranger dropping in to "look over" his wares.

He had also cut back on accepting carpentry-work in recent years, something he had found that he could do since his paintings were beginning to be known and sought after. This was largely due to Sarah who, whenever she had buyers come to her studio, would invite them over to see Jake's work. In time, Sarah's customers would become his, and buyers would often leave with both paintings and pottery in the backs of their cars. Jake — with Sarah's help — had rationalized the selling of his work by seeing it as an entirely different function from the making of it. By separating the 'product' from the 'why', he was persuaded that, by doing so, he was able to continue in the belief of the purity of his intentions.

Now that he'd become reconciled with the idea of selling his paintings as a means of income, he not only resented taking time away from his home and studio for the occasional carpentry job, but also found himself having to contend with a slow diminishing of physical strength and stamina. The years had taken their toll. He hated to admit it, but of late, spending long hours on his knees or bending over to build the lower shelves of cabinets was beginning to be taxing. Worse, the soreness that he would experience while at work would carry over into his free time, often getting in the way of spending any amount of time standing at his easel. And, forget about traipsing off to climb Overlook! He and Joe even found it tiring to drag out and set up their equipment in a nearby field — and it had been ages since they enjoyed a 'paint out' together.

Though they spent more time in each other's studios for a morning or afternoon chat, the fact that they no longer painted together out in the field was a loss that Jake deeply regretted. He sorely missed the free and easy exchange of ideas, the bantering, the mutual 'critiques,' and the sheer delight in being out of doors with a kindred spirit.

Neither would have thought of suggesting that they paint alongside one another while in their studios — it simply would not have been 'orthodox.' An artist's studio was a special place, a *private* place — the 'sanctum sanctorum' David Lehrer called it — and no self-respecting artist would dream of invading it during 'work' hours. Different, to come visit for a palaver — but that was not the same thing. Talking together about painting over a cup of coffee was not the same as one painter in attendance as another worked at his easel.

Joe once remarked that it was too much like being back in the classroom — something that Jake could not relate to, but he certainly understood the concept of privacy, of the need to maintain boundaries. One of the more important lessons he had learned early on from artists was that such boundaries were handed down from atelier master to student, from generation to generation. Along with the mantle that the instructor passed on when he "laid hands" upon his students, was a set of unwritten rules that the unwary only trespassed upon at their own peril. Certainly there were days when one's painting gear might be shoved aside for merriment and camaraderie — even, at times, for boxing bouts! — but every artist knew the sanctity of the creative moment, and during such times a fellow painter's studio was strictly off-limits.

Jake even knew one painter, a woman who had made her name and a sizable income by producing a steady flow of dramatic evening sky studies in the manner of the luminist painters, that had *two* studios. She had already had one studio in her home, but had asked Jake to build her a second one by remodeling a back room.

"I just had no choice," she told Jake some years after he had completed the job. "I was simply getting *so* many visitors — buyers, you know — that I found my workspace absolutely *defiled*. So, I turned *that* studio into my exhibiting gallery, and hired you to build the new one so that I could have my private *creating* space once again." She looked up at Jake with her large, dreamy eyes, and said in a breathy voice, "It absolutely *saved* my life!"

Jake never could warm up to what he considered her formula-like style of turning out paintings, but had no quarrel with her reasoning.

In time, he had discovered that artists' studios were extensions of themselves, and he could still remember the comments Joe made during that first visit to his studio. Even though it was still "in the making", he recalled Joe's assessment of it looking "professional". He would come to realize that the appraisal of artists' studios by their colleagues was in itself something of a fine 'artform.' Listening to one artist describe the studio of another could often be an entertaining — even, at times, informative — experience.

Many claimed that they could have guessed what some artist's studio would look like just by being familiar with the work they produced. Though Jake knew that you could often guess an artist's work by looking at the colors on his palette — it was a relatively easy matter, for example, to distinguish the palette of a landscape painter from that of a figure painter — but he never became adept at the finer points of predicting the looks of an artist's workspace by simply being familiar with the work.

Although he had never seen them, he had heard about some of the studios of the past. Some, like William Merritt Chase's, were more than simple places of work but were rather showplaces that were designed to impress the visitor-patron. The early American masters, fresh from their European experiences and instruction, knew that they had to make an impression on American buyers who, by and large, were still inclined to confine their purchases to European art. Not only did the artists bring to America their European training, but also a sense of the grand style, taking especial care to ensure their studios had the proper appointments that would reflect old-world tastes. Some less successful artists joked that such studios resembled 'Macy's front window', oblivious to the fact that it was precisely for that reason that it was purposely made so — to entice buyers to open their purses. From what he had heard or read, stepping into such a studio could be an awesome experience — for a would-be patron *or* impecunious colleague.

Of course, over the years, Jake had seen a great many studios first-hand through his eyes as a carpenter, and tried his best — *as* a carpenter — to avoid making judgments about their appearance or suitability. He might have put a shelf *here* rather than *there* — but this, he knew, was simply a matter of preference.

He saw some studios that had looked as scrupulously clean and orderly as any operating room in a hospital might look — and then some that appeared as if a tornado had just passed through. Some artists boasted elaborate and spacious affairs with expensive equipment such as wheeled taborets, a variety of palettes made of different materials, easels of varying sizes, and large, impressive north-light windows, while, on the other hand, some women artists he knew worked at their kitchen counters, pushing away dirty dishes to make room for their paint boxes when they were ready to paint.

Only rarely, however, would he have ever guessed that the work that these people produced might have come from the studios he had seen. The housewife who worked in her kitchen, for instance, might paint large-scale watercolor florals, while the owner of the roomy, well-appointed studio might turn out fussily-crafted miniatures that he could as easily have made in a room the size of a closet. He had even heard of a well-known figure painter who did not *have* a studio, simply setting himself up next to the picture window of his living room, content to pose his models as best he could in the confined space. Jake suspected that the set-up of an artist's studio had some relation to Birge Harrison's 'why' that lurked behind the painting.

Sarah's studio — though designed for the potter and not the painter — was as much a reflection of herself as was her home.

She had long arranged it to suit her needs, transforming Jake's original handiwork in the process. In a sense, she had 'brought up' her studio from the ground floor much in the same way as she would a vessel from a wheel. Whenever Jake entered, he felt 'surrounded' by Sarah, the smell of damp clay, the pervasive dust on her every tool and surface — even such feminine touches as fresh flowers in some of the pots on the shelves — exerting an unmistakable impact on him that was distinctly different from any other studio he visited.

He himself had long been in the habit of setting out his materials in a somewhat orderly fashion — a timesaving practice that he had learned as a day laborer — but still the most common description of his work that he had heard was that it appeared "spontaneous". Sometimes "good" — but *always* "spontaneous".

Joe's work, on the other hand, always appeared — at least to Jake's eyes — painterly, finished — "professional". Alongside his own paintings — which he had to agree seemed a bit rough around the edges — Joe's always seemed, well, elegant — even pretty. Not pretty in the same sense as those made by the lady with the two studios — Joe would have resented such a comparison out of hand. However, if a painting was supposed to be "beautiful," well, to Jake's eyes, Joe's would always fill the bill.

Still, he doubted if one might have surmised that either his or Joe's work had come out of their particular studios — as different as they were from one another. But then, that might have been simply because he was too familiar with them — it might be that he no longer really *saw* Joe's — or his own — studio.

This was not the case, however, for the artist who had just come from the studio of a new acquaintance — or from that of some perceived competitor. Artists have, of course, long measured their work against that of others, but the new spirit of commercialism had brought such measuring to a fine edge. Competition between artists seemed to Jake to be more pronounced of late, more hostile. He even knew of some cases in which fellow artists had become avowed enemies.

Part of this new combativeness, Jake well knew, had arisen from the almost daily vying for position that the commercialization of art had inevitably imposed on them all. Galleries were limited. Wall space was limited. Buyers were limited. Print, radio, television space was limited. So, getting your due was almost a constant concern. In all too many cases, an *overriding* concern.

Petty — and not so petty — sniping and backbiting between artists, therefore, cropped up ever more increasingly. Jake had once overheard some artist gleefully pointing out to a companion that he had seen photographs tucked behind some boxes in another's studio, a "sure" indication that the artist had been "cheating" — painting from *photographs* rather than from *life*.

Jake would try to ignore such comments and, as much as possible, avoid those artists who resorted to such pettiness. From his point of view, small-mindedness ought not be part of anyone's character, and he had little respect for those artists who openly demonstrated it. He had come across enough of such mean-spiritedness over the years when he worked as a laborer or carpenter with his fellow workmen and, rightly or wrongly, felt that artists, who ought to have had bigger fish to fry, should have been above it.

70

If narrowing down his time away from his studio and confining his companionship to his small circle of friends had presented no cause of concern, it was not as easy for Jake to ignore the gradual contraction of their "Third Thursday" group. To the dismay and sorrow of all, Sarah's mother had passed away without warning in the summer of 1966, her death surprising to Jake and Sarah since it unexpectedly preceded Cyrus's long-expected end. Apparently the constant care that Cyrus demanded in recent days had been too much for Mae, the anxiety and concern slowly sapping her resources until she had none left for herself.

"We should've taken your parents in with us years ago," said Jake. "There was never any trouble with them staying in the guest-room during the summer — and you know how I've always en-joyed the company of your dad." He put his arm around Sarah's shoulders. "We should never have let them travel back and forth like that the last few years — especially your mother. Even the few times they came were just too much. Having them move in here would have taken the burden from your mother's shoulders."

Sarah sighed. "Well, it wasn't as if we didn't try, Jake. But Mom was always reluctant to give up the house down there in Bayshore." Sarah's eyes filled up. "I don't think that she ever gave up on the idea that someday I'd take it over — you know, just up and move in."

Jake shrugged, finding no words to answer.

Sarah looked up at the ceiling. "Well, he's here now." She looked at Jake, then gave a short laugh. "And here I was the one who didn't want the trouble of having a child around. He'd been having the hearing problem for years, but now with the vision thing, he's almost helpless."

"Oh, he's not that bad, Sarah. I enjoy our morning walks around the garden." Jake smiled. "Each time we get to my studio, he asks me if I still keep chickens on the place."

Sarah gave in to one of her belly laughs. "And I suppose he really can't help it. Cal, now, used to act like a child on *purpose.*"

Jake chuckled, then put a serious look on his face. "Ever miss him, Sarah?"

"Cal? Not for a minute! Oh, of course he comes to mind now and then — like just now. You know, like whenever I have to face something unpleasant." She laughed again. "But *miss* him, Jake? Absolutely never!"

"Well, I certainly miss your Mom. Somehow her quiet presence always comforted me. To me, she was always what a mother *should* be."

Sarah said nothing.

"And speaking of missing people, how long has it been since we lost Myra? She's been gone for how long now — two years?"

"Not quite," said Sarah. She thought for a moment, then said, "Almost a year and half now. The last time she was here at one of our Thursday nights was in the fall of 1964." She did some mental calculating. "She died just before the opening of Morris's museum — just about a year before Mom."

"And then, shortly after we buried your Mom, it was Catherine."

"Yes," mused Sarah. "Time is taking its toll on all of us."

The thinning-out process that time imposed on them was not only evident at their Thursday night gatherings, but increasingly became the main topic of discussion each time they met. When they weren't talking about their personal losses, the gradual decrease in the number of the early Woodstock crowd would almost inevitably arise.

"Hardly any of us left anymore," Joe would say — the usual one who would first broach the subject — and the nods would run around the room.

David, the 'youngster' of the group, would invariably try to lighten the mood. "Look at Ed, now," he said. They all did, noting how much he had aged since losing his lifetime companion. He abruptly turned to Joe Bundy. "And you and Jake."

More nods, but a bit less emphatic.

"Well, nobody ever heard of an artist 'retiring'," said Ed. "We're not like bankers and plumbers and bus drivers who look forward to turning sixty-five and hanging up their boots. Artists just go on and on ..."

"Pure orneriness," said Joe.

"Right," said Jake. "Hard to give up our positions of power."

"I don't know about 'position of power'," said Ed Fielding. "But you certainly have standing in the old colony — a position of respect, I'd say." He turned to Joe. "Now that you and Andrea have your work in a gallery here in Woodstock — not to mention Andrea's representation down at that gallery in New York City ever since she had her show there — and Jake, here, selling like hotcakes out of his studio — you can't really complain."

"You don't really notice, though, how few of us old-timers are left until something brings it to your attention," said Andrea. "I noticed it last weekend when Joe and I went to that party at Harvey Fite's bluestone quarry over in High Woods. So many new faces! I almost felt like a stranger."

"I get the same feeling when I'm at the Association," said Joe. "I'm almost surprised when I run into someone I know at one of their opening receptions."

"Well, we're still here," said Jake.

"The remaining members of America's true school of home-grown painting," said Joe.

"Something to be said for that," agreed David.

"Here, here! To the remnants of the Woodstock School of Outhouse Painting!" joked Joe as he raised his glass. "May they go away quietly!"

"Speak for yourself, Joe," said Andrea.

"You know," said Lynn Lehrer, "we can joke about it, but Woodstock artists — all of them, from Birge Harrison and John Carlson to Arnold and Lucille Blanch — have played an important role in the history of American art. It took us a long time to break loose from the traditions of European art, and your 'Woodstock School of Outhouse Painting' — the Woodstock landscape artists — were just as powerful an authentic native voice as the so-called New York City 'Ashcan School' was."

"Well I predict that your voices will be heard for a long time coming," said Sarah.

"And you'd probably be right," said Lynn. "It's really surprising how many out there who are positively champing at the bit to get their hands on a John Speicher, a George Bellows, a John Carlson, or a Birge Harrison. They've become hot items, and some of my clients are having me scouring the woods for some of their early landscapes."

"Lot to be said for that," said David. "I hear the Association is planning a big to-do for its 50th Anniversary next year, and it's hard to see how they could do it without including early Woodstock work."

"What do you mean 'early'?" said Joe. He turned to Jake. "Sounds like we've already been relegated to the past, doesn't it? Have you stopped painting yet? *I* haven't!"

Jake waved off Joe's pretense of an intended insult from David. "I'm sure the Association has big plans, but we're not the only ones around. They'll surely include some of the past members — especially the important ones."

"Well, Andrea'll be a shoo-in, anyway," said Joe. "She's one of the last 'stars' living up here."

Andrea shushed him. "Well they have a whole new crop to choose from, don't they?" she said. "I certainly met a few new ones at Harvey's party. By the way, he's doing quite a thing with that quarry, isn't he?"

"He sure is," said Ed Fielding. "He originally intended it to be a foil for his sculptures, but the project of laying out the old quarry with paths and pools and whatnot has grown into an artform of its own. Something new for art historians to have to contend with."

"Already on the books," said David. "The one-night 'happening' is now becoming the fairly indestructible 'earthwork'."

"Not really much different from the ancient piece of sculpture created for a specific place," said Ed. "When you think of it, Michelangelo's 'David' is only a prototype for today's 'site-specific' work of art."

"What goes around, comes around," said David.

"Well, now, I wonder if things really ever do change," said Sarah.

"Food for thought," said Ed. "Food for thought."

* * *

"Ever feel like you were inspired from…" Jake pointed vaguely upward, "From above?"

Joe looked intently at his friend. "You mean, like hear voices?"

Jake's face showed his exasperation. "No! *Not* hear voices," he said. He pointed to the painting on Joe's easel. "You know what I mean. That your ideas come from — well, outside yourself."

Since they were sitting in his studio, Joe rose to play the host, and picking up Jake's empty cup, walked over to the coffee pot. "Oh. That." He filled both of their cups. "Thought for a minute you were going Woodstock on me — you know like one of them astrologers or tarot readers we got popping up in town."

"Hardly," said Jake sourly. "But David once told me about the Italians, and about how they believed artists to be divinely inspired. He said that that was the real meaning of the word 'inspired' — to be 'breathed into' — presumably by God."

Joe sat down. "You know, I don't really know much about that — I'm not even sure I take much stock in the notion." He leaned back in his seat. "Carlson, though, used to talk now and then about an artist having a calling — you know, like a priest."

"That's what I mean," Jake said. "Something like that. I suppose if an artist is 'called' as you put it, then he *has* to be hearing voices — of some kind."

Joe shrugged. "The only voices I know artists listen to is from their dealers — or buyers — or, heaven forbid! — the critics." Chuckling, he added, "David excepted, of course."

Jake sat quietly for a moment or two. Then he pointed again to the painting on Joe's easel. "I don't believe you were listening to any of those while you painted *that*," he said.

Joe scratched his beard.

"Come on — tell me you were doing that because some dealer told you to," Jake prompted,

Joe looked at the painting. "Well, I didn't say that *I* listened to them." He paused. "As a matter of fact, *nobody* tells me to paint what I paint. I suspect that if I *did* have a dealer he'd be trying to get me to paint something else." He laughed, then added, "Something that sells, probably, so that we could both make a living."

"So, OK. Then you're listening to yourself."

458

"Right. I paint what *I* want to paint — and if I want to waste my time painting that brook out back, then that's what I'll paint."

Jake nodded. "Did Carlson get you started painting brooks?"

"Not exactly — not *my* brook, anyway. He started me on painting landscapes." He thought for a moment. "You know, as far as I can remember, he never actually told any of us what to paint. He just told us to go out and use our eyes." He scratched his beard again. "I guess I turned to landscapes because *he* painted landscapes — I dunno. Anyway, today I paint what *I* want to paint."

"So, you just listen to your own voice."

"Yeah, I guess so."

Jake looked at him.

"Now I suppose you're gonna ask me where *my* voice comes from," Joe finally asked.

Jake nodded.

"How do *I* know, Jake?" He stood up. "If you want me to say that the voice in my head comes from …" He pointed to the ceiling. "…up there, then all right." He shrugged. "I guess you might say that I'm 'divinely inspired' then."

"*I'm* not saying it, Joe. I'm asking."

"Well, you always manage to ask the damnedest questions. Cripes! It's hard enough having to deal with tubes of paints, stretching canvases, lousy weather — the goddamned sun — and the *critics* without having to figger out where my *ideas* come from."

"Touchy, touchy."

"Ahhh, you and your damned *voices*! How do I know if I'm divinely inspired? I just *paint* dammit."

71

The year1969, depending on your disposition, was either the beginning of something new and great or the beginning of the end.

For the upbeat, ongoing peace negotiations in Vietnam, the active engagement of youth in the politics of their government, and the landing of a man on the moon — were all indications of a better world to come.

For the pessimists, the glass was surely half empty. Freedom had become licentiousness, the old standards were abandoned, politicians were more corrupt, education had been compromised, and everything from religion to culture had been commercialized. America had let in the barbarians, and was on the verge of its own decline and fall.

Jake did not feel he had the wisdom to determine which of the extremes would eventually prove right, and left the predictions to the experts. For him, 1969 just brought to him and Sarah one more loss in their personal lives — the death of Cyrus.

The old man — they had almost believed that he'd live to see 100 — had slipped out of the house unnoticed one morning in early May, and it was not until a neighbor came to tell Sarah that she had found Cyrus in her backyard that they were aware of his absence. He was sitting with his back against a freshly leafed maple, a peaceful smile on his face, his eyes still open to a sun that had almost risen to its zenith.

The Bundys and the Lehrers — Ed Fielding ailing and unable to make the trip — attended the small service at the funeral home in Long Island and, later that afternoon, the burial a bit further out on the Island.

But 1969 had also brought the excitement of choosing which

paintings to enter into the Association's upcoming Anniversary Show. Jake had asked Sarah to make the final decisions, unable after some hours in his studio to do so himself.

"Sometimes they all look good," he said to Sarah when he came over to the house for her help. "And other times they all look bad."

"Well," she laughed. "Let's go pick out the worst ones and see if they have the courage to accept them."

When the Thursday Night group heard the results of the jury selection, Joe was bursting with pride and excitement.

"I *knew* it!" he gloated. "Didn't I tell you we'd get picked? Three of Andrea's prints, and two each of our paintings! Didn't I tell you we'd be shoo-ins?"

Jake smiled. "Well, they didn't have too many of us old geezers left, you know. They needed some of the old-timers who could still walk around to show up at the opening."

"Spoilsport!" said Joe, then added with a grin, "You'd better not let Andrea hear you call her an old geezer!"

What better way, the board members decided, than to have an exhibit that celebrated not only the Association's 50th year, but also one that celebrated Woodstock's art of the past, present, and future? Unanimously agreed upon, they had eagerly set about preparing for the show.

There was certainly no problem in having an eclectic mix of 'past, present and future' — or at least, 'futuristic' — art. The Association's membership had long reflected the wide range of art that characterized the times since the '30s, with artists of all stripes eager to participate in the landmark show. The only problem was in jurying such an exhibit, since they had many more entries than their walls could accommodate.

Decisions made, the evening of the opening reception finally arrived, and to their great relief the steady flow of people showing up for the festivities promised a grand success.

Jake, as usual, stood outside the Association's front doors, avoiding as long as possible the crush of people. Every couple of minutes Joe would dash out in an effort to drag him inside.

"Geez! What a crowd! *Everybody's* here. — come on in and say hello."

He resisted Joe's urgings until Sarah came out and sternly reminded him of his "duties".

"Come on, Jake. Your niece has come all the way up from New York to see this show. The least you can do is show your appreciation by joining her — *and* by joining your friends. The Lehrers have been asking for you, and I've run out of making excuses." She grabbed his arm and pulled him inside. "Come on! No more stalling!"

Once inside, Jake enjoyed himself, hardly noticing the occasional elbow in his side or the jostling of the un-tasted wine glass slowly warming in his hand. Seeing Kirstin was especially pleasant — she planned to stay the weekend with them — her animated discussion of art, of the League, of her forays into the 'artworld' were both achingly reminiscent and joyously refreshing. He proudly introduced her around — broadly smiling when one or another would ask if she were his daughter.

It took little effort to bring her over to where David was holding court. When he brought them together, he was amazed at how quickly she engaged David in conversation. It took only a few moments of standing idly by and listening to them speak to make him realize how superfluous his presence was.

He sidled up to Sarah who stood a few feet away looking over the cheese choices laid out on the reception table. Nodding his head in the direction of Kirstin and David, he said, "She's sure something!"

Sarah placed a piece of cheese on a cracker and smiled up at him, happy to see the obvious pride he had for his niece.

"A couple of people asked me if she was my daughter."

"She *does* resemble you, Jake." She looked up at him. "In more ways than one. I already told you that."

Jake shook his head. "I *never* had that confidence."

The show was a resounding success, the Association realizing not only a boost in its reputation, but also a considerable increase in their sales. Lynn Lehrer had invited several of her clients, and from what Jake could tell some of them were responsible for many of the purchases. Buying was generally brisk throughout the reception, and as the evening wore on, the little red paste-ons put on the walls alongside works that denoted "sold" steadily grew in number.

Jake and Joe's paintings as well as all of Andrea's prints had been among the first works to be sold.

As successful as it was, for many, the resultant 'high' that the Anniversary Show had brought to the Woodstock art community was soon overshadowed by what would become known to the world as *the* Woodstock Festival.

Its coming had been in the making for over a year as the spreading sound of music increasingly drowned out any voices that were raised in objection to its arrival. Not content with the 'mini' soundouts that they could muster in and around town, the entrepreneurs were still chafing about having their ideas for bringing the Newport Jazz Festival to Woodstock nipped in the bud. Tireless in their efforts, the promoters capitalized on the success of the more modest attempts at "arts festivals" around town, and began touting a *musical* festival that would outshine all others.

The idea of "The Woodstock Festival" was born, grew into maturity, and soon became irresistibly unstoppable. So big did the project grow, in fact, that it soon became evident to everyone involved that such an event could not be contained within the limited confines of the old village of Woodstock. Undeterred, the promoters looked further and further afield until they finally decided on a location many miles away from town. Thus, the "Woodstock Festival" was held not in Woodstock — and not even in the same county — but in a town called Bethel, over in the adjoining county of Sullivan.

It seemed to many that, as far as Woodstock was concerned, the pessimists were absolutely correct. Not only was the town usurped by the barbarians — they had even taken its *name* away.

The old Woodstock art colony, they lamented, would *never* again be the same.

BOOK SEVEN

1979

72

FOR THE SECOND and final time, the Art Students League discontinued its classes at Woodstock in 1979, and for the perennial nay-sayers the shutting of its doors this time spelled out the final chapter on the old town as an art colony. Enrollment at the League's summer sessions had been steadily decreasing ever since landscape painting had not been the primary reason for artists coming to the colony, and the League's Board of Control could no longer justify the expense of maintaining a separate facility. Besides, travel being so much swifter, neither tourists nor artists deemed going "up to Woodstock" such a big deal anymore — not like back in the old days of large summer resorts, and a trip that entailed most of a day either by train or boat traveling upriver, followed by a stagecoach ride for the final few miles to town from the West Hurley train station.

"I, for one, think that as bad as it may be for Woodstock's businessmen, it won't effectively change it much for the artists who've chosen to become residents," David was saying.

The group — now reduced to the Bundys, the Lehrers, and Sarah and Jake — were celebrating Sarah's birthday at The Espresso, a spacious café on Tinker Street that was one of the more enduring contributions to the town from the hippie generation.

"I agree," said Lynn. "Movements come and go — have been, I suppose, ever since two artists got their heads together — but there's always been that overlap."

"True," said Joe. "The modernists think that they're the only show in town, and the traditionalists still claim their seniority — and validity — and all the time, they live side-by-side."

"No matter how hard they try to stay within their own cocoons," said Andrea.

"Still, they co-exist," said Lynn. "In New York City, galleries seem to cover the whole range, from ancient art to the very latest fad — all you have to do is look for what suits your taste."

"And, unfortunately, your pocketbook," added Jake.

Joe shrugged. "I suppose. But sometimes I think I'd just like to be shed of the whole thing." He looked around. "You know, just politely and quietly bow out of the ongoing competition."

"Now you're just showing your age," said Andrea.

"I guess — but it is a bit discouraging," he said. "Day after day going into your studio to do — what? One more painting that you're not sure is going to succeed — let alone sell." He turned to Jake. "How about you, Jake? Ready to hang up your brushes?"

Jake laughed. "Sarah won't let me."

"*I* won't let you! Hah!" She turned to the others. "You should have heard him on the way into town. But first, we just can't ride into town the *easy* way. *He* had to come from West Hurley via Zena and the Glasco Turnpike." She glanced around the table. "You know, so he can get that view of Overlook that he loves? 'Look!' he says. 'And in this early autumn light! I don't think I've ever quite gotten Overlook just like that.'" She turned to Jake. "Don't tell them *I* won't let you stop painting, you old fraud! You won't *ever* give up as long as that mountain is there!"

Jake gave a lopsided grin. "Heck, I'm lucky I can still *see* the darned thing."

"Besides, remember what Ed said. 'Artists don't retire!'" said Andrea.

Sarah sighed. "Poor Ed. He just kept going downhill after Catherine went."

"Hey, this is a birthday celebration!" said Lynn. "Enough of the gloomy stuff."

"Right! Here's to another hundred years!" said David.

"God forbid!" said Sarah. She looked at Jake and leaned into him. "Though I wouldn't mind a repeat of the *last* twenty-five."

Jake smiled and gave her a hug.

"So, what's this I hear about you two starting a new magazine?" said Sarah, changing the subject and turning to David and Lynn.

"Oh, nothing so ambitious as a *magazine*," David answered. "We're just thinking of a small publication."

"About art, I presume," said Andrea.

Lynn spread out her hands. "What else?"

The group smiled.

Jake signaled for another round of drinks, and David continued.

"With Lynn's business sense we might just make a go of it."

"We'll set up as a corporation," Lynn interrupted. "Neither of us is willing to accept the limitations imposed on a not-for-profit organization or follow the dictates of a board, so I'll be the publisher, and David will act as editor and art critic."

"Right," continued David. "I'm interested in a publication that takes the long view and, since we intend to cover all the arts — film, music, dance, theatre — I'll seek out writers who share that same view."

"The long view?" asked Joe.

"Yes, you know, a publication that doesn't concentrate on the latest trends. They're enough cutting edge art magazines out there now." He smiled. "They seem to go in and out of business overnight! Anyway, I don't like writing for them because they're mostly interested in a 'hook' — something that will pull in readers and viewers to a particular exhibit. It could be something about the artist, and not necessarily about the work."

Lynn continued. "Most of the time the hook is related to whether or not an artist or gallery has taken out an advertisement in the publication. If this is the case, the editor wants his writers to cover the show *because* they have taken out the advertisement — and not because of any intrinsic value in the art being touted."

David nodded in agreement,

"After all," Lynn continued. "They're in business — just as the galleries and dealers are — and businessmen don't stay in business long if they don't have their eye on the dollar. Can you imagine what it must cost for a gallery to rent space, say, on Madison Avenue? Who can blame them if there are times that money overrides considerations of quality?"

David smiled. "That's why *she's* handling the business end."

"There's no getting around the fact that art is big business. You hear more and more about its being an 'investment,' nowadays," said Andrea.

"Well, it *is*," said Lynn. "There's just no getting around it. Art today is like playing the market — and don't think that corporations and wealthy buyers don't know it. They're interested in bottom lines."

"Like those found on canvases," quipped Joe. "Lines like, 'Picasso' or 'Renoir' or 'Monet.' *Those* lines are what they're interested in when they buy art. Forget about buying for aesthetic reasons."

"Right — and that reminds me of the story Catherine once told me about Jean Renoir and his father," said David. "When Auguste — Jean's dad — was a young man scrabbling to make a living, he used to do knock-offs of Watteau — who at that time was a big seller — for some disreputable dealer. Renoir was good at it, and the dealer wouldn't tell his customers outright that these fakes were the real thing — only that they were 'attributed' to Watteau. Anyway, years later, when Renoir himself was a best seller, he visited one of his patrons and, during his time there, the buyer said he wanted to show him one of his 'treasures.' He led Renoir to a hooded easel and, carefully uncovering it, proudly said, 'Voilà — my Watteau!' Well, Renoir took one look and immediately recognized it as one of his potboilers. When he told this story to his son, Jean asked his father if he had told the gentleman that it was he who had painted it. 'No, I did not,' said Renoir père. 'Why not?' asked Jean. And here's the best part," said David. "'Because, my son, if he bought it because he loved it, then why should I take away his pleasure? If he bought it as an investment, *then it serves him right!*'" He looked around. "Don't you just *love* it?"

"Great story!" said Sarah.

"But still," said Joe. "Art has become strictly a business today, and galleries and art magazines seem to be kowtowing to that fact." He grinned. "Thank God that Jake and I have Sarah and Andrea — if it wasn't for their sales keeping us alive we'd have to be kowtowing, too." He looked at Jake. "Guess that makes us kept men."

"Okay by me," said Jake.

"Even though we intend for it to be a business venture," David continued, "we don't want to compete with the slicks — they appear to have major backing, and are only interested in what's selling — what they refer to as 'hot.' Living up here, we won't have the overhead that City publishers have."

"So, you'll write about what's *not* hot?" said Joe with a grin.

David smiled. "Well, I hope not. I would hope to convince people that what's not the latest thing out can also be 'hot.' I'd like to concentrate on quality — and what makes something quality."

"Hot continues to be hot, no matter how old it is," said Lynn.

"Up to a point, that's true," said David. "But there've been things in the past that were considered *very* hot that have since fallen out of favor."

"Isn't *that* the truth," said Andrea.

"The trick is to go beyond such considerations as 'hot' — a term usually given by the public, incidentally," said David. "Tastes change — as you both point out — but quality — excellence — usually endures."

Jake nodded. "Yes, excellence endures — but there's not much of that around these days."

"But, yet it does," insisted David. "As does art."

"The *real* trick is to be able to tell the difference," said Sarah.

"Oh, yes," agreed Lynn. "And that's why *he*'s the editor and artwriter."

"So how *do* you decide on what has 'quality,' as you put it," Jake asked as he turned to David.

David took a deep breath. "I wish I could give you an easy answer, Jake. The truth is, that I'm not always sure myself."

"Surely you don't just flip a coin when you decide to write about a show," said Joe.

"No, of course not." David stopped and stared off into the distance. "Again, I'm not so sure that I can explain how I arrive at such a conclusion, but here goes. You know that I go to see a lot of exhibits — some I'm invited to, others I just drop in on because I'm in the area. Anyway, I walk into a gallery and just sort of do a quick go-around. I don't consciously try to look carefully at any one picture, or attempt to make any definite judgments about the exhibit as a whole. Often, I just breeze in and out of a gallery because nothing stops me." He paused. "Now this is the difficult part to explain. When something *does* stop me, I seem to go into a different mode — my mind stops."

Andrea raised her eyebrows.

"But then," David continued, "my mind begins to engage. But just *what* it was that stopped me in the first place is something I haven't been able to explain even to myself. But something clicks inside — not in my head but," he pointed to his breast, "— in here. There is something in the painting — or the sculpture — or whatever — that communicates itself directly to me."

Sarah nodded. "I know what you mean."

"Again, don't ask me *what* is doing the communicating. At times, it's not the *whole* work, but just a part of it. Maybe something in the foreground of a painting, maybe a view of a piece of sculpture from a given point. Maybe it's the way the artist has handled light — or color — or shape. Now, I'm not speaking simply of technique here. Again, I don't know. But somehow I feel that *this* painter, *this* sculptor, is trying to say something beyond — or behind — or *somewhere* — other than the tree, or figure, or whatever the apparent subject is that the work represents. It's like whatever was obviously 'there' in front of the artist was not really the point. The painter is not painting the landscape for the sake of painting a scene, or the sculptor is not carving a figure for the sake of the model's form — they seem to be doing it for another reason — a reason that even they cannot express other than in paint or stone." He paused to look around at the group. "And, it's a reason that *I* don't know either — but it's unmistakably there, and it's what stops me in my tracks." He spread out his hands. "Probably doesn't make sense — but you asked, Jake, and there it is."

Jake furrowed his brow, but he felt he knew what David was trying to say. "I can follow that — sometimes — *most* times, I guess, I think I'm doing the same kind of thing when I try to paint Overlook. Like I'm trying to get *inside* or something. In any event, it isn't the *mountain* I'm trying to paint" He turned to Sarah. "No, it isn't Overlook at all — but it's *something.*"

"Sorry for the long-winded 'lecture'," David said as he noted Jake's knitted brows and thoughtful look. He turned apologetically to the others. "Anyway, if something in a gallery or museum stops me dead in my tracks, I want to take note — be with it for awhile. And even if I have trouble putting it into words, I want to let others know that *this* is worth their time to go and see. If it doesn't move them as it does me, so be it — but if it *does* — who knows? — maybe *that* person will be able to explain it."

"As vague as that all may sound, David, it clarifies what you mean by quality for me," said Sarah. She turned to Jake. "And I know *exactly* what you mean, too. I might tease you about your old mountain, but I know you're trying to get to something deeper."

"Whatever *that* means," said Jake with a laugh. "Maybe my father was right, after all. Maybe it *is* all nonsense. Even Birge Harrison once admitted that it all might be just 'kid stuff'." He leaned back in his seat and let out a long breath. "At least my father filled people's bellies — all I do is make pictures."

"And us? Andrea and me? All we do is 'make pictures'?" said Joe plaintively.

"Well it certainly isn't *all*" said Lynn. "Making pictures is a perfectly valid way to spend one's life."

"'Making' sounds like the operative word, here," said David. "Perhaps it's the *doing* that makes the difference."

"Something to be said for that," said Sarah.

Jake's mind flashed back to Cap'n Bob. "A wise old man once told me that it was process that counted. He thought that maybe we find meaning precisely in 'doing'." He looked around the table. "And after *we're* done 'doing', the next generation will take over." He smiled. "Maybe Kirstin will find what's behind Overlook with her "less is more" process — and if she doesn't, maybe some future offspring of the Forscher progeny will do it. After all, we can't all be as no-account as old uncle Jake, here."

"Anyway, it sounds like David and Lynn have both taken on quite a project," said Joe.

"Well, we'd like to give it a shot — you know, dedicate a small publication to steering the public — hopefully — in the right direction," said David. "To give back to art some of the dignity it once enjoyed."

"Speaking of directions," said Jake. "Anybody know where the gent's room is?"

David pointed it out to him, and he excused himself from the table.

"You folks go on," he said. "Just let me know what I missed when I get back."

When he entered the men's room, Jake found that it was occupied by two of the young locals. One stood by the sink combing his hair, while the other leaned against the wall, waiting for his friend to stop preening.

They ignored Jake as he went about his business, apparently continuing a discussion that had begun before he had come in.

"A *health* food store!" said the man at the sink. "Can you beat that? Now we have a *health* food store in town!"

The other man gave a short laugh. "So what does that make our regular grocery store — an *un*-health food store?"

The first speaker leaned toward the mirror and squinting at himself said, "I don't know — maybe." He stepped back to give himself a once-over. Satisfied with what he saw, he slid his comb into his back pocket and, turning to his companion, said, "You know, I don't know what the hell this town's comin' to!"

God! — Jake thought — *How many times have I heard that Woodstock was on its last legs? Still here it sits. Yep, it'll endure — just like Overlook and just like art will continue on. Who knows where or when it will really end?*

When he returned to the table, Jake sat down with a large grin on his face.

"What's the joke?" asked Joe.

"Yes, come on, share it," said Sarah.

Jake's grinned merely widened and he just shook his head. "It's a long story ...".